DIAMONDS & RUST

DIAMONDS & RUST

WONDERLAND WARS BOOK 2

SUSAN H. RODDEY

SHENANIGATOR BOOKS

SHENANIGATOR BOOKS

Name: Roddey, Susan H., author
Title: Diamonds & Rust: Wonderland Wars Book 2
Description: Third Edition. Phoenix & Fae Publications
ISBN: 979-8-9892292-5-3

Published by Phoenix & Fae Publications and Shenanigator Books
Printed in the United States of America

*For all the dreamers—anyone who has ever felt
like they belong somewhere far away from this reality.*

CHAPTER ONE

The man's head explodes in a shower of sparkles and blood. Damp glitter rains down around me, the tiny droplets soaking into my clothes and cobwebbing out along the threads. The blood spreads. The sparkles stick, turning me into something hideous.

Then I wake up screaming.

Sweat pours down my face and neck. My heart threatens to crawl up and out of my chest, desperately attempting to escape the source of my terror, though I'm not even really sure what it is. I can't breathe. Can't speak. Can't think. I'm dying, drowning in my own lungs, and scratching at my own arms enough to send bolts of white-hot pain along my nerves. I'm awake but the blood and glitter are remain, tainting my skin. It won't come off.

Manacles encircle my wrists, ripping my arms away from my shredded skin. I'm held in traction, unable to move. I'm screaming. I can hear the ragged sounds ripping from my throat but I can't control them.

Large, comforting hands land on either shoulder and urge me forward. I'm still blind with terror. Arms encircle me. Fingertips brush along my spine. The terror begins to fade. The manacles (hands, I realize) around my wrists ease up, then let go.

This has become a regular occurrence since the Mock Turtle tried to kill me. There's definitely trauma left over from that incident—I did explode him with magic, after all—but life has been much too busy to even begin to process it.

There also seems to be a shortage of licensed therapists in Wonderland.

I'm pulled down against a broad chest while another body presses up close against my back. My heart rate slows and the adrenaline coursing through my veins eases enough that my hands stop shaking. It's during moments like these that I'm so thankful for the presence of Rabbits in my life.

"You're bleeding again." Jerome says softly. He was the one who stopped me from clawing myself to pieces, but his hands are gentle this time as he reaches out and turns my arm over. A moment later, the sting of antiseptic bites into my skin and I hiss. He unrolls a bandage around my arm.

Ivan continues to hold me close, stroking his fingers along my spine. When I'm properly bandaged, I'm pulled down against him, tucking my head under his chin. Jerome presses his weight against the full length of my back. They say nothing. We hold onto one another, their solid presence comforting… until the jerking in my muscles ceases and I begin to relax once more. It doesn't take long for the nightmare to fade away enough that I'm able to drift off again.

Thankfully, I don't dream this time.

It's been six months since I led an army into battle, killed a mindflayer, and gotten married so I'd become the new White Queen of Wonderland. To say my life has taken a weird turn is an understatement.

Hi. My name is Alice, and I am Wonderland's White Queen.

Since that point in time, I've learned how to use a sword and a spear, had daily lessons in magic use with the Caterpillar and the Ace of Spades, and learned the inner-workings of a make-believe kingdom. The fact that I'm still technically a newlywed is the least of my worries. Said husband is also waiting in the throne room and I am desperately behind schedule.

In fact, I'm so far behind where I need to be that the White Rabbit's voice halting my progress actually startles me when I reach for the door.

"Stop a moment, Highness," Jerome says and I pause.

"You're usually the one telling me I'm late."

He smiles while he adjusts my sleeves and straightens my crown. At his nod, Ivan — the Red Rabbit and my left hand in all things Wonderland — opens the heavy doors to the throne room and I enter, Rabbits trailing behind. Tweedledee and Tweedledum — more commonly referred to as Tag and Nacht in this bizarre reality — stand guard at either side of the dais. They are large and menacing, a pair of vicious bookends protecting our court, and my heart melts with affection at the sight of them. The cavernous room gives me chills when I enter it, given this is where I nearly lost my life right before gaining a crown. Rows and rows of pews march along either side of the plush runner and a pair of tall braziers flank the closed entry doors at the other end of the room. Tall windows and intricate tapestries line the walls. It's warm enough, but still holds tough memories. The space is otherwise empty save for Felina and Talon, the aforementioned Ace of Spades and Caterpillar, respectively. King Phineas sits atop his throne on the dais; stoic save the small quirk of his lips as I take Jerome's hand for balance on the steps leading to my own throne.

These big productions are rare. Normally, I don't even try to look like a twisted fairy tale queen, much less act like one. But today is important for two reasons. First, we're appointing a new White Knight (no deck is complete without its face cards, after all). Second, we're receiving an emissary from the Court of Diamonds with a message from their King, The Carpenter himself.

He's already tried to kill me once too. I can't even lie about being excited about that visit. The only thing I can do is try to keep the fact that I'm fucking terrified off my face.

Which would be a lot easier if I wasn't dressed like a wedding cake from Hell.

"Husband," I say as I take my seat.

"Wife," Phineas response with a nod. "You look lovely as always."

"And you are dashing as ever."

He takes my hand and squeezes my fingers affectionately, then releases me with another nod — this one toward my Rabbits. Both click their heels together in a comically formal manner and bow with a flourish. For two people that hated each other half a year ago, they operate like a surprisingly well-oiled machine.

To anyone on the outside, we are the combined picture of perfect happiness. I suppose we truly are, when I think about it. The kingdom — at least the portion controlled by the White Court — is safe and peaceful. The King has a Queen. I'm not running for my life. And while my relationship with Phineas isn't romantic, we've become quite good friends. He even tolerates the fact that the Cheshire Cat comes around to visit and brings all the juicy gossip from the other lands. And despite the fact that trust is still a major issue, yes, Koji is just as flirtatious and handsy as ever.

What can I say? The damned cat is growing on me.

With one last, indulgent smile, Phineas turns to the empty hall and his stern-ruler facade slides into place.

"Bring in our guest," he says.

The doors open and in strides an absolute mountain of a man. My throat tightens at the sight of him. Dark hair, dark eyes, dark skin, and a pair of polished, sharpened tusks protruding from his mouth. A beast made for the sole purpose of destroying everything in its path. His very being is a void, drawing light and magic alike out of the air.

Those fierce, coal-black eyes take in their surroundings, and though he walks with the purpose of a shark circling its prey, he falters. There's a quiver to his stride which would be imperceptible were it not for the fact that I can feel the tremors in the magical currents swirling around us.

It's a facade. Bravado. It's not real.

Phineas stiffens. The movement as well is likely imperceptible to anyone else, but I feel the air shift again. These men are frightened of each other.

"The Carpenter has quite a bit of nerve," a familiar, disembodied voice whispers in my ear. "He chose to send the Walrus himself as a messenger."

A terrifying memory flashes through my mind at Koji's quiet observation—a desperate sprint through the Tulgey Wood, the thunderous sound of a synchronized march, the fear that the twins would die…

"Focus, Highness."

Just as easily as his words send my mind tumbling down that proverbial rabbit hole—get it? Ha ha!—Koji's simple statement pulls me back.

I swallow down my own fear and force myself to remain still. I'm in charge here. I'm the fucking White Queen and one day I will reunite the shattered shards of Wonderland.

The Walrus approaches and—reluctant though he may be to do so given the murderous glint in his obsidian eyes—bows to us.

"Most gracious rulers of the high court of Spades," his warbling voice booms through the nearly empty hall, a bubbly lisp present as he works to speak around the bone protrusions in his mouth, "I come to you with the offer of peace."

It takes everything in me not to laugh in his face.

He takes another step forward only to be halted by the crossed vorpal blades of my Rabbits. I have no idea when they even drew their weapons, much less flung them out to cross at the other man's throat. Unaffected, he drops to one knee in supplication.

"Most glorious and fair Queen Alice," he starts.

"Here it comes," Koji whispers into my ear. I bite back a snort.

"I humbly beg your forgiveness, both for myself and on behalf of my liege."

I look him straight in the face and let my mind spin for a minute. Is he really, really coming to apologize, or is this just another dirty trick in the Carpenter's arsenal? I have a hard time believing either of the two of them has a sincere bone in his body.

Either way, this is the most laughable situation ever. And I've already survived some seriously laughable situations.

"We were led to believe that you were a threat to Wonderland, but now we see you are here to help it prosper. Please, I beg of you, show mercy on a pair of hapless fools."

Yeah, dude. No. I read the books. I know better than to believe anything this psychopath says. I also know to keep my enemies close to keep an eye on them. These fuckers have a tendency to eat their followers.

"Test him," Koji says. "He's lying."

Of course he's lying. I'd be stupid to think otherwise.

Anxiety immediately spikes. I have a great handle on magic these days, but the last time I attempted this particular skill, I accidentally exploded three card servants. Talon immediately reversed time to stop it from actually happening, but since then I've been too afraid to try again. Murder in battle is one thing. Murder while dressed like a cupcake is something else entirely.

"You won't explode him," Koji says like he's reading my mind. For all I know, the damned cat is reading my mind. "And even if you do, then good riddance, right?" I take a breath.

Then I let my gaze lock with the groveling man and listen. The magic — tangible threads of light in my mind's eye — reach out toward him, twining up his legs and around his arms, stretching toward his heart. Colors swirl around him, refracted through the beams and coalesce into a pulsing, blackened aura. The light itself burns around the edges, curling like paper ashes. There is nothing genuine about this creature except the will to do harm.

As long as I'm aware of the truth, there's no harm in playing along…right?

"Kind Walrus," I say, causing both Rabbits to blink in confusion, "mercy is yours. Now tell us of your King's offer."

Phineas catches my eye and offers a small smile. This feels like a victory… until our guest starts to talk again.

"The Carpenter, the most gracious and magnanimous King of Diamonds, Lord Percival Rand, offers an alliance against the rule of the mad Red Queen. She is a blight on the beauty that is our fair Wonderland and must be stopped."

His aura pulses again, but this time, a pale blue light filters through. At least he's telling the truth about the reason for the alliance.

"An alliance may be of great benefit to both

courts," Phineas says. Not gonna lie, I swoon a little at the regal tilt of his head and the lilt of his voice. He's a damned fine King and he looks phenomenal in a crown. "What say you, my Queen?"

I try to emulate that air as I raise my own chin just a hair. I feel utterly ridiculous, but nobody needs to know that.

"I quite agree, my King. Present the terms, sir Walrus."

"The most noble and wise Carpenter, King of the Court of Diamonds and ruler of Wonderland's southernmost realm, offers a permanent alliance in exchange for a single request: the hand of The Alice to forge the bond."

Wait…what? The Carpenter wants to marry me? Sight unseen? This place never stops one-upping itself in fuckedupness.

"Steady, highness," Koji whispers and that invisible hand squeezes my shoulder.

"A most intriguing offer," Phineas responds when I don't. There's an unusual edge to his voice, but his face remains serene. He doesn't like the idea at all. "Please tell your illustrious King that we gladly accept a ceasefire to make way for a new era of peace while my Queen considers this most generous offer."

Oh, good…I don't have to turn him down flat.

The Walrus, clearly unhappy with the thinly-veiled dismissal, smiles with all the softness and comfort of bloody razor wire and bows deeply.

"Of course," he answers.

"Please rest and have something to eat before your journey back," Phineas says. "You are welcome here tonight."

No. No, he's not. Not really. But I can play nice for now. I hope.

"I do so appreciate the hospitality of the White Court, but I am afraid I must decline. My liege awaits my report."

"A shame," Phineas replies tartly. "Perhaps on your return then."

"Perhaps."

"Fair winds and clear skies to you."

"Much obliged." The Walrus — I realize I don't know his name — bows to my husband and turns to me. "We do look forward to your decision, Queen Alice."

"Safe travels, Walrus," I say in response. He smiles in a way I don't like and makes his exit.

The doors close behind him, and the tension drains from the room, visibly in some cases. Both Rabbits sag as if holding up their bodies has suddenly become a chore.

"I am not marrying that clown," I announce, like it wasn't already a foregone conclusion. "Didn't he go nuts and murder his last Queen?"

"Nuts is relative given where we are," Jerome says, "but yes. The Carpenter very much acquired his throne through regicide and false pretenses."

A shudder tears down my spine.

"How do we play this?" I ask.

"We discuss it in private," Phineas says, reminding me that even the walls have ears in Wonderland. Literally, in some cases. There's a wall in the east wing that just stands around all day and listens to everything said in the halls.

Sometimes this castle is such a busybody.

"So, next order of business, then?"

Phineas nods. "Send them in," he calls. This must be the new White Knight.

Nervous energy spikes when the doors open, but it's quickly replaced by curiosity. The creature that comes through the door is unlike anything I've seen before—tall and slender; the build giving no indication at all of gender. A faint blue-green hue to the skin of their hands catches my gaze. The face, entirely obscured by a gleaming, white helmet topped with a single, spiral horn, shows only a pair of jewel-tone blue eyes. I'm both fascinated and intimidated.

Phineas rises from his throne, but the strong, invisible hand on my shoulder keeps me seated.

A Queen rises for no one, they all said when I first took this throne, but it's hard not to do the "polite" thing when faced with a potential new ally.

Sometimes I think this damned cat really can read my mind.

"Welcome, friend," Phineas says, his deep voice booming in the quiet hall. "We are honored to be in the presence of the exalted Unicorn."

That deadly-looking horn dips as our guest nods slightly.

"It would be my honor and privilege to serve the one true Queen of Wonderland," they say. The voice is smooth and rich, also impossible to classify, and I'm curious to know what's under that helmet... "However," the Unicorn adds, "before I pledge fealty to anyone, I am afraid I must request a demonstration of ability."

They're cautious. I like that. One can never be too careful in these chaotic times.

I rise from my throne and, against the warning from Koji and the nervous glances from both Ivan and Jerome, step down from the dais to stand before the Unicorn. They tower over me even at the shoulder and getting closer reveals absolutely nothing about what's hiding beneath the armor.

I take a slow, deep breath and lift my hands, offering my palms up. The Unicorn places their cool, teal-colored hands in mine. Our eyes close. My hair flutters as the magic rushes up to surround us. Through that current, I offer up memories of my struggle to reach this moment in time—the tumble through the Rabbit Hole, the race across the battlefield, fearstorms, the Walrus' attack, the Duchess, the end of the Mock Turtle...

Those jewel-tone eyes flash open in a mix of horror and appreciation.

"You are a survivor," they say. I nod. They sink to one knee.

How Arthurian…

"Glorious Queen Alice, prophesied one of legend, I do pledge my services to you and you alone. Will you accept a lone knight into your service?"

The theatrics would make me laugh if the emotion brimming in those sparkling eyes hadn't already caught me totally off guard. I call on my training and mentally organize my words before speaking, hopefully with the appropriate level of formality for the situation.

"Dear Unicorn," I reply, "I am honored by your faith in me. Your service to the White Court would be a blessing to us all. Please rise, my Knight."

A ripple of fascination passes through the hall as the Unicorn rises to their feet. They fix me with that beautiful gaze and though I can't see it, I know they're smiling.

"Our Queen honors me with her favor."

Footsteps break this hypnosis and when I look up, Phineas is beside me.

"It appears our business is done," he says. "No need to announce it to an empty chamber."

"You should know by now that I hate formality," I reply, though my attention is far away from this reality thanks to the armored enigma before us.

"That you do," he answers with a laugh. "Tonight, we shall feast in honor of the White Court's Knight, The Unicorn. Until then, let us retire to a more private setting to discuss pressing matters."

There's a new door in the hallway of my suite. It's tall and pale; a shimmering white adorned with a glittering, gold unicorn horn. It sparkles in the soft light of the hallway, which makes me smile as we pass.

As he sometimes does, the Caterpillar has even seen fit to join us for the discussion. He stands patiently at the far end of the hall beside my bedroom door, though I'm not sure when he arrived. I shouldn't be surprised since he's prone to random appearances, but it always unnerves me when he shows up in unusual places unannounced. He has yet to admit it, but I'm pretty sure magic tells him secrets. He also claims to be impartial to any court save a unified Wonderland, but it also kinda feels like he's playing favorites. Not to be arrogant or anything…

I lead the procession of Wonderland's finest down the hall and into my room, which has expanded to include a table with enough chairs to comfortably seat this haphazard entourage. It's nighttime beyond the balcony doors. In the distance I can see the soft glow of the lights of Wabe. Jerome peels off to prepare several pots of tea and Ivan to retrieve snacks from that wild and wondrous magical sideboard while I disappear to the bathroom to change. The rest take their seats.

Leggings and an oversized sweatshirt later, I'm mentally running down the list of Important Shit to Discuss™ and starting to panic when a clean cup of tea appears on the table. Jerome's fingers slide across my shoulder and he leans down until his lips nearly touch my ear, pulling me out of my head.

"You're thinking much too hard, Highness," he says. "Very little beyond the time you spend in my arms requires such rapt attention."

Chuckles echo around the table and embarrassment floods my cheeks in the form of a blush when I realize that everyone heard what he said. My Rabbits are shameless. And so am I, it seems, since I enjoy their attention so much.

"It's not thinking hard as much as it is thinking about a lot," I reply.

While I'm responding, my tea is sugared and creamed thanks to Ivan's boundless energy. If he's awake, he's moving. He never sits still. Ever.

"Then share with us your thoughts," Phineas says, "for none of us can read your mind."

I'm not sure that's true.

There's true affection in his smile when he looks my way, which is a little disarming since he wanted to track me down to kill me right after we first met and right up until about an hour before we got married.

"Well," I start and take a sip of my tea—just tea today, thank you very much—and grab at my swirling thoughts. "First and foremost, I want to welcome the Unicorn. We don't stand on ceremony in private because I seriously cannot keep that act up for long. Please make yourself comfortable."

The tufted, horned helmet nods and those ethereal hands rise to lift it away. Removal of the helmet raises more questions than it answers.

That same teal skin covers the most perfect, beautiful face I've ever seen. The Unicorn's head is bald save a narrow strip of long, rainbow-colored hair marching down the center of their head. Sapphire eyes sparkle back at me and those perfect lips turn up into a gentle smile.

"Thank you," they say.

It takes a minute to restart my stalled thoughts. I shake my head to clear out the fog and refocus on whatever I'm supposed to be focused on. My gaze returns to the Unicorn time and again, fascinated by the beautiful confusion sitting at the opposite end of my table.

"Highness?" Ivan questions, no doubt sensing the clamor in my head. I tear my gaze away again and sit up a little straighter.

"Right, sorry. First question: who else thinks this invitation from the Carpenter is a big ol' trap?"

Nine hands immediately rise, the Unicorn's included. Good to know we're all on the same page.

"So what do we do about it?"

That question hangs in the silence, making it quite obvious that we're all at a loss.

Jerome is the first to move, his bright, amber eyes catching my gaze and reminding me of every memory we've ever shared, all at one time. My best-friend-turned-protector-turned-lover smirks, reading my thoughts like a naughty inside joke, which is totally not fair since he put those thoughts in my head in the first place.

"There are two viable options," he says, going stone-faced again. "One, you take a small contingent and go to meet with him face to face."

"How small a contingent?" I ask, not sure I want to play Jack to Percival Rand's beanstalk giant.

"No more than a dozen men," he answers, confirming my fears. "Any more could be seen as a show of force."

"I hate it. Next idea?"

Jerome turns to Phineas. "Has Hatta returned?" Phineas nods and Jerome turns back my way. "Then we send Haigha."

I pause and follow my thoughts through the stories to a point where that particular name comes up and draw a blank.

"The March Hare," Jerome answers the obvious confusion on my face. The naked bulb of intellect in my brain flickers on, startling the moth sleeping on it.

The addition of another two characters makes me nervous, though. I've seen and read enough weird adaptations to know that these guys aren't always who and what they say they are.

"Sounds like a plan, I guess?" I'll ask Jerome about my suspicions later. For now, I sip my tea and look around at my growing collection of… whatever they are. A King and his mage, a couple of Rabbits that aren't actually rabbits, a pair of twin assassins with some level of borderline personality disorder, a psychic, a cat-man, and a warrior. It's like the RPG party from Hell up in this magic room and somehow, I've become the dungeon master.

And this is by far not the strangest moment of my life.

"What else troubles my Queen?" Phineas asks.

I take a sip from a clean cup of tea and shake my head.

"I don't know exactly. I know our goal is to unify Wonderland and Talon has made it quite clear that I'm a vital part of the story now, but I'm still new to this whole concept of being a Queen. I don't know what I'm supposed to be doing or if I'm even doing any of it right."

Phineas nods in what appears to be understanding.

"Ruling a land is not easy," he replies, "and I would be remiss if I told you it was. As for what you should be doing?" He looks down the line of the table at the waiting faces. "You should be doing exactly the things you are doing now. Political negotiations take time, and wars are not won overnight. Handling this summons from the Carpenter is our most pressing matter. And no matter how it may feel, understand that you are not, and will never be, alone in your quest."

I nod and focus my attention on my teacup. His graceful words do make me feel a bit better, but at the same time, that weight of expectation remains on my shoulders. I'm feeling suddenly… inadequate.

"What else do we need to talk about?" I ask to drive the topic away from my leadership fallacies.

"Another request for an audience has been made, Highness," Koji says, surprising everyone. He doesn't usually speak during these pow-wows except to needle me.

"Who, pray tell, might want to speak with my wife?" Phineas asks. He really doesn't like this cat.

"Why, my mistress, of course."

"No," Jerome says.

"Hell no," Ivan echoes.

"Guys," I snap, silencing the whole table. I turn to the Cheshire Cat, who seems wholly unfazed. "I hope you don't mean the Duchess — as in the same one who invaded my castle right after we got there."

"Oh, but I do," he answers.. "You see, she is quite excited to meet the future Queen of Wonderland."

"I bet she is," Ivan mutters, but quiets when I hit him with a sharp glare.

"For what purpose?"

"Couldn't say."

Fucking cat…

"Then the answer is no," Ivan snaps.

"Why don't we let our Queen decide for herself?"

My Rabbit grumbles again but sits back and says nothing else. I don't blame him for being surly. I would be too if I were in his position.

"Let me think about it," I answer, watching Koji's face that, as always, gives away nothing. "It would help if I knew what she wanted going into it."

"I imagine it would," Koji says.

"Then why don't you find out what she wants? Then I can decide if I want to risk my life or not."

"The greater the risk, the greater the reward."

"Can I kill him now?" Ivan asks, not rhetorically.

"No."

I know Koji is trying to tell me something important, but I'm so annoyed by his stupid riddle that I can't even begin to parse out what the message might be. Besides, Phineas already said our most pressing issue is dealing with the Carpenter.

"I think we're done here," I say and rise from my seat. The others are slow to follow. "Lunchtime?" I ask.

"Sounds lovely," Phineas replies.

We begin the strange process of shuffling toward the door when the Unicorn appears at my side.

"Highness, might I have a word in private?"

Jerome and Ivan are both immediately on alert. If they had their way, I'd never be alone with anyone again. For more than one reason.

"Of course."

"Your faithful Rabbits may stay, of course," the Unicorn says in response to the death glares. That seems to soothe their murderous intent. A little. Koji, of course, slows, but before he can vanish and stay to listen, Phineas grabs him by the collar and forces him from the room.

"Private means without you, cat."

As the door falls closed behind them, Koji begins to yowl in protest. I want to laugh, but the serious look on the Unicorn's face stops the chuckle from escaping.

"I beg your forgiveness, Highness, but I must warn you," they say, "that one is not to be trusted. I have witnessed the Cheshire Cat's betrayal with my own eyes."

I'm both surprised and not. I'm pretty sure everyone has been a victim of his mercurial nature at least once. He's less than honest in any given scenario. Despite the fact that he showed up at the eleventh hour and helped save my skin when Phineas wanted my head to roll, there's still *something* about him that screams of trouble. But it's the look in the Unicorn's crystalline, blue eyes—a blend of concern and fear—that stops me from voicing my uncertainty.

We move back to the table as a unit and sit. I want to think that I can trust the magic to tell make a decision about Koji's door… but this is Wonderland and I know better than to really trust anything here.

Even myself.

"I do appreciate your concern—all of you," I add, indicating Jerome and Ivan as well, "however, things are rarely as they seem here, and the suite seems to thinkI can trust him. Well, at least as much as I already do."

Which, honestly, isn't all that much.

"Forgive my impudence, but magic often lies."

I'm sure it does.

"Please don't apologize for speaking your mind. As you've seen, I'm serious when I say we don't require formality here. At least, I don't." Some of the tension drains from the Unicorn's shoulders, but they remain formal as ever. "Speaking of, I still don't know your name."

"I am called Blade, Highness."

"It's nice to officially meet you, Blade." They bow with a flourish. I have too many questions. For the most part, everyone I've met in Wonderland appears mostly human. The Walrus is still a horrifying shock every time I see him, and Blade is an enigma. The color of their skin doesn't exist in my world in any capacity, much less on a person. "I promise you, I do not take your warnings lightly. I don't trust Koji as much as I'd like to. I'm always waiting for that betrayal—but I do trust my intuition where magic is concerned. Should the day come when my faith in my abilities falters, you three will be the first to know."

After a moment of deep thought, Blade smiles.

"You truly are amazing, Highness. The rumors of your greatness hardly do you justice."

The comment makes me blush. I'm not normally the blushy type, mainly because I'm not normally on the receiving end of compliments. In true Alice form, I brush it off with a snort and a wave.

"Enough of this sentimental nonsense. We have a banquet to throw!"

Jerome opens the door and we all file out. The one thing I can't leave behind, however, is the dread associated with the thought that Blade might just be right about that damned cat.

CHAPTER TWO

One thing about Wonderland I'll never get used to is the tea. For those that have never visited Wonderland, the tea is truly something. It's tea, yes, but it's also top-shelf alcohol, and the world's best designer drug all rolled up into one clean cup.

I'm on cup number four of whatever I've been handed, and I'm currently smelling sound—laughter sounds like warm snickerdoodle cookies—when the reverie is broken by a blood-curdling scream that smells like blood.

I'm immediately on alert and both Ivan and Jerome are in front of me, armor out and vorpal blades drawn, as the crowd parts to reveal a man lying on the floor, unconscious. His clothes are torn and bloody and he's not moving. Barely breathing. Magic pulses around him in time with his slowing heartbeat. He's dying.

"Felina!" Phineas shouts while moving toward the downed man. The Ace of Spades appears at his left elbow, but she isn't alone. Talon falls into step on the White King's right side.

"He's alive," Felina says as they draw near.

A handful of card servants swarm in and lift the unconscious man from the floor.

"Is that—?" Phineas asks.

"—can't be," Jerome answers.

The twins are across the room in an instant, following behind the procession of cards, magicians, and kings.

"What the hell is happening?" I ask, nearly shouting to be heard over the rising panic of our party guests, and the pair suddenly remember my presence.

"Alice! To Me! Now!" Talon calls. I rush to his side only to be pulled down to my knees beside him. He takes my palm and presses it to the center of the wounded man's chest. Warm, blue blood — Rabbit blood — pours from his chest, bubbling up over my pale skin before Talon's hands come down across the top of mine.

"Call up the magic," he says. I close my eyes, take a deep breath through my nose, and reach down into the ground. He immediately takes hold, pushing it into the rapidly weakening body. The faint, frantic pulse of this stranger's heart steadies, then regulates. When I open my eyes, my hands are stained blue, but the blood has mostly stopped flowing. On the outside, anyway. I can still feel the warbling cry of internal pain through the touch of my skin to both his and the Caterpillar's.

Seconds later I'm pulled away. My hands are sticky and my head spins. Too much big magic in one day. Too much... *everything*. I wobble, but hands slide under my arms and lift me up.

"Come with us," Ivan says as he and Jerome carry me from the hall. There's a buzz in the air that smells like rot; a thin, troubling, contagious vein of anxiety passing from person to person. I still have no idea what's going on.

At first, I expect to be taken back to my suite for protection but instead they lead me down a different hall. The acrid smell of antiseptic fills my nose, and the temperature drops a good fifteen degrees. Ivan takes my hand while Jerome pushes open the doors, and I realize we've come to an infirmary.

No... a hospital.

The room is a surprising blend of modern and medieval. There are machines that look like ones I'd see at home, but beside them are vials and IV drips loaded with swirling, magical infusions. It's the strangest thing I've ever seen. We have more important matters at hand, though—like the unconscious stranger.

When we reach the room where he is, I'm surprised to find everyone but Felina is waiting outside looking worried. Even Talon, who never looks anything but bored.

"He's going to live," the Caterpillar says when he notices us, though he keeps staring through the window into the surgical suite where Felina is working.

"Who is he?"

"Haigha," Phineas says. "Our messenger."

That crumpled heap of a man is the March Hare.

"He didn't make it very far," I say aloud, more to myself than anyone else.

"Ambush?" Jerome asks and Phineas nods. That's the point when I realize Talon is as covered in congealed Rabbit blood as I am. Maybe more.

"Felina is trying to recover his memories without waking him." When I meet his gaze, there's a haggardness there I've never seen before. His perfect refinement is cracking, and it's a troubling sight.

We stand there together, lined up like card soldiers on the battlefield, the excitement of the banquet forgotten. And we watch. It's a horrible feeling, being so helpless. I don't know him personally, but I don't like the idea of anyone suffering. Logically, I know he's alive because of Talon and me, but it doesn't feel like enough. It never does.

No matter how bad things get, nobody deserves to suffer. Nobody deserves to die. And they certainly don't deserve to die in such a traumatic way.

Phineas slides an arm around my shoulders and pulls me close to his side. It's a comfort having him there.

We remain that way for what seems like hours, watching Felina tend to him in both medical and magical ways. His pulse ebbs and flows like a tide, the monitor screaming in protest with each jolt of energy she sends through him. When she finally turns off the lights and emerges, she looks pale and exhausted.

I wonder how much of her sanity she just sacrificed for him.

"Any success?" Phineas questions. I'm not used to him being this impatient. Since the moment I've met him, he's been a pillar of strength and resolve.

"He's fragmented. Even for him, it's bad. There wasn't much usable memory in there."

I don't know exactly what that means, but I do know it's awful news.

"Will he remember when he wakes?" Phineas asks. Felina's expression darkens.

"I've no idea," she answers. "That mind is messy enough, and I won't know until we find out who wakes up. If he wakes up at all."

"What?"

"There is something else," she continues, bypassing my question, and leads us into the room.

The man in the bed looks small and weak, physically damaged by whatever attack befell him. But it's more even than that. The air around him also feels broken. Shattered, like the magic in the air is reflecting against the shards of the person lying in the bed.

"I could find no memory of this, and it's fresh."

Felina lifts his bandaged arm and turns it so that his palm is up. Another strip of gauze covers his inner arm, which she pulls back to reveal an angry burn.

No, not a burn... a brand.

In the shape of a heart.

"Where is that blasted cat?" Phineas asks, his voice a snarl.

"Probably still eating," I reply. Koji isn't here with us, but he's close enough that I can feel his energy. "He's been near me all day."

"He may not have done this, but he can certainly tell me who did."

"This is not the mark of my mistress," Koji says, indignant at the accusation after barely casting a glance at the brand on Haigha's arm. "She would not abuse another without cause."

"She's more animal than you," Ivan snaps.

"Perhaps," Koji replies, meeting my Rabbit's pointed glare with a firm gaze of his own, "However, I can assure you that she is not responsible for this man's situation."

"Can you prove it?" I ask. As it stands, I am the only one in this circle who doesn't have a weapon at the ready and aimed at the cat. The cat who, unsurprisingly, is more than willing to smile at me like we're alone in his bedroom. He's such a creep.

Is it bad that I don't entirely dislike it?

"Of course, Highness." Those long, narrow fingers move to the collar of his shirt and slowly begin to undo the clasps.

My mouth goes dry despite the many internal warnings to not ogle the cat. But when I asked for proof, I didn't know I ordered a striptease. There are many things very wrong here, the least of which is the fact that I'm certainly not *not* enjoying this. So much for being subtle.

And then I realize why he's taking his clothes off.

Aside from the fact that the majority of his body is covered in a blend of scars and tattoos, there is also a brand on his chest, just above his heart. And he's right. It's very different from the one on Haigha's arm.

"This is my mistress' brand," he says with a note of bitterness to his voice. The edges of his mark — a labyrinth-style heart topped with a tilted crown — are clean and crisp with little scarring outside of the mark itself. The mark on Haigha's arm is a solid heart; simple, blurred, and messy.

Silence descends on our group with a note of sympathy for Koji left unuttered. My mind spins over the options, but nothing solidifies.

Except…

"Where was he found?" I ask. My blood runs cold at the thought that grabs hold.

"Just past Wabe," Jerome says.

"Do you think—"

"The Walrus?" Koji asks. "He was my first thought as well."

"I didn't want to assume."

"Sometimes assumptions are worth a second thought," Ivan says. "It's not beneath the Carpenter to muddy the situation with false accusations."

"Quite right," Jerome agrees. "Felina says Haigha will recover," he continues, "let us return to the banquet and leave him to his rest."

"I'm not hungry."

"It is customary–"

"Fuck what's customary!" I shout loudly enough to make Koji flinch. Even Phineas—in receipt of the force of my statement—takes a step back. "I don't care about custom and tradition. We're under attack again, likely by the same asshole trying to corner me into a marriage death trap, so forgive me if I'm not interested in playing nice for the bourgeoisie!"

"Let us return to your quarters then," Jerome suggests. "I think we're done for the evening." I drag in a sharp breath through my nose and nod in agreement.

"I will see the others safely back to the dining hall," Ivan says as he hits Koji with an icy glare, "then join you soon enough."

And with that, I'm whisked back down the hall to my room.

The door is barely closed before my back hits the wall. Jerome's lips crash into mine, forcing my mouth open for his tongue to dip inside. Between the thundering of blood in my veins and the pulse of his desire through our Rabbit-Queen bond, I can no longer think straight. Which is good. Because I don't want to think at all anymore.

Jerome's fingers are quick to loosen the strings holding my dress in place and even quicker to find purchase on the bare skin underneath. I'm little more than a quivering mess when he lifts me from the center of the caged dinner gown and carries me to the bed.

"Jerome…"

"Stop thinking," he commands. The note of authority in his voice sends a shiver down my spine. He's only like this when we're alone, which is rare these days. But I do so love to see him take control. He strips me to the skin, then strips my authority, allowing me to just lie back and *feel*.

"Yes, sir," I whimper and my back hits the plush of the mattress with a soft bounce.

"Good girl."

Another shiver shakes through me. His quietly murmured praise is deliciously addictive. Jerome steps back, allowing me a full view of his body as he slowly strips away his coat and shirt to reveal the landscape of hypnotic, living tattoos hugging the curves of his body. The look on his face is pure sin, and I'm helpless to look anywhere but into his eyes. A smirk lifts one corner of his mouth. The whisper of fabric against the floor is both nearly inaudible and louder than any scream.

I spend the rest of the night trapped in his arms, mindless with pleasure and helpless to do anything but enjoy the deliciousness of his touch.

I barely register the rustle of bedsheets as Jerome extricates himself from my arms to open the door. Double-sided amusement filters through my head at whatever conversation passes between him and Ivan, then I'm wrapped up in two sets of arms, and my consciousness goes blank again.

It's late when I rise from that near-comatose state. The room is light enough to tell me the sun has been up for hours, and I'm alone, tangled in my sheets. For the first few moments of consciousness, I'm blissfully unaware of the reality outside my bed, but it doesn't last long.

There's a knock at my door and when I stumble over to open it, a cup of tea is shoved into my face.

"Gunpowder," Jerome says, then barrels past me toward my armoire to pick out suitable attire for the day. "We have a busy day ahead."

I look down at my cup, then back at my Rabbit. He's just handed me the Wonderland equivalent of cocaine straight out of bed…we're definitely in for a rough time.

CHAPTER THREE

The meeting room is full of excited chatter when I arrive. All of my nearest and dearest are here, including the new White Knight.

Jerome guides me the rest of the way into the room and for the first time in a while, the conversation doesn't stop when I sit down. Phineas and Ivan are wrapped up in a debate that sounds like gibberish while the twins do their best to confuse Blade. The Unicorn holds their own, clearly having dealt with nonsense before. Even Talon and Felina are quietly discussing magical matters while occasionally letting Koji speak.

For a few minutes I just listen, filing bits and pieces of the conversations away for later consideration while I finish my tea.

There's a lull in the noise right about the time the stimulant takes hold.

"What of Haigha?" I ask. Felina shakes her head.

"Still asleep, unfortunately."

"Well, where do we stand?"

"On our feet, obviously," Tag replies.

"And on the ground, clearly," Nacht adds.

"Though if one were to stand on their head, one might see things from a new perspective," Tag continues.

"Quite right, brother."

Now my head hurts.

"No one is standing on their head," Jerome announces even though we all know this already. Though, the mental image of everyone taking their heads off and standing on them is giggle-worthy.

Then it dawns on me...

"Perhaps not, but maybe a new perspective is in order."

Nothing is as it seems in Wonderland, which means that solving problems through traditional means is often a fruitless endeavor. There are options here not available in my world—Otherland, they call it—which means getting creative with my problem solving is the way to go.

"What do you mean?" Phineas asks as the strange idea takes root in my mind and grows into a plan.

"If we can't question Haigha, why don't we question the place the attack happened?"

Nine pairs of curious eyes blink as they parse out the meaning of my statement. I'm not even sure if it can be done…but if it can, it's the only real option we have.

Talon, of course, is the first to figure it out.

"A brilliant idea, Majesty, but certainly dangerous. A fool's errand and no doubt the purpose behind the attack."

"What other way do we have to figure this out? If the Walrus did this, then we can consider it an act of war."

"Alice," Phineas says with a sigh. He only uses my name when he wants to argue. "Have you thought at all about the reality where this is a trap meant to draw you into the open for assassination?"

No.

"Yes," I lie. But I am thinking about it now so it counts. "But look around. I'm the best-protected person in Wonderland."

"That you are," Phineas agrees, "but the Carpenter, he is…"

"Powerful? Mean? Sneaky? All of the above?"

"He raises the dead," Blade says.

Whoa. Not what I expected. I knew he was powerful and awful but… raising the dead? That's a thing here?

"He's a necromancer?"

"He's a monster," Ivan corrects. "More twisted and cruel than the bloody Red Queen and as powerful as any Caterpillar."

"I beg your finest fucking pardon," Talon snaps, clearly insulted by this. It's the closest thing to emotion I've seen ever from him and the only time I've ever heard profanity out of him. It almost sounds wrong in his gentle, singsong voice.

"Like it or not, it's the truth," Jerome says.

"So you see, Highness," Phineas continues, "it is far too dangerous for–"

"I'm going." The tea coursing through my system and I agree that we want results and we want them right this second. "We need to go now before they have time to finesse whatever trap they've set. Ivan, Jerome, Blade, Talon—you'll come with me. The rest of you will guard the castle. I can't imagine this would be a simple trap. Something is bound to happen here too."

I rise from my seat and reluctantly mumbled acquiescence follows me out the door.

What in the absolute hell was I thinking?

The attack site is not hard to find, and it isn't far from the palace at all. The part that makes me question this decision is the savagery with which the attack took place. Before I even open myself to the magic, I can feel the brutality. And see the blood. Oozing blue sludge coats everything in a five-meter radius, and bits of hair and skin litter the hard-packed dirt path. The air smells like death and even the ground seems to mourn the events that took place here.

"Animals?" Ivan asks out loud, more rhetorical than literal. Deep gouges in both the path and a nearby tree would lead one to believe it was a bear attack—do bears even exist here? If they do, I'm sure they're some weird flavor of bear-something-hybrid—but the finer details speak of human interference. Smudged footprints. Blade-shaped gouges. Blue blood.

"That is what they want you to believe."

The answer comes from an unfamiliar voice and is followed by heavy footsteps. Both Rabbits, suddenly fully armored, step between me and the approaching stranger.

"Apologies for startling you, Highness," he says and stops a respectable distance away, "but I have information that may be of use to you."

"Edwin," Ivan hisses. His helmet slides back, but he remains at attention, weapon drawn.

"Greetings, Ivan. So good to see you again."

"I wish I could say the same."

"Care to fill me in?" I ask.

"Edwin is the Earl of Mercia," Ivan growls through gritted teeth. "A loyal subject of the bloody Red Queen.

"Subject, yes," Edwin corrects. "Loyal? Only to the side of good."

Ivan laughs a hollow, humorless laugh. It sounds like a threat to my ears. "You, the great revolutionary, the fucking Red Court Beast, expect me to believe that?"

"I expect you to believe nothing," Edwin replies. He is completely unaffected. Smiling, even.

I'm missing a lot here, but I do see there is no love lost between these two.

"Can we get back to the point?" I ask and they all snap back to attention. "What happened here, Lord Edwin?"

"An ambush, Majesty." His gaze flickers to the battleground then back. "Two men dressed in Heart uniforms — though they most certainly are not men of the Heart banner — ripped dear Haigha clean out of his shoes while their leader attempted to tear him limb from limb."

"And how do you know these men are not of Heart stock?" Blade asks.

"Because, good Unicorn, I am the commander of the Red Army."

This is not good. It appears the ambush was a setup for an even bigger ambush.

Sensing my unease, Jerome and Ivan both move closer. Blade steps between Edwin and me, much more intuitive than I expected.

"Relax, Majesty," Edwin continues in a breezy tone, "though the enemy commander I may be, I am not at all your enemy."

"You do understand why she would have a hard time believing you, yes?" Jerome asks.

"Perhaps if you'd brought the Cheshire Cat along, you could have asked him as well."

"I don't trust him, either," I lie.

"He speaks the truth of himself," Talon interjects. He's so quiet and so motionless that I'd honestly forgotten he was here. I turn to look at him and see that his eyes are glazed and cloudy—he's looking at something only he can see. "The remainder of his statement shall soon be verified."

Talon steps up and offers his hand. There's a smoothness and refinement to him that draws a shiver along my spine. My personal headcanon says he's aristocracy. Close to royalty. Someone who was raised well, trained to have style, grace, and poise.

Or maybe that's just the fact that he's a fucking fairy.

"I assume this is why you asked me along, yes?"

"I-it is." I'm uncharacteristically bashful. I refuse to admit that I have a lingering crush on him. He's beautiful. Powerful. Completely unbothered by any of the bullshit around us. Raw pour hangs in the air around him; a magnet to my silly, lovesick heart. It wouldn't do either of us any good to dwell on something that is, in a world of impossibility, completely impossible.

"Then if you please." He nods toward the hand still hanging between us. Feeling foolish, I slip my fingers into his palm and brace myself as the magic starts to flow between us. Trusting my Rabbits, I let my eyes fall closed and watch time rewind.

The feeling is as disorienting as it was the first time. Talon's hand around mine is the only thing anchoring me in reality. Magic courses up from the ground and into my veins, a bottomless font for the Caterpillar's skilled manipulation.

Time lurches to a stop so suddenly that my body pitches forward into his chest. His free arm wraps around my waist to steady me and with what appears to be simple mental push, the vision reel ticks forward in regular time.

We're no longer surrounded by friends but rather standing alone beside the road. Talon assures me I'll be able to do this without his assistance one day, but the thought of controlling time itself terrifies me.

Focus, Highness, his voice echoes in my memory, pulling me back to the task at hand.

One moment, Haigha is on the path atop a domesticated jubjub and the next, the world around us is pandemonium. He's a whirl of armor and carnage, taking down one hooded attacker after another while the frightened bird flees into the forest, its massive claws leaving deep gouges in the well-worn path.

That explains one part…

The more assailants that come out of the woods, the harder Haigha fights, but there are just too many. He twists and whirls with singular focus, his eyes flashing bright with power against the faded landscape, but he's soon overrun. Weapons bounce off of his armor until they don't, and blood starts trickling between the panels.

My heart pounds in my chest as we move closer and closer to the inevitable outcome. Though it's not the influx of attackers that fells the March Hare, nor is it the pair of heart-armored assailants grabbing hold of his arms above the elbow and pulling him away from the fight. It's the magical shockwave that shakes the leaves from the trees and drops every living being to the ground. Even the vision itself wavers under the force of the impact. I flinch, but Talon's hand tightens around mine, reminding me to keep focus. If I don't hold the magic, we'll lose the story.

Willing away the pain, I turn my attention back to the scene before us and a dazed Haigha struggling to sit up.

Laughter fills the emptiness that follows, and the hollow, grating sound sends a shudder rippling through me. The… creature… (because I can't rightfully call it a man) that follows it out of the woods is one of the most horrifying things I've ever seen. Tall and broad-shouldered,. Its blood-red eyes glow beneath the gleaming black helmet and perfectly polished, segmented iron armor that covers him from top to toes. The armor is so dark that it seems to suck the light out of the air. He is something out of my worst childhood nightmares; the unnamed demon coming to claim my soul for his dessert. Even though he's not really there, I still find myself taking a step back as he advances. Talon's hand flexes around mine, reminding me that this is a vision; that the boogeyman can't actually get me, but even that doesn't help. My heart hammers against my ribs and terror pulses in my throat. I need to run.

I open my mouth to scream, but someone takes my other hand. The fear bleeds away enough to regain my composure. Sort of. . My mind slips back into focus and then Jerome is there, his eyes wide as he takes in the scene.

The imposing stranger has advanced enough in my distraction that he's now standing over Haigha, glaring down with those cruel, red eyes.

"No..." Jerome hisses. Clearly, he knows who this is. I'm too busy staring at the giant sword hanging from the man's left hand. It's easily as long as I am tall and probably as heavy, but he wields it as if it weighs nothing at all.

"You," Haigha gasps as he scrambles backwards over bodies in the bloody dirt. "The King of Clubs himself wants to disrupt the negotiations?"

The King of Clubs laughs, another hard, grating sound muffled by the iron helmet that promises terrible things.

"I've no need to tell you," he says, "because you will soon be dead."

He lifts that giant sword and brings it down hard, cleaving a massive divot into the ground where Haigha sat only half a breath before. The Rabbit-armored man is on his feet faster than a grievously injured creature should be able to move, but even that isn't enough. His attacker swings again and this time the blade not only shatters his vorpal sword into flying splinters, but catches him under the left arm, sending the Rabbit flying. His form sails toward us and I flinch away.

The vision breaks apart this time, dissipating at the moment of what should have been impact, and the magic leaves me in a rush.

When I come to, we're sitting in a small cottage with a steaming teapot on the table. I'm stretched out on a sofa, and my companions sit in nearby chairs, deep in some kind of discussion. I lie there and listen, unsure of what exactly they're saying or if I'm even able to move. Nothing hurts, but what their words makes no sense. Maybe I had a head wound. A concussion.

What they talk about sounds sort of like battle tactics, which always goes over my head.

I move to sit up, and both Rabbits are immediately at my side, guiding me.

"Welcome back, Highness," Edwin says and offers a smile and a nod. He makes no other move, as if he knows he's on thin ice.

"Where are we?" I ask. My voice doesn't sound like my own.

"A long-forgotten Rabbit Hole near the border of Mercia," Ivan explains, and my anxiety spikes given the fact that the last one was compromised. "It's safe," he adds. "We are the only ones here. This particular Rabbit Hole has been abandoned for quite some time."

"Could I…go home from here?"

It's not something I'd considered of late, but the thought of leaving this tangled mess is not without merit. I could just walk away. Go home and live my life.

"You certainly could," Edwin says, "though if I might be so bold, I am of the opinion that you are much safer on this side."

"He's right," Ivan mumbles. Grudgingly. It's almost like agreeing with Edwin causes him physical pain. "While in Wonderland, you are protected by us and by your position as White Queen. In Otherland, I'm afraid our rules do not apply."

So much for a quick exit.

Jerome places a cup of tea in my hands. "I made it," he whispers. That, at least, makes me feel a little better.

I take a sip. The warm chamomile and honey flavors coat my dry mouth, and the magic helps to soothe my raw nerves. The anxiety melts away under the effects of the low tea, but every time I close my eyes, the attack flashes through my head again. I shudder and take another sip. I'll see that in my nightmares for a long time to come.

"We have to stop that guy," I say out loud. "But I haven't the foggiest idea how to do it."

"Brute force, love," Edwin replies. "A united front would be best."

"Who do you mean when you say *united*?" I question. "You might've missed the memo, but everyone in Wonderland wants me dead."

"Which is precisely why no one would suspect an alliance. Particularly an alliance right under Lucinda's nose."

Ivan's mouth falls open. "Are you an idiot? Did you forget that that bloody Red Queen of yours would have your severed head served to us on fire just for suggesting this?"

"Oh, I am very aware. I simply do not care."

"At what point did this become an alliance negotiation?" I ask and all eyes in the room focus on me.

"By my estimation," Edwin replies, "The moment King Humphrey took up arms against the White Court's messenger."

Well… okay.

I take another sip of my still warm–weird magic there–tea. "How exactly would this work? What are you proposing?"

The smile that spreads across Edwin's face very much resembles Koji's expression when he gets what he wants, and I wonder if I haven't made a mistake by opening up this conversation.

"You and I want for the same goal, Majesty. My plan is not simple, but by grace and your faith and trust, it will work."

Subtle movement catches my eye and I glance over to meet Blade's whirling, hypnotic gaze. In those eyes, I read a clear warning: He is not to be trusted.

Hell, at this point, I don't even trust myself.

I nod once and, satisfied with my acknowledgment, they turn back to Edwin.

"Let's hear the details before I agree to anything."

Edwin leans back in his seat, relaxed and informal in a manner designed to put me at ease, but it doesn't.

"We must agree to share information," he says. "I shall keep you apprised of the Red Court's movements while you allow me to know your location at all times. If I know where you are, I may protect you from harm. And I shall help you avoid the Red Court until such time as we join together to take the Mad Queen's head."

Once again, all eyes turn my way for an answer. I can feel the anticipation in the bonds between my Rabbits and the Unicorn has made their position crystal clear.

"Talon," I say, holding Edwin's gaze, and a lazy smile spreads across the Caterpillar's face in my peripheral vision. "Show me the possible futures, please."

"As my Queen commands," he answers and slinks out of the chair to kneel at my feet. Every move of his exudes a fluid sensuality, and I have to remind myself again that he is that way by design.

One does not become the Caterpillar without an abundance of charisma and madness.

Talon takes my hands in his and his lip curls knowingly, like he can read my thoughts.

No, but he can see the futures. All of them.

"Majesty," he prompts, and I finally release Edwin's gaze to close my eyes and focus on drawing the magic up around us.

Anxiety creeps in with the visions. This one isn't as urgent, but the last was recent enough that I still haven't processed the pure violence we witnessed yet.

These new images rise up through a smoky haze in my mind. We're not transported anywhere. Fragments of visions flicker through my mind, barely enough to see, which means they're irrelevant.

Then one begins to play.

The fallen palace is restored. I look out from a throne onto four generals, one for each suit, and four faceless kings beside them. There is peace.

The images flicker again, like the faces of cards in a rapidly shuffled deck.

Edwin stands before me, a blade to my throat, while the Red Queen laughs. His eyes are cold and empty.

"Off with her head!" she shouts, and I'm forced to my knees.

Another flicker.

The Queen's suite. My Rabbits, King Phineas, the Cheshire Cat, the Twins, the Duchess, the Unicorn, the March Hare, Edwin. They stand around my bed. Talon rests on his knees. Wide, iridescent wings stretch from his back, showing my countless futures. I'm meant to make a decision.

Another flicker.

Chaos and carnage on a burning, bloody battlefield. Everyone I know and love dead at my feet while I hold the burning White Court standard. My dress, too, catches fire.

"Enough!" I shout—or try to. My voice issues forth as little more than a strangled whisper.

"There is more," Talon responds, and I can't tell if it's out loud or in my head. The vision changes.

A large, cruel-eyed man stands over me. Though he wears no armor, he's the same build as the King of Diamonds.

"One way or another," he says, "you will submit to me."

It changes again.

The Duchess stands far too close, her hands cradling my face.

"You will rule the world, my beautiful Queen," she says and kisses me.

The visions fade and the magic recedes, leaving me clinging to Talon's hand like an anchor to reality. When I open my eyes, my vision is blurry. I'm sweaty and shaking, and nothing about the world feels solid now that I've seen myself suffer in a dozen different ways.

The only thing in focus is Talon.

"All of that..."

"Is possible, yes," he says. "And may be determined by this one decision."

I'm the only one that can make this decision. In this moment, I decide my own fate. Everyone watches me, quietly waiting, and I have no idea what to do.

A pot of tea, a plate of cakes, and two hours later, I'm no closer to making this decision. The series of possible futures has left me rattled to the core and unwilling to move. My hands shake and nervous sweat trickles along my spine despite the fact that the air in the Rabbit Hole is cold. The fear of making the wrong decision is paralyzing, and the low effect of the tea has my head foggy.

This is not how I planned on spending this day. In the months since my arrival in Wonderland, I've carried the title of "Queen", but I've really been more of an apprentice to Phineas. I've let him lead political discussions and listened to his advice on affairs of court, making the decisions that needed to be made only at his urging. I've tried to learn the ways of this new world, to integrate myself in a way that will allow me to effectively lead, and thus far I've managed to avoid making any decision without first being well-informed.

Oh, well…we've all gotta grow up someday.

I had hoped that my first solo mission wouldn't be one that decides the fate of Wonderland as a whole.

Yay.

I swallow down my nervousness, place my teacup on the side table, and lace my fingers together to keep them from trembling as I look Edwin in the eye.

"Explain something to me, Lord Edwin."

"Anything, Majesty."

"How exactly do you suggest we pass information back and forth without being discovered?"

He smiles — a cagey expression full of teeth and unspoken threats.

"Why, the Cheshire Cat, of course. Who else but the Neko can move seamlessly between sides?"

"Do you trust him?"

"With my life." His answer is immediate and sincere. "A flight risk he may seem, but there is no other I'd have at my side in times of crisis."

I lock my jaw in place to keep from grinding my teeth together in frustration. If my time in Wonderland has taught me anything at all, it's to never take for granted that anyone here is telling the truth. Watching Edwin gives away nothing and talking to him gives away even less. Even a touch of magic pushed in his direction doesn't help at all. The man is as impenetrable as a fortress.

And the time has come, however, to make a decision.

...of shoes and ships and sealing wax, of cabbages and kings...

I shake my head to clear the sudden burst of poetry and focus on what appears to be an earnest smile on his face. I shudder.

"I agree to this plan—" his smile widens like he's about to jump up and dance, " —with the provision that if you betray me, I will tear you apart from the inside out."

"As my Queen desires," he answers with a half-bow from his seat. His smile is no less wide for my preemptive scolding.

Edwin then slides gracefully from his chair to one knee, prostrate as a knight before his liege-lord — or liege-lady in this case—and places a hand against his chest.

"Lady Alice of the White Court, Queen of Spades and rightful sovereign of the four kingdoms, I do pledge my faith and loyalty to your noble and just cause."

Well, that's certainly over the top. Might as well play along.

"Lord Edwin of Mercia, your Queen humbly accepts this show of fealty as your solemn oath to serve not just the Court of Spades, but the banner of a unified Wonderland."

There is as much magic in those words as there is free in the air. It wraps around both of us, binding us as if tethered. Almost as if Wonderland itself gives its blessing.

When Edwin raises his head, there's no edge to his smile — only a content, if not slightly indulgent, sense of calm.

"Enough of this formality," I say to break up this strange new tension in the air. "Now we need to figure out *how* we're going to accomplish this crazy plan."

"If you'll allow me, Majesty," Blade says, surprising me. What little I know of them means I don't know them to speak up unless asked, "but I may have an idea."

Well, if that isn't the most curious turn of events...

Chapter Four

By the time we return to the castle, it's well after midnight. My head is full to bursting and my bones ache from the magic, but my heart is strangely peaceful. The smell of dinner hits my nose as soon as we enter the foyer and my stomach flips in anticipation. Before I can get to the food, however, I'm swept up into a bone-crushing hug.

"You're safe," Phineas mutters into my hair. "Hearts and cards, woman, do you have any idea how worried I've been?"

"I'm sorry," I reply when my lungs reinflate enough to push words out. "It's been a busy day."

"Clearly." He curls an arm around my shoulders and leads me toward the stairs. "We've kept dinner warm for you. I'll have it brought to your room."

Six months ago, he held a sword to my throat and threatened to take my life. Now he holds my hand as he leads me down the main corridor toward the suite's door. I never would have thought this man capable of such deep and gentle caring, but he dotes on me as if I'm a precious treasure.

"That sounds good. Bring everyone up with us too. We have a lot to talk about."

Forty-five minutes later, I'm clean and dressed in comfortable clothes with a plate of food and a pot of tea in front of me. My room has adjusted itself in my absence to make room for my inner circle, which seems to keep expanding.

At the moment, I'm surrounded by two Rabbits, a pair of twins, a Caterpillar, a Unicorn, a Cat, and a King. Our court spellbinder is still in residence at Haigha's side, thus the empty chair.

Tea is passed around and those who want food have it. And once again, everyone is looking at me, which makes me so nervous that I can't touch the beautiful and delicious-looking plate in front of me.

"So," I start, unable to shake off the awkward nervousness that comes with being the center of attention, "a couple of things happened today." My stomach rumbles loud enough for everyone to hear. I pick up a small fruit that resembles a grape but tastes like pineapple custard. "First of all, how is Haigha?" I ask and pop the fruit into my mouth. The skin bursts with a satisfying pop and flavor explodes in my mouth.

"Stable," Phineas says. "Felina reports that he is no longer trapped in his fragmented memory. However…whether he wakes remains to be seen."

He bites back a sigh. He's trying not to show his fear, and that small hesitation makes the flavor sour in my mouth. "Do you know who attacked him?"

"We do," I reply, "but you're not going to like it."

I motion toward Jerome to fill in the blanks. He saw the vision too, which means he'll be able to better explain what happened than me. I lift my fork and begin to pick at my plate, but the frustration and worry remain.

"The King of Clubs, sire. He attacked our messenger then planted a Red Court standard, presumably to make us believe it was on the order of the Queen of Hearts."

Phineas' eyes darken and his mouth twists into an angry grimace.

"Humphrey did this?" Jerome nods. "He is a damnable fool if he thinks for one moment that we won't end the Clubs for this treachery!"

"Translate?" I ask Ivan.

"Clubs and Spades are in an alliance. The King of Clubs broke a hundred-year peace treaty."

"And none of you thought to tell me this sooner?"

"There wasn't time," Jerome interrupts. "And we had company."

Oh, right…Edwin.

"Which leads us to the next thing," I say against the lump rising in my throat. "We met the Earl of Mercia."

The temperature in the room drops a good twenty degrees. Phineas' gaze turns even sharper as he looks at me. He's not the only one. There is certainly no love lost between our newest ally and the men in this room.

"And our Queen survived," Tag mutters.

"Miraculous indeed, brother," Nacht replies.

Oooo...kay... Now I'm worried.

I look to Phineas for an explanation, but he's so flabbergasted that he can't speak. This moment shows just how little I really know about Wonderland's inner workings; how unprepared I am to lead. On one hand, it's troubling. On the other...if I don't know the danger I'm in, I won't know to be afraid of it until I'm dead, right?

"You look confused, dear Alice," Koji says. Figures the cat would be the one to come to my rescue.

"A bit," I admit. "The looks I'm getting say I should probably be in tiny pieces right now."

Koji smiles, his lips splitting far wider than they should and showing entirely too many teeth.

"Tell me, what do you think of Lord Edwin?"

Huh...what do I think of him?

"He's...odd," I admit, searching for words to describe my feelings. "Formal and cunning. A little — okay, more than a little — eccentric." I pause and take a breath. "I don't know...it almost seems like his good manners and proper conduct are a facade to hide some kind of beast."

"My, my…our lovely Queen is quite perceptive," Koji replies with a chuckle. "Did you know that Sir Edwin of Mercia is considered the most ruthless and deadly man in all of the four kingdoms?"

"Second to Morcar, of course," Ivan adds.

"Who?"

"The Earl of Northumbria," Koji says.

"And Edwin's older brother," Ivan finishes.

"The truth is, Majesty," Jerome says, "if Edwin had wanted you dead, you never would have seen him at all."

Cue panic attack.

"W-well, I suppose it's a good thing we now have a secret alliance with him," I announce, and a palpable shockwave passes around the room.

"Oh ho!" Koji laughs. Of course he's the first to recover. "I do believe, your Grace," he says to Phineas with a sharp clap of his hands, "that the student has become the master."

"So it would seem," Phineas replies through gritted teeth. "How did this come about?"

"Well…"

I launch into the story of him coming into the clearing, confirming that the Red Court was not involved in the attack on Haigha, and how Talon showed me the possibilities stemming from that meeting. My food still sits before me, mostly untouched and cooling. I'm not really hungry anymore.

"Then he knelt before me and swore an oath to me," I finish, to the feeling of eight mystified gazes trained on me. And half of them were there when it happened!

"That is… the most improbable story I've ever heard," Phineas says after a long enough pause to make me question everything about this situation. "But to return with such an alliance is truly miraculous."

"But did I make the right decision?"

Tag and Nacht blink at me in an alternating pattern, matching expressions of incredulity etched into their mismatched faces.

"To tame such a beast?" Nacht asks. "It was the best decision."

"Second only to death," Tag says, "Which would have been easier."

"But not better."

"Of course not."

"Our Alice is amazing!"

"And wonderful!"

"And–"

"Oh, stop it!" I yell, snapping the two of them back to reality with matching salutes before my face goes up in flames completely. "As much as I appreciate your weirdly inflated opinions of me, we have a lot of work to do." I sip my tea — still warm thanks to the magic in the air — and let the effects calm my nerves. "And I don't know if I can trust Edwin."

"Oh, you can," Koji says. "Bloodthirsty monster he may be, but Lord Edwin is not one to break an oath once made."

"He's right," Ivan confirms. "He did vow to end the reign of Queen Lucinda decades ago, but it appears he intends to make good on that promise now."

"He also said he trusts you with his life," I tell the cat, who blinks in surprise. "And he says you should be the messenger between the two sides."

Phineas makes a frustrated noise, like he wants to argue with me, but he holds his tongue. I know he doesn't trust the Cheshire Cat. But I do, and hearing Edwin's comment only solidified that trust.

"Well, if this isn't the most tangled of webs," Koji muses. "And what exactly might be done if I refuse the position of intermediary? After all," he buffs his pointed nails against his shoulder and pretends to examine them, "the last emissary from the White Court returned with his mind in pieces."

I can't argue with his logic, no matter how much I want to.

"The difference between you and Haigha is that you can go completely invisible when you want." I hope my argument is enough to convince him, otherwise I have no idea what I'm going to do. "Plus, by all accounts, you remain a member of the Red Court and have the ability to move freely among them. Nobody will suspect you."

He holds himself like he's considering his options, but the wicked gleam in his eyes tells me he's already made a decision and has a plan I'm probably not going to like. Koji is not one to do anything for the greater good. There's something he wants, and if he's considering anything at all, it's which thing to ask for first.

He holds my gaze, unflinching and unblinking until I speak first. I've played right into his hands, and we both know it.

"Okay…what do you want in exchange?" I ask, absolutely certain I don't want to know the answer. I can feel the fresh burst of anxiety rolling off of both Ivan and Jerome in waves.

"Is her Majesty willing to pay the price?" he asks. Stupid, brilliant cat, toying with me like I'm a mouse.

"That depends on what ridiculous thing you're about to ask for."

Extortion attempt in 3…2…1…

"You, my Queen," he answers, holding me captive with that swirling, laser-sharp gaze. His meaning goes sailing right past me.

"What about me?"

A scoff draws my attention down the line of the table, and the series of incredulous looks tells me everything I need to know. I'm an idiot, and I'm also a commodity, apparently.

"Surely my Queen can read between the lines," Tag says.

"Or between the sheets," Nacht adds. The brothers giggle.

My face goes up in flames and I growl to cover my embarrassment, both at the suggestion and at my own staunch refusal to understand. If this wasn't already the weirdest day of my life, it definitely is now.

"H-how is that even on the table for negotiation?"

"When you need something so desperately from someone," Koji tells me, still calm and collected as ever, "anything is on the table."

"He'll have her on the table," Tag stage-whispers to his twin.

"Among other locations," Nacht adds.

"Will you two shut up?" I hiss.

They snap to attention with another salute.

"What else do you want?" I ask.

"Only you, Majesty," Koji replies. "I do love the idea of being the Queen's favorite companion."

I growl under my breath, annoyed with myself because I don't exactly hate the idea. If the way he kissed me five minutes after meeting me was any indication of what I have to look forward to, then I can't say agreeing to his plan is a completely awful idea. A little thrill runs through me at the thought of what else he can do with those beautiful hands and that skilled tongue.

But no…this is insane. Nobody else at the table seems to be opposed to it, I realize when I glance around, except perhaps Phineas, but he's against anything involving the Cheshire Cat as a general rule. I'm not even certain why I'm opposed, except for the fact that this whole scenario seems so out of touch with the reality outside the castle walls and goes against everything I've ever been taught about propriety. Here we are, neck-deep in a four-sided war that shows no end in sight, and I've got the Duchess of Hearts' pet trying to bed me while a fucking necromancer is actively trying to wed me. I need to buy some time here because I can't think on the spot like this, and I certainly can't make an informed decision with this beautiful and mercurial shapeshifting man staring at me, waiting for an answer.

"If I say no, will you continue to try to extort a date out of me?"

"I would hardly call what I want from you a date, but most likely...yes."

Great.

Most of our companions laugh.

"This isn't much of a negotiation," I mutter.

"All is fair in love and war, is it not?" Koji asks.

"Maybe, but with you, I highly doubt this is either of those things, and it certainly is not fair."

A hint of emotion flickers across the cat's face and for half a breath, he looks...hurt.

I'm immediately on guard, weighing the options between a well-timed act and true emotional injury. Watching his face, I lean toward the latter because that single flicker of expression is now so well-hidden that I'd have a hard time believing it was ever there had I not seen it myself. Conversely, if he were playing wounded for attention, he'd really play it up. Koji is a master of wordplay and not at all afraid to shy away from weaponizing his words to get what he wants. This… is not that.

Now I feel like shit. Doubly so because this conversation is happening in front of everyone.

"Koji, can I talk to you in private?" I ask, mostly as a way to get out from under all of these far-too-interested stares. He makes no move until I stand. "Please?" I add.

A hint of a smile returns to his face, but it's damaged in the tiniest of ways.

"My Queen wishes to get me alone, does she?" His tone is as mocking as usual and there is no sign of vulnerability, save that barely perceptible air about him. It's… a shift in the magic, I realize. His emotions affect the flow of magic around us. It doesn't move as freely as it did a couple of minutes ago. "By all means…"

Koji rounds the table and breezes past me, fingers gliding along my exposed arm in the gentlest of touches, to open the door. As I move past him, I make a point not to acknowledge the snickering from the table behind me or the money passing between hands.

He pulls the door closed with a quiet click and takes my hand, leading me down the hall to the room with the crescent moon smile on the door. When it swings inward, I'm surprised.

I have no idea what I should expect, but it certainly is not the absolute feast of color and texture inside. Koji's bedroom is as extravagant as he is:

swaths of brightly-colored cloth sweeping across the walls of the round room in a sensual drape, cushions of various sizes and shapes scattered around the room, some near low tables while others simply exist. A huge, satin-clothed bed stands on a dais against the farthest wall, just as round as the walls and gloriously messy.

The sight puts me in mind of a Middle Eastern palace; in particular, the trumped-up Hollywood image of the quarters belonging to a Sheik's harem. The room smells sweet and musky, almost like nag champa, but somehow more, and an intricately carved table fits the wall on one side, pots of steaming tea and plates of cakes on top covered in decorative calligraphy that says eat me.

"Do come in, Majesty," Koji says. "As you requested a private audience, this seems the most appropriate location for delicate negotiations."

My jaw locks as I try desperately not to grind my teeth in frustration. This damned cat…

"Don't say it like that!" I snap, once again a little sharper than I intended. This time, Koji laughs. "Look… I like you. Probably more than I should And… and against my better judgment, I trust you," I say, carefully watching his face for any tell he'll give me. "Edwin trusts you as well. A-and you truly are the only one who could make this alliance happen."

"I am quite aware of these things, little Alice. What you've yet to tell me is your response to my request."

And again, my heart leaps into my throat. He's not going to be deterred from this.

"You're really serious?"

The question slips out of my mouth. One of his smooth, perfect eyebrows lifts just a hair, but he says nothing.

"I don't...understand," I continue. "What are you hoping to gain from this? Is it power? Some kind of control?"

"Oh, my sweet Alice," he replies. Koji doesn't appear to move at all, but he's suddenly right there towering over me while reaching one hand out to tuck a strand of hair behind my ear. His fingertips whisper against its curve, raising goosebumps on my arms. "Do I always have to have an ulterior motive?"

My heart races out of control and my cheeks burn with heat as I look up (and up, and up some more) into his beautiful face. It would be so easy to let myself be swept away by him, by the romance and the fantasy of this moment.

"In my experience," I answer, pulling his hand from the side of my face and holding it in both of mine, "yes."

He smiles again, but this isn't the razor-wire grin I'm used to. This smile is softer, more indulgent. Almost tender.

"Very smart of you, my Queen."

The backs of my thighs bump into the tea table, rattling the pots on their warmers, and I realize too late that I've been cornered by Wonderland's greatest predator.

"Case in point," he says in a low, purring voice that ripples up and down my spine in the most delicious way. "You should never let your guard down around me, Alice."

"Clearly," I answer, still held captive by his eyes as much as his long, lean body pressed against me from chest to knees. He leans in closer, the tip of his nose brushing against mine.

"Say yes, Highness," he whispers. His words gust against my lips, sweet and sinful and oh, so inviting.

"Koji..."

"Please, Alice." The sweet pleading in his voice is enough to unravel my resolve. The words linger in my ears, tickling something deep and private inside my brain.

Bind him to you.

The thought flows through my mind as naturally as any other idea, and equally as naturally, I rise up on my toes and press my lips to his. He tastes like tea and smoke and I am not prepared for the intensity of his presence or the heat that flares between us. This is the first time I've initiated contact, and the invitation is very well received.

I pull back just long enough for Koji to thread his fingers through my hair and draw me back to him, where he captures my lips in a fierce kiss. He holds me captive with one hand knotted at the base of my skull while the other arm bands around me, and for a moment I lose all sense of reality. He is a more potent drug than even tea; the taste of him intoxicating and so, so addictive.

He kisses me deeper, crushing my body to him until my head spins and I'm gasping for breath, yet he doesn't release me.

When we finally break apart, our heavy breaths and rapid heartbeats are in perfect sync. Long, slender fingers trace along the curve of my jaw, adding delicious shivers to the cacophony of sensation inside me.

"You are afraid." Koji gazes down at me with the softest of smiles and I nod in response. There's no sense in denying it. "But of what, I wonder?"

"I'm afraid you'll hurt me."

"No one can guarantee a pain-free existence."

"I know."

"Did you know that cats are among the most loyal creatures in existence?"

I blink up at him, trying to drag my brain around into this new direction. "Oh?"

"Once a cat's loyalty is won, it is forever." Koji touches his lips to my forehead. "My Queen… whether you want me or not, I am yours."

He is mine…

It's a thrilling thought. And a little scary.

Those long fingers continue to move over my skin—my jaw, my throat, up the back of my neck. He's sweet and tender, and despite the raw power just beneath the surface of this man, he's gentle with me. A single fingertip grazes over a sensitive spot along my shoulder, and a sigh falls from my lips.

"You look at me like you cannot get enough, yet you still refuse to say yes."

Because it's not that simple. Yes, I'm here and this is my new reality, but it's hard to shake off the chains of the society I grew up in. Everything is on its head here and though nobody but me views it as such, it feels somehow wrong. Like I'm somehow undeserving of pleasure. Of happiness.

"Tell me, Alice...what troubles you?"

I swallow hard, my dry throat scratching as I try to put the scattered pieces of my thoughts back together. I'm not entirely certain why I'm hesitating, but giving him an answer is hard. "My world... is..." I pause to think with great difficulty, "different. I'm not supposed to want you. Any of you... much less so many of you."

"That world is wrong," he replies. "It binds in ways we are not meant to be bound. Want what you want, Highness, and do not be ashamed for wanting it."

"Easier said than done."

"It's a simple word, really," Koji says with a laugh. There's that patronizing tone again. I was beginning to worry he'd dropped that part of his personality completely. "Three letters. One syllable. Y-E-S. Yes. You say the word and leave the rest to me."

My hand rests on his chest above his heart. His pulse beats beneath it, strong and steady, and much faster than expected. Slowly, I move my hand upward, over his shoulder, his neck, to cup his face. A rumbling purr issues from his throat and his eyes half-close in pleasure.

"I want to. But I don't think my heart is ready for all of you."

"Alice…" The way he says my name a half-plea, half-prayer, is like music to my ears. "You already have all of me."

"Koji…"

He swallows hard, and my gaze is drawn to the way the muscles in his throat move. "But I take no pleasure in forcing your hand."

The band around my chest relaxes. "I-I need more time."

"Time you shall have." He moves closer, his mouth just barely brushing mine. There's a tightness to the skin at the corners of his eyes, this unfulfilled desire tugging at him. "Just allow me to love you, Highness. Let me hold you. Touch you. Be close to you."

"I'm afraid…"

"Stay with me tonight," he whispers. "Let me have you to myself just this once." My eyes drift closed as his lips touch mine again. "No Rabbits, no Kings. Just you and me." He kisses my nose, my cheeks, and my forehead. "Say yes to this much, at least," he breathes again, those beautiful eyes catching and holding my gaze as mine peek open. Hard as I've tried, I can't deny this attraction anymore. Moreover, I don't want to.

"Yes," I reply, already breathless, and pull him close again.

He stops when I ask him to stop, yet by the time he's finished with me, I'm unable to do more than gasp for breath and let him pull the covers up over the two of us. That night, there is nothing more natural in this world than to fall asleep in Koji's arms. Unfortunately, he and I are both very aware that this fragile peace in which we sleep is only an illusion.

In a land where the majority of those in power are wicked, there truly is no rest for anyone. I have no idea where I am or what time it is when I wake — only that I'm warm and cozy, my body loose and lethargic.

A low chuckle rumbles through me, pulling me completely back to consciousness and the reality that yes, we really did do all of that last night. I hadn't expected the Cheshire Cat of all people to respect my boundaries… even if he did push them to the absolute limit with hands, lips, and teeth.

"Good morning, Alice." The smug amusement in his voice raises my hackles, but I'm too warm and comfortable against him to retaliate.

"Does it have to be morning?" I grumble, burrowing deeper into his arms as those long, sharp-nailed fingers slide through my hair and across my scalp in what may very well be the best massage I've ever had.

"Unfortunately, yes. While there may be a thousand ways magic can change reality, even it cannot stop the passage of time indefinitely."

Stopping time is off the table... good to know at least one thing is still impossible.

"We have quite a busy day today, Majesty," Koji says. "As much as I would rather keep you in my arms until the end of time, there are war preparations to attend to."

"War?"

Just like that, my happy, little bubble bursts.

"Of course. Surely you did not believe secret alliances and political intrigue alone would unify Wonderland?"

I grumble to myself. "I could hope."

"Hope, my beautiful, wanton Queen, is the destroyer of reality."

"Then let it destroy reality so we might rebuild it better."

A rumbling, purring laugh answers my statement and all of a sudden, I'm on my back with Koji's long, lean body over me. The slide of his skin against mine brings back delicious memories from last night, but his next words are as sobering as ice water.

"Hope is for fools," he says, and lifts one hand to cradle my face. The way he balances perfectly on one hand, bare muscles taught from the exertion, is almost distracting. Almost. "And you, my Alice, make me the biggest fool of all."

The gentle, sparkling kiss he gives me is too short. Then he's up on his feet, a symphony of ink and bare skin, pulling me up with him. The way his gaze lingers is both gratifying and embarrassing.

"Let us return you to your quarters. We should better prepare you for the struggles ahead... else I steal you away for my own forever."

I'm met at the door of the dining hall by a series of whistles and catcalls.

Stupid boys.

"Oh, shut up," I reply tartly as I take my seat, only to have an actual tart placed in front of me. It's warm and fragrant, smelling of fresh berries and summer breezes, and my stomach growls loudly. I never did eat dinner last night, so this time I don't wait.

The taste is more exquisite than the smell and that summertime sunshine aroma fills me from the inside out, a bright and exciting effervescence that truly makes me believe everything will be okay.

"Good news," Phineas announces as he enters the room, "Haigha is awake."

One of the many knots of anxiety releases and relief fills me. It's like finally, something has decided to go right.

"And how is he?" I ask.

"Much better than expected." Phineas doesn't look at me as he rounds the table and takes his seat. "Very little memory of the incident itself. There is still pain, and his mind isn't back to, well, even what it was, but he is lucid. He has quite a long recovery ahead of him."

"At least he's okay now."

We lapse into silence as everyone begins to eat, even though it's far from silent in my head. So much is happening at once and it has my head spinning. I'm still not completely trained in everything I need to know, but we are at least in a better position than when Jerome and Ivan brought me here six months ago.

The reality of my time here lances through my mind, and I realize yet again how much I miss my sister. Jerome assures me that our six months here translates into only days in Otherland and Edith is none the wiser of my extended absence. Yet it hurts to think that I've abandoned her on the other side of the divide with that horrible beast our father has become. And that makes me miss the man he used to be, when our family was whole and happy.

Jerome reaches out and squeezes my hand gently, reminding me of his presence, that he can feel what I'm feeling. Some of the sadness dissipates. I have to learn to put those thoughts out of my head. It does no good to dwell.

But dwelling on his ability to sense my emotions causes another wave of embarrassed panic to flood me. He hits me with a pointed stare and a smirk but says nothing of the discomfort that makes Ivan laugh from my other side. I elbow my Red Rabbit in the ribs, and his resulting grunt quiets his amusement.

After breakfast we move to the usual string of Kingdom business: requests for assistance, pending decisions regarding our neighbors, and other boring items that keep both Phineas and me occupied until lunchtime.

After lunch, it's the training hall, with yet another round of lessons in how to control and utilize Wonderland's magic. Then after a quick visit to Haigha's quarters—he has been moved from the medical wing—and an update from Felina that the now-sleeping messenger is, in fact, healing, we return to my room for the real discussion to begin.

One by one my men trickle into the room, all looking a little worse for the wear after the last few days, and take their seats around the table.

"I'm going to visit the King of Diamonds," I announce once they're all seated. Shocked expressions greet my statement. "I'll be taking the smallest possible group with me. After what happened to Haigha, I'm not going to sit by and wait for someone else to get stupid ideas."

"That is —"

"My decision," I reply to Phineas' attempt to interrupt so he can't talk me out of it. "Koji, I need you to pay a visit to Edwin and let him know that we're going. Tell him to mobilize an army to hunt me."

"What the hell are you thinking?" Phineas nearly shouts.

"I'm thinking deception is the best way to keep our enemies on their toes. Let the Red Queen think she has an advantage while we play our parts and line up the pawns."

"You're playing a long game, then," Koji says. "Smart. Dangerous, of course, but smart."

"It's the best way to keep the King of Clubs from thinking we might be onto him. An open declaration from the Red Court is the perfect smokescreen to draw out a false ally."

"That's all well and good, but you've yet to tell us what you plan to do about the Carpenter, though," Ivan says. Of everyone at the table, he's the most visibly frustrated. I get it. I do. He doesn't trust Koji or Edwin, and he's witnessed Red Court brutality firsthand. Participated in it, even.

"I'm going to spring the trap," I tell him. "It's obvious he plans to try to kill me, so if the Red Army just happens to be hunting me and they clash…"

"…you slip away in the confusion," Ivan finishes.

"Which leaves us open to do something about the Clubs while they're none the wiser."

Phineas' expression darkens. He's not happy about my idea, but he doesn't have any kind of real authority over me and he knows it.

"I won't deny the brilliance of your plan," he says after a long silence, "but I do hate it."

"Why?"

"Because you intend to offer yourself up to three opposing armies at once! You have to be mad!"

Well, yeah... that's kinda how it works here. Madness makes victories.

"Don't you want to end this war?" I ask. "Aren't you tired of the constant black cloud hanging over your head?"

His lip curls in annoyance but he can't argue. "Well, yes."

"Then why get in the way when I can try to end it?"

"Because you will die," he says, his voice a low, hissing whisper. He's not just frustrated or annoyed. He's truly angry, though whether it's at me or the situation, I can't tell. "You have to be methodical, Alice."

"Methodical is getting us nowhere. I'm not willing to sacrifice another messenger to dirty politics."

"But —" Jerome says, though I completely ignore him and keep talking.

"It's me the other kings want. If we give them what they want, we can make them go away."

"Or you die," Jerome says, echoing Phineas' sentiment.

Yeah, it's a possibility, I know. But looking around this room, I know I have the vast majority of Wonderland's elite at my side. I have two on the inside of the Red Court and a treacherous King who thinks he got away with his little murder plot. I might be young and untrained compared to these men, but we are at our strongest as a whole. Call me crazy, but this feels right.

"That's a risk I'm willing to take, Jerome. If I'm not willing to lay down my life, why should anyone else be willing to follow me?"

No one answers, and the ones that wanted to argue appear properly cowed. I mean, how can they fight back? A commander is a precious resource, but only a coward would hide away when everyone else's lives are at stake.

"I know what we need to do," I tell them. "But I need all of you to help with the plans and logistics. It's going to take all of us to make this happen."

We work late into the night discussing logistics and consulting the Caterpillar's internal crystal ball. There's food, tea, and more tactical planning than I can shake a stick at and by the time we break for the night, my head is spinning.

Equally as fatigued, the men shuffle out of the room one by one, but I stop Phineas with a hand to his forearm. This whole day has been a battle of wills, and the look of anguish in his eyes has been like a knife to my heart at every turn.

"Can we talk?" I ask as the door falls closed behind Ivan. It's rare that Phineas and I are completely alone, but we are now and I'm strangely nervous about it.

"Of course. Shall we sit?" He motions back toward the table we just vacated.

"Yes, but not there," I answer and lead him toward the pair of armchairs by the happily crackling fireplace. I really do love the ever-changing magical madness of this room.

A tiny smile turns his lips up and he takes my hand, curling it around his elbow to escort me over.

"Why are you so against me playing the bait here?" I ask, and he falters, stumbling to a stop. He doesn't look at me.

"Is it not obvious?"

"Are you going to tell me it's because I'm too valuable?"

"That and…" he hesitates, then finally turns to face me. "…and I, too, have grown fond of you."

Oh?

Oooohhhh….

"You are strong and fair, yet kind and gentle. Your heart," he cradles my face in a large, trembling hand, coal-black eyes softening, "it is beautiful."

Love and affection shine in those dark eyes, and my heart gives a funny little thump. What started as a political arrangement has shifted, but into what?

I have no idea.

After a moment, he smiles and draws me over to the—not armchairs now, but a sofa, where we sit side by side. The memory of his kiss from our wedding surfaces and now I'm even more nervous.

Why the hell am I nervous?

Once we're comfortably seated, he turns to face me.

"Now, what did you want to talk about?"

We kinda already talked about it. But there's more I want to know.

"Do you really hate the Cheshire Cat as much as you say you do?"

He's quiet a long time. Long enough that I begin to worry.

"...no," he admits. "I do not truly hate anyone."

"But you don't trust him."

"Not at all. Particularly with you."

We look at each other and say nothing else. I have questions, but words fail me completely when he holds my gaze like this. Phineas, the White King, is every bit as charismatic and hypnotic as the motley assortment of characters I've collected.

"I know," he says after a long silence, "I have no authority to stop you now that a decision has been made, but I cannot stand the thought of something happening to you."

"Phineas…"

"You are so much more than any of us expected, Alice."

"I'm glad someone thinks so," I reply, half-joking to try to lighten the mood, but my statement has the opposite effect. His forehead creases.

"Do you truly think anyone would be trying to kill you if you were not perceived as a threat?"

"People here tend to believe in magical prophecies. I don't have to be dangerous."

"They're smarter than you give credit for. You have real power and they sense it. Our enemies are afraid of you."

"They're afraid of the idea of me."

"Ideas are dangerous."

"That's strange," I say, more to myself. "Back home, everyone always overlooked me."

"People in your world seem to have trouble recognizing muchness. The fault lies entirely with them, not you."

Phineas rises and goes to the sideboard, coming back with two cups of tea. I find that as he works, I do quite enjoy watching him. He is calm and collected. Regal. Everything a fairy-tale king should be. I find myself drawn to him, harboring affections beyond the friendly as well, but something about him makes me shy.

Older man, younger woman...

He hands a cup over and returns to his seat with a smile.

"Can I ask you something?" I question.

He purses his lips into a perfect bow to blow across the surface of his teacup. "Of course."

"Do you think this plan will work?"

He takes a sip with a tiny slurp, then surprises me with his question. "Do you believe in it?"

"I do. Completely."

"Then yes. If you believe in yourself, you will be victorious."

That sounds like such a ridiculous, high school counselor answer, but it does make me feel better. A dark cloud still hangs around my heart, though.

"But at what cost?" I ask.

Phineas nods once and takes another sip. "That is the question. Only time will tell."

My tea is warm and sweet with a slightly sharp herbal taste. Almost immediately I begin to relax. My eyelids grow heavy and I realize just how tired I am. Not just from the tea, but from everything. My entire being is weary.

Sip after delicious sip, it carries away the stress and that soul-deep ache until I'm completely relaxed. I lean into Phineas' side, allowing myself to bask in his comforting warmth. He pulls me close.

"May I ask a question?" he asks softly. I nod against his shoulder. "Did you truly bed that blasted cat?"

There's no mistaking the jealousy in his tone. Its presence wakes me from my zen state.

"No," I admit. "I like him. A lot. He's fun to be with and surprisingly romantic. But I'm not ready to jump into bed with him."

Phineas snorts, but some of the tension drains

from him.

"But you did jump into bed with him," he replies, half teasing.

"I fell asleep beside him, yes, but there was no sex involved."

"There will be," Phineas announces as if it's already fact. He's probably not wrong.

"Probably," I admit with a yawn. My mind might be spinning but my body is done. "He made it pretty clear that he has no plans to stop chasing me."

"He is persistent if nothing else."

"Of course. He is a cat, you know."

"Speaking of sleeping," Phineas takes both empty cups and sets them to the side, "it's time we get you into bed."

I raise one eyebrow and smirk at him. Phineas at least has the good sense to look abashed, and his pointed glare brings a real smile to my face. He rises and pulls me to my feet.

"Are you gonna try to tell me you didn't think it?"

"Oh, I thought it," he replies, holding me close, "but now is not the time." Phineas cradles my face in his large, warm hand and draws me forward. My heart begins to pound in anticipation.

…is he…

At the last moment, he tilts his chin and touches his lips to my forehead. The tiny, maddening kiss is comforting, yet leaves me disappointed.

"Good night, my beautiful Queen."

I wrap my arms around him as he tries to pull away and hold on tight.

"Good night, my handsome King."

We part—reluctantly—after that lingering embrace, Phineas slipping quietly out the door while I climb into bed. It takes far longer than it should to calm myself enough to sleep and even then, I don't sleep well. I dream of bloody card battles and torrid affairs with handsome cats and mysterious kings.

CHAPTER FIVE

We stand in the courtyard of the White Castle in silence, the air thick and heavy. Everyone knows the stakes— Phineas briefed our soldiers well on the situation…the parts that are public, at least.

Our crew will be split for the foreseeable future, which actually makes me more nervous than facing the Carpenter unarmed.

As is custom for a "peaceful discussion" between enemies, I am only allowed my personal Rabbits and a guard of no more than a dozen soldiers. Taking Blade, I've been told, would be considered an act of aggression since they hold a high-ranking spot in the suit of Spades. They will stay with Phineas while Felina travels to Otherland in search of my family. Phineas decided it was too dangerous to not bring them to us, as any enemy worth half his salt would know that my sister is my ultimate weakness.

As it stands, Ivan and Jerome will accompany me, along with the twins and Koji, who will quietly "disappear" once we arrive in Brillig via the Wabe waystation. At least I'm allowed to take a pair of assassins into enemy territory. I'm not sure I'd have been able to talk my self into going if I wasn't. After all, Nacht is the single scariest thing in Wonderland.

Except, maybe, for a feral jubjub.

At the moment I have no idea where Talon is, but that means nothing. He's loyal only to his visions and as changeable as the tides. He'll reappear when he's ready. Or when I'm about to die and he wants to play hero.

The plot we've concocted here is ridiculously elaborate. There are almost too many moving pieces to keep track of, but if all goes well then the Club army should come for me by the end of the day. It sounds mad, feels even madder, and is now entirely unavoidable.

"Safe travels, my Queen," Phineas says. His big hand brushes over my hair and he takes a moment to straighten my crown. "Come back safely to me."

"I will," I reply and stretch up on my toes to kiss his cheek.

"Ready, Majesty?" Jerome asks, offering his hand to help me up onto the back of the massive black-and-white bandersnatch we'll be sharing. Then with one last glance at the castle, we set off.

I'm completely fucking terrified, even if I don't look it.

Brillig is the closest thing to a modern Otherland city I've seen. Buildings tower over us on either side as we step out from the quiet waystation, tilted and leaning cattywampus like stacked teacups that might tumble over at any time. It's beautiful and whimsical, the perfect blend of modern and medieval, and right in the heart of enemy territory, which makes it scary as hell. It's double scary because the city itself—what I'd expect to be a bustling metropolis—seems deserted. There are no people around us. It's like a scene from a post-apocalyptic action movie… all the trappings of civilized society sitting abandoned in the streets.

In the distance, Castle Diamond rises like a row of jagged, blood-tipped teeth—dark and menacing, like it's waiting to devour the world around it. The red and white pennants dancing on the breeze do nothing to soften its image. If anything, they remind me of blood spray.

That building is the physical embodiment of evil. Now I understand why Phineas hesitated to let me come here. The sight of it alone makes me second-guess this insane plan.

"I don't like this," I say to Jerome.

"Wise of you, Majesty," he replies. "Nothing and no one is safe here, least of all us."

Even the twins are silent. Sharp gazes patrol the area around us, scanning for any sign of incoming attack. Tag's fingers play over the knives hanging from his neck, and Nacht slowly flips a switchblade open and closed.

"Come quickly," Ivan urges, taking point and leading us through the empty city to the stables at the end of the street. Everything here is emblazoned with the Diamond Court crest, but the proprietor seems to be friendly enough as we pass through the gates.

"Welcome, Majesty!" he says with a broad smile and a clap of his wide, flipper-like hands. This man more closely resembles a seal than a person. "It is such an honor to meet the Alice in the flesh!"

"Well met, sir," I respond. "What's your name?"

"Orvice, my Lady." His waxy skin threatens to split in two from the pressure of his smile. "What brings you to our city?"

"Business with the Carpenter," I tell him. "He extended an invitation to visit. I thought I'd take him up on it."

Orvice's expression clouds over, like he's just realized something both important and terrible. He then seems to notice the more... notable... of my companions. The soldiers flanking us are intimidating on their own. Add in a pair of Rabbits, and we're pretty imposing. The twins are scary enough on a good day and today is decidedly *not* a good day.

"Perhaps Her Majesty might like to talk in private?" The question is accompanied by an odd hand gesture that I've not seen before. I'm not sure if he's trying for subtle or obvious, but either way, it grabs my attention.

"I do believe she would," Nacht responds before I can. He and his brother step up and curl their arms one over the other across my shoulders.

"Quite right, brother. She would."

What. The. Hell?

Before I have time to question anything at all, the two sweep me up between them, all but carrying me through the barn. Jerome and Ivan are left to follow along, clearly as confused as me.

"Stay with the retainers," Ivan tells Koji, who nods at him and winks at me. It's time for the cat to go. This plan is now fully in motion and we're getting ready to call down Hell on our own damned heads. I'm fucking terrified.

My Rabbits are nervous too. I can feel their anxiety, but they say nothing. Even the soft smell of hay in the air can't ease the fear. I feel like I'm missing something important here, but with no way to figure out exactly what that important something is.

We exit through the back of the barn and Orvice leads us down a narrow dirt path through a pasture to what appears to be his home. A small, studio-style house sits back among the trees, its wide front and tall glass windows pleasant and inviting. Flower boxes line the porch, the brightly-colored blooms bob on their stems in the gentle breeze. It appears far removed from the rest of this nutso reality, like it's inside its own protective shell.

"Now would be a good time to use your magic," Nacht whispers in my ear as they put me down just before the two steps leading up to the porch. I nod and, once my feet touch the ground, reach out into that ever-present current of magic. Never in my life did I think I'd actually learn a real-life *Detect Evil* spell, but here we are. I've used it more in the past week than I have in the whole of the last six months.

Magic certainly exists here, but nothing outwardly threatening. It grows stronger when Orvice mutters something under his breath—a magical passcode of sorts—and opens the front door. The comforting, yellow glow of happy magic greets us, inviting us into what I immediately recognize as a safe space. My Rabbits enter first, and the twins follow behind me, pulling the door closed and sealing the magic inside.

Orvice pulls a cord, and the tapestry above the fireplace lifts in a symmetrical drape to perfectly frame a large, familiar-looking crest. The metal shield holds replicas of the four Kings' swords, their blades intersecting one another in a perfect square. The icon for each suit rests at one of the four intersections, and a crown sits in the middle. I know I've seen it somewhere before.

"The crest of a united Wonderland," Jerome says. "Now a hidden symbol of the revolution against the split courts. It hangs in Wonderland Castle."

I'll take his word for it because I certainly don't remember seeing it there. Of course, I was a little more preoccupied with the crumbling castle and the smacker Koji had just laid on me at the time, too.

"Oh, such a frabjous day this is!" Orvice barks out, clapping his hands excitedly.

"What?" I ask. Ivan waves me off. I clear my throat.

"Majesty, it is the highest of honors to host your magnanimous presence!"

"That's very kind of you," I tell him. The sudden fannish display embarrasses me a bit. "But I don't require formality."

His rigid posture relaxes, and a genuine smile crosses his slightly elongated, waxy face. "Please sit, Highness." He motions toward a pair of armchairs. "You are safe here and may speak freely."

"Thank you, Orvice."

A small, mousy-looking woman appears from what I assume is the kitchen. She has tiny, rounded ears that sit high on her head and a narrow, whiskered snout in place of a nose. Her skin isn't the soft chestnut-brown it appears from a distance, but instead it's covered by a fine layer of fur. She carries a large tray loaded with tea service, cakes, and a pitcher of flower-infused water, and she executes a perfect curtsy without so much as rattling the stacked cups.

"My wife, Estrella," Orvice says, waving his flipper-hand toward her with a flourish.

"Pleasure, Mum," she squeaks, her tiny voice a perfect match to her appearance.

"Your hospitality is much appreciated," Ivan says, "but why have you brought us here?"

"For safety," Orvice announces. "Everyone in Brillig is aware of this week's events, and most of the people here are not on your side."

"I'm sure our Queen is aware of that, my love," Estrella says.

"Of course! But there is a plan to… to do away with…" he shudders, "…the White Queen and her court."

Of course there is. There's *always* a plot to do away with the White Queen and her court. I'm everybody's favorite punching bag these days.

"Do you have details?" Jerome asks. Orvice hesitates, then nods.

"The King of Clubs feels threatened by the presence of the Alice in Wonderland, and has made it his mission to destroy her before she can strip him of his power. The Carpenter, on the other hand, believes he can harness her power." Orvice casts me an apologetic look.

"Ah… that's why the Carpenter wants me to marry him."

Estrella gasps and clutches at her throat. "No, Majesty… you can't!" she squeaks. "He'll kill you!"

"He can certainly try," Tag responds. "Necromancer he may be, but a slit throat is not easily survived."

"Not if the slit is in the throat of a man who has also been poisoned," Nacht adds.

"Quite right, brother."

"What of King Humphrey's plan?" Jerome asks, turning our collective attention back to Orvice. The little man sighs, and the corners of his eyes crinkle in what looks to be sorrow.

"As soon as he is aware that the Alice is away from her castle—which by now he likely does—an army will march toward her. He knows of the meeting request with the Carpenter, which is why he sent one of his blades to dispatch the March Hare."

"He's still alive," I say, and relief relaxes Orvice's shoulders. "Damaged, but alive and on the mend."

"Thank the cards!" Estrella's hand lands on her husband's shoulder. He reaches up and squeezes it affectionately. "I've been worried about him."

"My wife grew up with Haigha," our host explains. "Their families have been connected to one another for generations."

"He's like a brother to me."

"So, this plot to march," Ivan navigates us back to the topic at hand with practiced ease, "when will it take place?"

"If my contacts are to be believed, it will be today. I've not received a messenger recently, which is just as troubling as having heard definitive word."

That makes sense. I sip my tea and have one of our hostess's cakes—honey cake with pressed flower icing, it turns out—and let the conversation continue around me. It concerns me that our false ally could already be on the move toward us when we'd expected to have at least a little bit of time to prepare. I hope Koji can get to Edwin and get their army on the move before it's too late.

Knowing this is happening makes me antsy. We're sitting in someone's living room, just waiting for the hammer to fall now. Only minutes ago, we thought we had the upper hand. Serves me right for thinking I can possibly be in charge of Wonderland, I guess.

I empty my teacup and place it back on the table.

"I appreciate your warning and your hospitality, but if it is as you say, then we need to be on the move as soon as possible."

"Yes, Majesty," Orvice says, dipping his head in deference. "I fear I have kept you too long."

"Not at all," I correct. "I would love to spend more time with the two of you, but I also do not want to put the two of you in danger if an army is coming for me."

"Then let us get you to your mount so that you might have a chance to accomplish your plans before the attack comes." He rises, bows formally in my direction, then makes that same curious hand gesture. A gesture which the twins return with perfectly-matched precision.

This day just got a whole lot more complicated, but at least I'm aware that there's going to be yet another ambush aimed in my general direction.

Jubjubs.

It had to be freaking jubjubs. There are few things in Wonderland I like less than giant feral lizard-birds with sharp teeth that would just as soon eat me as they would let me ride them. They're the closest thing to hellspawn I can possibly imagine, and knowing I have to ride one on my own makes my skin want to turn itself inside out. It makes sense, though… city streets aren't exactly wide enough for nearly twenty bandersnatches without causing all sorts of commotion. The birds are leaner, even if they are thrice as insane as their lion-dog counterparts.

Orvice takes great pleasure in helping me into the saddle, and as my four men fall into formation, he executes a tiny, formal bow and touches his fist to his chest. All four men return the salute, then they guide me through the stable gates.

Our guards fall in behind us as we start down the main road toward Castle Diamond, and as planned, I look around for the one person I know is already gone.

"Where's Koji?" I ask. The echo of my words in the empty street amplifies the ache in my heart at his absence.

"Good question," Tag says.

"Very good question," Nacht adds.

"No time to worry about him," Ivan announces, reminding me that this is all part of the plan. "Guards, stay sharp. We are in enemy territory."

The air around us grows thick with anticipation, and the rustle of curtains in windows amplifies the growing unease in my chest. The people here know something is about to go down. They're waiting and watching, hoping not to be seen by the people they perceive as the enemy. Right now, I'm the villain in their story: the interloper come to upset their status quo with my ideals and magical barbarism. They've been taught to fear me without knowing me. They don't trust me because I bring uncertainty.

The thought that in doing something for the good of the people, I could actually be hurting them sits like a lead weight in the pit of my stomach. The truth is, I don't know what these people have been through. What they've been told. What they expect. I'm not as well-versed in the sociopolitical side of Wonderland as I need to be in order to truly know what's best for the residents.

We crest a hill to discover a full-on view of the old castle, its gnarly towers and bloody, red flags appearing to suck the light and magic out of the air around it. Immediately my magical senses ping warnings. This place is so stained by evil that I'm not sure it can be saved. It's hungry for the light. It doesn't want to be fixed. It wants to devour.

The closer we move to the castle, the harder it becomes to breathe. Heaviness lingers in the air.

Darkness pulls at my skin, at my mind.

Wrong! Wrong! Wrong!

The bubble of anticipation reaches a crescendo. A high-pitched whistle sounds, deafening in this vortex of silence, and before I can even register the sound as a sound, an arrow embeds itself in the air just inches from my face. The shink of Rabbit armor and drawn swords follows. I stare at the razor-sharp point hanging in the air in front of me with absolutely no reaction. I'm too stunned to react. I simply stare, slack-jawed.

"A dirty tactic indeed," a familiar voice says and Talon appears beside me, one hand raised to hold the arrow in place. "A perfect shot, but dirty indeed."

"Indeed," both twins echo in unison, though their breathless voices carry no enthusiasm.

"I apologize for my tardiness, Majesty," he adds with a short bow.

"Where the hell did you go?" Jerome asks, angry.

"To announce the White Queen's arrival, of course." He's completely laid back. Unaffected, it would seem, by any of this. Perhaps he's madder than I first thought. Or perhaps he's so self-aware and confident in his abilities that he doesn't let the fear bother him.

"Why would you lower yourself to the position of page?" Ivan questions. Talon finally reacts with a tiny smile.

"Because no one, sane or mad, would dare harm a Caterpillar."

Okay… he has a point.

"Regardless of the reason," I say, sounding much steadier than I feel, "I'm glad you're here."

Talon nods his head, and the magical forcefield dissipates. The arrow falls harmlessly to the ground where he picks it up.

"Poisoned, too," he says. "Even if the marksman missed vital organs, you'd still be dead in minutes."

Great… they're upping their game and I don't even know the rules.

"You need to teach me that magic forcefield trick," I tell Talon. He smiles in response and swings himself up onto the jubjub behind me. His arms go around me and he gently lifts the reins out of my hands while his aura envelops me like the warmest, coziest hug. There is safety in his presence, and now that the initial shock of the attack has worn off, my limbs are starting to quiver.

"We'll work on that now. And we need to get to the castle quickly, before anyone else tries to be a hero."

CHAPTER SIX

I don't know what I expected of the Carpenter, but as seems to be customary in Wonderland, I'm quite surprised. I remember short, stub of a man from the cartoon with big lips, large nose, and a shock of red hair. That is absolutely not the person to whom I'm introduced. In fact, he's the exact opposite of that mental image: he's tall—very tall—and very, very thin. A wiry human with sharp features and even sharper blue eyes. Looking at him puts me in mind of a popular actor whose name is alliteratively similar to Beachbum Crumblypants. The thought makes me almost giggle.

Almost.

The Carpenter would probably kill me where I stand if I did. He looks like the stab-first-ask-questions-later type. Then he'd probably reanimate me and turn me into a marionette or something.

"Welcome, White Queen," he says, booming voice filling the empty expanse of the hall. "I do so appreciate the acceptance of my offer to visit." There is absolutely nothing warm about him or his presence.

"The invitation was much appreciated," I lie, keeping my head high and my shoulders squared. I'm not going to let this man know that I'm screaming in terror inside.

"You had no trouble on your way, I hope."

The way he looks at me tells me he knows there was trouble. Probably ordered the trouble, even.

"As a matter of fact," I start, and Talon produces the arrow from wherever he keeps poisoned arrows meant for my left eye socket. "This was offered to me just outside the castle grounds. Air mail, as it were."

One eyebrow lifts at my joke, but the feigned look of surprise tells me everything I need to know.

Yes, this asshole absolutely ordered the hit.

"Oh, my," he replies, pretending to be surprised. "I do apologize for my wayward subjects. You see, after hundreds of years of war, they've grown wary of outsiders."

"Clearly." Ivan and Jerome both tense at the implied disrespect in my tone, but the Carpenter laughs. "How about we skip the pleasantries and you tell me why you invited me here."

"Very direct," he answers with what appears to be a genuine smile. It's no less sharp for its realness. "I appreciate a no-nonsense ruler." He stands. And stands. And stands... this man is comically tall. "Let us retire to a more comfortable area for our chat."

All four men at my side turn into giant balls of anxiety and the pulse of their fear beats inside my head like a heartbeat. Yeah, I don't like this either.

"Might I remind his Highness that it is bad form to assassinate a guest in one's own home," Talon states, subtly interposing himself between us.

"Yes, yes." The Carpenter laughs, waving the Caterpillar away. "We'll save the bloodshed for the battlefield or the bedroom. I promise to be on my best behavior for our little Alice here."

I'd be lying if I said I wasn't scared shitless. This is one bad dude.

We're led through a door to the right of the dais and into a meeting room with a long, narrow table. The Carpenter, of course, sits at the head where a carved throne waits. I know I'm supposed to take a seat at the opposite end, but I really don't feel like yelling across the room. Plus, he needs to understand that I play by nobody's rules but my own.

I follow him to the far end of the table and take my seat three chairs away, much to the consternation of my four armed and angry guards. Ivan takes the seat between us and Jerome the one to my other side. An empty chair stands open between Ivan and the King of Diamonds. The twins remain standing in response to the red-clad Diamond guards around the walls. This time the Carpenter shows no reaction at all.

"So," I say, looking him square in the eyes, "your henchman said you were looking for a wife."

A sharp smile appears on his face.

"I seek a political arrangement," he replies. "Your goal is to unify Wonderland. For that, you will need four Kings."

"I am aware."

"This is a mutually beneficial arrangement, Majesty."

"Perhaps." I set my features and pray my poker face holds. "What are you proposing, exactly? What are your expectations for me, and what should I expect from you?"

"Mutual aid. I am sure you are well aware by now that both the Red Queen and your beloved ally to the east are coming for your head. Sooner rather than later, it would seem."

"You'll have to do better than that. It's not exactly news that everyone wants to kill me."

"Ah, but facing two of the deadliest armies in the four kingdoms without backup would be detrimental to your health, Majesty."

"Everything is detrimental to my health. Are you suggesting that you would offer protection?"

His chest swells with pride and he leans back against his throne. "As I am sure you are aware, my Oysters are an unparalleled force in Wonderland, and they are led by the bloodthirstiest of men."

"I've met your General."

His smile widens to an almost disturbing caricature of itself. "Then you understand my meaning."

"I understand that you want me dead."

"I do," he admits. "But not until I'm ready for you to be dead. You and I together would be unstoppable. I shall offer my army for your protection while you dispatch the tyrants and help restore order."

This sounds entirely too good to be true, but I don't see any cracks in his facade. Well, except that he wants to kill me after he's done using me. That part doesn't really sound like a good time, but very little in Wonderland does at the moment.

"Your thoughts?" he prompts. I continue to stare at him, looking desperately for any flaw, tic, or tell that would give me the upper hand. He's as flawless as a noh mask and at least three times as scary.

"Your logic is sound…" I pause, tilting my head to look deeper. "But I need to know why you are the best candidate to rule the Court of Diamonds, particularly since you've openly admitted to wanting me dead."

One eyebrow lifts and his mouth falls slack for half a breath. Ah…there it is. My challenge surprises him. This might be the first real reaction he's had.

"Is my current title not qualifier enough?"

"No."

He looks surprised again.

"Interesting."

"I'm not from this world," I remind him. "I come from a place that demands I be suspicious, particularly of men in power."

"A wise Queen, indeed."

Is that... respect... I hear? It may be grudging respect, but I'll take it. I'll take anything that isn't premeditated murder.

"As you are no doubt aware," he says, "I am from this world. It is very dear to me, and I do so love it." He's fascinating. There's a hard and scary edge to him, but he's probably one of the most fundamentally genuine people I've met on this wild journey. His conviction hums in the air between us, a near-tangible truth that binds him to this land and to the oath he took to guard it in whatever manner he sees fit. While I believe his methods could use some work, I can appreciate his dedication, and I believe him when he speaks of his love for his country. That appreciation doesn't make him less scary, though. "I took control of this kingdom to protect it, you see."

"Protect it from what?"

"The bloody Red Queen, of course. That woman is a nightmare. She'll bleed the land dry and behead those around her just for breathing."

"So I've heard."

"Unfortunately, my style of governance quite clashes with that of your beloved White King. Hence the lack of an alliance."

"You'll have to tell me your side of the story, then."

A cup of tea is placed in front of me, but I don't touch it even after he takes up his own.

"How curious," he says. I tilt my head in question. "Most of this land's rulers are unwilling to listen."

"We've already established that I'm not one of them." His evasive word games are growing tedious. "Is there a purpose to this conversation, or are we going to keep talking in circles?"

His smile returns.

"Governing the uncivilized requires a strong hand, as you've no doubt seen. Our world has existed in this dark age for so long that the people have forgotten how to get along amongst themselves."

"Funny...I don't see it that way at all."

"How do you see it, little Alice?"

Patronizing bastard.

"The people have no problem living their lives amongst one another. They're just people doing their jobs and spending time with their families; making ends meet and seeking simple pleasures where they can find them. They just want to exist. If you'd spent any time at all among them, you might realize that they don't want for power and wealth. They desire happiness. The rulers are the ones who can't seem to get along. Everyone is too afraid of losing power and status to be the one to compromise."

"Such a naive world view," he says. "The people are animals. Cattle to be bred and herded. The people–"

"The people," I half-shout, my fist landing hard enough against the table to rattle the china, "are the ones who matter! Without them, you would rule a wasteland!"

"Wonderland is already a wasteland!" he shouts back. "It is up to me to force the cattle to fall in line!"

"You..." I draw in a breath hard through my nose and rise to my feet. "You are not fit to be my King."

"You seem awfully judgmental for one who spouts such lofty ideals."

"You're royalty. Of course you've seen the power struggle, I know. But have you ever been at the bottom? Powerless? At the mercy of those in power who play dangerous games and demand deification?"

"Can't say I have." The smugness rolling off of him disgusts me.

"Then you will never understand what the people want or need. You have to come from nothing to appreciate anything." I take a step back from the table and both Rabbits rise, their gazes trained on the Carpenter. "If that's all you have to say, I'd like to go home now."

I'm not going to admit how nervous I am. I don't trust him at all, and I believe in his ability to be reasonable even less, because he is still perfectly rational about everything. My whole life, I've always been taught to never turn my back on a predator, but in this moment, that is exactly what I do.

I start for the door and the twins fall into step behind me. The walk is long and quiet, full of anticipation. Reaching for the handle, however, causes the Carpenter to call out.

"Wait," he says, though it sounds painful for him to stop me. I stop, but I don't turn around.

"Give me one reason why I should."

"Because there is more that you do not know."

Of course.

I pretend to consider it, then turn back around. I don't return to my seat, though. "You have exactly three minutes to convince me to stay."

His lips curl into a smile wide enough to rival Koji's, but there is absolutely no warmth in the expression. Jerome looks at his watch tattoo, as if starting a timer.

"You are correct in the assumption that I will one day take your life," he says. "I would not expect you to believe otherwise because beyond this negotiation, you and I are not friends."

"Not exactly a feather in your cap."

"No, however you and I will both struggle against our neighbors alone. When you and I wed and you take the crown of the Diamonds, you gain control of my not inconsiderable army."

"We've already discussed that. What, exactly, is in it for you?"

"When the time comes for you to die, little Alice, I will gain control of more than I will temporarily sacrifice."

"You seem awfully confident in your ability to kill me."

He doesn't respond to my statement. "Let us complete this alliance now," he says instead. "The sooner you take control of my army, the easier it will be to defeat your false ally to the east and the bitch in the north."

He knows about the murder plot. I suspected as much, but that statement confirms it. This guy has a serious information network. It makes me wonder if our new friends at the stables are as safe as they believe they are.

"And who knows," he continues, "with time, you and I may come to win each other's hearts as well."

Fat chance of that happening.

I look back and forth between Jerome and Ivan, wishing that telepathic communication came with the shared internal GPS of Rabbithood. There's so much anxiety pinging in my brain that I can barely think.

"A deal with the devil you know is better than leaving that devil in the dark." The voice in my ear scares the hell out of me. Koji was supposed to be gone. There's no way he made it all the way to Edwin and back in that short amount of time. "Seal the alliance now and bind that beast to you in every way you can," he says. "Lord Edwin's army is on the move and King Humphrey has come out to play."

"On one condition," I say aloud, my gaze trained on the Carpenter, "you do not leave this castle without my permission. You make no moves at all without my acknowledgment and approval. Should you break that condition, this union becomes immediately void and I retain all control of Diamond lands."

The nearly imperceptible lift of eyebrows precedes his single word reply.

"Done."

He rises and comes to stand before me. "As we have witnesses, the Cat included–" Holy shit... how? "Let us wed now so that you might survive the next seventy-two hours."

"Fine. Let's get it over with."

An hour later, I'm married to my second husband and headed back toward Brillig with the Walrus and two-thirds of the Oyster army with us. I'd be lying if I said I wasn't absolutely terrified of whatever lives inside that shiny black armor, but both Rabbits have told me more than once to trust the crown and let it lead the monsters.

Speaking of crowns, this new set of vows came with another crown: a silver circlet adorned with sparkling red gemstone diamonds. It fits seamlessly into my Spade crown, positioning the two central tines so that the diamond sits to the southeast of the spade, in the same layout as the split lands. I am the Queen of two courts now, and the whole of the army went to one knee in deference at the sight of me.

Koji rides on the back of my jubjub, still invisible since he's technically my enemy, but he's nonetheless warm and comforting against my back.

"My lovely Queen is more powerful than I thought," he says. He's teasing me.

"Yeah, who knew I'd be getting married again today, huh?"

"Marriage and death seemed the only two options."

"Oh, death is absolutely on the table. He already told me that. At this point he'll have to kill me to get his army back."

"Do not discount his ability to do so, Highness. The Carpenter is a capable mage in his own right."

"Is it fair to assume he can't be counted among the ranks of the Spellbinders?"

Koji snorts, the warm puff of breath against my ear rippling heat through me. Now that I know what that mouth can do…

"You are correct," he says. "He is a powerful curseworker. Not as deadly as the last one you dispatched, but he will be a formidable opponent when the time comes due in part to his unusual ability to raise the dead."

"Should I ask what's under the Oyster armor?"

"Not if you would like to sleep tonight."

Well if this whole conversation doesn't feel like foreshadowing, nothing does. We're not far when a messenger comes scrambling toward us on the back of an exhausted bandersnatch. The man is bloody and breathing hard. His clothes are in tatters, skin peeking out of the shredded holes and oozing a viscous, crimson substance. He looks terrified.

My new army ripples to a stop, and the messenger slides from the back of the beast with a groan. I'm off my jubjub and Talon and I are both at his side in a moment. He's badly injured–waxy-skinned and clammy from blood loss, and his unfocused eyes roll around in his head.

I lay my hand against his chest and Talon covers it with his own. Just like we did for Haigha, I channel the magic for Talon's use. The messenger's pain seeps into me, startling in its intensity, but Talon's steadying presence keeps me focused.

I follow his lead, directing the magic to different locations, feeling how it infuses into the wounds and lessens the pain. This is a skill I need to learn, seeing as how I've used it twice now in just a matter of days.

It's not long before the messenger regains consciousness. Talon helps him into a seated position, and the messenger immediately begins to thank me through his tears.

"What's your name?"

"Owen, Majesty."

"You're safe now, Owen," I say. "Tell me your message."

Agitation returns almost immediately.

"King Phineas sent me," he stammers in his sudden rush. "The Clubs... they attacked me before I could get to you."

"What's the message from the King?"

"I... I don't remember, Majesty. King Humphrey stole it!"

Talon doesn't flinch, even when I gawp at him. I'm surprised, yes, but well aware that anything is possible here.

"Any idea how to get it back?" I ask. Talon, again, remains emotionless.

"Yes...but it would probably kill him."

"Then let's go find Humphrey and get it back."

The Walrus is at my side a moment later, this red-haired beast of a man dropping to one knee in almost comical deference.

"Majesty, I await your command."

Yeah, there's no way loyalty shifts that fast... does it? I may be his Queen, but he is not my friend. I'm sure he's just looking for a soft spot to stick a knife.

"It appears our ally is not keen on keeping up appearances," I tell him. "Change of plans. We're going to pay King Humphrey a visit."

His face contorts into the most terrifying smile I've ever seen outside of a horror movie and he says, "I move on your command."

"Move."

"Oysters!" he calls as he rises, "Follow your Queen!"

A rallying cry shakes the air as it ripples through the army. Even the ground vibrates with the intensity of the shout.

"I shall inform Lord Edwin," Koji says in my ear beneath the cacophony. "Be safe, my lovely Queen." He kisses my cheek and his warmth slips away silently. Jerome catches my eye and raises an eyebrow in question, to which I respond with a nod.

"Let's move, Highness," Ivan announces, and we begin the process of turning a five-thousand Oyster army toward our new target.

Humphrey is expecting us, as Orvice said. We crest the ridge separating Club and Diamond lands. The sight of his front line, bedecked in a wall of flat-black armor, takes my breath away.

"A rat in the cellar," Nacht says.

"Indeed," his brother answers.

"There are a lot of soldiers over there," I add. Nervousness spikes.

"Steady on, Highness," Tag says with a big hand pressed against my lower back. "Sharks smell blood from leagues away."

I close my eyes and inhale deeply. The air around us is calm, smelling of fresh grass underfoot and damp storm clouds overhead. It's almost eerily silent. The occasional shuffle of armor from the army behind me rises, exaggerated in the stillness.

King Humphrey, atop a mottled brown and white bandersnatch, breaks away from the front line with a contingent of four guards.

"I guess that's our cue," I mutter.

"We're with you," Jerome tells me and as I break away, both Rabbits and both twins follow me.

The trek across the open plains is agonizingly slow, and no amount of zen breathing can calm the adrenaline jitters coursing through me. If there were going to be an assassination attempt, it would be now when I'm in the open and undefended.

The way the Club King carries himself commands attention in a patronizing, almost mocking, way. Even though I can't see his face, I know he's looking down his nose at me. Disdain rolls off him in waves, warping the air into something as twisted and cruel as he is.

Step by slow, painful step, we close the gap, coming to a stop a few dozen yards away. Humphrey's gaze sharpens, challenging us to run away. Then he lifts his helmet from his head. It shouldn't be possible, but he's even more terrifying without it. His skin is flawless, smooth and glossy as glazed porcelain. He's a menacing doll, emotionless and serene, still as stone and equally as unmovable.

"Well, well…if it isn't the Alice in the flesh," he says. His words rasp against my eardrums like coarse-grit sandpaper, and I involuntarily shiver with the memory of his brutality. His mouth moves only the tiniest bit as he speaks.

"King Humphrey," I say, "we finally meet."

"I heard a curious rumor about you, Highness." I lift one eyebrow in reply and wait for him to continue. "But it appears that nasty, little rumor isn't a rumor at all." His eyes rise toward my amended crown. "And here I thought we were allies."

"And here I thought that alliance dissolved the moment you attempted to murder my messenger in my territory and frame the Red Court for it."

A flicker of surprise lifts his shoulders, then the corners of his lips turn up in a tiny smile. The rasp of ceramic rubbing against itself fills the quiet, and I realize... he doesn't just look like porcelain. He is porcelain. It's why he doesn't have expressions. Why his mouth barely moves. He blinks and the quiet tap of his eyelids as they touch confirms my theory.

"A fair enough assumption," he replies, "but you must see it from my side." The King of Clubs tenses. I tense. My Rabbits go on alert. "You've wed the Carpenter – my sworn enemy."

"After you betrayed us!"

It's a struggle to keep the rising anger from my voice. Breathe, Alice, I tell myself. "And it was not the intent of my trip... not that I owe you any explanation at all, you traitor."

"If you were in the market for a new husband, all you had to do was ask."

"Why? So you could murder me in my sleep too?"

"Careful, Majesty," Ivan warns under his breath, "Never taunt the mad."

"We need to keep him talking until Edwin gets here," I mutter. "I'm going to need you to return that message you stole, too."

Humphrey laughs long and hard, like I've just told the world's funniest joke, but when he refocuses his gaze, his eyes are like knives. Never once does the smoothness of his face change.

"Oh, little Alice," he says, wiping at his teary eyes, "you amuse me. It will be such a shame to kill you."

The helmet in his hand slides over his head. What little humanity he has is completely obscured by that armor. It's the blackest black I've ever seen, not just dulling the light, but pulling it into itself. His aura is a black hole. The air shifts with his movement, and both Rabbits position themselves between me and my potential demise.

"Time to retreat, Majesty," Tag says.

"Quite right," Nacht sing-songs back. "Retreat, retreat, and live to eat!"

"That makes no sense," I answer, maneuvering my jubjub back a few steps.

"Contrariwise–"

Humphrey signals his army and —

"Highness, run!" they shout in tandem, forcing their mounts between me and my newest nemesis.

That army—a mixture of cards and people—spills down the far ridge and into the field with a thunderous roar. The noise doubles and the ground begins to rumble under us. My spooked mount squawks and tries to throw me off as the first of the Oysters scrambles past us to clash with the Diamond army with a deafening clang of weapons.

"Archers!" someone shouts and before I have time to react, an arrow strikes the bird I'm riding. It screams—a sound all too human for my battle-novice heart—and I'm thrown as it tumbles to the grass with a spray of blood. Soldiers continue to move past me, unaffected by the rain of death. They simply step over the fallen and keep pushing forward. I curl in on myself more tightly, tucking my head between my knees and covering my exposed neck with my arms.

Somewhere in the chaos someone screams my name. I unfurl, glancing around the bloody, shadowed field. Then I look up and know immediately that I'm going to die.

CHAPTER SEVEN

The arrows hang in the air, halted by the magic coursing through me. The haze of battle filters away, and I'm left in a tranquil bubble. It's quiet and peaceful; safe. The thrum of magic through my body is comforting. I can feel my sanity slipping away with each tick of the clock, but in this moment, I don't care in the slightest.

Somewhere inside my head, someone begs me to drop the shield, but that seems like a very bad idea.

A hand lands on my shoulder. The magic leaves my control. I become a siphon, drawing it up only to have it filter through me instead.

No! Stop!

"Let go, Majesty."

I'm not sure if the voice comes from above me or inside my head, but either way it's a long time before I process words themselves, much less the name of the one speaking to me. The magic is slowly drained from me and released into the air.

"You've done well," Talon says with a gentle smile. "Now let go."

My body craves the flow of magic, begs me to hold on and let it happen, but Talon's firm hand on my shoulder is a reminder that it is possible to pull too much. Even for a Queen.

Taking a deep breath, I relax my hold and let the current slip away. Even the Caterpillar lets the magic go, and I realize that while I can still hear the battle, I'm not right in the middle of it. It's disorienting.

"Focus, Alice."

It's Jerome who pulls me back to reality with both hands on my face, then sighs with relief when my watery gaze focuses on him.

"What happened?" I ask.

Jerome and Ivan share a dark look.

"You blocked the arrows," Ivan says.

"For the entire front line," Jerome adds.

"Are you serious?" My voice doesn't sound like my own in my ears.

"Your powers are growing," Talon answers. "You must now learn to temper the magic or face madness."

Oh, great...one more thing to add to the existential dread bingo card.

I lay back on the grass and close my eyes.

The battle rages to the south, a rumbling, shrieking cacophony that threatens to deafen us even from this distance. The air holds onto the charge of anticipation. I'd protected myself and our people... temporarily. Yet even from this distance, the smell of smoke and blood overwhelms the air. The reality of our situation threatens my better sense, and my already-racing heart speeds up even more.

"What now?" I ask in a tiny, gasping voice.

"Edwin will be arriving momentarily," Ivan says. "If history proves itself consistent, his brother will be at his side."

"Do you think Morcar will show himself this soon?" Jerome asks.

"For a chance at glory? Yes. At his brother's expense? Abso-fucking-lutely."

"His expense?" I question.

"Their rivalry is infamous. Morcar has longed to steal glory from his little brother and if killing the Alice will bring it, he will not let the chance slip by."

Because of course we need to add a sibling rivalry grudge match to the equation. Those always end so well for everyone!

"What do we need to do?" I ask. My strength is returning and my anxiety finally lessens.

"Absolutely nothing," Talon says. "Your plan is in motion and—" his eyes glaze over as he looks through the various futures, "—there is nothing you need to do at the moment."

"But Edwin—"

"—is still your enemy on the surface."

"—and Koji—"

"—is also your enemy and is perfectly capable of tracking you wherever you go."

"But what about—"

Talon doesn't even respond to my half-finished question. Of course, I know the twins will survive. I just want to hear it out loud. His single raised eyebrow is answer enough, as if to say why are you questioning the immortals?

"If there's really nothing for me to do here, then I guess we need to go to home."

"Not home," Talon says. "You, my Queen, will be going to Wonderland Castle. It is the closest, safest option. You need to be fortified when the Red Court Beasts arrive."

Jerome and Ivan both nod. Even Talon appears satisfied with my decision even though he swears he doesn't choose sides.

"Are you coming with?" I ask Talon while crawling to my feet. Going "home" is just as well because I'm exhausted.

"I will join you soon," he says. When I blink, he's gone.

The ruined castle isn't quite as ruined these days. Sure, it still has that mouth-full-of-broken-teeth look to it, but the turrets aren't missing shingles and the windows don't resemble oubliettes anymore. Even the land around it looks considerably less dead. The grass is coming back, and the water in the moat is no longer a thick, sludgy black. The brambles are also blooming into some of the prettiest flowers I've ever seen.

We walk into a lively and bustling foyer, filled with those creepy little card servants scrambling around to do things like clean floors and mend tapestries. There's little inside that resembles the condition in which we found it.

The servants, upon noticing me, turn and drop into a bow that puts me in mind of a fanned deck of cards. Murmured chants of "Welcome home, Majesty" echo in the quiet and I realize that I'm able to breathe deeply for the first time in a couple of days.

My gaze wanders over the uncovered tapestries, taking in the bright colors and the story they tell from one side of the room to the other. A familiar image catches my attention, and my breath leaves my lungs on a gasp. The crest—the one hidden in Orvice's house—hangs front and center between the legs of the great staircase. A visual representation of a unified Wonderland.

"Remember now?" Ivan asks and I nod, my gaze fixed on the powerful symbol. My heart beats just a little bit harder for its existence.

By the time we shuffle into the dining hall, a quadrille of battered bodies, the table is covered in food. I mean, not a single scrap of open space, save our empty plates, can be seen. It's more food than the four of us can eat in a month, but I'm in no shape to complain about the waste, especially when the dishes are jostling one another out of the way for my attention.

"Those magical card people are beginning to grow on me," I say as we take our seats. "Let the feast begin."

We eat and drink until we're bloated and sick, but this little sliver of normalcy is so nice that I don't want it to end. Two hours or so into the feast, I'm sitting here wishing the rest of my friends would show up when commotion in the foyer brings all four of us to our feet. The *shink* of armor echoes in the quiet room while memories of a previous ambush surface.

A moment later the twins appear in the doorway and I'm running toward them, grabbing both at once and pulling them into a three-way hug. It doesn't matter that they're dirty, sweaty, and bloody, smelling of death and steel. They're here and they're alive. Two pairs of arms encircle me and I'm momentarily lifted from my feet.

"Welcome back, you two."

"A warm welcome from our Alice!" Tag sing-songs.

"A warm welcome indeed, brother," Nacht answers.

"They didn't come alone," Ivan announces. I look between their shoulders and the shock nearly causes me to stumble backward. Talon has arrived as well, looking no worse for the wear. More startling, however, is the fact that the Walrus himself stands in the foyer, equally as bloody, with his helmet in his hands. Our gazes connect and he drops to one knee.

"We have brought you victory, Majesty," he says, his voice like gravel on glass. "The Club army forced a retreat and the Hearts..." he hesitates. I didn't know he knew how. "The Hearts protected the Oysters."

A smile spreads across my face.

"Then all is well," I say and hold my hand out to him. "Come rest, eat, and tell me the story."

Another small hesitation, then he rises, steps forward, and takes my hand. A jolt of electricity passes between our palms and tendrils of power twine around our hands, binding him to me.

He drops again to one knee and presses his forehead to my hand.

"My Queen," he says. That's all it takes. The Knight of Diamonds is now mine. An understanding passes through the occupants of the room. Did they feel the magic snap that bond into place? Or maybe it's just because I believe in it that they allow it to happen this easily.

"Rise, my noble Knight," I tell him. When he stands, he towers over me, "and welcome to my game." The beginnings of a smile crook his lips. "We're not formal here, so come on. And relax."

"My army—"

"—is cared for," Jerome says.

"The cards have already seen to them and will feed them as soon as they are settled," Talon says.

A look of gratitude passes across his haggard face.

"What's your name?"

"Torai," he says. "DeWinter."

"It is lovely to meet you, Torai. Now please have something to eat."

We move as a unit back toward the table and the three bloody newcomers quickly doff their armor and take their seats. We're back to eating and drinking and the atmosphere is relaxed despite the vortex of darkness emanating from Torai. I'm still wary of the hulking mountain of a man that tried to kill me my first week in Wonderland, but I also trust the magic to warn me of danger.

"Tell me about the battle," I say, intentionally not directing my statement to anyone specific.

Torai chews and swallows, then he speaks.

"Bloody," he says. His voice is firm and even, but there's a faraway look in his eyes. "King Humphrey is every bit as mad as the rumors say."

"How so?"

He looks up at me, his dark, beady eyes laser-focused. Something about him looks sad.

"A King—a commander—is meant to lead. He does not. He gives command to another and fights on the front lines. He thinks himself a god of war."

That's disturbing.

"Yet he called a retreat," Nacht says.

"Or the retreat called him," Tag corrects.

"Indeed brother."

"Indeed indeed."

"Do we know why?" I ask Torai. He gives a near-imperceptible shake of his head.

"No. Even after the Red Army appeared, he tried to push forward." He pauses to take a drink of tea. "Though something curious happened, Majesty."

"What's that?"

"The Red Beast and his brother only attacked the Diamonds. It appeared they had orders to keep the Oysters safe."

I fight to keep a smile off my face. This is a secret alliance, after all.

"What of our losses?"

"Minimal," he confirms. "Though I cannot trust his motive. Perhaps the brothers seek glory by attempting to take the Alice's head."

"Perhaps," I respond and return to my food.

The suite confirms what I already suspected. A new door stands closest to the entryway — gleaming black with a glittering pearl set into it.

"What?" Jerome gasps.

"It can't be," Ivan echoes.

"And yet, it is," Talon confirms. "You, my

beautiful Queen, have officially robbed the Carpenter of his right hand."

The fact that the Walrus has a door and the Carpenter does not is not lost on me. It's surprising, but at the same time not. Torai swore that oath; one I can feel simmering in the air around me.

"An amazing feat," Tag says.

"Indeed," Nacht adds.

"Somebody go get him," I say. I'm certain he's in the process of bathing and preparing for sleep, but I need him to know he's part of the team. "If he has a door, he has my trust." The Caterpillar nods and backs out of the hallway.

Four steps later, weariness takes hold of me and my shoulders start to sag. So much has happened in such a short amount of time, and I feel like I haven't slept in years. Were it not for the body behind me, it's very possible I might collapse right here in this hallway.

Food. Shower. Bed. Now.

Ivan and Jerome lead me to my room and stand guard as I stumble into the shower to wash the travel and the battle from my body, then help me to my bed because standing upright instead of leaning on the counter is entirely too much work. I'm just that tired. It has been a very long day, and I am so thankful for the key that allows me to sleep in my own bed tonight.

I snuggle down into the warm cocoon of my blankets, enjoying the peace and quiet that comes with being truly alone for the first time in days. It doesn't take long for the silence to drag me under, either. I'm just about asleep when a commotion starts up in the hallway.

Oh yeah, it's a gauntlet…

The memory of those words makes me hesitate rather than rush to yank open the door. I pause instead behind it and listen. There's plenty of shouting but no battle sounds. The voices are all familiar. Too familiar.

Wait a minute…

I snatch open the door before I can take another breath, hopeful that my suspicions are true.

"Phineas!"

"Alice?" He turns, shock written across his face. Once again, my feet are moving before my brain can catch up and I throw my arms around him. "How is this possible?" he asks, pulling me into a crushingly tight hug.

"Magic?" I ask. Because what other answer would there be in Wonderland?

"But…are you not at Wonderland Castle?"

"Yes. And you're still at home, right?"

"I am."

"We all have keys," Talon answers, swinging his around his pinky finger like it's a party favor. That… makes sense. Everyone who gets a key gains entrance to the Queen's Suite. Of course, their keys would work on any door, just like mine. And since they all take us to the same dimensional pocket…

Phineas is slow to release me back to my feet, and I'm equally slow to loosen my hold on him. There's comfort in his arms. Protection. A moment where everything seems right in the world and I don't have to be afraid anymore.

When he's beside me, I'm not making decisions alone.

"We need to talk," Phineas says and lets me go just long enough to lace his fingers through mine. I realize then that the hall is full of people and they're all glaring at each other. This was not how I wanted tonight to go.

"All of you. My room. Now."

I turn and pull Phineas by our joined hands. The rest dutifully follow behind into a room that is once again vastly different from how it was two minutes ago. My bedroom is no longer on display, having been replaced by a sitting room with the magical sideboard, the ever-expanding table, a sitting area with a fireplace (now that's an adorably quaint feature I didn't have before...) and access to the bathroom. The only one who isn't surprised by the change is Torai, but that's because he's never been here before. Whispers of awe rise as everyone wanders in.

Once we're seated, I look around at the collected mass—the Rabbis, the twins, Talon and Felina, Phineas, Blade, and Torai, the newest member of my assorted deck of crazies—and sigh.

"Next time you lot decide to try and kill each other, don't."

Muttered affirmations float up from them.

"A lot has happened today. I'm exhausted. I don't have the patience for any of this, yet here we are."

"Tell us what we need to know so you can get to bed," Phineas says.

"Our plan is working," I reply.

"Wait!" Felina cries out, "can we —"

"Yes," I answer before she finishes her question. "I trust Torai and so does the magic. He wouldn't be here otherwise."

"But…how?" she asks.

"Because I married the Carpenter today."

CHAPTER EIGHT

"Y ou what?"

Phineas' jaw drops. Every other expression in the room, save the four witnesses, matches his. A wave of incredulity ripples through the air. I can't blame them for being confused... I'm not sure exactly how we got here, either.

"Why?" Felina asks.

"Because it neutralizes the threat of the Diamond Court." I go through the door to my new bedroom to retrieve my crown and place it on the table in front of me. I point to the diamond circlet twined inside the Spade crown. I smile at Torai, who smiles back. The expression is stretched and his tusks are in the way, but he still seems happy. "And it has earned us a powerful ally."

"But... him?" she asks, gaze darting to the Walrus and back to me.

"He pledged himself to me."

"My Queen saved my life and the lives of my Oysters on the battlefield," he says in that gravel-on-glass voice. "The lives she saved belong to her."

No one else dares to argue. I mean, how can they? He's so sincere.

"You are absolutely mad," Phineas says.

"Comes with the territory," I mumble. Jerome smirks. He seems to be enjoying this. "Now as I was saying — the plan to draw out the King of Clubs was a success. We didn't end him, but he has openly declared war."

"And the unification of the Courts shows you have the power to affect real change," Phineas says. "Smart move."

"The Carpenter isn't my first choice for King, and he has sworn more than once to come for my head sooner rather than later, but he is right about one thing." I receive a series of curious looks. "Working together toward a mutually beneficial goal makes more sense than fighting each other and everyone else."

"A mindflayer and a tactician," Felina says. The Ace of Spades actually looks impressed. "There's more to the madman than I expected."

"So, the plan was to bait King Humphrey?" Torai asks.

"Yes."

"Why, if he's an ally of the White Court?"

"Was," I correct, "and this is where the story gets strange."

"I'll make the tea," Ivan says.

We sit and drink tea while we fill the Walrus in on the goings-on of the White Court over the last few weeks. I tell him of Blade's arrival, Haigha's attack and our subsequent meeting with the Earl of Mercia, my secret alliance, and the fact that the Cheshire Cat is an intermediary.

"...and that is why Edwin only attacked the Clubs."

When I'm done, he stares at me with a look of absolute incredulity. It's like I can almost feel myself sprouting a lobster from each ear. I've given him a lot to digest, but we still have a long way to go, and my energy level is nearly depleted. The gunpowder tea in my hand is literally the only thing keeping me awake right now.

"I never imagined someone might have the power to domesticate the Red Court Beast." Torai shakes his head.

"His honor was at stake," I say. "Humphrey tried to pin the attempted murder on his warriors."

He nods. "Fair enough."

"And I do believe I've had all the fun I can stand for one night," Felina says as she rises from the table. "It has been a very long day and I am exhausted."

"Quite right," Tag agrees, following suit and his brother rises with him.

They make it as far as the door before Felina stops.

"I forgot..." she pulls an envelope out of somewhere and brings it to me. "From Haigha,

Majesty." With a smile and a slight bow, she leaves.

At the sight of the envelope, Jerome and Ivan both groan. Loudly.

"What?"

"It's an invitation," Jerome says.

"Please don't open that…" Ivan begs.

"Okay? Why? And it's an invitation to what?" I'm already popping the wax seal despite the protests—purple with a steaming teapot in the center—as I ask and pull the contents out.

A tea party.

The Mad Hatter's Wondrously Wild Tea Party to be exact.

"A tea party?"

"Not just any tea party," Ivan mutters. Even Torai reacts to the invitation with surprise.

"I hope you've built up a very high tolerance to tea, Majesty," Torai says. "Otherwise, I do wish you the best."

"It can't be that bad," I respond but I know the words are a lie the moment they leave my mouth. "Besides, I look forward to meeting the Mad Hatter."

A look passes between the Rabbits that says so much more than words can. It quickly becomes clear that I've missed some vital piece of information. I do vaguely remember a conversation where Ivan called him something to the effect of an unhinged madman, but I don't rightly remember why.

"I do believe I need sleep," Torai says and rises, which causes a chain reaction of departures. When the door finally closes, I'm once again alone with Phineas.

His expression clouds as his brow furrows. Even brooding though, he's so handsome it takes my breath away.

"Do you want a clean cup?" I ask, but when I start toward the side table, he grabs my wrist to stop me. I turn as he rises, my arm spinning in the circle of his hand. We stare at each other.

"You did well today," he murmurs. He releases my wrist, his fingers sliding over my palm to twine with mine.

"Thank you. It was stressful."

One corner of his mouth lifts in a small grin. He looks twenty years younger when he smiles.

"I do not doubt that. You are very strong, though."

Heat rises in my cheeks at the compliment. This man is both good and bad for my heart.

"Contrariwise," the nonsense word falls from my mouth, "I don't think I'm particularly strong... just lucky."

"You don't even see it in yourself." He brushes my hair back behind my ear. The gentle look in his eyes short-circuits my brain. "You've tamed the most powerful magical beings in Wonderland. If that isn't strength, I don't know what is."

"I don't know that I've tamed anyone."

"You have earned the love of the Cheshire Cat and the respect of the Caterpillar. The Red Court

Beast and the Walrus have pledged themselves to you. What else should I call it?"

I'm at a loss on how to respond to that, but I don't have to. He keeps talking.

"In doing so, you have also bound our most dangerous threats to you."

"The Carpenter?"

"The Walrus," he corrects. "The Oyster army is an unrivaled and unstoppable force. With Torai on our side, even the Carpenter himself cannot win."

"He plans to kill me once this alliance is no longer useful."

Phineas's expression darkens. "He can certainly try. However, you also have the Red Court Beast in your pocket and that puts everyone at a severe disadvantage." His free arm slides around my waist, and he takes a step closer. "That mad fool has a hell of a fight coming if he thinks he can take you away from me." He holds me close. Our hands are still bound to one another. The look in his eyes is unreadable.

"I'm not going anywhere." I rest my other hand against his chest to feel his racing heart. Its wild tempo matches my own.

"Did he…" Phineas, for the first time that I can recall, looks uncertain though his meaning is clear.

"No. He didn't touch me." I offer a smile and some of the tension leaves his shoulders. "It is a partnership in name only. And temporary."

A sound akin to a growl leaves his throat. His grip tightens as his composure crumbles. He's gone feral–as wild and unpredictable as the magic around us. I don't ever want this feeling to go away.

"Phineas…" his name tumbles from my lips. I don't know what I'm asking for.

"My Alice…" he echoes. Then his lips are on mine.

The initial surprise fades and I'm transported back to the afternoon of our wedding, except this… this is different. So much more.

He tastes of tea and moonlight; an intoxicating blend of power and tenderness, and so much love. This kiss goes on and on until I'm weak in the knees and nothing exists but the two of us, body to body.

Phineas pulls away first, breathless and trembling. "My Queen," he breathes against my lips, leaving me dizzy and clinging to him for support.

"My, but jealousy is unbecoming of royalty."

Koji's voice echoing in the empty room startles a shriek out of me. The tender moment broken, I try to pull away, but Phineas holds me firm.

"I'm going to murder that blasted cat," he growls.

"Only if you catch me first," Koji replies. Invisible fingers graze the back of my neck, making me shiver. Who knew the Cheshire Cat was such a voyeur?

…only anybody who ever read the books…

"How long have you been back?" I ask.

"Not long," he answers, his disembodied voice bouncing around the room, making it impossible to pinpoint him. "I slipped in as the others were leaving."

"How very catlike of you," Phineas answers.

"Meow."

Phineas throws his arm out to the side, his big hand closing half-way like he's squeezing something, and a pained yowl fills the room. A moment later, Koji appears, his slender neck caught in Phineas' grip.

"Mother! Mother!" Koji shouts in melodramatic fashion. "I give! Let a poor cat go!"

The whole scene breaks me apart and I begin to laugh, long and hard. Clutching my middle, I fold over and fall to the sofa, tears streaming from my eyes.

It's official. I'm delirious.

"You said I had to catch you to kill you," Phineas announces and the arm around me pulls me just a little closer. "I suppose that means I get to follow through on my threat."

Koji does at least have the good sense to look worried.

"Now, now," I say as my laughter fades and I lay my hand against Phineas' arm, "let's not kill the cat. He'll just come back, you know. They do have nine lives."

"Then I'll kill him ten times."

"Then I won't invite you to anymore tea parties." Phineas hesitates. I harden my tone. "Let him go."

He growls as he releases Koji, who snarls in his direction before pulling me into his arms. This battle for dominance is so ridiculous that I can't stop laughing. Despite the stress of the day, my heart dances.

"You two can try to kill each other later," I say, more amused than worried. "Right now, tell me what I need to know, Koji."

"The plan is moving along, Majesty," he says. "Edwin was not able to dispatch King Humphrey, but the Club army left the battlefield significantly smaller. There is, however, one more thing."

"Phineas and I both take a sharp breath. Inside my head, both Rabbits go on alert, which causes me to glance at the door. Phineas pulls it open without any kind of acknowledgment and both men file through. Koji's fingers tighten into my hip just a little bit more.

"What's wrong?" Jerome asks. Ivan's face mirrors his concern.

"The inability of the younger Earl to destroy the Oyster army seems to have caused some discord among the brothers."

Uh-oh…

"Has Morcar finally decided to kill his brother?" Ivan asks.

"Not yet," Koji confirms, "but he is asking questions. It is not like the Red Court Beast to kill on the battlefield any other way except indiscriminately."

"Does Morcar know of the alliance?"

"No."

"That's good," I say.

"However—"

"...and that's bad."

Koji smirks. "Lord Edwin has extended an invitation to the Alice and her entourage to meet at the abandoned Rabbit Hole in three days' time."

Well, my social calendar is certainly filling up fast.

"I have no idea what any of this means."

My statement is more of a petulant whine. I'm tired. The post-battle fatigue has finally taken its toll. I can't absorb anything else tonight.

"None of us do," Jerome says as he removes me from Koji's arms and away from the gathered crowd. "We are living in unprecedented times. None of us—except, perhaps the Caterpillar—knows what the future holds." I sag against him, the strength draining from my body. "But the future is a problem for tomorrow." Then he's guiding me into my bedroom, tucking me back in, and kissing my forehead. "Sweet dreams, Majesty."

I'm vaguely aware of the door closing before I slip into oblivion.

Morning comes all too soon and I am not ready. Hungry, yes. Ready, not at all.

We eat breakfast together in my rooms in companionable quiet, though there's plenty of side-eye between Ivan and Torai. I'll be the first to admit that there are serious trust issues in our little blended family, but it's my hope that we'll all learn how to get along. I haven't forgotten that the Walrus tried to kill me at our first meeting or that his boss — former boss, I hope — still wants me dead so he can take my Kingdoms. And holy cats because — *plural*. I choose not to dwell on that.

After breakfast, the various parts of said family move out to prepare for the day and once more I'm alone with Phineas.

"My Queen," he says with a short, formal bow. There's a teasing glint in his eyes when he rises.

"My King," I parrot with a goofy curtsy. His lips lift into a lopsided smile. "Do we really have to go back to reality?"

He steps forward and pulls me into a hug. My arms go around him, and I press my ear to his chest to listen to his heartbeat.

"As much as I would love to keep you in my arms forever, we have a war to win and a land to save."

"Stop being reasonable," I joke and hug him just a little bit tighter. Phineas laughs and strokes my hair.

"Once we win the war, I will gladly hold you for the rest of our long lives," says. Phineas pulls back just enough to tip my face up with his fingertips and kiss me. The urgency from last night is gone, replaced by a warm, bubbling affection.

As with all the others, the kiss ends too soon, but we continue to hold onto one another until Jerome knocks on the door.

"Majesties, it's time," he says.

Time sucks. It's entirely too demanding.

"Well, here we go, I guess," I say."

"Come back to me safely." Phineas kisses me one more time before we turn for the door hand-in-hand.

Traveling by jubjub is much faster than traveling by bandersnatch, even if I really, *really* don't like the murderbirds. They're unpredictable and they make too much noise for me.

They do, however, make the trek through the Tulgey Wood much faster. It also helps that I'm only traveling with my Rabbits and Koji today. Our forces are scattering more and more, and I still don't like it.

Talon left early on his secret Caterpillar sneaky business. The twins are back at Wonderland Castle with Torai and the Oysters, likely discussing tactics. Phineas, Felina, and Blade remain in the White Court. This whole magic portal bedroom thing is useful certainly… but I don't like being away from my people.

I'm further disturbed by the fact that I actually recognize this portion of the Tulgey Wood. I mean, why shouldn't I considering the signpost up ahead is where I got lost while running from the White Court on charges of regicide? A shudder passes through me, drawing the attention of both Rabbits. I give a little shake of my head, which seems to satisfy them.

The Tulgey Wood creaks with the typical early-morning sounds of life—breeze rustling the trees, the various wildlife creating their harmonious backdrop, creatures snuffling through the underbrush—except for the vivid colors in the near darkness and the coziness bordering on suffocation, it's just a normal morning in a forest.

Except for the magic. Magic is concentrated here. Thicker and heavier and much more immediately dangerous. Wild magic... and a lot of it. I grip the reins of my bird a little bit tighter and urge the beast to pick up the pace so we can get the hell out of here.

Koji, currently napping in cat form on the back of my mount, raises his head.

"Something is wrong," he mutters. The hair on the back of my neck stands on end.

Oh good...it's not just me.

"Any idea what?"

And the Rabbit armor goes up. They close ranks, closely flanking me. Koji shifts, takes a seat, and slips the reins out of my hands all in one smooth movement.

"Just in case," he murmurs in my ear. The sound of his voice is so loud that it throws into sharp contrast the fact that the woods have gone deathly silent.

I'm glad to give up control and focus my attention on my surroundings. Koji seems less alarmed than the rest of us. Too calm and collected for the tension. It feels like there's something he's not telling me. I turn to ask him about it when I'm pitched forward, the three birds coming to an immediate halt.

"Well, well… what have we here…"

I don't recognize the voice, but the features of the man standing in the middle of the road are *very* familiar. He chuckles, the sound oddly mirthful in the forest's gloom. "A pair of traitors, a murderous Queen, and her lovesick fool." He scoffs. The sound pisses me off. "I knew my brother was hiding something."

Oh fuck.

"You must be Lord Morcar of Northumbria," I reply, holding myself steady only because of Koji's presence behind me and his arm banded around my waist.

"At your service, Majesty," he replies with a bow. "Thank you, Koji, for bringing me word of such a… tasty morsel."

The Cheshire Cat bows low around me. My heart begins to race.

No, no, no…

"At your service, your Grace."

Holy shit, they were right!

"Koji, what—"

"Hold tight to her for me until I rid the world of these flap-eared pests."

"Fuck," I hear Jerome hiss, but I don't have time to follow along before they both vault off their mounts, landing with an immediate clash of swords. Morcar's excited, maniacal laugh echoes through the woods in a way that makes me nauseous. He fights viciously and without pause, forcing Ivan back long enough to turn and take a swing at Jerome before starting the circuit over again. And again. And again.

"Relax, Alice," Koji whispers under the noise of the fight, "we have a plan."

Given our current predicament, that doesn't really make me feel better. I have no idea who this theoretical "we" is. The sound of battle rings out, deafening in the silence of the forest, but my Rabbits move like a well-oiled machine, quickly taking control of the fight and boxing in the Earl of Northumbria with a few swift and deadly blows.

"On my word, Majesty," Koji says and his other arm comes around my waist, holding me tight to him, "put your faith in me."

I nod, breathless, and watch as Jerome disarms Morcar and Ivan forces him to his knees. But instead of admitting defeat, he begins to laugh again.

And laugh.

And laugh more.

Then the cracking of bones echoes through the forest as he begins to shift. Human features give way to sharp, grotesque twists and turns. Skin sprouts scales and horns and Morcar's body grows, morphing before my eyes into a dragonlike creature, its long neck pushing its spike-maned head far above us as scaly, webbed wings burst from its elongated, snakelike spine.

"That would be our cue," Koji says and in the same breath he too vaults from the back of the jubjub, carrying me up into the air. "To me!" he shouts. Both Rabbits spring backwards, grabbing my hands midair, and we land more or less on our feet, somewhere far, far from the path. Belatedly, I scream.

Lucky for me, I'm with one of the only three beings in Wonderland who can navigate the Tulgey Wood without a path underfoot.

CHAPTER NINE

"What...the fuck... was *that?!*" I shriek as my feet touch down on the loamy ground. The shock of that transition drains every ounce of energy from me, and I collapse to my knees, my breath coming in shallow, sharp pants.

"Jabberwocky," Koji says, unfazed.

"Why didn't you tell me he's a fucking *shapeshifter?!*"

"You never asked, love."

That's an awfully big piece of information to keep to himself, but the damned cat doesn't seem the least bit sorry about it. I fall backwards onto my back in the grass, sending small, rainbow-colored bioluminescent sparkles up into the air — tiny firefly-like creatures, I realize, with big (relatively) googly eyes and full sets of humanlike teeth in their tiny mouths. They dance around, momentarily before fluttering into the darkness.

"Are there any other nasty shapeshifter surprises I should know about?" I ask as I press the heels of my hands into my eyes to block out the insanity for just a second.

"I assume you understand that the ability to change shape is a genetic trait?" The cat's voice comes closer, and the warmth of his body settles beside me.

"There is a reason for Edwin's sobriquet," Ivan says. "He's not called the *Red Court Beast* for nothing."

My eyes fly open and meet his steady gaze. "Are you fucking serious?"

"As a beheading, Majesty."

I let my head thump back against the soft ground and groan loudly.

"I cannot deal with anything else today. Or ever again. I quit. Get a new Queen."

Three men laugh at me.

Away from the path, the twisted wilderness comes alive. It's steamy and humid beneath the tumtum canopy and so dark that I can barely see my hand in front of my face. But here, there are also sounds and smells to rival any major city in Otherland. Sweet, salty, savory, clean and putrid. The damp flavor of petrichor lingers on the back of my tongue with every breath, and the warm scent of animal fur tickles my nose. My heart races and my skin feels clammy in the thick air.

Panic.

"I-is everybody okay?" I ask. My voice is louder now, free from the confines of the path's vacuum-like nature, and my mind is already so unhinged by what I just witnessed that it scares me to hear myself this loudly.

"Good," Jerome says. He sounds a little breathless too.

"I'm okay," Ivan adds, also not sounding as steady as I'd like.

"Oh, little Alice… I am *glorious*," Koji says right in my ear, and I realize he's lying in the grass beside me. His hands slide around me, and when my back hits his chest, my fear dissipates like dandelion fronds in the breeze.

Koji himself seems to glow in the darkness of the forest much like those bugs, emitting his own inner light. He illuminates enough of the forest around that I can see both Rabbits clearly, but in the same way an artist can see a cartoon character standing on a blank page.

"Well, gentle Rabbits… shall we continue on?"

Both Rabbits draw their swords, the vorpal blades adding their own glow to the area… sort of. It still more closely resembles that fourth-wall cartoon cut scene with Bugs Bunny scolding his inker. More concerning is that both Rabbits are handling this abrupt shift in reality much better than I am. Did… did they know what was happening?

If it weren't for Koji—a being literally made of magic—we'd be in serious trouble.

He pulls me to my feet and we begin walking, my hand clasped tightly in his and swinging between us like we're on the world's weirdest date. Koji starts humming. The sound rumbles through me, comforting in its familiarity, and my heart rate slows a little.

The Tulgey Wood teems with life. We see none of it, of course, because it stays well out of the circle of light, but we can hear it. *Feel* it.

Even the magic is different here. It's truly wild, moving about us in tempestuous currents. It's beautiful and terrifying all at once. Dangerous.

Between the unfamiliar flow of magic and my Rabbits' apprehension clanging inside my head, I'm not sure which way is up. So I follow along like a good little Queen, going wherever my attendants lead.

Speaking of…

"Where exactly are we going?" I ask as Koji leads us around the base of a tree wider than my car. "And what did you mean you have a plan?"

"To your clandestine meeting with Edwin, of course," Koji replies like it's the most natural thing in Wonderland and I'm a fool for not realizing it. "As to the other, I mean exactly what I mean."

"Which means what?"

He tugs me closer by the hand he holds. "It means, my lovely Queen, that you have nothing at all to fear."

Which means he plans to tell me nothing. This revelation surprises me more than it should. He is, after all, Wonderland's most famous secretive sneak.

"What about the two of you?" I turn an accusatory stare toward the Rabbits. Ivan gives away nothing, but Jerome's gaze flickers away. "You knew it was coming, didn't you?"

His lack of response is all the answer I need. My blood boils, nearly to the point of steam whistling out of my ears. They're all participating in these stupid mind games now. I shouldn't be surprised, but knowing even my Rabbits were against me on this one hurts.

"You all suck," I snap and turn away. The argument is already building in the air — they were protecting me, they needed me to be surprised, blah blah blah blah blah... Yet again I'm treated like a cowering child.

I give up trying to get answers from any of them. Koji is at my side, lazy smile on his face like he didn't just pull off a mini-betrayal. I want to know more, even though I know he's sealed up tighter than Fort Knox.

But isn't Fort Knox empty?

I tell myself to shut up. None of this is helping, so when Koji takes hold of my hand and leads me into the empty blackness, I let him. Rather than arguing, I muse curiously to myself instead on the many ways I might bargain for information. Though as I follow the trail down that particular rabbit hole — no pun intended... or is it? — something else comes to mind.

"Koji, you helped us in front of Morcar. Isn't it dangerous for you to return to the Red Court now?"

"Oh, my Alice...I am in danger no matter where I go." His smile tells me he's not the least bit sorry about this. "Not only am I an anomaly among the Wondrous, but I am also an endangered species."

What?

"You know the Neko are made from magic, yes?" Jerome asks. I nod, remembering that conversation from long ago. A manufactured race produced by a failed biology experiment.

"Yes."

"We are hunted," Koji explains, "for our parts. Even a bit of Neko fur is considered a vessel for blessings." My stomach turns, but he remains unaffected. "A whole Neko, still breathing? Why, those are invaluable."

"In a way, this one is lucky," Ivan says, nodding toward Koji, "because even as cruel as the Duchess is, she has a soft spot for wayward animals."

"Meow," Koji adds rather flatly. "This way." He tugs my hand again and we veer sharply to the left.

"Whoa!" I stumble over my own feet at the sudden shift in direct and nearly go ass over teakettle onto my face. The stupid cat laughs.

"If I'd known you wanted to dance, Majesty, I wouldn't have brought you to the woods."

"Shut up," I snap and tighten my grip on his arm.

We arrive at the Rabbit Hole none too soon. Even with the months of training, I'm not cut out for a day-long trek through an enchanted forest in high-heeled boots. I'm exhausted, panting for breath, and seriously annoyed by the fact that my three companions are tall enough that each of their strides equals two of mine. In Ivan's case, three.

We crest a hill and step out from under the dense canopy on the edge of the Tulgey wood. The sun is bright on its descent, the sudden shock of light temporarily blinding me and sends me reeling backwards against Ivan's front. He catches me with a laugh, sets me back on my feet, and curls an arm around my shoulders to guide me until I can see properly.

The Rabbit Hole itself is just that: a hole in the side of a hill that looks like it hasn't been accessed in years. I know it has been accessed, though, because we were just here a few days ago.

In yet another jarring transition, the door flies open and Edwin greets us with a wide gesture and an even wider smile. The sight of him, especially knowing what he is now, causes me to stumble. If he notices, he says nothing.

"Ah, welcome, Queen Alice! You are early!"

I can't help but glance at Jerome with amusement. He's usually reminding me how late I am for everything.

"It appears we took a shortcut," I say.

"Out of a coincidental necessity," Ivan adds. His lip curls up in a fake snarl. He's not really angry. This is a show. "You wouldn't happen to know anything about that, would you, Lord Edwin?"

Edwin's eyebrows shift upward. I'm not sure if he's more surprised by the necessity part or by Ivan's direct accusation.

Koji laughs, of course, but it isn't a mirthful one. "If you would, Majesty…" He nudges me toward the literal hole in the ground that is the door. "It would be wise to move this little gathering indoors."

"Oh, quite right," Edwin agrees and turns so that we can duck inside. And I do mean duck—the door itself is only four feethigh.

The inside, of course, is familiar; warm and cozy if just a bit dusty. Edwin already has tea and cake waiting for us, however before he can pour, Ivan snatches up the cups to wash them thoroughly.

"One can never be too safe with the Queen's life," he says upon return. "Clean cups are vital, after all."

"Quite right," Edwin repeats. There's no hint of malice in his expression. "Would you like to check the pot before I pour, Alice?"

"Uh…sure?"

So I do. This magical detector thing is useful. I don't find poison, spit, or any other contaminants, and the tea leaves themselves are just plain black tea.

"All good," I announce and let the magic recede. He pours. We drink.

"Now, tell me of the necessity which warranted your early arrival."

I can't stop the glare that pinches my face at his absolute audacity. All it takes is looking at that smug smirk to know he already knows exactly what happened. Probably where and when as well.

"You have a terrible poker face," I say. This time Edwin does look confused. Like he has no idea what language I'm even speaking. "Surely you play card games."

"Yes."

"But you don't know what a poker face is?"

"He cheats," Koji informs me.

"As do you," Ivan shouts.

"You're not exactly a pillar of truth yourself," I remind him. Jerome, wisely, says nothing. "That is to say, Lord Edwin, that you gave yourself away before you ever spoke. You know full well what happened."

The smile I receive in return is genuine. It's a stark contrast to the beast of pure carnage we met in the Tulgey Wood. Though the brothers resemble one another, I have a hard time reconciling the many faces they present in my head.

"Ah, about that. My brother is… how should I say it? Competitive?"

"Don't you mean a murderous hellbeast who wants me dead?"

He shrugs. "To be fair, Majesty, Morcar wants everyone dead. Quite possibly me more than you."

I roll my eyes and drain my cup. "Why do we need to add extreme sibling rivalry to the list of Wonderland fuckery?"

Edwin, of course, laughs.

"I was also told that his other form is genetic. Does that mean—"

"Yes, Alice," he says. "I can shift shapes at will as well."

"Good to know." Jerome takes the empty cup from my hand and presents a clean one. "And I do hope our urgently important business isn't so urgent that it can't wait until tomorrow. I'm quite tired after the fun we've had on this trip."

Edwin nods. "Understandable, Majesty. Feel free to use the Rabbit Hole as you see fit. If you would like to retire for the evening with the intent of continuing discussions in the morning, then I will have your dinner sent to your room by way of your dear Rabbits."

"I think that might be best," I hear myself saying, but my mind is already drifting to the thought of my bed. I don't get to spend enough quality time with it these days.

"I'll see our lovely Queen to her room," Koji says and lifts me from the chair with no exertion at all. For someone this fluid and sinewy, he's deceptively strong. He's also comfortable. The quiet rumble emanating from his throat and chest lulls me further into the darkness. It would take nothing at all to fall asleep right here in his arms despite the fact that I'm hungry and dirty and desperately want to take off my shoes.

A shower and a meal later, I'm perfectly relaxed and ready for bed. As much as I'd love to confer with the rest of my court, I'm just too tired. As it is, Ivan and Jerome have retired to their own rooms, and I'm stretched out across my bed with Koji at my side. He's shirtless and shoeless, and running his long-nailed fingers through my damp hair and down the line of my back. It feels heavenly. If I had that extra set of vocal chords, I'd be purring too.

"Might I ask you something, my Queen?" Koji asks softly, his voice low and sweet in my ear. The sound of it pulls me back from the precipice of sleep.

"Depends on how hard I have to think about the answer."

The soft chuff of laughter touches my ears. "Do you trust me?"

My eyes open and the look of frightened vulnerability on his face constricts my heart. This beautiful creature, so full of bullshit and swagger, looks terrified of my answer.

"Yes," I say without a second thought and relief washes over his beautiful face. "You've lied and cheated, played word games and spun me up again and again and again, but you came back when I needed you most. I trust you." The honesty surprises even me. "You've not once acted without good reason."

"And what would you say if I were to tell you that I'm planning to betray you?"

"I'd say that's quite a plot twist. It probably shouldn't surprise me, but it would." I reach up and run my fingers along the line of his jaw. "Besides, you told me yourself that I already have all of you. If you betray me, then that would be a lie."

A smile tugs at the corners of his lips, and he turns his face to kiss my palm.

"What do you know of the history of Wonderland?" he asks out of the blue. It takes a minute for my sluggish brain to make the turn into serious talk.

"Not as much as I should, I guess," I admit. "I mean, I know the stories of the original Alice, and I know the gist of what's contained in the prophecy, but I really don't know much about what came before."

Koji's gaze glazes over, growing distant like he's looking back through his own history.

"It's a dark and bloody story. Filled with hatred and fear."

"That sounds far too familiar."

"Indeed. Our world before Alice was much like yours—filled with opposing opinions, dissent, and those who would think themselves superior to others." He shrugs one shoulder in what's meant to be a nonchalant manner, but I can see it's his way of dismissing his own painful past. "There is still a good bit of that, I suppose. You never completely remove biases, and tyrants will always rise."

True, but it is possible to remove the threats." At least I hope it is. If we can't, then what's the point?

"Sweet, foolish, hopeful Queen," he says and leans over to touch his lips to mine. "Allow me to tell you a bedtime story. I cannot promise it will carry you to the land of sweet dreams but is quite the tale."

"By all means," I reply. My eyelids are already heavy and every muscle in my body begs for unconsciousness. Koji swiftly and gently rearranges me in my bed, then crawls in beside me and tucks us both in. I curl into his arms, letting his warmth seep into me.

"Once upon a time, there was a young cat who, like a fool, believed in a better world." With that one sentence, I'm fully aware again. This is his story. "That young cat, an adult by society's standards, was naive and idealistic. He wanted to believe in the goodness of the people around him. His mother always told him that in times of crisis, those around him would do the right thing."

The gentle way his voice lilts and twirls, even around these dark words, lulls me into a trance-like state where I'm completely prone, yet aware of every single word.

"His mother was a friend of the crown — the Red Crown — and thought herself and her family untouchable by Wonderland's standards. Oh, but was she ever so wrong."

Pain infuses his words. Grief. Anger. Centuries of unresolved emotion. This beautiful, dangerous creature in my arms is the walking wounded, forced to carry on despite horrible tragedy. I tighten my hold on him and am met by a single, sardonic chuckle. Long-nailed fingers trail through my hair again.

"The young cat watched his mother die, a Club-handled blade embedded deep into her heart on the steps of the Red Palace and dismembered into her requisite parts. Because you see, darling Alice, we Neko are considered lucky charms. Even *pieces* of us are valuable beyond belief."

I want to ask questions, but whatever spell he's cast over me makes it impossible for me to move, much less speak.

"The young cat, horrified and grief-stricken by the sudden and violent loss of the most important person in his life, hid himself away only to discover that the damnable Queen of Hearts — the woman his mother trusted and loved above all others — ordered betrayal for financial gain."

Tears seep from the corners of my eyes as I'm overwhelmed by this shared grief. I can feel the pain radiating from him as he speaks. My heart breaks for him though he speaks of himself as little more than a character in a fairy tale.

"It was the Queen's daughter who found the orphaned kitten. Little more than a child herself, the girl took him in and cared for him. She and her sister loved and protected the little cat despite the danger. For you see, their mother, in her madness, announced the eradication of the Neko from Red territory and the sale of their parts in order to fund her next war."

My heart constricts. It makes sense now why he is the way he is.

"The sisters cared for him as if he were their child, though they were younger than him by several years. The girls believed in a peaceful future, where all races were equal and all creatures could live freely and without fear."

As Koji talks, his fingers card through my hair, long nails scratching gently against my scalp. I'm convinced this alone is what keeps me from falling to pieces.

"It took several attempts for the Alice to defeat the Red Queen and restore peace. Once it was done, however, the girls and their cat lived happily on. It wasn't until The Alice chose to take her family to Otherland that things turned sour. For you see, The Alice chose her successors, but did not take into account the power she relinquished. For power is addictive, and when not handled properly, it corrupts."

"What about the cat and his people?" I ask, keeping my question shielded by that impersonal lens of a third person point of view.

"The cat survived, of course. Thrived, even. His people, however..." Koji takes a breath that leaves his lungs on a sigh. "His people were not so cunning as he. And not at all lucky." He leaves his statement hanging at that, and I do my best not to let my mind fill in the blanks with the true meaning of his silence. My tears intensify and I tighten my arm around his middle. He starts to purr.

The soft vibrato issuing from his throat helps ease the pain. His presence is magic of its own, and despite the fact that he's broken my heart in so many hundred words, all it takes is a taste of his sweetness to make me whole again.

I fall asleep tonight nestled in the Cheshire Cat's arms, my ear pressed to the base of his throat.

Chapter Ten

"Shall we move onto our business, then?" Edwin asks? I nod.

"I'm ready to know why I've been invited into enemy territory, please and thank you."

"It's simple, really."

Koji, having wandered off somewhere, returns to perch on the arm of my chair then artfully drape himself around my head.

"I quite regret to inform you," Edwin continues, "that this is an ambush."

I have exactly one-quarter of a second to process before both Ivan and Jerome are on their feet and armored with weapons drawn.

"Wait!" comes the slightly panicked feminine voice.

My head turns slowly, like I'm encased in jelly, and terror seizes my heart.

"Give it a chance," Koji says while wrapped around my neck. "She has her reasons."

"Majesty, let me introduce the Red Duchess, Lady Aeromi Dreadlow."

I glare at Edwin and his introduction, then turn my attention back to the Duchess. She executes a perfect curtsy while nary a hair on her head moves.

"An honor," she says, but the words feel false thanks to the smirk on her face.

She's pretty, but with a hard, cruel edge. Dark hair falls in perfect waves around her pale face, and dark lashes frame the palest blue eyes I've ever seen. Her very being radiates subtle violence, from her expression to her stance. The most shocking of all, however, is the tiny pig—not much larger than a teapot—tucked under her left arm.

"My Lady," Koji purrs. I see red.

"Good kitty," she answers with an indulgent smile.

"What the hell is this about?" I ask, trying desperately to keep the fear and fury out of my voice. I fail pretty miserably.

"Lord Edwin says you can be trusted." I don't respond. "I want to propose an alliance," the Duchess says. Her words pour out of her in a rush, like she's afraid she won't be able to finish her statement before she dies. Considering my Rabbits have their blades at her throat, it's possible. "You see, my sister is quite mad, and she fails to see reason at every turn."

"That may be the largest understatement I've ever heard," Koji says in my ear.

"I can no longer stand idly by while she allows Wonderland to burn. I need help, Majesty. Please." Her voice cracks on the last word.

"Stand down," I tell my still-armed and still-angry Rabbits. "At least let me hear what she has to say before you kill everybody in the room." Both swords return to their sheaths, but both Ivan and Jerome remain standing. "Have a seat and let's talk."

The Duchess wants to team up with me to get rid of her sister because she wants to keep her title after Wonderland is unified. That's all well and good, but it feels like there's something she's not telling me.

Then again, it always feels like there's something someone isn't telling me.

Despite her cruel countenance and Ivan's thorough distrust of her, Aeromi Dreadlow seems to be a fairly kind person. She's whip-smart and knows the history of Wonderland, which she has easily demonstrated over the last two hours of discussion.

"Let me get this straight," I say, trying to sum up our negotiations while wrapping my head around yet another curveball, "the only thing you want from me is to keep your title as Duchess of Hearts?"

"Unless, of course, you would grant me the title of King."

There's something sheepish about the way she asks. The slightest hint of color stains her cheeks, and her smile turns bashful. The idea is off the wall, but... not a completely awful idea when I think about it. Just way out in left field.

"I feel like I'm missing something here." I feel like I say that a lot. I can't seem to catch up to where everyone else is, no matter what I do.

"I promise you, Majesty," she replies, "I have no ulterior motive and no plan to betray you." She sighs, and the sound is so forlorn that it nearly breaks my heart. "I have never known a world of peace. This war has stretched far beyond my ability to remember, and I, like many who live here, am weary because of it. I am an advocate for the common people, My Lady."

That sounds suspiciously good. All of the higher-ups in the Heart court seem a bit too pious for my liking. But then again, revolution often succeeds on the back of subversion. Cogs in the machine have to break for the turning to halt.

"Can I ask you a question?"

Aeromi blinks at me like she didn't expect rational discourse or something. She nods. "Of course."

"Was your sister always mad?"

Watching her expression change tells me more than words ever could. The sharpness fades from her features. Her lips draw together. And her eyes — so much sadness lives behind them.

"No," she says. "She had the softest heart when we were young. She tended a garden for the bread-and-butterflies. Taught the flowers to sing. My Lucinda loved the land. Loved her people. But..." Aeromi pulls in a shaking breath with a tiny hiccup trapped inside, "but power is tempting and magic is addictive." Her voice hitches. "She wanted to help."

"What happened?"

"The magic. It changes people. We're taught from a very young age not to abuse our abilities. We are trained as children to accept the fact that the more we use our magic, the less of ourselves we retain." A single tear slides down her face. She swipes at it with a delicate finger. "The more she used it to do good, the more it took from her. And took. And took...until there was nothing left."

I have no words. Edwin and Ivan wear matching expressions of subtle grief. Of all the things I expected to come of this conversation, this was not one of them. Seeing the Red Queen as a reflection of my potential future self is frightening. Could I truly become so corrupted? Could I grow addicted to magic? Would that addiction shatter me?

I want to help end this war and bring about the peace she craves, but now I'm afraid I may not make it.

"Stop worrying, Majesty," Jerome says. "That sort of madness is centuries in the making."

"For the Wondrous," I counter. "I'm also human."

"Part human," Koji corrects. "You do have quite the advantage."

Aeromi reaches out and gently places her hand on my arm. Her touch is gentle and warm. "I did not mean to frighten you, Majesty. I only wanted you to understand a bit about my sister. There used to be a person behind the madness. A good person. But her mind is gone."

"I'm sorry," is the only thing I can think of to say.

We're all still and quiet, the only sound the ticking of a clock somewhere deep in the rabbit hole. Aeromi dabs at her eyes with a handkerchief.

"So, Majesty," Edwin says, breaking the tense silence, "do we have an alliance?"

There's certainly hesitation from both Rabbits. I look at Ivan for guidance since this is his former court. "Your thoughts?" I ask.

Ivan is slow to respond. When he does, he surprises me.

"Lord Edwin has proven himself. We should afford Lady Aeromi the same chance."

"Your thoughts, Jerome?" I turn to look at him.

He holds my gaze for a long time then nods. "An alliance would be beneficial."

"A wise choice from both Rabbits," Koji says. "Say the word, Majesty, and the alliance is yours."

I truly hope I don't regret this.

"We have an alliance."

My return to the White Palace is met with an excited squeal and an even more excited teenager wrapped around my head. I stumble backwards and think I'm going ass over teakettle. Ivan's hand between my shoulders keeps me from hitting the ground. He laughs. I don't care. My sister is here, wrapped around me. She's safe.

"Oh, sorry," Edith says when she releases me and then drops into an awkward curtsy. "I probably shouldn't assault the Queen."

I laugh and pull her back into a hug. "It's okay, Edith. It's your right as my sister."

She burrows deeper into my arms and squeezes me tightly. "I'm glad you're home. Miss Felina was telling me that you were in a war. And another one."

"I was, yes. The last one was more of a skirmish. And as you can see, I'm perfectly okay."

She squeezes me even tighter. "Please don't die," Edith says with that naked vulnerability that only young teenagers have. It twists my heart into knots.

"I don't plan to."

Once I extricate myself from my sister's grasp, I'm pulled into another hug.

"Welcome home, my Queen." Phineas's low voice flows over me like warm honey, and the comforting feel of his arms surprises me. He's not usually physically affectionate, and certainly not outside of the Suite.

"It's good to be home."

And waiting behind him...

"Aunt Margaret!" It's my turn to run at her and grab her up in a big hug. She wraps her arms around me and suddenly all is right with the world. "I didn't know you were here!"

"Well," Aunt Margaret says as we pull away, "your King here can be very persuasive, and his messenger really didn't give us much of a choice."

I smile at Phineas who grins back. "I'm so glad," I say.

"Shall we go inside, ladies?" Phineas asks as he begins herding us into the castle.

"I have to say, Alice," Aunt Margaret starts, "I am quite surprised by all of this."

She gestures around at everything. The castle, the people, the jubjubs, the cards... it's a lot to take in. I'm still stunned by it, and I've been here half a year now.

"Me too."

"I knew of our connection to the original stories, but I never imagined that it was more history than fairy tale."

"It is amazing," I say. This whole adventure has been surreal. I have no idea what I'm doing, but I'm doing it nonetheless. And the people I've met have been nothing short of amazing. Having my family here grants me a sense of peace I didn't realize I was missing. They're close by and safe. I don't have to worry quite as much. My court will protect them.

"Have you had fun?" I ask my sister, while reaching out to grab her hand, and I'm met with a big, bright smile.

"So much fun!" She squeezes my arm even tighter. "Felina is teaching me magic. She says I'm a natural."

"Of course you are," I answer even though fear grips my heart. "We are Liddel blood. We're powerful women."

"I knew we were witches! Jason Collins can eat his heart out." She throws her head back and cackles. Loudly.

"We aren't witches, Edy."

"If we can do magic, we're witches."

She has a point, I guess. I smile at her happiness.

We meander through the castle, giving Aunt Margaret a tour while Edith prattles on about her studies over the last week. The things her tutors teach here are nothing like what she's accustomed to. No reading, writing, and arithmetic here. She's learning magic, medicine, and battle tactics.

They're training my baby sister to be a general, and she is one hundred percent here for it. I'm certain Aunt Margaret will figure that out for herself soon enough too. That, however, is a conversation I am not looking forward to. One of many, if I'm honest. She's going to rake me over the coals first chance she gets.

The closer we move to my suite, the more crowded the hall becomes. Blade and Felina join us, along with various members of the court who stop to welcome me home. It's nice to be seen. But it also makes me nervous. I seem to be pretty okay at this Queen-thing so far, but I'm very aware that I still have a long way to go. I just hope I'm not deluding myself.

Tag, Nacht, Torai, and Talon are all standing in the hallway waiting for me as we enter. I'm immediately on full alert.

"Welcome home, Majesty," Nacht says with a deep, comically formal bow.

"Is everything okay?" I ask.

"Quite well, indeed," Tag says. "Now that our Alice has returned."

"Well, we have a few hours until dinner," I say, "Should we catch up?"

No matter how many people I have in my room, it never feels cramped. Magic is such a wondrous thing. There are currently thirteen of us around this table. The tea and cakes never run out. All the people I care most about in two worlds are here with me. I couldn't be happier.

Oh, but you could, my cruel mind reminds me. There is one conspicuous absence from your life.

A pang of sadness seizes my heart, and my breath rushes away. I don't want to think about my father; about the cruel things he's done to us.

But that voice is right. He is absent, and I do want him — the person he used to be, that is — back in my life.

Shake it off, Alice, I tell myself and actively try to focus on all of the good around me.

I make introductions for those that need them and take my seat at the head of the table. Edith looks around with all the wonder of a child, but Aunt Margaret looks concerned.

"How was your latest meeting, Highness?" Torai asks. I can't stop the sigh that escapes me.

"The two ambushes notwithstanding —" I hit Koji with a glare, to which he responds with a smirk, " — it was quite productive."

"Two ambushes?" Phineas is up and out of his chair, but I wave him back.

"Only one was violent. And now I understand why Edwin and Morcar are referred to as beasts."

"What did he —"

"Morcar, not Edwin," I nod to his vacant chair and Phineas sits. Grudgingly. "He came after us in the Tulgey Wood, so we had to take a short-cut."

Phineas growls. "I do hate acknowledging that cat's usefulness, but just this once, I am thankful he was with you."

Koji, never one to miss an opportunity, disappears and appears in cat form on Phineas' shoulder, rubbing his long-whiskered snout against the King's face. There's a snarl and a yowl and the next thing I know, Koji is dangling by his very human throat from Phineas' hand.

"A-and here–*koff-koff*– I thought you l-liked me," Koji gasps.

"Appreciation and likeness are very different things." Phineas squeezes harder. Koji gasps.

"Let him go, please," I order. The cat crumples to a gasping heap on the floor. Phineas smugly returns to his seat.

"He said if I catch him, I can kill him."

"You're not allowed to kill him."

"Jealousy… is so… unbecoming," Koji chokes out while trying to regain his breath.

I facepalm. We've had this conversation before. Now the cat is just needling the King.

"Jealous?" Phineas raises one eyebrow. "Of you?"

"Oh, yes," Koji goads as he rises a little unsteadily to his feet. "Our King is jealous that I bedded our Alice first."

And that statement triggers pandemonium in my bedroom.

Edith's jaw drops. Aunt Margaret shrieks in surprise and clutches at her throat. Both Rabbits jump to their feet. The twins howl with laughter and begin exchanging money. And me?

I'm ready to die of embarrassment.

"I cannot believe you!" I shout. My face burns with shame as Aunt Margaret's laser-sharp gaze lands on me. I do my absolute best not to look at her. Koji, of course, laughs like a loon, delighted by both the chaos and my personal embarrassment. Rage boils off Phineas with every breath he takes.

"You did not bed me, you idiot!" I yell, but it's no use. I've lost all control. Koji drapes himself over my shoulders and licks a stripe up the side of my neck. I refuse to admit how much I like it.

"Correct me if I'm wrong, Majesty, but did you or did you not spend the night in my bed after having been pleasured to the point of delirium?"

"That's... well, that's... quite beside the point," I mutter while praying I suddenly develop the Neko ability to turn invisible at will. "It wasn't like that at all."

"Oh, but it was," Koji whispers, "and it will be again. I am well aware that I am irresistible."

I cast a terrified glance at my family, hoping they didn't just hear him. Edith, of course, is eating up the drama. I'm certain she'll be asking all of the inappropriate questions later. Aunt Margaret looks both amused and quite uncomfortable. She is a southern lady of a certain age...this whole conversation has certainly scandalized her.

This is not how I expected this reunion to go.

"Okay, I'm done. Everybody out!" The chaos freezes. "I need a minute, please," I add in what I hope is a less psychotic tone.

"You heard our Queen," Jerome says. "Everyone take your leave. Now."

"We'll reconvene in a few minutes if that's okay."

"Of course, Majesty," Torai agrees, and is the first to move for the door. His egress sparks a chain reaction.

I catch Ivan's arm as he stands to leave. "You and Jerome stay with us, please." He nods and taps Jerome's shoulder.

Soon it's just my family, my Rabbits, and me. And boy, is it awkward.

"This was not how I expected any of this to go," I say, falling back into my chair. I run my hands through my hair and sigh.

"What exactly did you expect, *your Majesty*?" Edith asks, falling into a dramatic and somehow totally wrong curtsy while grinning like an absolute fiend. I'm never, ever, ever going to hear the end of this.

Ladies and gentlemen, my loving sister.

"This is an unusual situation," Aunt Margaret says. "I know this is a different world with different rules. And I know you are a grown woman..."

"But?" I prompt.

"How many boyfriends do you have, Alli?" Edith asks.

Now the questions start.

"Our society operates quite a bit differently than yours," Jerome says. He's even-tempered and has a calming effect on all of us. "Here we are less concerned with the human concept of propriety because our people are not bound by the same social constructs."

"What does that mean?" Aunt Margaret asks. Her voice carries a hint of accusation.

"It means things that bother people in your world have little to no effect on our people here."

"Alice may have as many lovers as she pleases, though it is expected that she will take four husbands as her Kings," Ivan says. Aunt Margaret's eyes go wide. "She is the most powerful woman in Wonderland, after all."

The gentle admonishment leaves my aunt gaping and flustered.

"I am not judging anyone," she stutters while collecting her thoughts. "It's just a lot to take in."

"You're *totally* judging, Aunt Mags." Edith grins again. "I know you are because I am too. I just happen to think that my sister breaking down social barriers and being free is pretty sick."

"Sick?"

"It's a good thing," I say. "I think. Anyway… I know it's a lot to take in. All of it. Believe me, there are still days I question everything I know. But the last six months—"

"Six months!?" Aunt Margaret shrieks. "It's only been a week and a half!"

"That's another thing. But yeah, my time here has been scary, but also wonderful."

Jerome busies himself making fresh tea while Aunt Margaret thinks through everything we've talked about. It's clear that she's having trouble reconciling what she knows with how this place works. I can't fault her for that though. I did too. Hell, there are still days when I have trouble believing my life is real.

"Just tell me one thing, Alice," she asks. "Are... are you safe?"

Safe? Safe how? Safe sex? Or is she asking if I'm physically safe? Because the answer to both of those, if I'm perfectly honest, is no.

"I'm okay," I tell her because it's the best I can do. "I was more worried about you. You and Edie could easily be used against me. Now that you're here, I know you're safe."

"Used against you? How?"

"Aunt Margaret... we're at war."

This revelation, of course, neither surprises nor excites her. Her face is a calm mask of stoicism, but I can tell from the fire burning in her eyes that she's furious. Edith has checked out of this part of the conversation—she doesn't really seem to care except for the fact that she's been given the chance to study magic over the last few days.

Of course she took to it like a natural. She's my sister and we Moncoeur girls are nothing if not resilient.

An hour and two pots of tea later, Ivan escorts my family to their rooms while I collapse in an exhausted, stressed-out heap on my bed. Jerome chuckles while he clears the table.

"This afternoon seems to have been a struggle for you," he says. "I've seen you quail less facing down wizards and mad kings."

"Yeah, well wizards and kings didn't change my diapers."

"Point taken, love." He moves to sit beside me, perching on the edge of the bed beside my head. "We have roughly two hours before dinner. Would you like to nap before you dress?"

"Can I?"

"You are the Queen. You can do anything you like."

"Except make people stop fighting."

"In time, you will even do that."

"I'm glad one of us has faith in my abilities."

Jerome leans down and kisses my forehead. It's such a sweet, simple gesture and it fills my heart with love. "I have always believed in you, Alice. Even when you didn't believe in yourself." I sit up and wrap my arms around his neck. This wonderful man has been saving my life for years and he doesn't even know it.

"Thank you for being you," I mutter into his neck.

"Get some rest, Majesty. We have a long night ahead of us."

When I finally do emerge from my room, I'm dressed and ready for dinner... -ish, because no one is truly prepared for a Wonderland banquet.

They're fun but they're also a lot. As is generally the case, I'm met by portions of my entourage. Phineas is dashing as always in his regal finery and of course, my Rabbits clean up well. They escort me to the dining hall where everyone else currently located in this castle waits. I'm silently thankful that the twins are half a land away because the last thing I need is one of them trying to give my kid sister their favorite kinds of tea. Again.

There is a surprising addition to the party tonight. Haigha sits beside Felina. Physically, he looks good—better than I've ever seen him, actually, but he keeps his eyes trained on the table in front of him.

"Majesty," Felina says as they all rise, "might I formally introduce Haigha, page of the White Court."

He rises, turns, and gracefully falls to one knee in complete supplication. "Queen Alice, I humbly and very sincerely thank you for your generosity and kindness." His voice begins to waver, and he has yet to look at me. "You saved my life, and so my life is yours."

It dawns on me a moment later that this cowering man before me used to be a Rabbit. And a quite powerful one, if the stories are to be believed.

"Please rise," I reply, realizing I sound near hysterical. The theatrics, man... this place is nothing if not dramatic. "I am relieved to see you are up and about. I worried for you."

Haigha struggles to his feet–the pain shows when he moves. Still, he won't look at me.

"Thank you, Majesty."

"You really don't have to be so formal," I tell him. "I do hope that, like everyone else here, you and I can be friends."

My statement shocks him. Dark, sharp eyes snap up to meet mine and his jaw falls, his mouth forming a perfectly-round O. Haigha is more rugged than most of the men around me–pale skin and dark features intersected by jagged scars. His face shows thin lines and the weight of years of battle. But his eyes are what truly fascinate me. Hollow and haunted, and nearly black, like parts of him are missing. He knows they're missing, too... but he has no idea what, exactly, those parts are.

"I... I don't know that I've ever had a friend before."

"Then I would be honored to be your first."

"Majesty..."

"Now come on." I lace my arm through his and pull him toward the table. "Tell me everything there is to know about you."

Jerome shifts a seat without my asking, allowing Haigha to take the chair beside me. The look on his face is unreadable, and anxiety pings inside my head. It appears I'm missing some vital information here. I make a mental note to dig for that later. I have a whole list of mental notes in my head about this guy. I really should make time to ask the questions.

Tonight, however, we sit, we eat, and we drink. We enjoy ourselves to the fullest because if I have learned nothing else from my time in Wonderland, it's that nothing is guaranteed. Least of all tomorrow.

As our dinner winds down, my family is escorted to their quarters while I take my inner circle and head for our suite. Since our afternoon meeting was interrupted by a certain smartass cat, we still have a lot of work to do. Jerome and Ivan knock on everyone's doors in passing, and soon my room is filled with my entire council. I swear this is the most twisted round table I've ever seen. Not that I've seen many others, but still. Now it's time to get to work.

Our evening council is uneventful as well.

Evening tea, some good-natured ribbing between Felina and the twins, and all the affection I can stand from Phineas in Koji's absence make for a swell of happiness in my heart. Strangely enough, though, Felina is the one to hang back as the others retire to bed.

"Might I have a word, Majesty?" She seems hesitant.

"Of course! Let's sit and talk." I lead her to the spontaneous armchairs and we take our seats. She is a truly lovely woman—feminine and delicate with dark hair and pale eyes, yet she carries an air of power about her that's both attractive and intimidating. She has that same ethereal breeze around her that affects Talon, and it gently ruffles the ends of her unbound hair. "What's on your mind?"

"Even though it has only been two days, I wanted to update you on your sister's training." She twists her fingers together in her lap like she's nervous. "Lady Edith is doing quite well, you see. She has the same aptitude for magic exhibited by others of your bloodline. A star pupil to be sure."

"But..." I take hold of her hands and gently pull them apart before she picks her cuticles raw. "You can be honest with me, Felina."

"She is youthful and stubborn, Majesty. She thinks her freedom in the castle means freedom from observation. And earlier today I found her skulking around the barracks. Questioning our officers about battle. I think she may be planning something."

I can't stop the sigh that escapes me. "Of course she is. She's a teenager, after all."

"I'm sorry, Majesty."

"You have nothing to apologize for. I'm glad you told me."

She nods and her shoulders relax a little.

"Have you told anyone else?"

"No, my lady. Only you."

"Good. We'll let Phineas know, but keep it quiet from there, okay?" She nods. "Would you be willing to continue observing her in secret? I'm pretty sure she's looking for ways to sneak into the ranks, but I'd like to know for certain."

"As you command."

"Not a command... I only want you to accept if you're comfortable. If not, I'll put a stop to it first thing in the morning."

"I believe your idea is wise, Majesty. I shall watch her. I'd like to know what she's up to myself."

"Wonderful!" I clap my hands together, then tuck my feet under myself. "Now that that's over, you've gotta fill me in on the new Kingdom gossip."

Felina smiles wide and makes herself comfortable. "Well, word from the dodo is..."

CHAPTER ELEVEN

I feel like I'm always walking away from something half-finished. I guess that's the way it is when one is in charge, but it's frustrating to say the least. I realize as I make my way down the hall to the throne room that I've become a walking pile of cliches and stereotypes, and it annoys me. I'm perpetually late — as Jerome loves to remind me — and usually only half-aware of what's going on around me.

I know my sister is plotting something. I know I'm married to a man who wants to kill me. I know half of my allies are on the other side of the war. And I know that we have something of a loose plan in place, but I don't really know how to execute it. We've reached the murky middle of the story. It just feels like it's all downhill from here.

They've only been here a week, but today I leave my family in the care of my husband — my first husband,

I remind myself — and return to Wonderland Castle. Koji has plans to return to Aeromi and will keep us in contact with the secret alliance in the North. Talon has duties to the various courts, so he will remain behind. My sister is still under Felina's guardianship and tutelage. Blade, however, will join Jerome and Ivan as my security detail. I hope to use the trip to get to know them better.

Then there's Haigha. He is by far the oddest piece of this giant jigsaw puzzle. He's up and moving well, and set to depart in three days' time. He'll be delivering status updates to the Carpenter on the majority of our public affairs, then moving to the High Tea Grounds south of Brillig to help prepare for the upcoming tea party. As I enter the courtyard, prepared to depart, I have to remind myself that we each have roles to play and responsibilities to carry out. Our separation is vital to the success of the plan. That doesn't mean I have to like it.

Edith comes running the moment I step out the door and wraps herself around me, sobbing.

"Do you really have to go?"

"I do," I tell her, taking hold and hugging her tightly. "But I will come back soon. And Felina will bring you into the suite so we can hang out."

"Why can't I just have a key?"

"That suite is a magical defense mechanism. If you have a key and a room, then you're in the line of fire if things go wrong. Besides, the suite picks the residents."

"But I want to protect you too."

My heart twists in my chest. Hard. She's so sweet and so earnest. But she's also very naive.

"And you do. Everyday. You are what I fight for, Edie."

Tears well up in her big, blue eyes, but watching her face is like watching the sun emerge from behind the clouds. My sister is learning the meaning of bittersweetness. "I'll see you tonight, okay?"

"Okay," she says on a sniffle. I hug my sister one more time, then return her to Felina's care before turning and hugging Aunt Margaret.

"You're safe here," I tell her. "Phineas will take good care of you."

"I have no doubts about that," she says. "Will these boys—," she gestures toward my Rabbits, "—take care of you?"

"Absolutely. You know Jerome already. Ivan is as dedicated to my protection as Jerome. Plus, I'll have Blade. Our Unicorn is more than capable."

She reluctantly releases me, and I turn directly into Phineas' arms. He kisses my forehead. "Safe travels, my lovely Queen." Even he is reluctant to let go, and I'm equally as reluctant to make him.

By the time we mount our jubjubs and move out, I am an emotional mess. This plan has to work. I have to save my family. I can't let my friends down.

I just hope I'm as capable as they think I am.

The trip to Wonderland Castle takes two long, uneventful days. We stop for the night in Tarrytown and find the quirky tea-party village in the middle of its annual harvest festival. The gingham grass has shifted from red and white to orange and white, and the air smells of pumpkin spice tea. It's just as delightful a place as it was the first time, far removed from the politics of war and heavily steeped in the whimsy that is Wonderland.

We stable our birds and take our belongings — or rather, Jerome takes my bag and his — and as we exit the alley into the main square, salutes and cheers fill the tea-scented air. Everyone in town is aware of our presence and thrilled that their Queen has come to join the festivities. Hands are shaken, hugs are accepted, and people part with curtsies and deep bows as we move toward the stage they've built in front of the inn.

My heart swells and warms as a girl with flowers in her hair takes my hands and pulls me into the circle. Another of the ladies drapes a ring of flowers over my head, encircling my crown, then curtsies with a sweet smile and backs away. A moment later, a young man offers his hand and asks me to dance.

I hesitate, but the mental nudge from both of my Rabbits breaks down what restraint I possess. The people are having so much fun, and it has been so long since I've been able to simply be free. I don't know the steps and I'm not at all graceful, but nobody seems to care. I'm tugged along in a wild dance that seems to grow faster and faster with each twirl from the young man holding my hand. The joy radiating from the revelers is enough to remind me why I'm doing what I'm doing.

These are the people I'm fighting for. This simplicity. This happiness. There are no politics here. No war. No death. No existential dread — or if there is, they do a fantastic job of hiding it.

This way of life is what I want to preserve.

Ivan and Jerome are eventually pulled into the revelry, where they take turns spinning and swirling us around the dance floor while Blade looks on, their sharp, mysterious eyes taking in everything so that I don't have to.

We drink too much tea and dance until we're dizzy, and that's the point when Blade catches my attention again. They seem to be enjoying themselves, even if the stoic expression on their face might say otherwise. There's a twinkle in those hypnotic eyes that I've not seen before.

I'm also drunk as hell and not entirely control of my body or tongue when I skip over and offer my hand.

"Come dance with me."

"Majesty…" Blade balks, but not out of disgust. That much is apparent. Their eyes cast a wide circle around the firelit square, then land on me. "Someone must stand watch."

"I can't imagine our enemies will be able to launch an attack in the time a single dance takes."

I shake my hand a bit toward them and smile. "Please? I appreciate your willingness to care for me, but I do want there to be more to life than a sense of duty that leads to death."

That stiff facade cracks for the first time, and a small smile slips through. My White Knight slips their hand into mine and immediately takes control, spinning us back into the fray with the practiced ease of a professional dancer. Delighted laughter bubbles up from my chest as cheers rise around us, and in no time I'm thoroughly dizzy and breathless with joy. When the song ends, Blade spins me around three times in rapid succession, then drops to one knee at my feet as the entire square erupts in cheers and applause. The scene is like something out of a Renaissance painting.

"Thank you for the honor, Majesty," they say. Jerome and Ivan come up behind Blade and, smiling ferociously, take them under the arms and lift them straight up into the air. In such a position, they're helpless to resist despite their immense strength.

"See, I knew there was a person under that mask!" Ivan shouts.

"Good to see you are, actually capable of something other than a hard stare," Jerome adds. They place Blade back on their feet who whips around, scowling at the two of them.

"You two are disgracefully drunk," they reply tartly. "And our Queen's favor is the only thing staying my hand at the moment."

"Oh come on," I reply, threading my arm through Blade's. "They're just trying to get you to loosen up. We're *all* drunk right now, and I, for one, was happy to see you smile."

Their expression softens a little as those swirling eyes turn in my direction.

"Anything for you, Majesty."

I lay my head against their shoulder and allow them to lead me toward the inn. By the time we retire to our rooms, the tension is gone, and we're all horribly drunk and very happy. I'm not certain how I get down the hall to my room or who might witness me at my worst, but I'm also too inebriated to care. At some point, I manage to kick off my shoes before I fall into bed with a goofy smile on my face, my cheeks aching with joy. That night I fall asleep without a care in the world or a thought in my head.

The next morning, however, is a very different story.

Blade waits at my door the next morning with flower-infused water and a lovely hangover remedy, and I am glad for both their protection and their forethought. Even with my terrible influence, they appear no worse for wear… unlike myself. At this moment, I'm not entirely certain I'm alive.

Without a responsible adult on this trip, I fear my Rabbits and I may end up in a ditch somewhere.

Once the buzzing in my brain fades and I'm able to stumble into clean clothes, my entourage and I descend the topsy-turvy teapot stairs to the main hall, where the lovely, little owner, a portly, moon-faced woman named Nailini, places steaming bowls of scrambled jubjub eggs and some kind of spotted, sweet-smelling meat in front of us.

When I attempt to pay for our board and breakfast, she waves me off with a pretty blush.

"That our Queen graced our town with her presence and was so kind to spend time with our people is payment enough," she says with a curtsy. "It has been an honor to serve, Majesty."

I look over at Jerome, who nods in understanding. Her open adoration is certainly cause for embarrassment in my head, and I'm not entirely sure how to respond. Words fail me. Jerome gracefully steps in.

"Your kindness and hospitality are appreciated, Miss Nailini," he says with a smile. "But it would not be right for the Crown to take without return. Please allow me to pay you for the room and this lovely breakfast."

"I-I couldn't possibly," she stammers, looking at flustered as I feel. She wrings her hands together tightly enough that her fingers turn white, and without thinking I reach out and cover them with my own.

"Please," I say. "Even if you say no, we'll leave the money on the counter." I smile at her, which brings a bashful smile back to her face. "Let me take care of my people, please."

"Your Majesty is…" she trails off, tears filling her eyes. "Please, Majesty," she adds, her voice just above a whisper as she reaches out to take my hand in both of hers, "end this war and let peace return."

"I will," I tell her, squeezing her fingers in mine momentarily before we let go of one another.

I truly hope I've not just told a lie.

By the time we're on the road, I almost feel like a person again. A hungover person, but a variation of a person. My head and heart are full from the morning spent amongst the citizens of Tarrytown, and I realize that my hair and clothes smell like rich, black tea long after we leave. It's a pleasant reminder of what exactly I'm fighting for. Being able to return to Tarrytown year after year for their harvest festival is definitely on my list of things to do once this war is over.

My heart aches a little as we mount up and ride away.

Blade leads the procession, and the Rabbits bring up the rear. It's a gently sunny morning and the various creatures of the Tulgey Wood provide us with a happy backdrop of sound. There's nothing threatening this morning—except the remnants of the headache even medicine can't erase—so I settle into my saddle and just enjoy the peace. None of us are particularly talkative. Even the magic is silent.

I don't remember the last time I was this relaxed while outside.

Hell, I don't remember the last time I was this relaxed at all.

We arrive at Wonderland Castle late in the evening and I'm greeted by over-enthusiastic hugs from the twins and a stiffly formal bow from Torai. He still looks at me like I'm a strange and wondrous creature and I'm not as afraid of him as I was. It's a little unnerving, but it's quickly wiped from my mind as Tag lifts me clear from my feet, my stiff back crackling as I'm folded nearly in half.

"Blade, good buddy!" he calls out and is met with the unmoving blue facade that is their face. He stops in his tracks, arm half-raised. I'm not sure if he was planning a handshake, a high-five, or a hug, but he stalls and his smile falters. "Okay, then..."

The way Tag's head hangs makes me chuckle.

Nacht is equally happy to see me, but much more subdued than his twin.

"Welcome home, Majesty," he murmurs in my ear and takes me into his arms. The knives at his neck clink together just above my head. Everything about him screams danger, but there are very few places I feel safer than at his side.

I look up at the castle—still in disrepair but somehow even *less* so than when I left, and smile. Nacht's words resonate in my mind. For the first time in a very long time, I finally feel like I truly am *home*.

"Shall we go inside?" I ask. Nods and murmurs of acquiescence are followed by an en masse movement inside. The twins have already commissioned a lavish feast, and I'm thankful for that, because I need the fortification.

It's funny, I realize as we take our seats around the massive table, but we spend a lot of time eating and drinking. It's almost like...I don't know. Like somehow the introduction of food, however bizarre and colorful, makes the situation feel a little more normal. Like we're not on the precipice of war with betrayal closing in on all sides.

I note as I look around the table that there could not possibly be a more well-protected person in Wonderland than me. Rabbits, assassins, a Walrus, and a Unicorn, all loyal to me and waiting to move at my command.

And oh, how I love each of them with all my heart.

The evening is slow and without conflict. Surprisingly cheerful. The problem with these quiet, happy moments is that they never last.

CHAPTER TWELVE

I'm sitting on Wonderland's throne with my newly upgraded crown on my head, accepting visitors despite the fact that literally any of them could be an assassin, yet somehow this is the most normal I've felt in a very, *very* long time. Most of our guests are common folk, come to wish me well and beg me to end the war. Some attempt to bring gifts scrounged together from their town's crops, but I can't bring myself to accept those. I'm not taking anything from anyone if I can help it.

But then… there's Bill.

My darling lizard friend from a lifetime ago appears in the doorway, his tattered hat crumpled in his scaly fingers and a nervous tic at his temple. Tag and Nacht's heads tip to the left in tandem as he stumbles his way up the aisle, his tail somehow getting tangled up around his feet and nearly throwing him down several times. Seeing that he's well does my heart good. He was the first non-Rabbit person in Wonderland who truly felt like a friend.

"Bill!" I say, rising from my throne and moving to meet him at the bottom of the dais. His beady eyes go wide and his lizardy jaw trembles.

"M-Majesty…" he stutters out as I reach for his hands.

"It's so good to see you!" For a moment I forget that I'm supposed to be a Queen and he, my subject. I want to hug him, but I'm pretty sure his head will actually explode if I do that. I settle instead for squeezing his cold hands and offering a kind smile. "I hope you've been well."

"Yes, mum," he mutters, clearly flustered. His cheeks turn a funny shade of brown and I take that as my signal to release his hands.

"I'm sorry if I made you uncomfortable," I say. "I was just happy to see a friendly face."

"Understood, mum." He smiles. "I-I came to give a message."

I grudgingly return to my seat after a pair of admonishing glares from the Rabbits, and as I turn to sit I catch sight of Bill making that same funny hand gesture that Orvice made. It looks sort of like sign language, but not any sign language I've ever seen before. Nacht offers a similar hand signal in response. My gaze narrows and Bill snaps to attention.

"What's the message, Bill?"

He clears his throat and thumps the side of his hand against his forehead in salute, then bends at the waist in a sharp, formal bow.

"The Black has stepped away from his throne," he says, his voice low and ominous, not at all like the Bill I know. "The Red has left her fortress. Clandestine planning awaits. Red and Black twine, combine. Blood feuds laid to the side mean blood for secret allies. High Tea will decide who lives and who dies."

Well, I'm confused. The twins seem to know exactly what it means, which worries me more than my not understanding the message. Their matching dark expressions are downright scary.

Then Bill's hand drops from his forehead. He bows again, and the severity that had taken over his face softens. His eyes relight and he smiles.

"I hope this message is useful to you, Majesty," he says.

"Yes…very useful," Tag answers in my stead. "Her Majesty shall plan accordingly."

O…kay?

It appears my savage assassins are playing a game of their own, and I don't think I like it very much. I want to ask them what it means, but again… the walls have ears around here and whatever reading between the lines they did is probably best left not spoken outside of our safe space.

If I had to fathom a guess, though, I'd say that the Red Queen and the King of Clubs are plotting against me with each other. Not that it would be much of a surprise. Everybody still wants to kill me.

"I must be going now," Bill says, pulling me from my contemplation. "The Waystation won't run itself, will it?"

"Probably not," I say and offer the most genuine smile I can. "I'm happy to know you're well. Please take care of yourself, Bill."

"Always, mum," he answers with a broad, lizardy smile. "Please, mum…please continue to make this old lizard's dreams a reality."

"I'll do my best. Be well, my friend."

His face flushes again, and he offers another of those sharp bows before scrunching his hat up in his hands again and scurrying out the door.

The rest of the day passes in relative quiet, but I'm so distracted by that weird riddle that I can barely focus on my duties. More than once, Jerome has to remind me what I'm doing and explain how, exactly I'm supposed to respond.

I just can't stop thinking about it.

High Tea will decide who lives and who dies.

That, I decide, is ominous as fuck. I need to talk to my council about it, but by the time we manage to escape the line of visitors, it's well after midnight and I'm too tired to think anymore. Those questions will have to wait until later.

I barely give Phineas a weak wave as I stumble past him in the hall of the Suite, pausing only long enough that he has proof of life, then push into my room and collapse face-first into bed. I think Jerome may have followed me in, but I'm not at all aware of anything once my nose scrunches into the sheets.

I wake up some time early in the morning to a soft tap on my door. The sound isn't loud enough to wake me up, but maybe that's why it does. It's gentle and quiet. Almost like... claws? The sound is hollow and ethereal, like it might escape if I don't listen hard enough. Hell, right now I'm not even really sure if I'm awake at all. This could all be a dream. It wouldn't be the first strange one I've had since landing on my ass in Wonderland.

I quickly realize it's not a dream. The floor is cold under my feet when I stand, shocking me into full wakefulness. I don't remember taking my shoes off. The window is open, the cool, fresh breeze rippling across my skin and raising gooseflesh. My hair is a tangled mess, loose around my shoulders. I'm still in the same hearts-awful dress I wore all day. It's itchy and annoying, and the insistent tapping beats against the back of my brain.

Said tapping turns to scratching as I draw near, slow and raspy against the wood. I'm not surprised to find Koji standing on the other side of the door, dashing in the low light and purring loudly enough to hear.

"Good evening, my lovely Queen," he says. His

voice is soft and seductive, perfectly tuned for my ears alone. I haven't seen him in days, which makes the sound of his voice that much sweeter.

"You're back."

"I am." One side of his mouth quirks up in a half-smile. "Did you miss me?"

"What time is it?" I ask, my own voice raspy with sleep.

"Late enough for our meeting to have a singular purpose, yet early enough that we need not wake anyone for tea and breakfast." His smile widens, turns predatory. "Unless, of course, my Queen enjoys being watched?" I don't miss the challenge in his words. I also don't miss the way my breath catches at the thought of someone else knowing what we're doing.

Wait... what are we doing?

Are we doing... *this*?

He stretches one long-finger out and traces it along the curve of my cheek. A singular, maddening touch that sends me up in flames.

"Are you going to let me in, Majesty? Surely you have no intention of leaving a poor cat out in the cold."

Carried along by the magic of the moment, I step back and allow Koji entrance. My heart starts to pound, and when he closes the door with a quiet *snick*, a shiver runs down my spine. I've been alone with Koji before. I've even been in bed with him. His hands and mouth have been all over me. But the ring of finality in that sound has me quaking in my ridiculous dress.

Koji turns and slides one hand around my waist, drawing my body flush against his. I can feel his heart beating hard in his chest through the corset, hear the purr rumbling from his throat. I lift one hand and press it against his chest.

"Did you save this... rather stunning... outfit just for me?" he asks, looking me over.

"I was too tired to change."

"How attached are you to this particular dress, Majesty?" His eyebrow quirks up in a challenge. My already flushed face heats even more.

"Not very... why?"

"Oh, no reason." The singsong tone in his voice means he *definitely* has a reason. The ideas that wicked grin put in my head are entirely too delicious to ignore.

Forget propriety. Forget whatever moral values and standards I brought from my world. Forget all of it... I want this and I'm tired of dancing around the truth. I want him. In any and every way I can possibly have him.

"Koji ..."

"Yes?"

" ... yes."

Koji's lips land against mine with unrestrained urgency. He pulls me up tightly against him, his tongue pressing inside and twining with mine. I know I make a sound, but I'm caught off guard by his presence — larger than life yet so very intimate — that I can't be bothered to care how it sounds. Heat flares in my belly when he threads long-nailed fingers through my hair and tugs me hard against his body. One hand slides over my hip and curls under the swell of my ass, bunching the layers of fabric up in his fingers. He growls into my mouth, hands sliding up my back to twine into the laces there, and yanks hard. The sound of tearing fabric fills the room and my chest expands on a gasp. Cool air rushes over my skin. The remnants of the gown pool at my feet, leaving me in my underthings.

His lips find my throat, kissing and nipping a fiery trail down to my chest, where he lingers, tongue drawling lazy patterns on my skin. My head falls back on a moan. Those beautiful, long-fingered hands slide down my sides, over my hips, then up my back to press against my shoulder blades. My back arches, pushing my chest toward his waiting mouth, and the first wet pull of his lips against my aching nipple rips the air from my lungs.

A chuckle rumbles up his throat while those hands move lower, closing around my hips. Koji rises to his full height, pausing only long enough to take control of my mouth, drawing me back into a deliciously aggressive kiss. Without releasing my lips, he tightens his grip on my hips and pulls upward. I jump, wrapping my legs around his waist as he moves to support my full weight one-handed. His other hand slides up my naked front to close around my throat, holding me captive.

"Good girl," he murmurs between kisses. I shiver in delight, the sound turning to a moan when my back hits the bed. Koji's long, lithe body slides over mine, radiating heat that sears straight through me.

I love everything about this.

He's startlingly efficient at ridding both of us of the remainder of our clothing, then he returns to his previous goal: killing me with pleasure. The thought that I want to touch him, to taste him, floats through my mind and is promptly driven out when he shoves my thighs apart and buries his head between them. The shock of blinding pleasure that accompanies his lips on my most sensitive parts bows my back upwards. He's methodical and relentless, driving me higher and higher toward the peak of ecstasy.

The peripheral vibration of his vocal chords as he purrs against my skin sends me tumbling off that cliff, my body seizing as bolts of pleasure lance outward through my body. I think I scream, but the pressing weight of blackness at the edges of my consciousness take what little focus I have against the pulsing waves of orgasm.

I'm still twitching, my body primed, oversensitive, and desperate for more when his tongue plunges between my open lips to tangle with mine. The taste of him mixed with my own flavor makes me shiver again, and my hands find their way into his hair. It's soft and silky, against my fingertips, and my fingers curl into the locks, crunching them, as he settles his hips against mine.

I want to touch him, to bring him the same pleasure he brought me, but I'm completely at his mercy. He's long and lithe, but very strong. Despite the fire raging inside me, I have no desire whatsoever to escape his hold.

"Koji..." his name leaves my lips like a whimper and a shiver raises the fine hairs along his skin. His lips curve into a grin against mine.

"I do so love it when you moan my name... do it again." Koji flexes his hips and another stuttered whimper falls out.

"Koji... please..." My fingers flex, nails digging into his neck and shoulder. He purrs louder, sweeps his tongue against my lips.

"Please what?"

Please... everything. I can't think with his fingers dancing over my skin, his heat pressing down into me. I can't stop myself from writhing under him, craving more of him. I can't form words; only small, broken sounds of pleasure.

"Please... more..."

His fingers slide under my neck to the back of my head, and he fists my hair to make me look him in the eyes.

"More what, Majesty? I won't know what you want if you don't tell me. Be *very* specific."

"I want…" I pant against the onslaught of sensations his hands cause. "I want… you…" I gasp when he finds a particularly sensitive patch of skin beneath my left breast. "…all of you."

Those wicked lips curve up into a beautiful smile, and my eyes fall half-closed. "Then you shall have all of me. Do not close your eyes."

Koji's hips shift. He holds me hostage by the hair, his swirling gaze locked on mine as he takes me in one long, smooth stroke. I gasp at the sensation, the fullness as he seats his hips firmly against mine, and my fingers flex against his skin. A quiet, rumbling curse leaves his lips. He's the first to break eye contact, his lids fluttering closed before he claims my lips in another deep, languid kiss.

Every movement of his body is slow and deliberate, perfectly timed to drive me out of my mind while keeping my body teetering on the precipice of ultimate pleasure. His kisses are interspersed with quiet murmurs and growls, the vibrating rumble of his chest against mine, and gentle tweaks and touches. He is as unhurried in this lovemaking as he is in every other aspect of his existence. I am a wash of sensation; no longer corporeal but a pawn of magic and lust. Phantom fingers caress my skin as our combined power rises around us, a swirling vortex of desire and need.

A cresting wave of pleasure crashes down on me. My body tightens and pulses, heightening the feel of him as he moves inside and around me. It lasts forever, ebbing and flowing with my breath and the beat of my heart; one climax rising into another, then another, until I'm delirious from pleasure.

Koji finds his own release, body tensing and pulsing with a keening cry, but he's relentless, not stopping even as I fall again, until tears blur my vision and even the slide of his skin against mine is too much to bear. All the while he whispers words of love and devotion, interspersed with vocalizations of his filthiest desires.

I know he's nearing his limit—a thing I've long-since surpassed—when he hooks his elbow under my thigh and lifts my hips at a sharper angle. The shift in position allows him to delve even deeper. His thrusts become sharper, more frenzied, and he nearly bends me in half as he sweeps down to kiss me again. The sharp slap of skin fills the space between my near-breathless cries. I cling to him, desperate for more, for less, for anything and everything and nothing all at once.

"Ko… ji…" His name, a broken plea, sends him over the edge and I fall with him, this last climax the most intense sensation of my life. I think I'll die right here from pleasure.

He lets my body down, continuing to kiss me as if he can't get enough of my taste, and rolls us to the side. We're still pressed together, connected in every way possible. His lips break from mine and he pushes my sweat-slicked hair back from my face, dropping tiny kisses to my forehead, my cheeks, and my nose before returning to my lips.

"You, my beautiful Queen, are the most magnificent creature to ever exist."

Devotion shines in his eyes when he looks at me, and the soft, indulgent curl of his smile makes happiness bubble up inside me like carbonation. From my belly to my brain goes fizzy.

"Come, my love…" he pulls away, the sudden emptiness leaving me bereft, then gathers me into his arms and carries me toward the bathroom. "Overexerted muscles require warm water and lots and lots of bubbles.

By the time he carries me back to bed, I'm dozing on his shoulder. I fall asleep in his arms, sated and near-boneless, somewhere near dawn, his long fingers combing gently through my hair.

Breakfast is awkward, and not just because this damned cat left me covered in very visible love bites. It's awkward because we have several guests in the suite. Not only have my aunt and sister joined Phineas and Felina, but Koji has also brought both Edwin and Aeromi to visit. This table is getting hella crowded.

The only one absent is Talon, but he also tends to be harder to pin down.

A pained yowl sounds and I have to physically remove Koji from Phineas' grip. Again.

"Can you two please not kill each other before tea?" I ask while trying to stifle a yawn. Phineas releases Koji, who wraps himself around me. "And you," I say to the cat while reaching up to scratch behind his very feline ears, "can you please not antagonize my husband?"

"I've done no such thing," he says, pretending to appear scandalized.

"The hell you didn't." I bite the inside of my cheek to keep from smiling. "Go sit down."

Laughter rings out around the table. Everyone is far too amused by this scene, and I am far too tired to care. Echoes of last night shiver along my spine, and it takes every bit of focus and control I possess just to keep from moaning at the memory.

"We have a few visitors, as you've no doubt seen. Many of you already know Lord Edwin of Mercia. The lady with him is —"

"The Bloody Red Duchess," Phineas snarls.

"You got a problem with me?" Aeromi replies. Her lip curls up in a snarl of her own.

"Should I not?" Phineas, hands planted hard on the tabletop, begins to rise from his seat. "Or am I supposed to forgive the murders of thousands to soothe your ego? You should rot in the Underlands."

Aeromi rises to meet him. "Says the man not fit to rule a dumpling cart."

"Will you two please sit down?" They're nearly nose-to-nose across the table, but my quiet request causes both to pull back.

"My apologies, Majesty," Aeromi says softly. "I should know better than to let fools get the best of me."

"Phineas... " I warn when he opens his mouth to argue. "Sit. Down."

He does, though he makes it very clear through glare alone, that he's annoyed, too. The fact that I'm ordering a King of Wonderland around like a child is not lost on me. But to be fair, he's acting like a child.

"The Duchess has sought an alliance with us alongside Lord Edwin. As Lord Edwin has proven himself a valuable ally, I've chosen to accept her terms — on a trial basis."

"My Queen," Aeromi answers with a nod. "You are very kind."

"I want to trust you," I tell her. "So please help me to do that."

"Pretty hard to trust the Red Queen's left hand," Phineas mutters.

"Then let me do the trusting while you stay suspicious." Normally watching him pout out of jealousy would be amusing, but all of this is tiresome now. He's jealous of Koji almost to the point of irrationality, and while he's legitimately distrustful of the Duchess, I really need him to back off a bit. I'm also tired of all of my interactions with people taking place in this room with little to no real action resulting from it. It seems that the only time things get done around here is when I stand up and do them.

I turn my attention back to Aeromi. "Now tell us your plan."

The Duchess closes her eyes and takes a breath, her thick curls shuddering with the movement of her shoulders. She's clearly nervous, which makes perfect sense given the fact that she's sitting in enemy territory with a dozen proverbial weapons pointed in her direction.

"The first thing we have to do," she says, "is make my sister think she's winning. She's not stupid, but she is prideful and she will let it get the best of her."

"So, we're supposed to hand our Queen to her?" Phineas asks, a scoff clipping his final word. "There is no chance of that."

"Not exactly," Aeromi replies despite his derision. "My sister would see through a sham such as that. She has to think she's the one winning, and it needs to be a bloody battle before she takes her prize." She pauses, looking uncertain about her next statement. "She needs a hostage to trade for your head, Majesty." Her gaze flits to Phineas then back to me. "The more powerful the better."

My brain immediately flatlines while Phineas's fury spikes. He sucks a hard breath in through his nose and his eyes narrow to angry slits. His expression is absolutely lethal.

Logically, I know what she's saying. But my head and heart immediately begin to argue. Is she seriously insinuating that I need to betray my King?

The thought of leaving him bound and powerless in her hands sends a ripple of terror through me. Bile rises in my throat. I am completely and utterly speechless.

"It is a gamble," Edwin says, taking up the mantle of conversation when I let it fall. "But Queen Lucinda loves a gamble, and she is intelligent enough to know that your love for your King would bring you to her side without question."

Realization dawns on the rest of the table, and the ensuing chaos is enough to knock every coherent thought out of my head. At this point, I can't do much but let them yell. They've got to get it out of their system.

With everyone squawking at once, whether in excitement or outrage, I can barely focus. I reach over and tap Aeromi's arm, then motion for her to follow me.

It's not much quieter on the other side of the room, but at least they're not right on top of me with their yelling. Phineas follows. As we take our seats in the magic chairs, I find myself sitting between them while they glare at each other once again.

"Is there really no other way?" I ask. "Can you guarantee she'll return him to me?"

"I can guarantee nothing where my sister is concerned," Aeromi says, "but I do know that she wouldn't irreparably damage a pawn when it may net her a Queen."

"Excuse me? A pawn?"

"Figure of speech," I say, patting his hand to calm him. "But there is a big difference between returning him *alive* and returning him *intact*."

"There is. And those of us at her side will do our best to ensure his safety if this idea becomes reality. She is well aware that killing one of The Alice's Kings would lose her the adoration of the people she craves. With Edwin and I stationed in the palace, we can help moderate her mercurial whims."

"I don't like this," I say. Phineas says nothing, but the dark expression on his face tells me everything I need to know. He's pissed off just by the suggestion that he be stripped of his power, even if only temporarily.

"My King," I say, turning my gaze fully on him. He meets my eyes, but his expression doesn't soften.

"My Queen," he replies, terse.

"As this conversation suggests a gamble with *your* life, what say you?"

"I say this plan is absurd." His tone is flat. "I do not trust *your*—" he emphasizes that word in a way that shows he's not happy about any of this, "—allies in the slightest, which means I do not trust that they would protect me if the Bloody Red Queen came for my head."

"That's fair," I say.

"It is," Aeromi agrees, then turns her full attention to Phineas, "which is why I want the opportunity to earn your trust before we enact this plan, Highness."

"And how, exactly, do you expect to do that?"

"Through time and actions. My heart and my loyalty belong to your Queen. If the prophecy is true, then soon our beautiful land will no longer run with blood. I would give anything to see peace in my lifetime."

My eyes prickle and burn at the sincerity in her words. She's either serious, or Wonderland's greatest *scheisster*…though I'm not yet sure which.

"My sister wants to chase her prey before she pounces," Aeromi continues. "It will be the job of myself and Lord Edwin to funnel information to her about how best to capture you. That does, unfortunately, mean I will need to inform her of your alliance with one of her generals."

"You mean to out the connection with Edwin as a double agent so you can control the information?" It seems logical, but as the words leave my mouth it also sounds like the plot of a bad spy movie.

"Yes. She's proud enough to believe it, which will work to our advantage. If we can secure the scene of the 'ambush' using Lord Edwin's men, I can guarantee your King will remain unharmed."

Phineas scowls, deep lines carving themselves into his face. He's furious about this plan and honestly, I don't blame him. It's risky. It could also go very, very badly.

"When exactly do you expect to 'ambush' me?" Phineas asks. He's trying very hard to keep the fury out of his voice and failing pretty miserably.

"Not right away," Aeromi says. She turns her pretty gaze toward my husband and offers a soft smile. "As I said, I want to earn your trust before we put this plan into motion. I want you to know that we will do our utmost to protect you."

Phineas snorts.

"It's a solid plan," I say when it becomes clear that he isn't going to speak. "And I appreciate the time it will take to plan it, particularly since we have other, more pressing issues."

"Certainly, Majesty," she replies with a deferential nod of her head. "It would not do to take on too many enemies at once."

"Not at all."

"I hate to tell you, ladies, but even more pressing than our enemies is the little matter of High Tea. We have to survive that before we survive the war."

Her eyes go wide at the mention.

"Oh, that is scary."

CHAPTER THIRTEEN

What I didn't realize about the upcoming tea party is that it means everyone who is part of my court is invited. All allies, public and secret. Even the Carpenter.

While he doesn't have a key, he is one of my husbands. He gets an invite.

My Aunt and Sister are not invited, however, and will stay in my room with express orders not to open any door for anyone that doesn't have a key to get in until we all return. I'm not sure how I feel about my entire inner circle in one place and exposed, but it seems we have no choice but to let it happen. After all, an invitation from the Mad Hatter is inescapable.

"It is customary for all new regents," Jerome explained as he helped me dress for the day. "And lies are not permitted."

That, at least, is a sliver of good news.

But it's also the reason why I'm standing in the middle of my bedroom, completely terrified. We're scheduled to leave for the High Tea Grounds in moments, and I have no idea what's about to happen.

"Honestly, J., I'm not sure if I'm more afraid of lies or of the truth."

"The truth is often harder to accept," he says. Always the sage, that one. Drives me nuts sometimes.

"Don't we have enough going on? Why did the invitation have to come now?"

"You saved Haigha's life. I suppose Hatta saw it as a fitting thank you."

Speaking of…

"So what's the deal with—"

A knock sounds at my door and my heart leaps into my throat. I'm not ready for this. I'm not looking forward to this. I'm back to being that scared, little girl on the battlefield being chased by a bandersnatch general. The problem is, I can't afford to be that little girl anymore. I can't afford not to face this.

We're all due to gather this afternoon. This party is apparently a huge honor. And dangerous as hell. And yet again here I go stumbling blindly into danger like I don't have the good sense of a slug on a stick.

At the door stands my family, accompanied by the husband I actually like. Aunt Margaret looks worried, but Edith looks angry. Pretty typical for a teenage kid, I guess. Or rather, it would be if she were any other teenager in the world. This particular teenager looks like she's ready to murder me where I stand. I choose not to engage with that since I'm already the human equivalent of a live wire. Edith storms in and flops into a chair.

"I guess this means it's time?" Tons of questions float around in my skull that I don't have time to ask. Then I catch sight of Ivan standing just behind Phineas. He smiles, but there's a hard, bitter edge to it.

"It is," Phineas says. "Felina and I will arrive at the waystation soon enough. You, my Queen, have a much longer journey ahead of you."

"So I gathered. I guess that means I should go, huh?"

"Is this a good idea?" Aunt Margaret asks when she steps into the room.

"Probably not," I admit, "but I've been told I can't turn down an invitation from the Hatter."

"You certainly cannot," Phineas confirms. "His invitations are absolute."

"That doesn't make me like this," she says. My brave, big-hearted aunt turns and levels my husband with a glare while talking to me over her shoulder. "You won't be safe."

"No, probably not. At least one participant actively wants to kill me, and at least one other has already tried."

"Alice--"

"It is what it is. I'll be fine. I think."

"Majesty," Ivan urges.

"Coming," I say and hug Aunt Margaret. I cross the room and bend to hug my sister, but Edith leans out of my reach. Yeah, she's pissed. But I'll have to find out why later. "Love you, Edie."

"Yeah," she mutters and adds something that sounds a little like a declaration of love.

Phineas follows me out the door, and Jerome pulls it closed behind us. The walk to the end of the hall is long, but it's also not long enough. The Rabbits do at least exit the hallway first, giving us a moment of privacy.

"You and Felina, please be safe," I tell him. "There's no telling what might happen today."

Phineas smirks, proud and confident as ever. "I have the best protection in the four kingdoms."

"Second-best," I correct, "because I'm the one with the Rabbits."

"Fair enough," he concedes. "I will see you again in a few hours. Stay safe until then, my Queen."

"You as well, my King."

Phineas catches my wrist and pulls me toward him. It's easy to trust myself to his arms and the soft touch of his lips on mine. It's gentle and easy, and it wouldn't take much at all to let myself fall for his charms.

"Be well, my love," he mutters as we break apart, then pushes me toward the door.

The High Tea Grounds are nothing at all like I expected. There is no white picket fence surrounding a table layered with steaming teapots. There is no disembodied, happy music. There are no tea set-shaped buildings.

What it is, I discover, is a fucking nightmare.

We're back in the Tulgey Wood, off the main path, and standing in front of a door carved into the trunk of a giant Tumtum tree. It blends in except for the shiny, metal latch and the oval window with a curtain behind the glass. It's just so…weird. And those trees really are multipurpose.

"What do we do?" I ask my entourage. "I've never done this before."

"It is a door, Majesty," Blade says. "General courtesy suggests one would knock to gain entry."

So the Unicorn is a smart ass. Good to know the dancing loosened something up.

Swallowing the nervous lump in my throat, I step up and knock.

What happens next is like one of those weird fantasy movie moments. The small gap between the door and the trunk begins to glow with a faint, blue light and mist curls out through that crack. No, not mist. Steam. The scent of warm, black tea fills the little clearing, and a wave of placid contentment washes over me. All of my nervousness vanishes, and suddenly it feels like everything is going to be okay.

There must be something in the steam, because right now I should be anything but calm.

The door opens inward, and the blue glow would be blinding if not for the figure silhouetted in the center: tall, slender with broad shoulders, and the most ridiculously tall top hat I've ever seen. The shadowed head tips to the left—my left—and the hat goes with it, remaining anchored in place in spite of gravity being a thing. The sight brings a smile to my face.

I realize that I've been so busy with war that I haven't had much time for whimsy.

"Welcome, your most glorious and grand Majesty," the Hatter says with a dramatic, flourish-filled bow, "to my humble abode." His voice sounds strangely familiar though we've never met. When he steps back to allow us entrance, I see why. A familiar, weathered face floats in front of us; a patchwork of scars, both old and new giving him away.

"Haigha?"

Confusion clouds his features. He looks at me like I've lost my mind, and the expression on his face is... offended?

"I beg your pardon?"

Yep, he's offended. What I don't immediately understand is why.

"I-I'm sorry. I mistook you for someone else."

"Hatta, old friend!" Jerome shouts and steps up beside me. Seems a little exaggerated... but what the hell do I know? This is why I should have found more time to ask the questions I needed to ask. "You are looking well!"

"Yeah? 'Cause I feel like shit."

Now it's my turn to be confused. The man standing in front of us is Haigha. Am I really going mad? Have I gotten myself somehow mixed up? The scars on this man's face and hands are identical to those on Haigha's body. He sounds the same, looks the same. Moves the same! I wasn't with the March Hare for long, but identifying marks are called such for a reason.

"Come in, come in," Hatta says and steps out of the way. I enter first, obviously, and only because both Ivan and Jerome have knuckles in my back, urging me along.

Well, this is a first, I think. I've never been inside a tree before.

Of course, it's nothing at all like I expect the inside of a tree to look. The walls and floors are made of wood, yes, but the space is surprisingly modern—all clean lines, broad panes of glass, and metal accents. It puts me in mind of an industrial New York high use. The hallway leading from the door is wide enough for four people and three times as tall.

Hatta moves past us with a fluid grace contradictory to his size and leads the way through the house without a word. I try not to gawk on the silent tour, but this is fascinating. It's only the third time I've been inside an actual house in Wonderland, and Jerome's house doesn't exactly count.

We also don't stay inside long. We're led to the back of the house, out a set of accordion doors, and into a garden. It's lush and green, filled with chittering flowers and fluttering fireflies and lazy little bread-and-butterflies. Bioluminescent vines hang from the trees—we are still IN a tree, yes?—giving the High Tea grounds an eerie glow.

I know we've reached the High Tea Grounds because a table large enough to seat at least thirty stands in the middle of the clearing, and it is covered with plates of cakes and steaming pots of tea.

"Are we the first?" I ask.

"Of course you are," Hatta replies with a put-upon huff. "The others know it would be rude to arrive before their Queen." He motions not to the head of the table, but to the throne in the middle of its longest side. The table, I realize, is not a rectangle.

Someone else knocks on the door, pulling the Mad Hatter—for mad he certainly seems—away from the garden.

"Have I finally gone completely mad?" I ask quietly once we're alone.

"Be more specific, please," Ivan mutters back.

"Is that not Haigha?"

"Yes and no. Now sit, Majesty. No one else can until you do."

So many rules! My brain is full. I don't know how I'm going to remember more.

As if to urge me on, Blade pulls out my chair and Jerome takes my hand to help me into it. I go where I'm supposed to be, but when all three take a step back and remain standing, my nerves spike.

Then the garden becomes chaotic. Boisterous laughter startles the insects into flight, and a moment later the twins come bouncing into view. Torai follows behind, tolerant but clearly frustrated, and immediately comes to kneel at my side.

"My Queen."

I reach out and place my hand on his bowed head. "It's good to see you."

Torai rises with a fragile smile. He looks nervous. I can't really blame him considering the situation. To be fair, I'm still a little nervous about him, too. I pull on my magic—there is an abundance of it in this place, so it's easy—and cast it toward him to find a curious sight. The aura of the Walrus is no longer solid black. The center, closest to his body, glows bright green, as if the new light were beginning to heal the withered blackness of its edges.

Hatta clears his throat and glares at me. I avert my eyes and let the magic drop. Probably broke another rule, if his expression is any indication. It would be helpful if I knew them going into this, but it's a little late for that.

Phineas and Felina are the next to enter, followed by Talon. The entire party goes silent when Koji appears, mainly because of his companions. Edwin and Aeromi follow behind him, Edwin as confident as ever while Aeromi looks nervous.

As they filter in one by one, they position themselves behind chairs, but no one else sits. I feel strange being the only one seated, but I tell myself it's all part of the ritual. Everything here feels like some kind of ritual; dark and dangerous.

Everyone stands around the table, Phineas to my right, but the chair to my left is conspicuously empty. My stomach drops when I realize why.

I'll be flanked by my Kings.

In absolutely no reality am I okay being this close to the Carpenter again. I'd like to think he wouldn't shiv me under the table, but nothing is outside the realm of possibility with that man.

So we wait. And wait. And wait some more. In fact, we wait long enough that everyone starts to get restless.

"Well, this is quite rude," Hatta says, and grabs Jerome's wrist to look at his watch tattoo. "Just as I thought... we're late."

I have a smart comment, but I keep it to myself for propriety's sake. It would do no one any good if I got in trouble for snarking about a genocidal maniac who also happens to be my second (and least favorite) husband.

At last, a series of three hard raps echoes through the overcharged silence. My anxiety spikes. Hatta huffs again, indignant that he's been made to wait, and turns for the door. I look around at the assembled cast of characters and bark out a stilted laugh when I realize that they're arranged by chess rank. I know just enough about the game to understand that this High Tea is, in fact, just another battle. Another battlefield. Another chance to win or lose. That realization sends a shiver down my spine.

Seeing my other husband in the flesh sends terror scrambling through me. Percival Rand is one scary motherfucker. That feeling intensifies as he nears us. Everything about him screams violence. The smile on his face is designed to unsettle me. It works.

He comes to stand in the empty space beside me, a sharp gaze moving over my choice of companions. When he lifts my left hand and bends to kiss my knuckles, I have to actively fight not to scream in disgust.

"What curious company my Queen keeps," he murmurs, then lets go of my hand. Of course that would be his first observation. Leaving people off balance until he can devour them is his M.O., after all.

"No stranger than you, I'm afraid," I reply with a smirk of my own.

"Fair enough."

"Ahem... may I have your attention, please?" Hatta calls out, clapping his hands to draw everyone's gazes. Those swirling, familiar-yet-not eyes positively sparkle with excitement. "Welcome, Queen Alice," he continues with a formal bow, "to the High Tea grounds and the first High Tea Celebration in far too long." He executes a perfect forty-five-degree bow. The others follow suit, turning toward me in the process.

"Thank you," I reply and hope it's the right thing to say, "I am delighted to be here."

Seeming satisfied with my answer, Hatta nods. The others take their seats in an unrehearsed yet perfectly synchronized motion that puts me in mind of those professional water dancers. The fact that the most powerful men and women in Wonderland move at his command is also not lost on me. wonder exactly what kind of hidden power he really has. I make a mental note to ask Jerome about that later. Along with every other question I have about this person—or these people. Because the Mad Hatter and the March Hare are supposed to be a pair.

But right now, it feels like they're the same person. I'm confused.

For now, my attention turns back to the Mad Hatter and those swirling, mysterious eyes. He remains standing like a good host, but the look on his face is anything but pleasant. He's predatory almost, like a carnival barker turned cannibal. His smile is sharp, like he wants to eat me up and pick his teeth with my bones. Then he winks, startling me. With a flick of his wrist, a fat, steaming teapot hops down the table toward me. Nobody else finds this strange, so I keep my mouth shut and watch as my tea makes itself to my exact preference.

Once mine is ready, the rest of the teapots take up their posts in front of the others' cups and pours.

"A reminder," Hatta's voice cuts the silence like a knife, "for those who may not remember the proper way to have High Tea," his gaze pauses on me only a fraction longer than on the others. He snaps his fingers and a giant roll of parchment drops from the leafy canopy overhead. It unfurls itself into a three-foot long (give or take) list of rules.

1. One may only tell the truth at the table.
2. One may not kill another at the table.
3. One must answer any questions asked of them.
4. One must drink an entire cup to earn a question.
5. One must use a clean cup after every question.
6. One earns an extra question if today is their un-birthday.
7. One may not fall asleep at the table.
8. One may not leave until the Queen leaves.
9. The Queen may not leave without permission from her host.

And now I am more confused than ever. This sounds more like a frat party than a tea party, but what do I know? The answer to that, by the way, is nothing.

I read through the list a second time. Hatta snaps his fingers again, and the list rolls itself up. It disappears with a pop and a shower of paper dust and sparkles. Everyone else claps so I do too, which seems to be the right thing going by Hatta's satisfied expression.

"Now, if everyone is quite ready," he says and motions in my direction. A pulse of energy accompanies his words, inviting itself close enough to twine around my arm when I lift my cup. Everyone looks at me.

Well fuck.

I have no idea what's going on, so I say the first thing that comes to mind.

"Bottoms up!" I shout, lifting my cup just a little higher in salute. Everyone else follows suit. I drink. They drink.

The effects of the tea are immediate, slamming into my senses with the force of a freight train. One minute I'm completely sober and rational and the next...

Well, I don't really know what I am. Intoxicated, certainly. But this is not a type of intoxicated I can easily describe. I'm not drunk. I'm not high. But after one sip, I'm so far out of my head that I'm not sure I'll ever remember my own name. But the tea is yummy and when I look down into my cup, it's empty.

"Your first question, my Queen," Hatta prompts. His voice serves as an anchor in the vast sea of my tumbling mind. Everyone else, I realize, appears far more composed than I feel.

"Oh... me first?"

"A proper tea party always starts with the Queen," Hatta replies with a feral smile. "Highness," he nods to Phineas, "your question."

Wait.... that was my question?

Phineas places his empty cup back onto its saucer and turns a sharp eye on the Carpenter.

"Why have you married Alice?" he asks. Percival smiles that same sinister smile I've come to despise.

"The closer I get to her, the easier it will be to kill her."

"You would think that," Ivan says with an annoyed snort.

"I do think that," Percival replies, "otherwise I would not have said it." He dangles the empty cup from his middle finger in a subtle salute before slinging it against the wall where it shatters.

"That was not necessary," Hatta grumbles.

"Oh, but it was."

"Next question goes to the Unicorn," Hatta says with a sniff.

Blade empties their cup and turns their hypnotic gaze down the table. "Sir Walrus," they say. Their voice is smooth and even as always, with no hint of emotion. Torai leans forward and looks down the length of the table, the bend in the sides just long enough that he doesn't have to lean far. "For whom do you fight: the crown or the people?"

"Both," Torai replies. "I fight for my Queen so that she may defend the people."

The questions continue on; this odd verbal combat where everyone is on the same side yet clearly trying to catch one another in some kind of lie. I lose track of what, exactly, is happening until Hatta draws attention to the man to my left.

"Your question, my Lord," he says with a disturbing level of reverence. Percival turns to me with a shark-like grin. His gaze is as friendly as a drawer full of sharp knives.

"My Queen," he says, a mocking echo of Hatta's statement, "tell me why you want to unify Wonderland. And do use small words, as I may not understand your greatness."

I could hear a pin drop in this garden, were one to fall. As much as I hate to admit it, it *is* a good question.

"It's my family legacy," I say, which is the truth.

"That is not an answer, and you and I both know it."

He's right. It's the truth, but not the whole truth. The unsaid part lingers in my mouth, begging to be set free.

"I've never actively thought about it," I say, thinking through my words. "I suppose… because I love the people here. In my world—" that phrase feels so foreign on my tongue, "—I was a nobody. A powerless victim of circumstance. But here, I have power and influence. I have the ability to make the world a better place for the ones who don't have a voice."

A smile—a real one—spreads across Percival's face and for just a moment he doesn't appear quite as scary.

"A fine answer, Majesty. Now, how do you plan to accomplish that goal?"

"Well, I—wait a minute! You already asked a question!"

"I certainly did not," Percival replies with mock indignation. "I directed a statement toward you, but I did *not* ask a question."

I look over at our host, who nods. In fact, he looks a little bored. "It's as he says, Majesty. Answer the question."

"Oh…you shifty bastard…"

"Now-now, compliments will not exempt you from an answer."

He has me, damn it. This time I have to stop and think. It's a good question, and one that requires more consideration than impulse.

"I… I don't really know for certain. But the first goal is to stop the fighting. If the world is constantly at war, the people can't trust their leaders."

"But fear makes life precious," Percival says.

"Maybe, but it also makes the people weary. Constantly fighting for your life makes it difficult to do more than just exist. Once the people can rest, then we can move forward in establishing fair laws that make fighting inefficient."

Silence reigns as I finish speaking. When I dare to glance around, everyone stares back with mystified expressions. Even Hatta's glare has softened. He stares at me, eyes wide and mouth agape for several long moments before visibly shaking himself.

"Clean cups, everyone," he says, though much more subdued than previously. "Drink, then it is your question, Majesty."

When I look down, a different teapot is pouring steaming pink tea into a new cup. The strange intoxication clings to the walls of my mind, but I lift the clean cup to my lips and drink, as the rules dictate.

The effects are slower this time, but no less intense. It starts as a light effervescence in my belly that works its way up to the space behind my eyes. My whole brain goes fuzzy and fizzy, and I grab onto the edge of the table to keep from floating away. Yet, despite the bubbles, my brain feels sharp.

Like… the kind of sharp one might find on the edge of a knife. Or maybe the jagged edge of broken glass.

"Your question, Majesty," Hatta prompts.

I look around the table at the equally intoxicated faces. Everyone appears eager to jump at my command, but strangely I can't think of a single question. Except one.

"Koji."

When I call his name, his spine straightens and a lazy smile spreads across his lips. I shiver. That look reminds me all too well just how dangerous the cat is.

"My Queen."

"When you betray me—" the words surprise even me as they pop out of my mouth, "how do you plan to do it?"

Curious murmurs rise, but the swift smack of Hatta's cup against the table stops the chatter immediately. Everyone's eyes turn toward Koji, who remains absolutely unruffled.

"Oh, my darling Alice," the Cheshire Cat says, "you are right that I fully intend to betray you. But... not for the reasons you may expect." He pauses and my eyebrows rise. I'm very drunk and he's very dramatic. "When I sell you out to the Red Crown, it will be to save your life."

"That makes no sense."

Rather than answer, Koji lifts his cup to his lips and empties it in one smooth, fluid movement, signaling the end of his statement.

Silence returns to the table and holds long enough to grow uncomfortable. That... answers one question, but not the one I asked. And it raises so many more. At least I'm secure in the knowledge that what he said was the truth.

"Majesty, if you will," Hatta says, indicating Phineas, who glowers at the cat and his confession.

"Lord Edwin," he intones, turning that sharp gaze across the table.

"Yes, Majesty?" Edwin is, naturally, unruffled.

"Are you planning to help the cat betray us?"

"Not planning to, no. But if such a need arises..."

A snarl tears from Phineas' throat, like he's ready to leap across the table and tear Edwin to shreds.

"Let him finish," I say quietly and rest my hand on his wrist. The touch seems to calm him. Some of the tension drains from his body.

"Thank you, my Queen," Edwin says with a dashing smile. "Now, as I was saying: should the need arise, any betrayal will be solely for the purpose of protecting little Alice's life and will, I believe, be but temporary."

"Oh, dear," Percival mutters beside me, "with such a declaration, how ever are we supposed to trust the truth, I wonder?" The flat monotone of his voice can't mask the question. Nobody answers it, though.

It's not his turn.

Hatta clears his throat. "Moving on…"

The questions—mostly benign and ridiculous—continue on. We drink more. My head grows increasingly fuzzy. By the time the questions make it back around the table, I'm wobbling on my throne, and the colors of the world are inverted and singing children's songs. Percival has needled me nearly the entire time and I'm starting to feel a little spiteful. Somebody needs to put him in his place, and right now I am the only one with the power to do it. Looking down the wobbly lines of the table, a question pops into my head and out of my mouth before I can stop it.

"Torai."

"Majesty?"

"To whom are you truly loyal?"

"You, my Queen," he answers without hesitation. The temperature seems to drop twenty degrees with that confession. Percival is *pissed* and everybody in the garden knows it. "A truly noble ruler willing to give of herself to save the lives of an entire army is certainly worthy of loyalty. You saved my life, Majesty. That life is now yours."

If looks could kill, the glare aimed at me from my immediate left would make me explode. It's this very moment that we all realize just how powerful the declaration of the Walrus truly is. He has single-handedly shifted the balance of power in Wonderland in my favor.

"I'd like to use my bonus question," I announce. "It *is* my un-birthday, after all."

"Of course," Hatta replies. "Ask away."

"King Percival," I can't keep the mocking tone out of my voice, "how do you feel about your right hand becoming mine?"

"I hate it and would love nothing more than to remove your head from your shoulders at this very moment," he answers through gritted teeth while hitting me with the full force of his angry stare, "but Torai is right that a Queen willing to protect the people is worthy of loyalty. That nobility is what stays my hand. For now."

"But you are not loyal to me." Not a question.

He smiles just a little. "Absolutely not. I *will* kill you, Majesty." Also, not a lie if said here. "It is only a matter of *when*."

CHAPTER FOURTEEN

We've been invited to stay the night with the Hatter, which is fine. I'm totally wasted from the tea, and none of my entourage is in any shape to defend me in the Tulgey Wood, so we pick a door and file through one-by-one.

No sooner do I walk through the door of my suite than my sister is wrapped around my head, arms tight enough behind my neck that I can't breathe. Her body convulses with silent sobs and when my arms close around her, she squeezes tighter.

I look up to find Aunt Margaret standing just behind her, a look of relief etched into her features. The fact that they're emotional is curious, but I remind myself not to panic, or it'll only make whatever's wrong with them worse.

"Did something happen?" I ask when Edith finally lets loose enough for me to draw a breath.

"Not really," Aunt Margaret says. "It's just... you've been gone three days."

Three days?

I turn my attention to Ivan, standing just behind me on my left in the narrow hall, and he nods. "Time moves differently here," he reminds me, but even that doesn't compute in my brain. Were we really high enough that we sat around that table for three whole days with nothing to eat and no word to the outside?

That's...weird.

"We should move everyone inside," he urges, a rare look of distress flickering in his eyes. "We have much to discuss."

Edith and Aunt Margaret turn toward my room, my sister glancing back over her shoulder every few steps, as we move down the hall. Once inside, Ivan not only closes, but locks the door behind him before coming to sit beside me.

There's tea—plain tea, because I'm not going to get my little sister high—and tiny honey cakes shaped like bees waiting for us. The thought of drinking more tea turns my stomach a little, since I can still feel the effects of whatever the hell it was we drank in that garden. I have a thousand questions, but I'm not sure where to start.

"Three days is surprisingly short for High Tea," Ivan says. "That long-winded fool usually keeps the game going for a week or more."

"But it didn't feel like three days," I say. Lame, I know. But I'm having a really, *really* difficult time reconciling this in my head. I'm having a difficult time reconciling any of it, actually.

"I can't believe you were gone for three days having *tea*," Edith spits, her fear morphing into anger. Teenagers are so much fun.

"It wasn't three days for us. It was only a few hours."

"Well it wasn't here!" She huffs loudly. Aunt Margaret places a hand on her shoulder, but Edith shakes it off. "You are *so* inconsiderate!"

I open my mouth to ague, but... I also hesitate. Am I inconsiderate? Do I really have the right to say I'm not when I can't really remember what even happened?

"I'm sorry," is what finally comes out of my mouth, small and feeble.

"Now you wait just one minute," Ivan demands, but I hold a hand up to stop the indignant rage threatening to break loose.

"It's okay," I tell him. "She's right. I haven't thought about her feelings at all."

"There are more important things—"

"No, there aren't," I tell him. We exchange a look that I hope he understands. I need my sister to be safe and happy. If she's angry, she'll be reckless. "Edith," I turn to my sister, "I am sorry. And we need to talk about this in depth, but I have business to attend to. Can you give me a couple of hours to get everything sorted?"

My sister cuts her gaze away, but she nods.

"Perhaps you would like to rest away from official business?" Ivan offers, turning his attention more toward Aunt Margaret than Edith.

"That would be lovely," she says, "thank you."

Ivan rises and leads them out of the room, only to return a moment later with Jerome and Blade with him. I don't ask where he took my family, and he doesn't offer the information; only takes a seat beside me as the others file in.

"Well, that was quite the tea party," Jerome says. "Hatta was in rare form, indeed."

"I still don't understand how we lost three days."

"The High Tea Grounds exist in a place outside even our time," he explains, patient as ever with my astounding lack of knowledge. "Only available by invitation and not exitable until the host releases us."

Speaking of the host…

"You said Hatta and Haigha are kind of the same person. What does *that* mean?"

"Exactly what you think it means."

"Which tells me exactly nothing, J."

Jerome's lips lift at the corners. He's teasing me. Probably to try and make me feel better. But it's the way he looks at me that makes me anything but calm. There's heat in that gaze that has nothing at all to do with the warmth of the tea in his hands. I clear my throat loudly and bring my own cup to my lips to hide the blush creeping into my cheeks. All this time and he continuously makes me feel like a giggling schoolgirl.

Hatta and Haigha occupy the same physical vessel," he says once he's done with the visual foreplay, "but they are very much different people."

"Split personalities?"

"A fractured mind," Blade interrupts. "Haigha, as you may already know, was a Rabbit to the Queen of Diamonds some years ago. Their current state is the result of her death, and the most extreme outcome of a Rabbit's survival."

My gaze cuts back over to Jerome, who remains perfectly stoic, and my heart aches for him. It's been roughly eight months since the previous White Queen was murdered by her knight, and her loss nearly split him in two. He came through it and remained whole — despite the fact that he lost not just his Queen, but his mother as well — though changed. There is a darkness to him now; a haunted look in his eyes when he thinks nobody is watching. The trickle of grief along our bond also tells me he's thinking about the same thing.

"Their bond must have been deep," I say.

"Very," Blade continues, their low, melodic voice like candy for my ears. "A Rabbit-Queen bond when the two are also lovers? That is the most powerful magic in all the realms."

My heart aches harder when I look at my two Rabbits. Infuriating as they may be, I love them both dearly. The thought that they could become like Haigha if I were to die…

Well, better not die then.

"So, Haigha is the person and Hatta is the manifestation created from her death?" Blade nods. "Is… is there a way to fix him? Haigha seems a lovely person, but Hatta…"

"Haigha is as bloodthirsty as any Wonderland warrior," Ivan says. "Don't let the politeness fool you."

"And nobody will disagree that Hatta as scary as fuck." I shudder at the thought of those crazy eyes focused on me. "But to *fix* them…"

"Such a thing has never been attempted," Blade says.

"To be fair, there's never been a schism quite as severe as theirs either," Jerome argues.

"True," Ivan adds. "A bond that deep has always ended in the death of the Rabbit."

"Which begs the question: how, exactly, does one go about repairing a fractured mind?" Jerome asks.

"With love and patience," I say. All three of them pause and turn to look at me, mystified. "I've spent years in therapy thanks to the things that have happened in my life, and every therapist I've ever had has always said that patience, forgiveness, and love are the keys to helping a person heal." I'm not gonna lie, I have a whole lot of anxiety about this half-cocked, malformed idea, but I also can't stand to see someone suffer. "I'd like to get to know both of them better. Maybe that would help us find a way to help them."

"My Queen truly is magnanimous," Blade says, awe in their voice. The compliment makes me squirm, and my cup is empty. "And also quite mad."

"I wouldn't go *that* far," I argue. "Mad, yes. Magnanimous? No. I just don't like seeing people hurt."

Our conversation is interrupted by a small knock at my door. All three of the warriors at my table are instantly on alert, but I wave them away. I know that knock.

"That's my sister," I tell them, and dive for the door before any of them can greet her with a sword to the neck. As it swings open, her wide, tear-filled eyes float into view. "What's wrong?" I ask, my heart constricting in my chest at the thought of anything happening to her or Aunt Margaret.

"I... I'm sorry, Alice. I'm sorry I was so mean to you. I love you, you know." The tears standing along her lower lashes spill down her face and a sob wracks her small body. I pull her into my arms and hold her tight.

"It's okay, Edie. I never doubted you for a minute."

She sniffles and sobs against my shoulder, squeezing tighter with each convulsion of her lungs. I pull her into the room, and the door closes behind us, then Jerome's hands are on my shoulders as he guides us to sit. My sister climbs all the way into my lap like she did when she was a little girl. She doesn't fit as well as she used to, but I don't care.

Right now, we both need this closeness.

It takes a while but Edith finally cries herself out. My shoulder is soaked with her tears and my lower back aches from sitting for so long. When she lifts her head, her face is puffy and red, with salty tear tracks over the curves of her cheeks. She looks like a little girl again, and it serves as a good reminder that while she may look grown, she is not, in fact, grown.

She's sixteen and scared shitless.

After one more hug, she slides off my lap to sit beside me and takes the handkerchief and the cup of tea Jerome offers. A cup appears in my hand as well, then he returns to making himself scarce on the other side of the room. When I look up, I discover that Ivan and Blade are both gone.

"Are you okay?" I ask, feeling a little silly.

"Yes," she says, then, "no. I don't know."

"Tell me what's going on in your head."

Edith sighs and leans into my shoulder. She draws her knees up and tucks her feet under her body, then starts to fidget, picking at her fingernails.

"I don't really know," she admits. "Everything is just changing so fast. I go to Savannah on Friday and a week later you're a Queen with a whole history that I didn't even know existed. I guess... I guess I'm just having a hard time catching up."

"Makes sense," I reply. "When they first told me you were coming to Wonderland, I thought you were going to be furious for my being gone so long. Then I found out you thought I was only gone a week… it was weird on this end too, knowing I've been through so much. But Edie," I turn and take her by the shoulders, making sure she's looking at me and paying attention, "there is nothing more important to me in either world than your safety. I'm sorry if I'm making you feel like a prisoner, but you are a target, and one I am not willing to sacrifice under *any* circumstances."

"I'm trying to get stronger!" That defensive edge creeps back into her voice. I drop her shoulders and take her cheeks in my hands.

"Stronger is great, but I need you *safe*." I search her face, watching tears well up along her lower lashes again. "I have no doubt in my mind that you can protect yourself and that you will one day be my strongest, most powerful general. But right now, you are the one *everyone* will go after to get to me, because everybody knows I will do anything to protect you."

"That's not fair," she mutters, bitterness far beyond her years embedded in her voice. "How come you get to do all the reckless, stupid things while I have to hide like a sheltered little girl?"

"Because, unfortunately, I'm the Queen. I didn't ask for any of this, and it scares the hell out of me every single day. But this is our family history, our legacy. And maybe by the end of it, we'll both know exactly where we belong."

Edith is quiet for a long time. Her head lands on my shoulder, and I curl my arm around her, holding her close. For so long it's been the two of us against the world...now it feels a little strange to have an army of allies and protectors. And as much as it may hurt her to be kept away, it's the safest.

My eyelids are growing heavy when I realize that my sister has fallen asleep on my shoulder. Without my asking, Jerome appears at my side and gently lifts her into his arms. She murmurs something and smacks her lips once—just like she did when she was a little girl—then snuggles down into my bed as he tucks her in. A moment later, he's back at my side, offering his hand.

I take it, and he pulls me into his arms. The feel of his body against mine is a comfort for my weary mind. He kisses my forehead, then my lips, then lifts me into his arms the same way he did Edith, only to tuck me into bed beside her.

"Sleep well, my Queen," he murmurs and after one last, lingering kiss, disappears to his own room for the night.

The next morning dawns clear and cold. I leave Edith curled up in the center of my bed and open the door to find both Rabbits waiting for me. Jerome hands me a cup of tea and Ivan pushes some kind of bread-based food into my other hand.

"We have a busy day ahead," I'm told as I go about getting ready for the day. "A return to Wonderland Castle in time for Court this morning, then a meeting with the Carpenter. We should soon receive word from Koji about the state of Red Territory as well."

I head into the bathroom to wash up and change my clothes, and when I come back, I'm greeted by a second cup of tea and more of the same.

"This evening, we'll gather for dinner and a strategy session."

"So business as usual."

Ivan grunts. "Except for the part where we let that murderous psychopath in through the front door."

"If he comes in through the front door, I would think he's less likely to kill me. After all, the Red Court stands and I'm still useful."

"Fair enough," Ivan replies. The look of distaste on his face could stop a clock.

Once I'm ready, I turn back toward the bed. My sister, of course, has slept through all of this. Sometimes the power of a teenager to ignore things amazes me.

I leave her sleeping in my bed and allow my escort to lead me out of the Hatter's house and back to the waiting jubjubs.

Four hours later, I'm travel-weary and stumbling into the throne room of Wonderland Castle, which feels strange since nobody is there waiting for me. The twins, however, enter as I take my seat. They're followed by Blade and Torai, who come to stand at the ready like mystical and, quite frankly, frightening bookends. It's a balanced scene for the moment, and one that will be thrown out of balance by my presence.

The balance of power tips in favor of the Queen.

I take my seat with the help of my Rabbits. Tag turns and kneels, his head touching his one upright knee. There's something majestic about him like this. Six months ago he was nearly feral, but now he's more or less a refined, graceful gentleman. Nacht, however, remains a complete mystery. Literally tall, dark, and mysterious, he's the polar opposite of his twin in every way. He catches my eye and nods, but the look in those nearly black orbs is one of unhinged ferocity.

Tweedledum clearly hasn't re-acclimated to society as well as his brother.

I offer a small smile, repress a shiver, and turn my attention back to Tag.

"When you are ready, Majesty," he says. I take a deep breath and nod.

The card attendants pull open the doors and the last person in the world I want to see stands behind them.

Percival Rand steps over the threshold, and the cards drop to one knee in perfect synchronization as he makes his way up the center aisle. Murderous psychopath or not, he *is* still a King. The shit-eating grin on his face is infuriating. If it weren't for the fact that he's promised to kill me at some unknown point in the future, he might almost be handsome…

But not now. Now, his lanky figure puts me in mind of the grim reaper without his robe and sickle.

"My Queen," Percival says as he reaches the dais. His words and expression have all the softness and affection of a hungry shark who smells blood.

"Why are you here this early?"

He raises one eyebrow and the corner of his mouth follows it upward into an amused expression.

"My darling bride is without a King at her side to advise her this morning." He feigns care and concern moderately well, but not well enough that I believe him. "Why, I simply thought I would fill that empty seat at her side and offer moral support as she handles the affairs of state."

He's mocking me.

"You're such an asshole. Sit down and shut up."

This seems to genuinely amuse him, but he does as he's told, taking the last three steps up to the empty throne. The Diamond crown sits neatly atop his head and, as he sits, the hard lines of power and spite soften into what almost looks to be a contented expression.

If there was any question among the people that I have two kings, there will be none at all after today. I drag my attention away from the homicidal enigma beside that is Percival Rand and turn my attention back to my court.

"Proceed," I announce. The doors swing open again and the first in a long line of visitors steps inside. Strangely enough, Percival and I fall into a comfortable routine. He does exactly what he said he would do by advising me on affairs I am not completely aware of and offering suggestions on how to alleviate the problems plaguing the people. For all his taunting and terrorizing, he takes this part of the job very seriously. Despite his need for control, he defers final judgment on every situation to me.

The doors close behind the last visitor, and I relax against the back of the throne with a sigh. The questions we've answered are the most mundane of problems, yet it feels good to know we could help in some small way. Whether it was providing the resources to help with farmland irrigation or settling a business dispute between siblings-turned-rivals, every person who came through those doors today left with a satisfying resolution. I smile.

"As much as it pains me to admit it," Percival says, pulling my attention back, "you are quite good at being Queen."

There's no hint of malice in his voice and when I turn to look at him, there is no savagery in his expression. "It's not easy and it doesn't always feel like I'm doing it right but thank you."

A genuine smile spreads across his face. "Humphrey is daft, but he was right about one thing: it really will be a shame to kill you."

Of course he has to add that little jab at the end. But there's no venom behind it. It's almost as if he's trying to make a joke.

"Then don't kill me," I answer.

Something has happened here. I can't put my finger on what exactly, but something between us has shifted. It doesn't quite feel like we're mortal enemies anymore. I'm hesitant to call this *friendship*, but it certainly seems like we may have a chance of winning one another over.

"Majesties," Tag says snapping his heels together and pulling me out of my contemplation, "lunch is served."

Percival rises first, then turns with a slight bow and offers his hand.

This evening's council is... strange. And strangely lacking. Despite my hesitation, Percival has accompanied us into the suite—his first look at my personal space and the fortification he will likely have to fight his way through when he decides the time has come to assassinate me—but so many others are missing. Felina is with my family, Haigha is off handling sneaky messenger business, and Koji has yet to appear with Edwin and Aeromi.

The longer we wait, the more I begin to worry. It's ultimately Percival who calms me down.

"There are any number of reasons why your

pussycat may be waylaid," he says. "If I recall correctly, he and his companions *are* considered your enemies by the general public."

"You're right," I say reluctantly. But I am able to take a full breath once his words sink in. "Thank you." I smile at him and it seems to surprise him. The change in his expression is nominal at best, but I do catch the slight rise of his eyebrow. This is a man who has experienced a lifetime of cruelty and betrayal. It appears kindness may be his ultimate weakness. Or he's a really good actor.

I file that bit of information away as we set about the task of discussing the day's events. As they pertain to both White and Diamond territory, everyone *must* be involved. We're also set to begin the tedious portion of Project Fool The Red Queen — logistics. Though that's hard to do without the primary players present. So, I fill in the rest of my crew as best I can. The more I talk, the darker the twins' expressions grow.

"Don't like it," Nacht says.

"Not at all, brother," Tag echoes.

"Is there really any other way, though?" I ask.

"Use force, of course," Percival answers.

"But that puts our friends in danger."

"Casualties of war, Majesty," he replies. "When fighting for one's life, one cannot be too sentimental."

And with one sentence, he reminds me why we will never actually be friends. While I can appreciate the brutal efficiency with which he conducts his business, I can't condone it. Needless sacrifice is not my style. Especially not with someone I've—oh, hearts and cards— *grown to love.*

"In my experience," I say, struggling to find the right words to stay civil, "sentimentality is what makes a nation thrive. Every life is precious, and I'm not willing to actively sacrifice a single one."

This feels like a repeat of our very first conversation, except this time we have a much broader audience. Percival grunts but he doesn't outright argue. Sort of.

"We shall see which philosophy proves to be more effective."

"I shouldn't be surprised by your position, considering you've threatened to kill me with nearly every other breath you've taken in my presence."

"Just a reminder of where the power truly lies."

"Yes. With me."

He opens his mouth to argue but ultimately says nothing. There's nothing he *can* say because I'm right. As long as I breathe, I am in control.

We hold another's gaze for a long time. There *is* kindness and caring in him, but it has become twisted by the power he wields. I see glimmers of it in his actions, despite what words spill from his lips.

My mind trips back to the original poem and how the Carpenter…

Wait.

No, there wasn't a single thing about him that was good then either. He was the mastermind behind luring the oysters in to eat them. He was also betrayed by his right hand, who he apparently subjugated after the incident, only to be betrayed again as he moved into my service. I have questions. So many questions. And I can answer exactly none of them. There's a lot more here to unpack than I realized, and staring into his eyes—into the empty pit of simmering rage behind them—reminds me that there is nothing at all that he won't sacrifice in the name of his ambition.

I also wonder what he's seeing inside me as he stares back.

We wait and stare, and we get nothing done. I'm ready to call it a night and start over later when someone knocks on the door. It doesn't exactly break the tension, but it does provide enough of a distraction that I'm able to look away. Jerome moves to open it and on the other side waits Felina, a look of concern on her face.

"Majesty," she says, nervous, "there's something you need to see."

By the time I make it to the door, Jerome is already halfway down the hall, staring at something with the most confused expression I've ever seen on his face.

"W-what is that," I say, half-breathless, as I sprint toward him. The rest of my council is on my heels. Jerome's arm rises, and one long, graceful finger points toward the emblem crowning the new door.

A shining, red heart with the silhouette of a Jabberwocky.

"Are you fucking serious?" Ivan snaps and follows with a groan.

"Well, well…" Percival says, laughing, "it appears our little Queen truly has tamed the beast."

"Don't make it weird." My words are half-hearted at best because my mind is wholly occupied by the internal celebration. Putting my faith in Edwin has paid off. He has a door. He's on my side.

But that celebration is short-lived. No sooner do I start making plans for presenting the key to him, I remember that I've seen none of my Red Court allies since High Tea. Koji's door is still there, and I find myself staring at it, wondering what could be keeping him. It's not like him to be gone for so long.

Part of me wonders if this isn't that betrayal he promised.

But part of me also worries that something terrible has happened to him. Especially now that I know his story. Now that I know what he's sacrificing to be at my side. I know what the Red Queen and her sister mean to him. I know that they know him as well as he knows himself. Possibly better.

I reach out and close my hand around the knob on Koji's door. It's locked. Of course.

"Try your key," Jerome suggests.

Their keys are made from the same magic as mine, and mine is supposed to be all-powerful. A skeleton key of sorts. I pull the chain out from beneath my shirt and take the small, gold key between my fingers. It slides into the lock soundlessly, and when I turn, the mechanism disengages.

The door swings open, and I'm met with a rush of not-for-polite-company memories, followed by a wash of absolute panic.

The lights are off. The room doesn't smell of incense. There is no tea on the sideboard. Koji has not been here for some time, and it's painfully obvious by the emptiness inside. Not a shred of his magic lingers in the air. I can't feel him here. It's almost like...

...like...

...like he never even existed.

My breath catches, and immediately I have two sets of arms wrapped around me, pulling me back between two large, warm bodies.

"Don't overthink it," Ivan says. "He's the most transient being in all of Wonderland. He will return."

I want to believe him, but I don't. Alarms ring in my head. Something is wrong. Really wrong. I know it, but I don't know what. I don't know how I know, but I know.

It's the magic, I think wildly. The magic is telling me something is wrong. The emptiness in here insists I'm looking in the wrong place for him.

My Rabbits' arms are the only things keeping me from going to pieces right here in this empty room. They're also the things that pull me out and lead me back down the hall to my own room. I fall into what feels like a trance; a spiral down into despair then back up to consciousness. Over and over again, council and my allies forgotten, until I finally don't remember anything at all.

CHAPTER FIFTEEN

I move through the world in a fog for days on end; my mind consumed by the startling disappearance of the Cheshire Cat. There are things I should be focusing on, but I can't seem to escape the specter of his absence. Targeted attacks from the Clubs have forced us to rethink our easy-does-it strategy, and for this I've allowed my generals to take control of the decision-making. Tag and Nacht, Blade and Torai — a pair of assassins and two of the strongest fighters in the four Kingdoms — work together day and night to strategize an effective plan for us. Phineas and Percival come and go, updating me on various issues between the two lands, but I'm… more or less useless at this point. I'm not a strategist and most of what they say goes sailing right over my head.

I'm reminded again that I'm just some throw-away girl from Otherland, doomed to a fate for which she didn't ask. The only thing that keeps me grounded is my sister, who hovers close in the evenings but doesn't question. Even she can feel the tension in the air.

The flurry of activity continues in the same manner while I feel stuck in the mud. There's so much coming from every direction so fast that I can't focus on any of it. People and cards skitter to and fro. If I try to watch it all, I'll be dizzy.

This is what it's like to prepare for war.

This castle hasn't seen such a crowd in at least a hundred years, if the Twins are to be believed. The whole thing is awake and alive and will soon be bursting at the seams. The Black army has already arrived, Blade leading them across the bridge in the most glorious and terrifying parade I've ever seen. Thousands of soldiers, both humanoid and card, stacked in neat rows and marching in time enough to shake the ground beneath our feet long before their arrival... it was both horrifying and beautiful.

The Walrus and the Oysters are still here as well, having been stationed as a defense against... well... everything.

Phineas and Felina are due to arrive this afternoon and Percival in the morning. It will be the first time I've had both of my kings in one space since High Tea, and that makes me nervous given how that event concluded. Despite his stated declaration of regicide—mine, in case that wasn't clear—I've developed a tentative friendship with the King of Diamonds over these last weeks, but I can't put my faith in the union. It is too new and he is far too chaotic.

As I sit and take stock of my allies, a pain twists my heart. I'm reminded yet again that I've heard nothing at all from Koji in weeks. Neither has Edwin, if the Red Court Beast is to be believed based on the messages I've received... and I do.

Everyone tried to warn me of this betrayal. Even Koji admitted it was coming. Yet as I wander down the hallway of my suite, I can't help but stare at the door with the crescent moon smile on it. If he truly betrayed me — sold me out to the King of Clubs, if Nacht's newest intel is to be believed — then why does he still have a door?

Because he said when he betrayed you, it would be to the Red Crown, and it would be to save your life.

I continue to puzzle through it as I exit the suite and start toward the throne room. Tag falls into step beside me, his lips drawn into a tight, thin line. The stress of running this castle in my stead weighs heavily on him. It's like if I look hard enough, I'll be able to see weights visible there and the cracks forming in the creases they leave.

The underlying current of anxiety has the hair on my arms standing on end. Everyone in the castle feels it, too. Even though we're all here together, closer than ever, we're isolated in fear.

I thread my arm through Tag's and lean into his warmth as we walk. It helps to push back the loneliness in my heart. Even though we say nothing on our walk, just being close to him, to that strong and steady presence, makes me feel better.

The throne room is oddly quiet when we arrive, despite its many occupants. in addition to my inner circle, my generals are also present—a disturbing mix of humans and cards, all of which stand at attention and bow low as I pass. Tag snickers despite the fact that his face is tightly drawn.

"What?"

His grin widens. "Just find it funny that someone who hates formality so much so often engages in it."

"Only because you lot make me."

"You could say no."

Sometimes I wish I could… but then where would we be?

Tag escorts me up the steps and to my throne. It's when he steps back that I realize his brother is missing.

"Where's Nacht?"

"Handling a situation," Tag answers and the accompanying look invites me not to ask questions.

I nod toward the page at the back of the long room—a two of spades—and it steps forward, reaching into the magical cavern of its playing card belly to retrieve a fancy scroll. That sight shouldn't still make my skin crawl the way it does. I blink away the memory of the bandersnatch generals with their gory guts and focus on upcoming court business.

"Announcing Orvice — of Brillig."

My mood perks up considerably at the sound of his name, but quickly plummets as he stumbles in, a walking stick the only thing keeping him on his feet. His clothes are bloody and torn, and dirty bandages coat both arms and the visible part of one leg. He manages four more steps before the injured leg buckles and he tumbles forward. Blade and one of the cards are at his side to catch him, however, and the Unicorn lifts the injured man into their arms.

Jerome produces a chair from somewhere, and I'm at his side, taking his hand, before Blade can release him.

"Majesty..." Orvice breathes, his voice rasping against his short breath.

"What happened?"

"Clubs... soldiers... he took her..."

He falls limp, slumping to one side. He would fall to the floor if not for Blade's quick actions. He's carried away, but his message hangs heavily in the air.

Jerome helps me to my feet and urges me back to the throne. I feel his worry, but he says nothing out loud. We all know the her is his wife. It's the *he* portion that's concerning. There's more than one option for who he could be.

The page continues as if the ground didn't just fracture under our feet. I suppose it hasn't for most because to the majority of my court, he's just a

Diamond Court citizen who fell out. I want to rush after him, but I'm led back to the throne instead with a quiet reminder that I have business to attend to.

So, we meet the long line of locals and travelers alike, accepting well wishes and gifts, and searching for solutions to problems until late in the afternoon. It's nearly tea time when the last visitor is seen out, and I collapse back against my throne in the most undignified position Wonderland has ever seen with a loud sigh.

Being a Queen is exhausting. I have no idea how I'm supposed to do this for over a hundred years.

Phineas and Felina accompany Blade to the infirmary to care for Orvice while the rest of us retire to the library for tea. There's an air of anxiety hanging over us that we can't seem to shake. Even the call of the light and fizzy intoxication accompanying the pots of gunpowder tea on the table isn't enough to make me forget the heartbreak in Orvice's eyes as he passed out.

I must be building up a tolerance to tea.

I glance over at Jerome's ticking wristwatch tattoo. One hand says we're late for something. Another says it's nearly time for Phineas to arrive, but he isn't who walks through the door when it opens.

"Aeromi?"

What the hell is the Duchess doing here? And unattended, no less?

Something is very, *very* wrong. She has a wild look about her. Her hair isn't perfectly curled. There are dark circles under her eyes, like she hasn't slept in days. She's also not carrying her pig.

"Have you seen Koji recently?" she asks. Her voice trembles. Tears gather along her lower lash line.

"No," I reply. "He hasn't been back in weeks. I figured he was with you."

She stuffs her fist between her teeth to stop a sob from escaping. It comes out as a thin whine, and her shoulders shake. "I think something's wrong. It's not like him to be gone so long from me with no communication." Her voice is tiny and fragile.

I'm immediately on alert and so is Ivan.

"Lord Edwin?" I ask, hoping he's told her something different than the messages I've received say, but she shakes her head and the first tears spill down her cheeks.

If Koji hasn't checked in anywhere...

We have to find him.

Before I can issue the order, Haigha kneels at my side, head bowed. His quick movement startles me. I'm not finished reconciling the broken pieces of him into one man. "Allow me to carry your message, whatever it may be, to our allies, Majesty."

Allies? With Aeromi here, Percival at my left elbow, Koji missing, and Orvice incapacitated, what other allies do we have?

"I appreciate that Haigha, but there is no message yet. We have to figure out where he went first."

Now would be a very good time for Talon to magically appear and save the day, but he doesn't. He's still technically neutral in this war and as much as I wish he'd choose our side, I also know it's not in the nature of a Caterpillar to do so. My teeth grind together in frustration.

"Tag..."

"Majesty?" He bows low, then kneels at my right hand.

"How does one go about finding a missing cat in the whole of Wonderland?"

"Quite carefully, one would imagine," he replies.

"We don't have time to be careful," I say, to which he nods.

"Then we must start—"

"—at the beginning?" My eyes narrow and he smiles.

"When did you see him last?" Aeromi asks.

"High Tea. He left with you."

Her mouth turns into a thin, flat line, and the color drains from her face.

"Koji left me two days after that, headed here."

"From your home?" Ivan asks. She nods. Some sharp, dark emotion hits him. It stabs into my brain like a dull, serrated knife. This new fear has teeth, and they shred my mind as it slides through. "And you are certain Edwin has not seen him?"

Aeromi shakes her head and sniffles.

"Jabberwocky? "Jerome's voice is small and fearful.

"Their community does lie between the courts," Tag adds.

"But they are under Red control," Aeromi adds. "They generally are not aggressive toward allies."

"Perhaps your sister learned the truth of this alliance," Percival says to Aeromi, joining the conversation for the first time.

"He hasn't exactly been quiet about it," I remind them. My cheeks flush as memories of his very public displays of affection surface.

"Koji has always had his own agenda," Ivan announces. "He's rather… mercurial."

"Very true," Aeromi says, "but he has never gone missing like this before."

"Maybe he's just hiding," I answer, but the words feel wrong on my tongue.

"Or there's something nefarious afoot," Tag says, "which is the way of Wonderland."

We sit for a long time in stiff silence, everyone trapped in their own thoughts. My own imagination circles the drain, conjuring up the worst possible images from the dark recesses of my brain. The idea of Jabberwocky terrifies me. Morcar's twisted, serpentine body flashes through my mind, and I shudder, an involuntary reaction to the unspeakable horror that he is. That image is followed by a series of terrible hypotheticals — Koji captured and in a dungeon somewhere, his body lying broken in the depths of the Tulgey Wood, fingers and toes and familiar strips of tattooed skin hanging for sale in a vendor's stall somewhere, his head in a basket at the foot of the Red Queen's guillotine…

I physically shake myself out of these waking nightmares and refocus my attention on the people around me. Each of them looks worried. And it's their worried faces that give me an idea.

"Haigha?"

He clicks his heels together and bows low. "Majesty?"

"Can you get a message to anyone in Wonderland?"

"Naturally."

"Can you find the Caterpillar and have him come to me?"

Haigha clicks his heels together, salutes, and turns for the door. The thought of having Talon here alleviates some of the anxiety swirling in my chest. If anyone can find Estrella and Koji at the same time, it would be him.

I take a deep breath, which works as a signal for everyone's attention.

"For the moment we must assume that our plans are compromised," I announce. "With two allies now missing, I cannot simply assume coincidence." Worried murmurs of agreement float up, popping like bubbles over the table. "However, we are not going to give up. Orvice is counting on us for help, and if Koji truly is in danger…"

"What do you suggest, Majesty?" Tag asks when I trail off.

A fresh wave of anxiety washes over me. The idea coalesces in my mind, bright and shining like a vicious star, and as I realize what I'm about to say, I also realize that there is no other option.

"While we wait for Talon, we're going to find Koji."

"How amusing that her Majesty thinks I would make her wait."

That rich voice, low and seductive right in my ear startles a shriek out of me. I'm out and out of the chair, whipping around to face my would-be attacker only to find… nothing.

"Majesty?" Tag asks. He and both Rabbits are on their feet, weapons drawn.

Laughter echoes through the room. Or maybe it's just my head. Then a hazy mist appears, and the Caterpillar coalesces from within it.

Of course the first thing Talon thinks to do is mess with me. It seems to be a favorite pastime of these knuckleheads—jumpscares and shrieking contests. The snickers floating up from a few of my companions tell me they not only saw it coming, but actively did nothing to assist.

How cheerfully he seems to grin, I think, looking at those hooded, swirling eyes. *How neatly spreads his claws, and welcomes little fishes in…*

"Traitors," I mutter while I glare at those gently

smiling jaws. There is no doubt in my mind that this creature would devour me whole and leave not a single crumb if given the chance. "All of you." The resulting laughter at my outburst is ultimately what drags me back to center, and I resume my seat once Talon moves away. Annoyance buzzes in my mind, while my Rabbits sheathe their weapons.

"How might I be of service, Majesty?" he asks taking a seat.

"I need help locating two people." The fact that he's already here and it hasn't even been half an hour is…astounding. "I can't believe Haigha found you that fast."

"He didn't," Talon says. "It seems a happy coincidence that you were searching for me in the first place."

"Does he know you're here?"

He pretends to think about my question, then raises one shoulder in dismissal. "Not likely."

"In that case, won't he have a hard time finding you?"

"He certainly will."

This sounds like history I don't want to visit. I clear my throat and take another sip of my tea — from a clean cup, of course.

"Talon, I need to know where a woman named Estrella is being held. She's—"

"—the wife of the man in your infirmary," he finishes.

"Yes."

"You also desire the whereabouts of our wayward pussycat, do you not?"

Aeromi sits up a little straighter. "Do you know where he is?"

"No," Talon says flatly. "However, with the help of our Queen, I may be able to locate him."

She looks at me for clarification.

"It's a thing we do. I harness the magic and he uses it. It's like the ultimate party trick."

She nods like she understands, but the look in her eyes is firmly skeptical. I don't blame her. If I wasn't part of the fun, I wouldn't believe me either.

"This evening, in the garden," Talon says. "After you've eaten well and rested."

"Sounds like a plan."

I lift my cup to my lips and empty it, allowing the fizziness of the gunpowder tea to infuse my body. The thought that two people close to me are missing is troubling, but this little bit of intoxication helps curb the anxiety enough that it won't eat me alive for the next few hours.

"Are you quite ready, Majesty?" Talon asks, holding his hand out as I enter the garden. It's near dusk, and the flickering of tiny, burning-sugar firefly bodies gives the garden an ethereal glow. The flowers have bedded down for the night and twilight wraps around us like a cocoon.

Appropriate, considering the strangely magnetic man standing before me.

"As ready as I'll ever be," I reply, then kick off my shoes and step into the cool, dewy grass. The garden is in bloom, but sparse. Most of the plants have turned green, but very few of them beyond the beds of possessed flowers actually bear fruit and flowers. It's a hopeful sign, and I let that hope infuse me as I step up and lay my palm against his. Talon's skin is warm and a tingle of magic races up my arm. He's already drawing on my abilities. Testing me. It's an odd sensation but not unpleasant, and the current of magic helps focus the scattered parts of my mind.

"Take," he says and offers the hookah hose to me. I take it with a tiny, wild giggle — here I go doing drugs in the garden of my own castle with a magical being who plans to crawl inside my mind and use me as a vessel to do his bidding. Or my bidding... his way, though.

Yeah, this is a *totally* normal Tuesday in Wonderland. I draw the sweet, spicy smoke into my lungs and the effects are immediate. Magic races up through my body from the grass under my bare feet, taking control of me. I remind myself to breathe and not fight it.

I close my eyes, the vision of his smirking face lingering in the darkness behind my eyelids and reach down into the currents. The bottoms of my feet tingle and warm, and a pale yellow glow takes over inside. It's comforting, but with a deadly undertow which teases the fringes of my consciousness, begging me to let go. I don't. Talon's presence moves through me by way of our linked hands, tapping into the magic and pulling it up and out. It's a simple touch, but more intimate than any other experience in my life. We're no longer touching; we've become part of one another, if only temporarily.

"Majesty," he calls, his voice low and gentle. My eyes drift open to find a set of hazy, ethereal wings have sprouted behind him, a veil over which visions play. I'm vaguely aware of Ivan and Jerome nearby, and of their roiling emotions inside my head, but the magic has taken over and compartmentalized their curiosity and jealousy.

Talon's gaze is distant and unfocused; his pupils flickering back and forth as if he's watching a movie at quadruple speed. Blue-green light pulses in the distance of my mind. A familiar beacon, flickering like a rapid heartbeat. We move toward it together, the Caterpillar and I, as he guides me through the twisted labyrinth of thought and magic. Fragments of images flicker across the surface of his wings, stopping and starting, skipping and glitching, until the speed slows to something close to real-time.

A cavernous building made of stone, and rows upon rows of metal bars separating small, mostly empty cells. A few emaciated prisoners peeking out of the rags of their clothing, one hanging on the bars, weekly crying. Near the end of the wall, a small slip of a woman weeping softly into her hands.

I gasp as the familiar face comes into view. Estrella looks terrified but mostly unharmed. She's dirty and shaking, though whether cold or scared, I can't tell. I can't hear anything, but I can see the pulse of grief flickering in time with the magic.

"She is safe," Talon says, his voice a faraway reverberation. "Find the Cheshire Cat."

Even the magic feels frightened as the title falls from his lips. It hesitates, flickering in that nonsensical way again before coalescing once more into a mostly clear picture.

A village set deep in the mountains. A pair of guards on either side of the rough gates. No weapons. One nodding while the other glances into the woods beyond their clearing.

It skips.

A cave set into the hill rising behind the village, blocked by two more guards. Darkness seeps out from inside. It's…cold. Damp. I can almost feel the mold taking root in my lungs from the moisture inside. The pulsing light is stronger here. Brighter.

Scared.

"This is not good," I hear Ivan say distantly. "Not at all."

I'm not at all in control of my body, mind, or mouth, otherwise I'd ask why. The problem is, I think I already know. I've never been to the place flickering in Talon's wings before, but I know *exactly* where and what it is. The fact that it exists is horrifying.

Down we go into the vision and into the tunnel. It turns sharply to the left and the grade turns steep; steep enough that if one were to lose their balance, one would certainly tumble ass over teakettle all the way to the bottom and land in a broken, bloody heap.

At the bottom, the blue pulse nearly blinds in its intensity, but it shows us exactly where to go. We follow the beacon, floating along in this magical trance, into an alcove. Far to the back of the cave, recessed into a far wall and masked by tattered curtains, it houses a series of cages. Above these, the light flashes one last time and goes out.

My eyes are slow to adjust and, at first, the cages appear empty, save rags and cloth scraps at the bottom of one or two.

Then something moves in the farthest cage. Barely perceptible as it is, I notice the shiver of moving fabric. It happens again when we're halfway across the room, and it becomes clear that the cage is not, in fact, empty.

From inside the pile of rags, an arm emerges. Long, graceful fingers and elegant bone structure, wrapped in all-too-familiar tattoos.

"Koji…"

I gasp and, in my surprise, let go of Talon's hand. The wings burst like a bubble, leaving behind a shower of sparkling magic which falls to the grass like so much discarded glitter. Talon winces but otherwise shows no sign of discomfort at the sudden severance of our connection. The magic rushes through me, up and out, and draws my unguarded strength with it. I collapse to the ground, unable to stop the sob that ribs from my throat.

Jerome and Ivan are immediately at my sides, hands tucked under my arms as if to pull me back to my feet. I hold up a hand in silent protest. Even if I were to stand up, I'd only fall down again. My chest aches from the tumble of fear and grief, and my muscles quiver from the magic-fueled adrenaline rush.

I stretch out my hand. Talon, sensing the meaning, kneels in front of me and takes my outstretched fingers in his. We hold onto one another, our racing heartbeats gradually slowing. I'm vaguely aware of the swirl of magic beneath the sadness, and it takes far too long to realize the Caterpillar is siphoning it off of me.

The moon is high in the sky and the night birds deep into their song when I begin to feel better. Three sets of hands offer support as I stand.

"Well… at least we know where our cat is," I say, but the joke I try to make falls flat.

"The question now is how do we get to him without dying?" Ivan asks.

"We have a beast for that."

The four of us turn at the sound of the new voice. The Red Duchess stands in the doorway of the castle, looking small and scared. The lack of color in her cheeks tells me she probably saw more of that vision than she needed to. I can't blame her, though. She loves Koji as much as I do.

…wait…

Did I really just think that?

I mean, I love all of my friends and allies, but for that thought to roll through my head so easily is certainly cause for concern.

"Let us go inside," Talon urges and I remember that he still has hold of my hand. He likely knows everything I've been thinking. "It has turned cold, and we do not need our Queen under the weather on the eve of her next big adventure."

CHAPTER SIXTEEN

"How the hell do we get our Cheshire Cat back?" I ask as I look around at the faces of my assembled council. Everyone sits stiff and silent, looking at one another. At the end of the table, Aeromi looks even smaller and more fragile than she did in the garden. It is also she who speaks up.

"He's being held by the Jabberwock clan," she says. "Blackridge isn't a normal city. It's a stronghold."

"So, no easy in and out with this one?" I ask.

"Not at all." She gives her head a little shake. "It's the most well-guarded location in Wonderland, second only to the Red Palace. It's impossible to get in."

"There are ways," Talon says. Everyone immediately turns to listen. "Though they may be dangerous."

"Dangerous comes with the territory," I reply. "Tell me what I need to do."

The Caterpillar's gaze drifts toward the mirror standing against the far wall.

"Why are you looking at my mirror?"

"Do you know what that mirror is, Majesty?"

"I was told it's a Mercian Looking Glass."

"That it is. Do you know what it does?"

"It connects to a Rabbit Hole?"

"And do you know which Rabbit Hole?"

I'm already tired of this game. I want my cat back. I don't want to answer questions.

"Which Rabbit Hole?"

"The Alice's Looking Glass was tied to a Rabbit Hole near Callowary, the Capitol of Mercia," Aeromi says. "Lord Edwin's home," she adds when she sees my confused expression. "Majesty, that mirror you possess was as much mythology to us as we were fiction to you. We thought it destroyed decades ago."

I look at the heavy mirror and its decorative scrollwork. "Will it work if I'm already in Wonderland?"

"A Looking Glass will work anywhere, though inside of its own Rabbit Hole may be a bit of an adventure," Talon says. I need a minute to catch up to his line of thinking, but when it clicks, it *really* clicks. He smiles at me when he notices I've caught on. "You see, Majesty, as long as that Rabbit Hole and your mirror continue to exist, you will *always* have a way into — and out of — Wonderland."

I see where he's going with this conversation and he's right... it *is* dangerous. It's the fastest way to get to our Allies to the North. It's a crazy idea, but it may just be crazy enough to work.

"So we go through the looking glass to meet up with Edwin. Then what? Walk up to the gate and demand our cat back?"

"No," Talon says. I wait, but he doesn't elaborate.

"Then what?"

Jerome and Ivan exchange a look. Their thoughts feel muddled and anxious, and I'm unable to glean any understanding from them. Even Aeromi winces, seemingly catching on when I don't.

"It's the only way," she says aloud, but her words are heavy with a sigh.

I continue to watch the verbal ping-pong match with great interest because I know they're talking about me, but I don't know exactly what they're saying. I'm still not as up on my Wonderland battle tactics as I should be, and I know next to nothing about the Jabberwocky in general. I also don't like the idea of running headlong into Heart territory without a solid plan in place.

But something tells me I'm not going to like the plan we're concocting.

"Absolutely not," Jerome snaps. Anger radiates off of him, slamming into me through our bond.

Yep. I'm not going to like it *at all.*

"How else will we get her into the dungeons?"

Aeromi asks. "The Jabberwocky trust no one."

"And I certainly do not trust them!" Jerome shouts back.

"But you do trust Lord Edwin by this point, yes?" Her voice remains smooth and even, but the look in her eyes as she stares at Jerome could stop a clock.

The lightbulb in my brain flickers to life. They're talking about using me as bait. He's Jabberwocky, so it would stand to reason that he could move among them easily. It's honestly not a bad idea for more than one reason. It would get us inside, but it would also solidify his place as the hero of the Red Court since he'd be imprisoning me. It also isn't the first time I've been on the plate as a pawn.

"Am I correct in assuming you're going to ask Lord Edwin to transport me to Blackridge as a way of getting inside?"

"I'm sorry, Majesty," Aeromi says, "it's the only way. The Jabberwocky are extremely suspicious of outsiders, but it is not unusual for my sister to request they hold prisoners for her."

"And I'm the ultimate prize, right?"

Jerome grumbles under his breath.

"What?" I ask. "Spit it out."

"How did the plan go from offering King Phineas as bait to handing our Queen over without a second thought?"

"Because Koji's life is on the line and I refuse to let him die for me."

Jerome is clearly not happy, but as much as he'd love to protest, he won't because he knows it's ultimately my decision. It also sounds like there isn't much of a decision to be made if we're to get Koji back in one piece.

"How do we get a messenger to Edwin quickly?" I ask, much to my Rabbits' chagrin.

"First things first," Talon interjects with a mischievous smile, "through the Looking Glass we go."

"We?" I ask, raising an eyebrow at him. His smile widens.

"Of course, Majesty," he says with a flourish and a bow, "how else am I to record the deeds of our illustrious Queen of Cards if I am not in attendance?"

Wow... just wow. This bitch disappears for weeks on end only to turn up and taunt me by saying he's going to *watch* what happens? He's really lucky he's pretty. And useful, I suppose.

"Okay, let's go."

"When?" Aeromi asks.

"Right now. The sooner we get there, the sooner we get our cat back."

"I'm going," Jerome demands. The protective way Ivan moves closer tells me he's going too. Talon has already offered his astounding lack of services, and Aeromi is our guide. Our party is set and for once, Phineas isn't here to convince me it's a bad idea, not that he needs to.

I'm well aware that it's not just a bad idea... this is a *phenomenally* bad idea. I realize too late that I've yet again allowed myself to be placed in an utterly stupid position for the sake of someone else, but I reach out where directed—a cleverly-hidden rosebud carved into the ornate scrollwork on the right-hand side—and flip the switch that will activate the portal.

The mirror doesn't look like a magical portal.

Upon passing through the Looking Glass, we find Edwin waiting on us in the Rabbit Hole. It's like he knew we were coming, yet nobody can explain to me exactly how that happened.

I'm worried about this entire process. I'm worried that I'm going to disappear and the rest of my council won't know where I am or what happened... except that Blade has remained behind and will surely be on their way to tell my husband.

"Time is of the essence, I suppose," I say aloud as I look around at our crew for this heist. This... *cat*-napping. A hysterical giggle bursts out of me at the thought, and five pairs of confused eyes turn my way.

"Did... did she hit her head?" Edwin asks.

"No," Jerome and Ivan reply in unison.

"But she did think something funny," Jerome adds.

I pace across the room, stopping in front of Edwin. "What's the plan? Can we go ahead and go now?"

"Absolutely." Edwin holds out a length of red silk rope. "If you please, Majesty…allow me to bind your beautiful wrists."

"Um…"

Okay, this just took a left turn into *really fucking weird.*

"You are meant to be a prisoner," Talon reminds me, though he does so with his lips at entirely too close a proximity to my left ear. Now they're messing with me. I want to not like it, but I can't quite get to that point. My libido is clearly in overdrive.

"Don't ever say it like that again," I reply, tilting my head away from Talon while glaring at Edwin as I hold out my wrists. "Damned Jabberwocky."

"I am aware of my place in the food chain, my love," he replies without missing a beat and drapes the rope over my arms. In a few quick movements, my hands are immobilized, and there's no way I can break free from the intricate and, admittedly, pretty knots.

I'm then led outside like the good little prisoner I'm supposed to be, and I get my first really good look at Red Territory. It's peaceful looking, just like the majority of Wonderland. I'm not sure what I was expecting, exactly, but as is usually the case, I'm wrong. I really do need to stop expecting the worst. We're far enough away from the city that it's little more than a misty backdrop, and here on the edge of the Tulgey Wood, the air isn't as thick. It's peaceful.

I'm so fascinated by my surroundings that I miss the moment when Edwin transforms from man to beast. The action is soundless and nearly instant. When I turn my attention back to him, Lord Edwin of Mercia is gone, replaced by a giant lion-serpent-weasel-*thing* that makes my heart stutter in my chest.

Edwin's Jabberwock form is exponentially bigger than Morcar's. His beastly body is long and lean—more snake than dragon—and covered in iridescent gold scales. His head resembles that of an Eastern-style dragon with the long, narrow snout and feathery beard, and four long, spindly legs tipped in deadly-sharp black eagle-like talons. At first glance, his delicate, feathered wings don't appear to be load-bearing, but they now stretch wide on either side of his body into roughly a thirty-foot wingspan. The sight of him is *terrifying*.

"Majesty, if you would," he says. Edwin's voice issues from the beast, but there's a reverberation behind it; an extra undertone of intimidation. It sounds like him, but also completely foreign.

"Um… how?" I hold up my bound wrists.

"Simple," Ivan replies, sweeping me up into his arms. I'm not sure how he does it exactly, but he scales the side of Edwin's body and deposits me neatly between those wings. Jerome slithers up the dragon's side and takes up the space in front of me, then reaches back and clamps one hand onto my thigh. Ivan keeps an arm wrapped around tightly me as we lift into the air.

Traveling by Jabberwocky, I discover, is one of the strangest experiences of my life so far. And that's saying something because Wonderland is a series of strange experiences all fighting to one-up each other at every turn. The sight of Edwin in beast form was enough to startle my heart into a full panic-gallop alone but actually *riding* him—all jokes aside—is just as intimidating.

Yet…here we are.

I'm sandwiched in by my Rabbits, who have to hold me up since my wrists are still bound—the flight would probably be much more enjoyable if I weren't trussed up like a goddamned turkey—and we're up so high that wisps of cloud pass every few moments.

"Relax, Majesty," Ivan says in my ear. The arm around my waist curls even more tightly, pulling me back against him and his lips brush against the cuff of my ear, making my shiver. "I won't let you fall."

I expect not, but that doesn't ease my anxiety at all. There are entirely too many factors at play for me to be comfortable, and the teasing from my Rabbit doesn't help either. The one consolation is that if we pull this heist off, everyone will be back together again, safe and sound. I'm just worried about what condition Koji will be in when we find him.

Ten minutes or so later, we land soundlessly inside a small clearing. Of course, Talon is already there, sitting cross-legged with his back against a tree, looking completely and utterly bored.

Ivan lifts me into his arms again and swings himself down to the ground. A moment later, the beast is gone, replaced by the man I know, though he looks a little more feral than I remember. Like the shift is stealing his humanity. I blink again and even that look is gone. He's back to being refined aristocracy, only with windblown hair.

Jerome is on alert, circling the perimeter of the clearing, but it appears to be just us. Once he completes his circuit and returns to us, Talon opens his eyes and rises.

"It is time," the Caterpillar says. His hair lifts and flutters in an invisible breeze, and the sight sends a shiver down my spine. He looks more mirage than man, like that magical breeze of his might up and blow him away.

"One more thing." Jerome steps up, kisses me softly, and lifts the crown from my head. "I cannot go with you, but I will keep this safe for your return."

The rope connected to my bound wrists rests in Edwin's left hand as we reach the gates of — well, I can't really call it a city. It's more of a fortress; the stone walls an extension of the mountain looming just behind. Two large, angry men stand guard, one with a spear and the other with a war hammer. At least, I assume it's a war hammer given the nasty-looking spike curving away from the rounded, blood-stained head. These dudes are scary in ways they have no right to be, and I am completely defenseless.

Their weapons cross with a *shink* as Edwin leads me up to where they stand.

"Identify," the one with the spear says, and his already-angry expression deepens into a scowl.

"Prisoner from Queen Lucinda," Edwin replies. "Maximum security."

He examines me, pausing to note the rope binding my wrists and forearms. He's probably checking to make sure I'm scared, which I am. I'm absolutely *terrified*. But I'm not going to let it show if I can help it. Me being scared isn't going to help us find Koji or get out of whatever's about to happen alive. He appears to find whatever he's looking for and the weapons un-cross.

"Proceed," he says. Edwin nods and tugs the rope just hard enough to jolt me forward.

It's relatively early in the evening, but with the height of the mountains around us, it's almost too dark to see clearly. A few scattered torches burn, casting pools of watery, orange-tinted light around the entrances to some of the buildings, but for the most part we're stumbling blind. Night vision must be a Jabberwocky thing.

Edwin leads me through the deserted town. There is *no one* around. Not even faces in the windows. This place is the epitome of *mind your own fucking business.* A slight breeze rolls down from the mountain, cold and biting, and the bare skin on my forearms prickles. My fake captor tugs the rope just hard enough to cause me to stumble and I tell myself it's just for show, that he's not actually playing a long game to lock me away from right under my allies' noses.

He has a door, I remind myself. *The magic wouldn't lie to me.*

But even that doesn't make me feel better.

The walk is long and hard, with just enough of an incline to keep me stumbling and make my legs ache. As we move through town, the buildings thin. The air grows even colder. And then I see our destination: A yawning maw of inky blackness carved into the base of the mountain, its entrance illuminated by the dancing light of two mounted torches.

My steps stutter to a halt, and this time Edwin pauses as well.

"Do not fear, Majesty," he whispers. "No harm shall come to you."

"I trust you," I reply, my voice small and shaky.

"Come." He tugs the rope. "Stay close and stay quiet. Keep your head down and believe nothing I tell these beasts."

I nod and cast my gaze to the ground just before my feet. It's so dark out here that I can barely see my feet, but I follow along obediently, right up to the second pair of guards, which provide a near-identical repeat of the first.

We move into the mountain by way of a narrow, humid tunnel. It's well-lit, and the firelight is almost blinding given the darkness outside. This path slopes downward, deeper into the mountain, and curves around in a wide, disorienting spiral. We walk… and walk… and walk… and walk some more. We walk so long that the constant downward grade makes my calf muscles ache. Yet Edwin continues to silently drag me along, playing the part of victorious Jabberwocky captor.

The deeper we get into the pit, the heavier the air becomes. The torches continue to flicker on the walls, but their halos of light grow tighter and tighter. Somewhere in the darkness, a bird sings a carefree melody, which only adds to the vicious ambience.

Then, the torches stop and the walls begin to take on their own light. It starts as a dim, blue glow but quickly grows into an ethereal rainbow of undulating, ambient light. It's hypnotic. Beautiful. I want to get closer, to run my fingers through the swirling illumination and see if it feels as pretty as it looks.

In my fascination, I stumbled. I would faceplant, but a strong hand closes around my upper arm and steadies me.

"Careful, Majesty… a scene we must not cause."

I shriek in surprise and immediately smack my bound hands over the hand that's suddenly covering my mouth. By doing so, I also hit myself in the face with the tail of rope and would knock myself over again if it weren't for the strong hand on my arm and the large body into which I slam when I lose my balance again.

A low, deep rumble of laughter responds in the strange twilight, and I look up into a familiar face. His big hand slides away from my mouth, fingers trailing along my jaw before moving to my waist to steady me.

"Nacht," I hiss when I realize exactly who and what has hold of me. "How the hell did you get in here?"

The look he gives me indicates *exactly* how stupid he thinks me.

"My lovely Queen questions my abilities," he says, his voice trained so that only I can hear it. It doesn't echo off the walls the way mine does, which unnerves me for a whole other set of reasons. "Wounds my fragile heart, she does."

"Oh, please," I snort, "the only way to wound you is with a weapon… if one could get close enough."

One corner of his mouth hitches up. "Her Majesty speaks the truth."

His grip on my arm loosens, but he doesn't let go. He does, however, move away from me so I can walk unhindered, though his fingers remain along the ridge of my hipbone, guiding me. The sudden loss of his warmth behind me sends a chill through my bones, and I realize just how much colder it has become in this tunnel. We're pretty deep into the mountain now.

"We are almost there," Edwin says, nodding to Nacht as if he expected him to be there. "Just a little further, now."

We start walking again, but my attention is drawn back to the iridescent light display along the walls. The colors ripple as we walk, and I realize that the surface of the tunnel is actually moving.

"What—"

"Mome raths," Nacht says in my ear. "Bioluminescent lichens with the ability to rearrange themselves as they see fit. Quite the pernicious little buggers."

I squint and look harder. That's when I realize he's right. The colors aren't cycling. The smooth tops of the individual creatures are moving with us. They're packed so tightly that there's almost no definition to their little mushroomy bodies, but when I look *very* hard, I can just make out their tiny, dark outlines.

"Venomous, too. Very."

"Wait… they *bite?*"

"Majesty," he replies, pitching his voice low, "everything in Wonderland is designed to kill. If it doesn't bite, it stabs, suffocates, or drowns. Either way, if it wants you dead, you *will* die."

Something tells me he's talking about himself more than the critters on the walls. I am well aware of his lethality. I'm also very glad he's on my side and that I don't know the details of where he goes when he goes off to sneak his secret sneaky business.

"A curious lot, they are," Nacht adds, pulling me back from that brain spiral. "Never tell a secret you do not want the entire world to know if a mome rath is in range."

"They gossip, too?"

"Terribly."

A bark of laughter tears loose from my throat. There is absolutely nothing funny about this situation, but the thought of gossiping mushroom-creatures his freaking *hilarious* to me. Nacht's arm slips from my waist and goes around my neck. His hand covers my mouth, reminding me of the thing he *just* told me that I, in my hysteria, have forgotten.

"Quiet," he hisses in my ear. I nod in response and after he's certain I'm not going to either talk back or laugh again, loosens his grip on my mouth. "The mome raths have no eyes, but their hearing is exceptional. Best I can tell, they have yet to figure out I am here. I would like to keep it that way, if you don't mind."

I nod one more time and we start moving again. Edwin's and my footsteps echo in the narrowing tunnel, but Nacht moves silently. He's close enough that his arm brushes against my shoulder every few steps, but I can't even hear him breathing. I have so many questions for him that my chest is practically about to burst, but I can't ask any of them. I can't give him away.

After another hundred or so steps, the sloping tunnel opens into a wide, damp cavern. The mome raths stop at the entrance and torches replace them, lining the walls and posted sporadically around the space. It's dim, the air is thick, bitter, and bitingly cold, and there is absolutely no movement. It feels like a tomb even though the occasional pained groan rises from one of the two dozen stone cages littering the space. Based on their construction, I realize this entire place was carved out from the interior of the mountain with the specific purpose of being a prison. The iron doors aside, these cages appear to be naturally occurring features. I shiver, though whether from the cold or the horror of this sight, I am not certain, and lean closer into Nacht's side.

Edwin drops the rope and removes the lasso from around my wrists. The thinner cord binding me remains in place—a safety net, I realize, even though there are no guards in this place.

Nacht nods toward the middle of the room, urging me forward with a silent order. I follow along obediently, though I wish with every fiber of my being that we didn't have to be here.

Several cages with closed doors host piles of rags that might have once been bodies, so there appears to be no need for them. The stink of death permeates the air, flavoring it with a particularly tangy flavor of rot. It's not particularly strong, but acrid enough to curl my toes. This is the place the Red Court sends people not just to die, but to be forgotten about. My heart sinks. I just hope we're not too late to save our cat.

CHAPTER SEVENTEEN

We find Koji buried in one of those rag piles in a cage near the far wall of the cavern. At first, the pile doesn't move, and my heart sinks at the sight of yet another empty cage. Fear rises like a hard lump in my throat as I realize that it's the last cage. We've looked into every other one, and of the occupied ones, only two appeared to be alive. A shudder runs up my spine, and tears burn at the corners of my eyes at the thought that we've lost him.

"No…" I wobble, my knees trying to buckle, but Edwin places a steadying hand under my elbow to hold me up.

Then, the pile of rags groans. All three of us freeze. My heart takes off at a gallop in my chest. Nacht turns and moves behind me, but I dare not turn around. I can't, just in case it's not Koji. The rustle of fabric echoes through the quiet chamber.

The rags groan again. A moment later the hinges on the heavy door squeak open, and I turn just in time to see Nacht reach into the shivering pile.

Another groan rises; this one pained and breathless. Weaker. I watch, my jaw clenched and my hands balled into tight, anxious fists. Nacht pulls back and gently lifts a limp form into his arms. I gasp as Koji's battered, bruised body unfolds, dangling from the arms cradling him. His clothes are in tatters, and scabbed-over gashes coated in crusted blood mar the beautiful tattoos decorating him.

A startled cry escapes my mouth, and I smack my tethered hands over it to quiet myself, but it's too late.

The alarm sounds.

It starts as a single, ear-piercing shriek but quickly rises to an ungodly cacophony.

"Fucking mome raths..." Nacht growls. "Move. *Now.*"

Edwin sweeps me up into a bridal carry and takes off across the room, right on Nacht's heels. My shout of surprise is lost underneath the noise of the screaming mome raths, not that it matters. Nacht and Edwin run. Fast. Upward and outward, directly through the center of the glowing, screeching tunnel. We move around and around and around until I'm dizzy, and the ambient light of the mushroom creatures fades back into watery torchlight. Edwin, who has taken the lead, skids to a halt and fluidly slings me around behind himself, where he sets me down on my feet and pushes me toward Nacht.

Four things happen at once, though I'm not entirely certain what order they happen in.

1. Nacht lifts me up in one arm while holding Koji with the other.
2. Several guards rush into the tunnel.
3. Edwin shifts.
4. Lightning strikes just outside the entrance to the tunnel, sending bright white streaks through my vision.

"Protect the Queen!" Edwin shouts in that strange double-voice and lets loose a sound roughly akin to Godzilla from the old 1950s movies.

I can't see anything, but I hear growling, groaning, and shrieking as we somehow go airborne—at least I assume we're airborne by the feel of wind rushing past me—and then...silence. I'm deposited (more like dropped, really) on a hard surface. Koji whimpers and his head lands in my lap. Instinctively, I loop my bound arms around him and hug him close to me. The rapid, weak flutter of his pulse under my fingers and the small sounds of pain from his throat are concerning, but enough to tell me he's alive and fighting to stay that way.

"I've got you," I murmur, and much like the cat he is, Koji inches closer. My own heartbeat starts to slow, and my breathing regulates, but I'm still scared. "Nacht?" I ask against my blindness.

"Quiet," he hisses back from somewhere nearby. I comply. I can't see him, but at least I know he's there. "Take care of him. Quickly." There's an urgency to his voice, but I can't see anything, so I have no idea what might be causing it. I feel along Koji's torso as far as my arms will reach, but find nothing save a few damp spots where his wounds seem to have torn open again.

I settle in, my back to a wall, and hold onto my cat while I blink furiously against my blindness and the panic it causes. Once the streaks of pain fade from behind my eyes, I realize we're once again in the darkness of a cavern. It's not the one we came from but similar in structure, albeit on a smaller scale. This space is long and narrow, but instead of cages, the iron doors are fitted into alcoves carved into the walls of the room itself. Nacht stands watch at the entrance, his head cocked to listen to… something.

Koji shudders in my lap. When I look down, I realize that he's wearing the same clothes I'd last seen him in, and several of the cuts are, in fact, oozing blood. One arm is curled around his midsection, and the dark red spilling over his fingers catches my attention.

"What…" I reach over and pull his bloody hand away. A gash roughly four inches long and wide enough to show me the soft meat of his belly pours a river of crimson and I gasp. It must have torn open during our attempted escape. Even in the dim light of the room, I can see the color draining from him. He's waxy and pale, his beautiful face twisted in a scowl of agony. "No... no, no, no, no...." This is bad. So very, very bad. "Hold on...please hold on..." I hear myself begging.

If I don't do something right now, he's going to die.

"Hush," Nacht hisses from the other side of the room.

"He's bleeding," I hiss back, but I go ignored.

From my bound and twisted position, I struggle free from my shoes, then use my toes to peel off my socks. Every movement jostles Koji and he howls in absolute agony, but I can't help it. He's heavy enough that I can't easily move him and with my hands and wrists tightly bound to one another, my range of movement is severely limited.

Cold stone meets the bottoms of my bare feet. I don't know if this is going to work. I don't even know *how* to make this work, but if I don't do something, he's going to die.

"Hold on," I whisper to Koji, then place my hands flat against his skin — as close to the wound in his belly as I can reach — and press my feet hard into the floor.

My eyes close and I take several deep breaths, focusing on my heartbeat, then reach out toward the magic. The flow is weak, but it's there. The stone of the mountain muffles it, makes it hard to draw up. The first time, I lose my hold and the flow snaps back into place below me. The release is painful and I bite down on my tongue to keep from shouting.

I try again.

It's easier this time, now that I know what to expect, but I wouldn't call the process at all *easy.* The magic and I struggle to connect through the density of the stone. It wants to come to me as much as I want it to rise, but the path through the hard floor is cloudy at best. It weaves through tiny fissures, stretching and pulling at me almost painfully. When the magic does reach my body, it's less of a stream and more of a diffused puddle… but it's enough. The tingle starts in the bottoms of my feet—and, curiously, in my rear-end which is also touching the floor—and I grab on the way I was taught, drawing it up and into me to shape as I need. The magic is slow and sluggish after its trek. I take a deep breath and pull harder, lending my strength to help it move more freely.

Everything else falls away, my focus narrowing to the blue-tinged stream of energy running through my consciousness toward the weak thump of Koji's heart under my hands. Now that I have a good grip on the flow, I direct it down my arms and into the Cheshire Cat through my palms. My skin warms and tingles, and the deep, jagged laceration in his side glows in my mind. I've not actively tried to heal someone before, so this is new and frightening.

I don't know what Talon sees when he does it, but I know the way the magic feels when it flows through me. That feeling is what I try to recreate. I don't want to push too hard and hurt him, but I need this bleeding to stop.

I follow the outline of the wound with the magic, watching in horror as it curves upward from the point of entry, cutting through his body at a sharp angle yet somehow missing nearly every vital organ. The tip of the wound, however, is embedded deep enough that his left lung is punctured.

This is bad.

My connection to the magic falters under the weight of rising panic, but I grab on again at the last second and keep it tethered. I take a breath, press my hands more tightly against Koji's chest, and remind myself that if I let go, he dies.

Focus on the magic. Focus on the magic. Focus on the magic.

The panic recedes. I pull the magic back to myself, then push it back into the wound. The edges are raw and pulsing. I can feel the pain where my consciousness touches, and each weak beat of Koji's heart makes me flinch. It's now that I realize I have no idea how to do this. I've watched it done. I've held the magic for someone else. But I've never been the one to heal someone.

Stop it, Alice, I chide myself and force myself to take another breath.

There is no other option. I have to do this.

I refocus again, feel out the edges of the wound, and turn my attention to the puncture in the bottom of his lung. Air whistles in and out of his nose, a thin, reedy sound that grows thinner with each new inhale. The magic is also there, wrapping around the shredded edges of the organ, awaiting my command.

Breathe, Alice.

I focus my attention on those tattered edges and will them to pull together. The magic resists at first. Frustratingly so. I push harder, forcing my will into the tissue and finally, *finally,* the shreds start to come together. My whole body grows hot with exertion. My head grows fuzzy. Koji's body convulses under my hands. Sweat slicks his exposed skin, and he groans in pain, but the tissue slowly rebuilds itself. The gash closes and I push more magic into him to reinflate his lung. Koji's whole body bows upward as he gasps in a hard breath.

My hold on the magic slips and he groans in pain as it tries to pull away. Catching the connection again, I inhale deeply and push the last of my shreds of my will into his healing. The wound pulls together enough to stem the flow of blood. It's ugly and messy and will probably scar, but his erratic heartbeat eases and his body relaxes in my arms.

The connection breaks, and the magic pulls away from him and flows out of me in a hard, fast rush. Pain flares through every part of my body. I cry out against the onslaught and the world goes dark.

I wake cradled in Nacht's arms. I have no idea how long we've been in this cavern, how long I've been asleep, or if I'm even truly alive. All I know is his body is large and warm, and for the first time since leaving my suite, I feel safe.

My consciousness floats back up, and I take mental stock of myself. I'm drained and exhausted, draped carelessly in Nacht's lap with his arms tight around my waist and shoulders and my head lolling against the side of his neck. He smells like woodsmoke and blood, and in my haze, I don't remember to be just a little afraid of him. It's comfortable here, and I don't really remember much of why I've wound up in this position until suddenly, I *do* remember.

I try to sit up but my lethargic body refuses to move at my command. There's nothing left inside me except my own life, and even that feels a little suspect at the moment.

"Ko—" I try to call his name, but my voice comes out like the broken croak of a frog. Nacht shuffles me a little closer and shushes me.

"He will live," he says quietly. "My Queen is quite wondrous, indeed." There's real affection in his voice, which makes my face tug itself into a smile.

"Thank… you…" I whisper, and I'm not sure if any sound actually happens.

"Can you stand?"

Nacht is gentle as he maneuvers us both to our feet. My head spins when my feet touch the ground—still cold, since I've kicked my shoes and socks somewhere—but the dizziness quickly clears. This is the first time I've been on my own feet since we found Koji, and the rubbery feeling in my legs is quick to remind me of this fact. My body holds, though, and I only wobble slightly when he lets go. I realize that my hands are no longer bound.

"We must leave now," he says, lips close to my ear to minimize the sound, then moves away to pick up Koji. I locate my shoes and socks and stuff my feet into them quickly, then run my hands down my rumpled clothes as if the action will do anything at all to make me look like I didn't just harness more magic than my body is capable of holding. When I turn back around, Nacht has Koji over his shoulder and is coming at me quickly.

"This way," he orders, catching my left bicep in his big hand to tow me along toward the far end of the narrow chamber. A dull, blue glow emanates from a small crack in the wall. As we move toward it, I realize that not only is it an actual passage— narrower than the entryway, of course—but there are additional cells carved into the rooms. These actually have live bodies in them. These people are conscious and groaning, their bodies hunched and their eyes wild. They've all been here awhile, but they've been well-taken care of.

"Do not look," Nacht says. There's an urgency to his voice that begs me to follow his directions without complaint. I lower my head and cast my gaze at his heels, but not before something terrifyingly familiar catches my attention.

It's a pattern. A simple set of colorful, granny square rows. It could be any crocheted afghan anywhere in any world, but it's the specific color pattern that drags my feet to a halt in the middle of the passage and pulls me toward the locked door in front of it. Dread coalesces in the pit of my stomach like a malignant seed, radiating fingers of horror outward as a series of memories flash through my mind in rapid succession.

A split thread.

A shout.

Screaming.

A thump.

Blood on the living room floor.

The heap of cloth lying on the floor of this particular cage is the blanket Aunt Margaret made for my dad for Christmas when I was little. The alternating rows of orange, brown, and green are meant to reflect fall colors and match the woods where we'd go hiking all those years ago. I used to love it, but now the sight of it turns my stomach.

It represents every single thing I lost, and the split corner, hastily tied back together in a rough knot confirms everything.

"Alice, come," Nacht orders, but I can't. I move

closer, narrowing my eyes in the dim light to take in the details.

Why would this blanket be here of all places? I haven't seen it since the night Mom died. I always assumed he burned it when he burned her clothes.

A whimper escapes my throat, and the tattered lump of cloth moves. The body inside groans. My heart beats sickly in my chest, knowing what I'm about to see but refusing to accept it as reality.

No, no, no, no, no… this can't be. No. NO!

The bundle shifts, and a dirty face floats into view. It's thinner than I remember, the hair longer and the eyes duller, but they fixate on me as intelligently as they did when I was a small child. Gone is the anger and hatred, the cloud of whiskey vapor, and the air of intense malice. My brain can't keep up as I look into my father's face.

"Dad…?"

Those clear, blue eyes widen with recognition and his mouth falls open.

"…Alice?"

And then, I'm airborne again.

My mind is such a swirling vortex of anxiety that I barely notice the transfer from Nacht's shoulder to Edwin's winged back, except to say that I fight against it while screaming obscenity-riddled, unintelligible nonsense. I am entirely consumed by the violent memory of my father's face, aged and worn, and dirty from his time spent in that cage. His voice isn't rough and angry, but instead wondrously confused.

Next you're going to tell me my father was replaced by a Jabberwocky or something…

As the air rushes past me, the pieces click into place one by one, painting an ugly, painful picture of reality. The man I ran from less than a year ago was not my father. The man in the cage *is*.

"We have to go back! We have to save him! Save him!" But someone holds tight to my waist, pinning me in place as we soar through the darkening sky. I scream, my throat raw and ruined, my body heavy from exertion yet pulled taught with anxiety and adrenaline. The flash of surprise in his expression plays through my mind over and over and over again. I fall absolutely to pieces.

Then I'm placed on a sofa inside the abandoned Rabbit Hole.

Strong arms wrap around me, and I'm dragged into the familiar warmth of Ivan's embrace. He holds me close to his chest, stroking my hair like I'm a child as tears I didn't realize I was crying roll down my face. Years of pent-up frustration and heartbreak flow out of me, leaving my already exhausted body lethargic and lost, and my heart shattered into a million tiny, sparkling shards.

I don't know how long I sit there and cry. When the tears finally stop falling, my whole being is spent. Ivan and Jerome have a conversation over my head, but at this point I'm so empty that I can't follow along. Koji is alive. My father is here. And I am helpless to do anything else for either of them, as much as I want to.

My skin aches when Ivan uses his sleeve to wipe away the remaining dampness from my cheeks. I cough, then hiccup. Someone pushes water into my hand and I drink it. I hiccup again.

"Welcome back, Majesty," Ivan says in my ear and carefully lifts me into his arms. His voice is warm and affectionate, which only causes emotion to well up again. "Time to go." He brings me back through the looking glass, then carefully places me on the edge of my bed. Around his large frame, I see Nacht carry Koji out of my room with Talon and Felina close on his heels. A pained gasp sounds, and that's the point when I realize my room is full of familiar people.

Jerome quickly fills those waiting in on the details while I lay back at Ivan's urging.

"Don't...tell my sister..." I manage to squeak out before I close my eyes and let the lethargy of sleep drag me under.

CHAPTER EIGHTEEN

When I wake up, it's to the sound of arguing voices in the next room. My head and body are heavy from sleep and from exertion, so I'm not immediately aware of who's speaking, or what any of the words actually mean. I listen from my foggy stupor, trying to make sense of anything they're saying, but it doesn't work. There are a lot of voices and they're all talking over one other. *Yelling* over one another, actually.

I'm honestly not even sure I'm awake at this point, because it feels more like dream nonsense than reality. Not that anything here is ever something beyond nonsense.

But then all the voices stop.

"Oh, she's awake," one of them says.

Next thing I know, someone is brushing the hair away from my face with gentle fingertips. I struggle to open my eyes, and as soon as my gaze focuses on the sharp planes of Percival Rand's face hovering above me, every alert and alarm in my body begins to scream.

I struggle and scramble backwards away from his dangling hand until my back hits the padded headboard. My heart hammers in my chest, and my entire body breaks out in a cold sweat.

"What the hell are you doing in my room?" I ask, sounding just as hysterical as I feel through my clipped, panting breaths.

"I am simply caring for my Queen," he replies with that wicked, snarky smirk on his lips. "Am I not allowed to show concern for my lovely wife?"

"You'd only show concern if it got you close enough to find a good place to stick a knife," I retort and draw in a deep lungful of air. The room smells of tea and the acrid, metallic undertone of blood, mixed with the sweet scent of the Caterpillar's smoke. The Carpenter stands in the doorway, grinning at me like he wants to eat me—and not in the happy, fun way, mind you—and somewhere behind him, someone sighs.

It's Tag who comes to my rescue.

"Let her up, now," he says, his voice stern, but calm and even. His big hand lands on Percival's shoulder and urges him away. The way the fabric of his shirt crinkles under those long fingers says that there's enough force to remind even a King that this request is not optional. The vision of this mini-war reminds me yet again just how glad I am that the twins are on my side.

The standoff comes to an end, and Percival rises. My breath leaves in a rush, and I collapse in on myself, my shoulders rolling forward toward my rising knees. The one good thing is that I am completely and utterly *awake*. There's no doubt at all that I have nine additional people in my room.

Tag pushes the pair out and closes the door behind them, then comes to stand beside the bed silently, watching me as I calm the panic raging through my body. When I finally uncoil and look up, he offers a gentle smile and a hand. It hangs there between us patiently. He doesn't force me up and he doesn't demand anything of me. He simply waits. Once the shaking in my hands stops, I place my palm against his and allow him to help me stand. Every muscle in my body is sore, but Tag holds onto me until I'm steady on my feet.

"Perhaps you'd like to wash up and change your clothes?" he asks, glancing down the length of my body at...

Holy shit.

I'm still covered in the Cheshire Cat's blood. It has darkened over the hours; a brutal wine color leaning toward black. The fabric of my shirt is stiff and now that I'm looking at it, my skin itches where patches of the substance have dried on. It's a nauseating reminder of everything that happened.

"I-is he—"

"Alive," Tag confirms. "Sleeping. He lost quite

a bit of blood."

I sag against him, allowing the lighter twin to take my full weight for a moment while I let his words sink in. Koji is alive. I did it. I saved him. But that revelation has the potential to lead me down a very dark path of thought. One I'm not quite ready to explore yet.

After several long minutes, I regain control of myself and my legs and push off of Tag's chest. He holds my shoulders until he's certain I'm going to remain upright, then pulls his hands back.

"Wash up, Majesty," he says. "I will wait for you."

A shower sounds like a lovely idea. I retrieve comfortable clothes from my armoire and slip into the bathroom, locking the door behind me for good measure. I *mostly* trust Tag not to sneak in...but there are others in the next room who I *don't* trust not to show up unannounced.

The water is heavenly, though the first thirty seconds or so are frightening as the layers of dirt and mud slough off of my skin, mixing into a sickening slurry against the white marble backdrop before sliding down the drain. It's not the first time I've had to wash the aftermath of battle from my skin, but this particular fight just feels much more personal.

For one, the Red Queen nearly took Koji from me. The cat she swore to love and protect...and she tossed him to the Jabberwocky like he was worth nothing at all. The realization angers me to the point where I can feel my blood boiling in my veins. The shower is hot, but it feels like steam is coming out of my ears as I scrub my skin clean.

I'm still mad as hell when I smack the handle down to kill the spray. The mirror is cloudy enough that I can't see my reflection, so I haven't the foggiest idea whether I'm actually steaming like a teapot or not.

By the time I dry myself off, move through all the finicky parts of personal hygiene, and dress, I feel like half an eternity has passed. It feels good to be clean. My rattled nerves are somewhat soothed. My muscles don't hurt from the exertion. Even the rope burns on my wrists have lightened to the point where I have to look hard to see them. Yet I don't want to open the bathroom door, because it means I have to face whatever comes next in this weird as fuck reality.

Tag leads me to the sitting room where I look around at my assembled guests while he stuffs a teacup into my hands.

"How is Koji?" I ask again, hoping for more of an update than I got from Tag. Talon offers a small smile while the skin around Aeromi's eyes tightens.

"Healing well, Majesty," the Caterpillar says. "Resting in his room. You saved his life."

"That you did," Edwin adds with a broad grin. "Truly exceptional, you are." Something is off about him. His tone isn't… him. It doesn't sit quite right with me.

"What has gone wrong since then?"

Edwin blinks at me and Aeromi gasps. It's a tiny sound, but it tells me I'm right to ask. Phineas also makes a strange sound; almost like *he's* hesitant to tell me the truth. He has *never* hesitated to tell me anything, even the worst of the worst news.

"What is it?" I ask when I realize nobody is going to elaborate. I mentally tick down the list of outstanding fuckery in the hopes that something will click into place. "Has Humphrey moved again? Do we have news of Orvice's wife? Or is it because the Red Queen thinks Koji is a traitor?"

Edwin tenses.

"Right field, Majesty," Percival says. "Wrong sport."

"What?"

"It is not Koji the Red Queen thinks a traitor," Nacht says, clearly tiring of the hesitation, "but Lord Edwin. After your…rather wondrous display at Blackrock, she believes she has you cornered. You see, Queen Lucinda still believes our darling pussycat is innocent of all charges save being bait dangled in front of this court in order. She believes she truly has placed her double agent at *our* Queen's side."

"It's true," Aeromi says. "My sister is horribly paranoid, but she believes she has cornered you,

Majesty." She swallows, like the next part is going to be bad. And it probably is. "The fact that the Jabberwocky have reported Lord Edwin's assistance to the Alice means he is no longer welcome in the Red Court." She sighs. "This… this is my fault." Her voice is tiny and afraid. "I never should have come to you about Koji."

"Absolutely not," Edwin replies, indignant. "You speak as if I have no agency of my own." He huffs, then clears his throat. "The Cheshire Cat is *not* expendable, Duchess." Edwin turns his gaze toward me. "This development just gives me a reason to do away with my fool of a brother once and for all."

I choose to ignore the bloodlust sparkling in his eyes with that statement. I've had enough death for one day. Of course, my mind immediately goes to my own sister. I would do anything in the world for her… but it's not like that for everyone. This is a stark reminder of that fact. It also reminds me of another thing I'd forgotten to announce in the chaos of Koji's rescue.

"Lord Edwin, would you please hold out your hand for me?"

"Certainly, Majesty." He does so without hesitation. He doesn't even question my motives. I'm not sure whether to call that loyalty or foolishness. Probably some of both.

I pull my key from around my neck and work the tiny, gold replica beside it off the ring. The movement gains the attention of everyone at the table, which makes me feel super self-conscious as I hold it up in front of me.

"I suppose this means you're officially one of us," I say.

Edwin splutters, his gaze tripping back and forth between the key and my face. His mouth opens and closes several times while he works to gather his thoughts. Then he pauses and sighs.

"When I learned the news of my eviction from the Red Court, I'd hoped to seek refuge with my allies." He pauses, looking like he's searching for the right words. "I... I never dreamed the welcome would be quite this warm." He dabs at one eye with a handkerchief. "It is a fortuitous development, particularly since my army is currently en route to Wonderland Castle's barracks as a peace offering."

The smile he offers is as bright as the sun, and I find myself smiling back at him as I reach over Phineas and drop the key into Edwin's palm.

"I'm glad you'll be joining us on a more permanent basis."

"There is nowhere else in this crazy land I'd rather be, Majesty."

"How sweet a scene it is," Percival says, mock-sniffling and wiping his completely dry eyes.

"Shut up, asshole," I reply, to which he laughs. "No key for you. You keep threatening to kill me."

"That I do," he admits with a good-humored chuckle. "But not yet. This discussion has been quite enlightening. You, my darling Queen, are still very useful."

"Didn't I tell you to shut up?"

"Yes."

"So shut up."

"As you wish, Majesty."

The dickhead winks at me but doesn't say anything else. I roll my eyes as loudly as I possibly can, sigh, and then turn back to Edwin.

"Shall I show you to your room, Lord Edwin?"

"Her Majesty honors me with such an offer and I would be a fool not to accept."

I wobble when I stand, but Phineas' hand under my elbow steadies me. He offers a kind smile before allowing his hand to slide down my forearm and catch my fingers. He brings them to his lips and kisses my knuckles gently, then offers me a wink as he releases my hand. My face heats up, as it always does when he flirts, and I have to focus so my knees don't buckle.

Then Edwin is beside me, and I thread my arm through his offered elbow for support. Both Rabbits rise and follow as we move into the hallway, and I marvel at how long it has grown. Decorated doors line both sides, and Edwin's is at the very end, nearest the outer door.

"Thank you, Majesty," Edwin says softly as we walk, "truly. Not just for this, but for everything you've done."

His sincerity leaves me speechless. I nod and

continue walking, but the silence between us doesn't feel right. He deserves a response, but none of the words in my head are adequate. This man has lost so much — *everything*, as it were — to help my cause. That sacrifice deserves respect.

"I am truly grateful that you are on my side in this war," I say, though the words feel choppy. "I hope I am worthy of your sacrifices."

Edwin tugs me to a stop in the middle of the hall and turns to face me. His big hands close around the sides of my face, and he looks down at me with all the sternness of a father about to reprimand a child.

"Understand this if nothing else, Majesty," he says, and I catch the flash of… not anger, exactly. Frustration, maybe? — in his eyes. "You. Are. Worthy. Of all of this and more." The hard lines of his expression soften into an indulgent smile. "If only you could see yourself the way the rest of us see you. Your pure heart. Your tenacity. You, darling Alice, are so much more than we ever hoped for."

Tears slip down my face. These people and their faith in me is both humbling and empowering. Terrifying. He tugs me forward and kisses my head the way my father used to, which only makes the raw emotions swell more. His arms close around me while I cry into his shoulder. I can't help it. Hearing praise from Jerome and Ivan are one thing, but to hear a man that's supposed to be one of my greatest enemies treat me like I'm a precious treasure… it's too much.

When I finally regain control of myself and pull back, he's smiling the sweetest smile.

"Any number of people in Wonderland would do any number of things to protect a heart as pure as yours, Majesty. *We* are fortunate that you've chosen to share your power with us."

"I'm afraid your faith in me is misplaced," I admit as he curls his arm around my shoulders and we start walking again. "It's like…" I try to breathe through my suddenly runny nose and end up coughing out a hard breath. A handkerchief appears in front of my face, and I take it from Edwin's fingers with a smile. "It's like I'm playing a game that I don't know the rules to, and I'm scared I'm going to mess up."

"Fear is what keeps us focused, Majesty," he says. "Without fear, we become complacent. And complacency is when atrocities abound. So long as you remain fearful, you remain powerful. Do not *ever* let anyone rob you of your power."

"Are you afraid, Lord Edwin?"

"Every day of my life, love. My people are currently without a leader, and I do not trust my brother to protect them properly. Their lives are mine to guard, and I cannot guard effectively when the price on my own head is death."

We arrive at his door. Edwin places the tiny key into the lock and it swings inward just as my door opens and Aeromi steps out. She looks a bit frayed around the edges and freezes when she sees us at the other end of the hall.

"Duchess," Edwin calls across the open area, "care to join us for a quiet moment?"

"Absolutely," she replies on a relieved exhale. "They're trying to kill each other in there again."

Jerome and Ivan snort to cover their laughter, but their combined amusement in my head causes me to snicker.

"That's nothing new," I tell her. "Those idiots are always fighting over something."

"Yeah, well right now they're fighting over who's more loyal to you. Strangely enough, I think the Carpenter may be winning the argument."

"That is terrifying."

Once Aeromi catches up to us, we move into Edwin's new room. I'm not surprised to find a Spartan setup: bed, desk, chair, lamp, sofa, empty bookshelf. Nothing else. Maybe it's just because he hasn't officially moved in yet, but it feels like this is pretty close to how he actually lives.

"Yes," he says, glancing around, "this will do nicely." He turns and looks down at me again with that same sweet smile. "Thank you again, Majesty." He places a fist over his heart and bows formally. "I am your weapon to wield."

Appreciated as that announcement is…

"I'd much rather you just be my friend."

A surprisingly boyish grin splits his face. "That was a foregone conclusion, love."

When Aeromi and I exit Edwin's room, the twins escort Percival out of the suite. The remaining members of my court return to their own rooms, all pausing to acknowledge me in some way. Even my Rabbits offer wishes for a good night before moving to their own rooms.

"Should we check on our cat?" I ask, and she nods.

"I hoped you'd let me see him before I have to leave."

"When you're done, come back here, Duchess," Edwin calls through the open door. "You may stay in my quarters for the time being."

Her gaze flashes to mine, but I nod in agreement. "It's for the best. You're safer here. No offense, but I don't trust your sister at all."

"Neither do I," she admits.

Side by side, we walk back down the hall to the other end, pausing at Koji's door. I suck in a breath, uncertain of what I'm going to find inside. The last memory I have of him is... not good. I don't want to relieve that. But I can't live in this hallway forever. The door swings open, and memories flood me. The heavy scent of tea. The feel of arms closed around my back. The taste of tattooed skin...

A shiver slides across my shoulders as I step inside, noting that the steaming pots of tea are gone, and the room has a sterile, antiseptic smell to it. The low light flickers, drawing my attention. A pair of sconces on either side of the bed light the space enough for me to see the narrow outline of his body under the dark covers. Aeromi sniffles beside me, then reaches out and takes my hand as we move closer. Her fingers tremble against mine.

"I've never seen him this still," she whispers. I feel her anxiety just like it's my own. Maybe it *is* my own I'm feeling. I don't know. Maybe they've intertwined. Either way, my knees nearly knock together by the time we reach the edge of the bed.

He looks... *normal.* The dark rings around his closed eyes are the only indication that he might not be entirely okay. There are no bloody gashes, no scrapes and cuts. The rhythmic rise and fall of his chest is a small relief, but the fact that he doesn't move at all when I perch on the edge of his mattress and lay my hand makes my heart drop into my belly.

"How is he really?" I ask. I reach out to touch him but hesitate. Images of him bleeding out under my hands flash through my mind. The memory of his wheezing breath and weakening heartbeat rattles through me, and I reach out for that connection to prove to myself that he's alive.

Koji's skin is warm under my fingers; his heartbeat is strong and steady. But he also doesn't respond to my touch. He has *never* not responded to my touch. I pull my other hand free of Aeromi's death-grip and reach up to wipe the tears from my face.

"The Caterpillar says he's going to live," she whispers. "There will be physical scars, but he's alive." She inhales sharply through her nose, and the breath stutters out between her parted lips. The Duchess sits facing me, her knees against mine, and reaches out to brush Koji's hair away from his face. "But the one thing they can't tell me is when he'll wake up. Or *if* he will."

It was the same with Haigha, but my heart still plummets. We worked to fix him, but there was no guarantee he would come back. It was different with him, though. Haigha was a stranger when it happened. Koji is…

Mine.

My heart cracks and emotions bleed out. My breath hitches.

"He will come back, Majesty," Aeromi announces, but it sounds like she's trying to convince herself of the fact as much as she is me. "He *has* to come back. We need him."

I need him.

The raw vulnerability in my mind's confession rips a sob from my throat. Arms go around me and I'm pulled into a warm embrace. The clothes under my cheek smell of sugar and summer rain, and gentle fingers trill up along my spine, trying to comfort me. The gesture is sweet, but it does little to soothe my tattered soul.

"He will come back to us," Aeromi whispers against my ear. She tightens her hold on me, hugging me close, then gently pushes me back into an upright position. "While we wait, we need to figure out our plan."

"You're right." My voice is like gravel, my throat raw and parched from my tears. I cough, sniffle, and wipe my face with the heel of my free hand. "We need to figure this out." I glance at Koji, still asleep, and shift my fingers to curl under his palm. "What can you tell me about the Red Army now that Edwin is no longer part of it?"

Aeromi shifts her posture to lean back against the wall. The way she settles in says it's going to be a long night.

"Morcar's brutality is legendary. He's the kill-first-and-don't-bother-to-ask-questions type. Edwin, though quite beastly, is infinitely more reasonable than his brother. The Earl of Northumbria will kill everyone and leave nothing but scorched earth in his wake."

"I believe that." The memory of the giant, angry Jabberwocky in the woods makes me shudder. "What do we do about it?"

"As much as it pains me to say this, I believe Morcar is best left to his brother. There is nothing you or I can do to stop him, no matter how badly we might want to." Aeromi strokes Koji's forehead gently, like a worried mother. "May I speak freely, Majesty?"

"Of course. I would have it no other way."

"You and I need no secrets between us, Majesty,

if we have any hope of surviving." The look she shoots my way is hard and cold. Ruthless. The complete opposite of how she looked at Koji. "My sister is the most dangerous thing in this upside-down world. I will do my utmost to protect you, but I need your trust."

"It's yours," I say without hesitation, though I probably *should* hesitate a little. Trusting her feels as natural as breathing and her aura is as clear and bright as a Rabbit's. There are no red flags beyond her affiliation with the Red Court, yet for the first time since coming to Wonderland, I find myself questioning whether the magic would lie to me or not.

"Thank you, Majesty," she replies, and her gaze falls away. "Because I have a confession."

Uh oh...

"I want you to hear it from me before he wakes—"

Oh, no. No, no, no... don't... don't say it...

"It was my idea to send Koji to the Jabberwocky."

Fuck.

My mouth falls open. I can do nothing but stare at her, dumbfounded. How... how could she?

"I swear to you, Majesty, it was not my intention to see him harmed!" Tears stream down her face. A shaking hand reaches toward me, halts, then curls against her chest as a sob tears out of her throat.

Pure rage fills me, and magic rises to meet its level, swirling in a vortex of fury. My vision goes red; darkens at the edges. His on mistress nearly sent him to Koji death... for what? To win brownie points with her psychopath of a sister? My hair lifts from my shoulders, caught in the cascade of anger. Raw electricity crackles at my fingertips. It would be nothing to reach over and...

"If I had known what she would do to him just for being near you, I never would have let it happen!"

The devastation in her voice stops me dead. The rage falls away. The magic recedes, taking with it my breath.

What the fuck did I almost do?

I glance between Koji and Aeromi, then close my eyes and drag in a breath that goes down like shattered glass. It stutters out of me, but it also helps to clear my head. I'm still... *angry* isn't quite the right word. I certainly have anger, but the way my heart constricts also feels a lot like grief.

"Did...did you know my father was down there?"

Her gaze falls. "I didn't know, but I suspected."

That feels more like a sucker punch than the knowledge that she sent Koji to his doom.

"I need you to explain all of this to me. And use small words."

And she does. Over the next hour and a half, Aeromi lays out the plans of the Red Court in startling detail, beginning when her sister decided the best way to remove the threat of Liddel blood returning to Wonderland would be to eradicate the entire family. I listen to the story of how her agents sent a high-ranking officer from the Jabberwocky Corps to Otherland to abduct my father, leaving an assassin in his place. Lucky for me—relatively speaking given my mother's fate—the assassin wasn't very good at his job and developed a taste for Otherland vices. He reported my mother's death but left the details ambiguous enough that Queen Lucinda believed us all dead.

"Why did she keep him alive, though?" I ask as the story draws to a close. "Why not just kill him too?"

"Lucinda is vain, Majesty," she says. "She loves a trophy nearly as much as she loves precious jewels and cherry tarts. Capturing The Alice's father was the ultimate trophy."

That...makes sense. I don't like it, but it's an absolutely believable story. If this woman is at all as mad as everyone says she is, then every bit of this story is exactly what I should have expected from the start.

"And how, exactly, did you end up sacrificing your own cat?"

Her cheeks flush and she looks away again. I swallow hard against the lump rising in my throat and tell myself I'm not going to annihilate her before she explains herself. She's been forthcoming enough, but it takes all my willpower to keep from doing something stupid right here and now.

"Koji and I discussed it, and we thought it best if we share information to make it seem like he's still on her side. She's always been partial to him, but I didn't expect the news that he'd gotten so close to enrage her the way it did." It's her turn to swallow whatever's crawling up her throat. Aeromi won't look at me. "The little braggart let slip that he'd shared your bed."

Oh, for fuck's sake... though the revelation isn't all that surprising. Koji's favorite game thus far *has* been to use me as a weapon to ruffle feathers. And for a woman who prides herself on her trophies, losing one to the enemy would be the ultimate sucker punch.

"Will she try to kill him again?"

"No," Aeromi says matter-of-factly. "That was a punishment, but it also gave her results in the form of Lord Edwin. She's had enough cruelty to satisfy her sadism for a moment."

"Well, that's good...I guess."

"It means we have time." She reaches out and brushes Koji's hair away from his sleeping face one more time, then bends and kisses the spot she cleared. "Get some rest, Majesty. We'll get through this as long as we stick together."

Aeromi rises with the same fluid grace Koji carries and straightens her skirt that doesn't need straightening. As she passes, she pats my shoulder gently.

The door *snicks* closed behind her, and I'm left looking at the sleeping cat. He looks so peaceful. So innocent. So *not* nearly dead. The tears come again and I let them slide over my cheeks freely. My heart hurts, both for the man in front of me and for the man I left behind.

My father is alive. I have a chance to get him back. I might be able to salvage *something* of my family... but right now, I'm exhausted despite the fact that I've only been awake for a few hours. Heaviness settles into my extremities, and instead of going back to my room, I lift Koji's limp arm and curl up at his side. The steady thump of his heart under my ear calms me, and it's not long before I fall asleep.

I go from sleeping peacefully at Koji's side to airborne so abruptly that I scream.

"Oh, don't be so dramatic," I'm told as I'm thrown over a shoulder like a sack of potatoes. My scrambled, panicked brain whirls and spins and takes entirely too long to put the pieces together and tell me the voice belongs to Nacht. There aren't many in my court who would manhandle me like this, and the fact that he's doing it *again*...

Well, I suppose I can't be *too* angry at him for this since he has saved my life more than once in the last forty-eight hours. Once my racing heart slows enough to speak without puking down his back, I turn my head and look at where we're going.

His long strides have already taken us out of the suite and into one of the lesser-used corridors. Cobwebs adorn the artwork on the walls and the carpet runner under Nacht's feet still has that dull, half-asleep look to it. There's a slight crunch with each footfall, and the air is colder here.

"Where are you taking me?" I ask because I have no idea where we even are.

"Training," he says. "Caterpillar's orders."

"I can walk, you know."

"More efficient this way."

I sigh and settle in, letting him carry me like the good little sack of potatoes I've become. I'm not sure if I'd call this gallantry or misogyny, but here we are. I'm over his shoulder and there's nothing I can do about it.

When he finally puts me down, it's an un-ceremonial drop to my ass on a very hard floor in a *very* cold room. There are two vaguely person-shaped dummies at one end, and Talon stands next to me, looking phenomenally unruffled. I'm sure, given the fact that I was snatched out of a dead sleep less than ten minutes ago, that I look like some kind of bog witch by comparison.

"Good morning, Majesty," he says with a deferential nod of his head while I climb to my feet and rub at my sore tailbone. "Or should I say *good afternoon* as it is well on the way to dinnertime? Shall we begin?"

"Begin what, exactly?"

"Surely Master Tweed shared our itinerary with you?"

"He said something about training after he tossed me over his shoulder and brought me here against my will, but that was it. Care to fill me in on the purpose of this abduction?"

Nope.

"Let us begin."

I don't even get an answer...lovely. It's going to be a great day, I guess. No coffee, no tea, no breakfast *or* lunch, no shower...not even a toothbrush. What I do get is Talon's hands on my shoulders as he bodily moves me into position.

"What are we—"

"Knock down the target," he says.

The post-and-hay target standing roughly forty feet from me looks almost comical. It's canted to one side, the wooden left "arm" significantly lower than the right. Straw pokes out of the sack which comprises its head, and someone has seen fit to draw a lopsided smile onto it. I almost feel guilty about beating it up.

I toe off my socks and kick them somewhere behind me. The motion earns a snicker from Nacht, who in turn earns a glare from me. I get the feeling he's doing everything in his power to rile me up, and it's working. I'm highly annoyed already. And more than a little hangry.

"Focus, Majesty," Talon says, pulling me back to center by dropping his hands to my waist. He's also great at getting under my skin, but he does at least know how to be serious when it's required. I nod, then close my eyes and take a deep breath.

The magical currents rise much easier here than they did inside the mountain, and that first touch of raw energy inside me sends a familiar shiver up my spine. I stand for a moment and let the swirl consume me, infusing itself into every part of my body. My blood and skin warm and the lethargy of interrupted sleep recedes, leaving only a gentle, blue glow inside my mind. Taking mental stock of my body, I note no damage beyond superficial bruising, and Talon's hands on my sides are a bright spot ringed in a dark outline. He's not helping; just observing.

I open my eyes, my vision ringed by the shimmer of magic, and shape my hands as I was taught — one up and one to the side, fingers curled to help focus my intent. Casting my gaze away from the awkwardly adorable face, I focus on the barrel that comprises the dummy's chest and draw pure energy into the space between my hands.

Just as I prepare to let the attack fly, my vision morphs and the face of the Mock Turtle appears, mouth wrenched open in shock in the half a breath before my attack landed, and I feel the magic buckle. The training dummy explodes in a rain of hay and splinters. Talon and Nacht take cover, throwing their arms over their heads as they dive behind larger pieces of training equipment. The magical fireball is so out of control that it singes a cometlike streak down the center of the training room's floor before fizzling out near the far wall. Bits of hay and wood rain down on Talon and me.

"He told you to knock it down, little one," Nacht says as he stands, "not destroy it."

"At least I hit the target," I answer, matching my glare to his amused grin.

"Your aim has improved," Talon cuts in, and when I turn he's completely unruffled. "Now, you learn to control your power."

"I haven't had that happen in awhile," I admit through a shudder.

"You saw him again?"

I nod and swallow around the lump lodged in my throat. "I don't like being reminded that I'm a murderer."

"And yet, that is a title you must live with," Talon replies. His tone is gentle, but his words are not. He doesn't baby me. Never has. I appreciate that. "You must train yourself not to react to the memory. Always keep your focus on the present, or your past will consume you."

It's good advice. But good advice is rarely something I follow.

He waves his hand and a new training dummy appears in the middle of the carnage that was the first. "Start again."

I take a deep breath to clear my head, plant my feet, and move my body into position. As the magic gathers between my hands, Talon steps behind me again, curving his arms around mine. When he speaks, the words sound inside my head rather than out loud.

"Forget about the past. Focus on the target. Let the magic tell you when it is strong enough. Lead it. Do not let it lead you."

Same as last time, awful images intrude, but Talon's nearness and his voice echoing through my mind remind me to keep myself focused. I swallow the bile rising in my throat and return my attention to the fireball in my hands.

"Open your eyes."

I do. The hazy, blue glow of magic rings my vision, but the target is clear in the center. I follow his instructions.

Focus on the target. Feel the magic. Release.

The fireball flies true, exploding against the barrel-chest of the dummy and knocking it over. A scorch mark is the only real damage when the currents and smoke clear, and a sense of accomplishment fills me.

"Remember that timing," Talon says out loud. "Your skill has improved considerably, Majesty."

"Don't get cocky," Nacht says and steps in front of me. "The remaining King and Queen of these gods-forsaken lands will not topple as easily as a wooden dummy. Keep your wits about you and you *may* live."

"I'm aware," I reply. "Believe me, I'm well aware I'm not strong enough for this."

"Contrariwise, I never said her Majesty was not strong enough," Nacht continues. "A bit wild and unrefined in her ways, perhaps, but also... rich in muchness."

I think that's a compliment?

"Thanks," I mutter, a little bashful under his watchful gaze.

"Once more," Talon announces, taking me by the shoulders and returning me to position. "This time without assistance."

I manage to hit the target five of the next seven attempts, which seems to please him. By the time he releases me from this particular lesson, I'm well awake and pleasantly exhausted. My whole body is warm from the magical currents, and for the first time in a long time, I feel like I may actually have what it takes to be a proper Queen.

Unfortunately, the Caterpillar refuses to let me get comfortable.

"Your next lesson begins now," Talon says. He smiles, turns, and plunges a dagger deep into Nacht's belly. "Do not let him die."

The blade exits as smoothly as it entered, and Nacht, with barely a grunt, stands and watches as wetness darkens the black fabric of his shirt. I stare at the damp bloom in utter shock. This impenetrable trickster is... wounded? It just doesn't compute.

"Majesty," Nacht says, and I look up into his face. The ashen tone to his brown skin is the only indication that something is wrong. "Not to rush you, but… if you would?"

I look back down, and it's ultimately the blue-green blood dripping onto the floor from the hand clutched around his wound that brings me back. Urgency fills my chest as the dripping intensifies. I take a step forward and pause. I'm still exhausted from my attempt at saving Koji and today's training and I… I really don't know what to do.

"Help me," I ask Talon. "I don't know how to do this the right way."

"You saved the cat, did you not?"

"Barely."

"Almost destroyed herself in the process," Nacht mutters through clenched teeth.

"Show me how you did this before," Talon says, watching me with those swirling, laser eyes. I nod and move closer to Nacht.

The magic is easier to draw up in here since there isn't a whole-ass mountain in the way and comes eagerly when I call it. I lay one hand against his belly, covering the open wound and feeling the warm pulse of blood as it pushes out of his body, then place my other hand along his waist to steady both him and myself.

I'm not used to willingly being this close to Nacht and, unsurprisingly, it makes me nervous. This man is absolutely lethal in so many ways. He's also a whole lot more aware of his surroundings and what I'm doing than Koji was, so the expectancy level is much higher. I meet his gaze and he nods. A thin line of sweat has sprung up on his forehead.

I nod back and close my eyes, willing the magic forward. It reacts much the same way it did the first time, seeping into the open crevice and illuminating the raw edges of the wound. I'm vaguely aware of Talon's hand when it presses between my shoulderblades, but I'm *very* aware of his consciousness twining with mine while he watches the magical currents.

I will never, ever get used to the feeling of having someone else inside my body with me like that.

Reminding myself to focus, I turn my attention back to the dull, blue glow in my brain, pulsing in the shape of the wound in Nacht's stomach. It hasn't hit anything vital—not like Koji's collapsed lung—but it's bleeding pretty steadily.

The source is… there. An artery nicked by the blade.

Nacht's heart rate is way up. I can feel the fear inside him. That startles me more than the amount of blood he's losing. Until this moment, I didn't think it was possible for this man to be afraid of anything.

He's afraid of dying, I tell myself. *Don't let him die.*

Turning my focus back to the wound, I find the edges of the artery and push my energy into them, willing them to knit cleanly. It takes a good bit of pushing and tugging, but the raw meat eventually starts to move, pulling together and reconnecting itself. It's messy, and it draws so much of me out that my legs begin to shake, My knees go weak, like they're going to buckle and pitch me to the ground. My head buzzes and pain flares between my eyes.

"Stop," Talon says, his voice crystal clear both inside my head and beside my ear. It's so easy to let the thread of magic go that I nearly collapse — would were Talon's arm not around my waist. Nacht grunts in pain, his half-healed wound still bleeding, though not nearly as badly. "You've the right idea, but the wrong method," the Caterpillar instructs.

I open my eyes and glance up at him, my head lolling against his shoulder as weakness overcomes me. He guides me gently to the floor, pulling my back against his chest to cradle me in his arms. Nacht kneels beside us, hand clutched to his stomach. I notice through the fog that he doesn't look as pale, which seems like it would be a good sign. But it's hard to hold onto any kind of thought as the edges of my vision waver.

"You are using your own life to heal," Talon says. His voice is gentle in my ear, and my body is warm where his arms lay around me. "You are sacrificing yourself, Majesty. You can only give so much of yourself before there is nothing left for you."

That makes sense.

"Come with me and learn." He takes one of my hands in his and, drawing magic through me and into himself, places his other hand against Nacht's skin. I close my eyes and through that connection watch and feel the way the currents move around the wound. It doesn't pull itself together in the clumsy way it did for me but rather melts back into itself like the knife never even happened.

With Talon it feels different. Moves differently. The difference is that he's manipulating the magic itself. He's not giving his own life force... not that I realized what I was doing as I was doing it... but still.

"Try through me," he says, holding the magic in place while I attempt to reach out for it. I follow the current through my fingers to his, up his arm, and out into Nacht's body where I find it pooled in anticipation. It's warm and gentle, unlike the frenetic mass gathered at my will. "It's waiting for you. Tell it what to do."

I nod and, tapping into it, ask the magic to continue healing the wound. To let it melt together. To repair itself and Nacht. In a matter of minutes, the wound is gone and only smooth skin remains. I'm the one with beads of sweat on my forehead now.

"Very good, Majesty," Talon says and draws the magic back. I release my hold on it and, despite the fact that I feel very much like jelly, I feel strangely refreshed. Like the healing power somehow transferred to me on its way out.

Nacht collapses flat on his back, a sigh of relief floating upward. I, on the other hand, really, *really* want another nap.

CHAPTER NINETEEN

The throne room of Wonderland Castle is tense. There aren't many guests, which leaves a whole lot of time for *just us*. Percival sits beside me, lost in his own thoughts while both Rabbits and twins stand still as statues. Edwin and Aeromi are nervous, and rightfully so. Edwin's army was expected to arrive hours ago. He has just about paced a hole in the floor despite the fact that I've already dispatched a pair of scouts to look for them.

It's doubly strange this morning since both Blade and Talon have removed themselves from the palace in an attempt to fill the informational void left by Koji, and as far as I'm aware, they're on the hunt for Orvice's missing wife. Orvice himself is up and about in the infirmary, which was good news this morning. He's pretty beat up, but the healers tell me he'll make a full recovery. Now if we can find Estrella and reunite them, I'll be happy. So will he.

We continue to wait in strained silence until the ticking of the clock in the hall threatens to drive me mad. My eyes swing from side to side with each distinct *tick* and *tock*, putting me in mind of that old black-and-white cat clock my grandmother used to keep in her kitchen. If I had a tail, it would probably be swinging, too.

Some indeterminate amount of time later, after I'm far beyond ready to climb the walls and Edwin has gone from simply pacing to pacing *and* growling, the doors swing open and in steps one of our scouts with a dirt-caked, bloodstained soldier clinging to him for support. The strangled sound from Aeromi and the breathless curse from Edwin are signal enough.

This is one of his men.

The twins are already at his side, assisting him up the aisle and into a seat. He's exhausted, but doesn't appear to be badly injured. I get the feeling the blood isn't his.

"I apologize for the tardiness, Lord," he says, and attempts a formal bow from a seated position. "We…were ambushed not far from the border of Mercia. Lord Morcar, Sire… he…"

"Let me guess," Edwin half-snarls, "my brute of a brother set my army upon itself." The soldier nods, then lets his head hang. "How many?"

"Roughly a quarter of the army turned, Sire. I've no idea how many are dead."

"Are there more of you?"

"Yes, Sire. Scattered throughout the hills and the wood. Waiting, as planned."

Edwin lets go a string of curses to rival any American sailor, and when he turns to face me, the blend of grief and fury in his eyes would cause me to take a step back if I weren't already seated.

"Go," I tell him. "Take the Oysters with you."

"They'll never make it in time," Percival says from beside me and I startle. I'd forgotten he was there. "Morcar will hunt down and kill every last Red soldier who doesn't swear fealty to him."

"That is… regrettably true," Edwin agrees.

"What about the Looking Glass?" Torai suggests, and every head in the room swivels toward him. "It would take a fair amount of time to move an entire army through a single glass, but it would be infinitely faster and safer than a forced march."

Also true.

"Torai."

"Yes, Majesty?"

"How long before you can mobilize the Oysters?"

"We shall be ready to depart by this afternoon."

"Good. We'll bring the Looking Glass down to the courtyard when you're ready."

Torai and Edwin bow and depart together with Aeromi on their heels, taking the Red soldier with them. My remaining companions all turn to me, a mix of concern and curiosity etched into the lines of their faces.

"A suggestion, Majesty," Tag says, and I turn my attention to him. "Perhaps it would be prudent to send a deck or two with the fleshlings for support."

Send card soldiers too? It's not a bad idea. We don't know the condition of the Red Army, which means the Oysters *are* going in more or less blind. Any additional support we can send with our allies might be enough to turn the tide of whatever battle they face upon arrival. But only two decks? That would only be two-hundred-four cards. We have two-hundred decks in the castle... surely we can spare more.

"Good idea. Send five decks and a pair of scouts in case they have need of more."

The relief on Edwin's face is immediate. He presses a fist to his chest and bows.

"Thank you, Majesty," is all he manages to say before emotion overwhelms him.

"Go save your people," I reply.

The Earl of Mercia and the Walrus perform a perfectly synchronized bow before turning on their heels and marching out of the throne room. I look around at the remaining members of my court. Everyone, even Percival, looks concerned. The twists and turns of Wonderland politics have taken us to some strange places, and I fear it's only going to get worse.

"Well," I say as I rise from my throne, "shall we retrieve the mirror and give our soldiers a proper send-off?"

The phrase "controlled chaos" comes to mind when I look out across the courtyard. There are soldiers everywhere, though they stand in neat, silent rows, awaiting commands. That pearlescent black armor is no less frightening for belonging to me, and it takes every shred of resolve not to turn tail and run for the safety of my suite at the sight of those... well, zombies. I've been told more than once not to ask what's under that armor, so I don't. But nobody said I had to like it.

Which I don't.

Tag appears from a door to the east, leading five neatly stacked decks of card soldiers. A Queen of each deck faces forward, the obvious unit commander, and he, the General of Wonderland's card army, calls them to a stop in a new column beside the Oysters. They're just as intimidating as the ranks of the undead, but more easily transported.

Tag comes to stand at my side, executing a perfect about-face as he turns toward the gathered forces. "Now would be a good time for the Queen to offer words of encouragement," he says out of one side of his mouth.

Um... Fuck.

Edwin and Torai appear from *somewhere*, standing before me in front of the gathered army.

Both are perfectly calm and collected and watching me with placid expressions.

"What do I say?" I ask. "I've never done this before."

"I don't fucking know," Tag replies. "You're the Queen. Tell them to live. Bring glory to our banner. Rescue our allies. Dance a jig. Just *say something*."

"Soldiers!" Percival's voice booms out across the courtyard from my right, startling me. He steps up and offers a cheeky wink. "It is your duty to not die. Allies are in danger, and it is up to you to bring them home. Save those you can save, end the lives of the traitors, and put an end to the Bloody Red Queen's viciousness."

A round of cheers rises from the gathered ranks, and he turns to me with a grin that could cut glass. "Your turn, Majesty. Grant them your favor before you send them off to die."

That's what I'm doing, isn't it? Sending them off to die?

"Your lives are irreplaceable," I say even though I know it's a lie. My voice shakes and I hope they can't hear it. "Fight smart. Fight well. Bring victory when you return with our allies!"

Another cheer rises from the army, and with that I turn and activate the looking glass, then step to the side. Edwin leads the decks through first, pausing only long enough to offer a formal salute. Torai follows, stepping up to the side and watching as line upon line of Oysters in shining, black armor march through. Their synchronized steps are enough to shake the ground under my feet. My pulse elevates with the exhilaration of watching them move.

The excitement quickly dulls. Mobilizing an army of thousands in a single-file line through a mirror takes considerably longer than I thought it would.

Who am I kidding? I didn't even stop to think about how long it would take. It was different when it was half a dozen of us ducking through. But this? Even in perfect formation and moving without pause, it takes *hours*. I stand shoulder-to-shoulder with the King of Diamonds and General Tweedledee without complaint and watch the procession. Somewhere into the fourth hour, the final column falls into step and passes before us. I'm near delirious from a combination of boredom and hunger when Torai falls in behind the final Oyster, offering the same formal salute Edwin did at the start, and disappears through the looking glass.

I disengage the mechanism and immediately sag, allowing Tag to support my weight for a moment. My feet hurt. My knees are stiff. My hips and back are screaming. But we just sent ten thousand soldiers to their potential doom, so I refuse to complain.

At Tag's suggestion, we turn toward the dining hall, but we never make it. Standing just before the doors is Talon, a grim expression etched into his face.

"Majesty, we have a problem."

"Humphrey has her?!"

The words burst out of me in an angry rush as bile rises in my throat. Why the hell would he have taken the stablemaster's wife? How would he even know how to do so? The entire situation reeks of betrayal, but I don't have a single clue who would do such a thing. I turn to Percival, whose expression is as dark as mine feels.

"He entered my territory to take this woman." His words are little more than a snarl, so I don't correct him on the his-versus-mine topic. "Shameless *and* honorless. I should expect no less from Humpty Dumpty himself."

"At what point do we get to throw his ass off a wall?" I ask. One corner of Jerome's mouth quirks up, but everyone else looks at me like I'm insane. Clearly, he's the only one familiar with the nursery rhyme.

"Give the word, wife, and I will rip him limb from limb and present his heart for your dinner."

That's… descriptive. I take a nervous step away from my second husband.

"That won't be necessary," I say. "Let's get Estrella back first. Then you can kill him if you like." I look to Talon, who somehow manages to both look worried *and* bored at the same time. "How do we get her back?"

"Short of laying siege to Castle Club?"

"Don't you *dare* tell me I can't," I say before one of them can finish the thought. "I went into Blackridge with rope around my wrists to get Koji back. Don't you think for one single goddamned second that I won't go get this woman too."

"Majesty," Percival says, his eyebrows rising in surprise when I turn my angry gaze on him.

"What?"

"Why is this one woman so important that you would risk life and limb for her?"

I... don't have a good answer. Why *is* she so important? She was nice to me, sure... but there has to be more to it than that. I'm not daft enough to think that I'd go charging into enemy territory to save every person in Wonderland... but maybe I would. Then again, all I can see when I close my eyes is Orvice, bloody and abused, begging me to save her. It's not her specifically. It's the *idea* of her. The idea of *any* person suffering when I have the power to help them.

"No life is worth sacrificing," I say. The words come from somewhere deep inside me. I feel like I'm floating above myself as the realization comes together on the fly. "Her husband came to me as his Queen and begged for help. If I'm not willing to put myself in danger for the people I'm supposed to rule, then I'm no better than Humphrey or Lucinda. If it is within my power to rescue her, I will rescue her."

A lazy smile spreads across his face. It appears I've passed whatever test this was supposed to be.

"How do I get into that dungeon?"

Talon and Tag look to one another, then at Nacht, who leans against the wall, one ankle crossed over the other while picking his teeth with one of the daggers around his neck. He looks completely and utterly bored.

"You," he says, pointing the blade toward me and somehow managing to make even that motion belittling, "do not. Your muchness is *entirely* too loud for espionage." Nacht pushes upright; his ankles still somehow slouched against one another in a move that defies gravity. "And you have a terrible habit of wanting to save every pitiful creature you see."

He's not wrong, but his assessment of my darkest wishes annoys me all the same. I glare at him and he stares blandly back.

"How do we get her back, then?" I reply while punching my hands into my hips hard enough to bruise. "I won't leave her there."

"There are ways," he answers, one side of his mouth lifting into an infuriating smirk, "but it's best if you don't know what they are."

"Are you saying you'll handle it?"

"Do not I always?"

He's toying with me... the jerk. Part of me wants to punch him in the stomach, but it has also been less than twenty-four hours since I learned how to repair the gaping wound in his side. Hurting him again seems silly in comparison. I settle for rolling my eyes.

"Go do whatever it is you do that I'm not allowed to know about despite the fact that I'm your fucking Queen."

His smirk turns into a full-blown grin, no less lethal for its playfulness. "My *fucking* Queen... sounds delightful."

Yep. I walked into that one.

"Get the hell out of here!" I half-shout and groan loudly to emphasize my annoyance. "Go do whatever it is you do and bring her back!" I turn on my heel and storm past them toward the dining hall, followed by the sound of Nacht's gleeful cackling.

By the time Percival and I make it to the table, everyone else is finished eating and half-delirious. He's grinning as he pulls out my chair and helps me into it, and the smile I offer in return is more like a snarl. I wouldn't say it's easy between us, but it's certainly not as contentious as it used to be.

I don't trust that at all.

The room is quieter than usual as I eat my lunch, which gives me too much time to think of all the horrible outcomes facing us if either of the teams we've dispatched fails. There's too much at stake in either direction. If Nacht is caught, Humphrey will kill him. If Edwin and Torai can't subdue Morcar...

I can't even imagine what those losses would look like.

After lunch, we return to the throne room for round two of public appearances, and by the time I make it back to my bedroom, my mind has completely spun out. All I can see when I close my eyes is carnage. Before I'm consciously aware of where I'm going or what I'm about to do, I'm knocking on Jerome's door.

He answers half-dressed and rubbing at his eyes like he'd already been asleep for hours, stepping back as I enter without waiting for an invitation.

"I need to know that Edwin is okay," I spit. He's slow to respond through his sleepy haze, and before he can speak, another voice sounds from the doorway.

"I shall take you, Majesty."

Tag stands at attention, back ramrod straight with his chin lifted high. A perfect gentleman soldier, if perfect gentleman soldiers were one-hundred percent feral. It's almost like he was waiting for me to ask.

"Is that really such a good idea?" Jerome asks. Only one eye is open, and it's not entirely focused as he looks down at me.

"Good idea or not, I can't rest not knowing what's happening."

"Majesty," he says patiently, like I'm an impetuous child who needs reprimand, "I highly doubt the Oysters have had time to reach the front, much less engage in battle."

"Then our Queen will not have missed anything vital," Tag retorts. It's not like him to advocate so strongly for, well, *anything*.

"It's the middle of the night, Tag."

"And battle knows not how to read a clock."

Jerome looks at me, exasperation etched into the lines of his face. The glare in his eyes screams, *will you please put a stop to this madness?!* But I'm inclined to agree with Tag here. I want to go. I need to see it for myself. When he realizes I'm not going to back down, he sighs loudly and his shoulders slump.

"Lord Edwin is smart enough not to attack at night, particularly if his brother is expecting him — which, I assure you, Morcar is." He glances between Tag and me and sighs again. "You need to sleep, Majesty. We'll leave at first light."

"First light it is," Tag agrees with a nod and a salute, then turns on his heel and disappears into his room.

"Come on," Jerome says when we're alone and curls an arm around my shoulders. "Let's get you back into bed so you'll be able to travel tomorrow."

When I step through the looking glass into the Rabbit Hole, I'm greeted by a sword at my throat.

"Stand down, you idiot!" Jerome shouts while batting the blade away with his own. "Beheading your Queen would be a terrible idea."

"And it would ruin my fun," Percival says as he steps out into the cramped living space behind me.

"Shut up," I mutter while stepping to the side to allow him all the way into the room.

The black-armored soldier drops to one knee, head bowed in supplication. It doesn't speak — I'm not sure it's capable — as it offers its sword up. I'm not sure what's happening.

"Its life is yours should you decide to claim it," Percival says. "It nearly killed you. It's only fair you punish it accordingly."

I whip around to glare at him. "Seriously? It makes a mistake, so I have to kill it?"

"Yes."

"You're a monster."

"We already knew that," Tag supplies...not helpfully.

"I'm not killing a solider." The thought of it turns my stomach.

"Fine. I'll do it." Percival reaches for the sword.

"No!" I step between him and the soldier.

"Why?"

"It's wasteful." I turn back to the soldier. "Stand up, please." It does but otherwise it doesn't react.

"You do realize they're zombies, by now, right?" Jerome asks into my ear. "They're disposable."

"Reanimated or not, I'm not killing *any* creature if I can help it." I move away from the cluster of bodies, toward what I assume is the door. "Can we please move on from this? I want to get to the front before something awful happens."

Ivan, the last to step through the portal, deactivates the looking glass from this side and weaves through the gathered crowd to stand at my side. There's a tightness to a features and a stiffness to the set of his shoulders now that we're on this side. I wonder if it has anything to do with being back in Red Territory, but I don't question.

"Are you certain you want to do this?" he asks. His tone is careful, even. He's almost delicate in the way he handles me. "It's going to be bloody. Morcar is more monster than you know."

"Bloody I can handle. Standing by and doing nothing while one of our allies risks his life is unforgivable."

He nods once and moves for the door.

A pair of card soldiers stand guard outside the Rabbit Hole, their thin, paper bodies tucked into the overgrowth that masks the door. The last time we were here, I was herded onto the back of a Jabberwocky, so I didn't really have time to look around. It's…definitely abandoned. Very well hidden, even from the path that sits an arm's length away from the gates.

"Where exactly are we?" I ask once we're all on the path.

"The edge of the Tulgey Wood," Ivan explains. "A few hours from Calloway. Looks like we'll have to walk for a bit."

"I can handle walking."

And we do. We fall into a comfortable rhythm, moving quietly through the thinning forest. The woods are still and silent; not at all like the Tulgey Wood from earlier adventures. Perhaps it's because we're in Red Territory, but even the air is different here. Thick. Heavy. Strangled, almost. The magic is stifling. Too close.

After an hour — though it feels like so much longer — we crest a hill and the forest opens up onto wide, rolling plains. I'm instantly transported back to the horror of my introduction to Wonderland, to that grisly scene of bloody grass and burning bodies. We're back on the edge of that checkerboard.

The mountains to the east wind down toward us. My heart races, and my palms slick with the same cold sweat that trickles from my hairline all the way down my spine. If I close my eyes, I can see the snarling chasm that is the bandersnatch general's hollowed-out card face. Only this time…

"Alice!"

Jerome's voice cuts through the panic as effectively as if he'd splashed ice water on me. I startle out of the waking nightmare and look up at him. The edges of my vision are fuzzy with panic, but he's completely in focus in front of me. He's so close that I can see the specks of color swirling in his irises and smell the clean wind-and-rain scent of his skin.

"Whatever you're seeing, it's not real." His voice is pitched low and gentle. His hands are firm around my biceps but not tight enough to hurt. Just steady enough to ground me in the moment and pull me away from the fear bunching up in my throat. "It's in the past. It can't get you."

"I-I know," I admit. My voice doesn't sound like my own.

"This was a bad idea," Ivan says over his shoulder. "We shouldn't have come."

"Do *not* underestimate my Queen," Tag half-snarls, half-hisses. "She knows her limits and you *will* respect them."

Well that's new. Not surprising, exactly, but new. He steps up and offers his arm as an escort, which I take. The harsh glare softens into an indulgent smile when he looks down at me.

"We must cross the checkerboard to reach Callowary, and then we will find transport."

"Sounds good," I reply, but my voice is a dry husk. The idea of setting foot back on that checkerboard — a checkerboard that shows no sign of the bloody, vicious battle from half a year ago — terrifies me. It's yet another moment when I have to choose to face my fears head-on, whether I like it or not.

I'm on alert all the way across. We're open and exposed, and my personal trauma threatens to rip me apart, but nothing happens. At all. The sky remains clear; the individual ten-foot squares untouched save the impressions of our footprints in the ankle-high black and red grass. It's the silence that truly frightens me. Just like in the forest, the air around us is tense and anticipatory, like the earth itself is prepared for whatever attack may come. And I suppose it is. This land has been war-torn for over a century.

The sun is high in the sky as we near the end of the field and the ground begins to slope downward. The first spires of Calloway's skyline come into view, but that awe is quickly outshined by the heavy rumbling of running feet in the valley below.

Oysters and cards alike rush forward into the lowland, led by the familiar, terrifying sight of Edwin in his Jabberwocky form. And equally familiar, yet slightly smaller, version of that form races toward him, leading its own army of red-clad soldiers.

"I see we made it," Percival says just as the two sides clash in a deafening roar of voices and screeching metal. The two giant beasts rear up and go on the offensive, serpentine necks bending at odd angles and massive claws swiping at one another. From this distance I can't see their exact movements, but my heart thuds loudly in my ears as I watch them rip one another apart.

The front-line ripples back and forth; new soldiers pushing forward to fill the gaps as participants on both sides fall to blade and club. It's raw and vicious and the sight makes me nauseous. Tears stream down my cheeks as the feeling of helplessness takes hold, and the only reason I don't collapse to the ground is because of Tag's arm firmly around my shoulders.

The fight seems to stretch on forever while the sun crawls across the sky at a snail's pace. Edwin and Morcar launch skyward, jaws snapping at one another. The beat of their big wings forces gusts of air toward the ground, knocking over soldier and card alike and sending dirty, bloody clouds billowing toward us. I throw up a shield at the last minute, watching in a mix of fascination and horror as the angry mist boils around us.

As the dust settles, I drop the barrier and the battle comes back into view. Down in the valley, it's a writhing mass of bodies punctuated by the shriek of metal on metal. Even that, however, is drowned out by the reverberating shriek that draws my gaze skyward again.

The two Jabberwocky circle each other in the sky, claws extended while their wings hold them level. One of the pair opens his mouth and the sound that issues forth is reminiscent of Godzilla ready to level Tokyo, except ten thousand times louder and wrapped in magic that pulses with each beat of my racing heart. The other lunges, giant jaws snapping closed around the throat of the screamer, and an audible gasp rushes out of me. At this distance I can't tell which monster is which. My fists curl into tight knots, fingernails digging into the soft meat of my palms as that big head shakes, cutting off the screech and sending the other spiraling across the sky. Those big wings shoot outwards, billowing like sails and the monster levels out. Its head snaps toward its adversary, and the monster shoots forward with more speed than I would ever expect something that large to have. It slams its head into the other's body like a battering ram. Wings tangle, claws catch on scales, and more of that horrendous shouting fills the air.

The pair spins together, winding to a halt with one's jaws closed squarely around the other's throat. The captured head is bent at an unnatural angle. The victor shakes its head like a dog, the body of his victim shuddering under the pressure, and then he releases.

The giant dragon-thing drops, increasing speed until it slams into the ground with an earth-shaking *thud*. Once again, the battlefield's participants lay down, their legs rattled out from under them on impact. The Jabberwocky on the ground doesn't move.

The airborne monster lets loose a victorious screech loud enough to be heard all the way across Wonderland. My hands fly to my ears but not quickly enough, and warmth trickles between my fingers. I have no idea which Jabberwocky is which... until my ears stop ringing and my vision refocuses. The red-clad soldiers are either retreating or surrendering. They're doing their best to lift the fallen Jabberwocky, but his body is so big, so heavy, that they're struggling to move him.

My mouth hangs open, the tang of spilled blood dancing across my exposed tongue, as the field clears. Our soldiers remain on the field, moving the wounded. Aside from the trampled, scorched grass, there's very little wrong with the valley once they start to clear the field.

The battle is finally over. I have exactly two-point-eight seconds to appreciate that fact before my vision goes black and a giant, bloody beast lands in front of me. That big, serpentine head drops down, and warm, golden eyes blink at me before it performs what I can only imagine is a formal bow.

CHAPTER TWENTY

One moment I'm staring into the face of a battle-scarred Jabberwocky and the next I'm staring into the face of the very bloody, very naked Earl of Mercia. He kneels, wincing as his knee touches the ground, and clutches at a wound in his side. Blood pours over his fingers and down his chest from the raw meat of his throat, but a satisfied smile sits on his lips.

"My Queen," he says, his voice as shredded as his skin, "we have brought you victory."

I glance over the top of his head at the immobile pile of scales and claws in the middle of the mostly empty battlefield. Morcar's soldiers are having trouble moving him.

"Is he...dead?"

"Goodness, no!" Edwin exclaims as if we're talking about suddenly stormy weather and not the mutilated body of his brother. "Merely incapacitated. It takes significantly more than having one's throat ripped out to kill a jabberwock, Majesty."

"Do you maybe need a healer?" I focus my attention back on the General at my feet—er, on his eyes, that is. "Can I help?"

"Not necessary," he says and rises to his full height. Ivan shoves a coat at him. I have no idea where he got a coat from. "We heal fast." His throat already looks less like ground meat, which makes me feel marginally better. I'm relieved that he's okay, gory flesh wound notwithstanding.

"So... what does this victory mean?"

"It means I retain control of Mercia, and that it exists under the banner of Wonderland, not the Red Court."

"I can't imagine the Red Queen will let that stand."

"Not at all, which is why we shall advance into Northumbria and take control of my brother's lands as well. With the beast out of commission for at least the next two days, I have the opportunity for a mostly peaceful transition."

"But the soldiers appear to be retreating...and trying to take him with them."

Edwin chuckles, the sound sort of like razorblades on glass, and looks over his shoulder. The wound rips again and fresh rivulets of blood run down his pale skin, but he doesn't seem to notice.

"Those who are loyal to my brother won't get far. The Walrus and his Oysters are already on the way to his castle. And don't worry about Morcar… he won't be moving for a while, no matter how many of those fools try to lift him."

"Perhaps it would be prudent to reconvene with the army," Percival offers over my shoulder, startling me. I forgot he was behind me.

Dangerous, I know.

"An excellent idea," Tag agrees and offers his arm as if to escort me.

"Perhaps her Majesty would like to fly?" Edwin asks. I immediately shake my head.

"Absolutely not. Once was enough." Everybody laughs at me. Jerks. "Besides, you're injured."

"Merely a flesh wound."

I nearly choke on my tongue, then hold my breath to keep from launching into a movie monologue that would certainly earn me even stranger looks than the ones I've already received this afternoon.

So once again, we walk. The hill is steeper than it looks, and by the time we reach the edge of the battlefield proper, I'm exhausted and breathing hard.

"Should have flown, Majesty," Edwin jabs with a cheeky smile. "Stubborn woman."

"I am… your… Queen," I wheeze, squeezing my side to loosen the stitch there.

"You're still stubborn as a brooding bandersnatch," he says, then sweeps me up into a bridal carry like he's not beat absolutely to shit and bleeding from several open wounds.

"Will you put me down?!"

"No. Now hush before I drop you."

"You wouldn't dare!"

"One would think," he replied, stone-faced. "Be still, woman."

I would say I'm getting really tired of being hauled around like a sack of potatoes, but right now I'm thankful for the break. And because there's so much blood on the battlefield that Edwin's shoes splash and squish through it.

The problem with being carried, I discover, is that I have plenty of time to look around at the carnage. Shredded cardstock and pieces and parts of bodies are strewn everywhere, some mostly intact, others… not so much. There are more severed limbs than my brain can process. There are also surprisingly few black-armored bodies, which makes me feel marginally better. We don't seem to have lost many soldiers.

Edwin gives the still-fallen body of his brother a wide berth, and I'm glad of that. I don't ever want to be up close and personal with Morcar again. Still, as close as we pass is too close for comfort, and I make an effort not to crane my head all the way around to look as we move along the high ground nearby.

By the time we reach the far ridge and Edwin settles me back on my feet, the sun is creeping toward the horizon. How these men can keep going without complaint is beyond me. I'm exhausted, and I was carried for half the time.

As my feet touch down, the first thing I notice is the quiet. It's not surprising for a battlefield, but the silence is unnerving all the same. Then I turn and let out an audible gasp. Every single fallen Oyster is once again vertical and following along behind Percival like an obedient puppy.

Oh, yeah… Necromancer.

I definitely don't want to see what's under that armor, because I don't want to know how many times these battle poppets have been reanimated. They've also picked up dropped weapons along the way, so we now have our own little battalion. Having the undead at my back does *not* make me feel better about this situation.

At the bottom of the ridge, the ground levels out. The abandoned Red Army camp still houses a few stray animals, and the Oysters appear to have taken it over for ransacking. The soldiers snap to attention as we pass, and a wave of Percival's hand has two… men? Creatures? I'm not sure what to call them. Either way, a pair of soldiers brings over a few of the remaining animals — a bandersnatch and three jubjubs. Then I'm airborne, deposited onto the bandersnatch with Ivan at my back.

"This is where I leave you, Majesty," Edwin says. His voice is closer to normal, but still not right. The majority of his wounds have scabbed over, though the one at his throat dribbles blood. "We shall reconvene at Coving." He pauses, clears his throat, and casts his gaze to the ground. "I should warn you, Majesty… Coving is not what one would expect from a city."

Nope, don't like that.

"What does that mean?"

"You'll see," Ivan says, letting Edwin off the hook. "It's not good, but it's not something we can explain unless you see it for yourself."

"Be safe, Lord Edwin," I offer in a small, meek voice, because what else can I do? I have no idea what we're walking into, and no idea how any of this is going to end. We're also close enough to the Red Palace that I can feel the rot seeping into the magic around us.

They're absolutely right. Coving is *not* at all what I expect, and I've had plenty of time to dream up all sorts of scenarios. What I never once thought to imagine, however, was the Auschwitz-like prison that stands before me. High, stone walls topped in vicious-looking blades ring the city, and a medieval-style drawbridge that's broken open. Rows and rows of drab, windowless block buildings march in stiff rows along a dusty road. The only thing it's missing is the wrought-iron *arbeit macht frei* slogan above the entrance. My skin threatens to get up off my body and crawl away at the sight.

This is not a city to which an entire army has retreated. It doesn't just look empty; it looks *abandoned.*

"Something is wrong," I say from atop the bandersnatch. Ivan's arm tightens around my waist and Jerome's nervousness spikes in my brain. "Torai isn't here."

A quiet obscenity draws my attention toward Tag. The color has drained from his face, and he looks like he's going to vomit.

"This… is a trap."

Fuck.

The sharp snap of a bowstring breaks the silence and before I can even turn, an arrow splits in two and falls to the dirt road. My heart stutters with the realization that I've avoided yet another close call… only this time, the man who ordered the previous hit is the one who saved me from the new one.

Percival's glare is dark as he focuses on something I can't see on the other side of the wall. His hand lifts, fingers curled like claws, and someone screams. The sound abruptly stops. Then, a body falls from the top of the nearest building, disappearing behind the wall with a sickeningly final *crunch* of bones on ground.

"Get her out of here," he snarls, not bothering to look in my direction as he raises a hand and signals the resurrected Oysters forward. The troops file through the broken gate in perfect rows, salvaged weapons at the ready, then follow behind while Ivan turns the big beast. Edwin launches back into the sky with a roar. Jerome places himself between us and the gates. Tag whistles four pitch-perfect notes—a code of some sort—and takes up a battle stance. Nothing happens. He nods toward Percival, who waits just inside the gate. The King of Diamonds nods back.

Doors are forcefully thrown open, buildings searched. Edwin circles overhead, dipping low then regaining altitude. In a matter of minutes, the city is cleared of all living beings, and the body of the would-be assassin has vanished.

Edwin lands in front of Tag, the shift so fast I can't see what happens.

"Empty. Everything. For quite a stretch, too."

I can't see the look on Tag's face, but I feel the shift in the air when he comes to a horrible realization.

"Callowary."

Edwin immediately launches back into the air with Tag on his back. Then they're gone.

"What…just happened?"

"The Red Army is likely trying to take Callowary without Morcar's leadership," Ivan says.

"Is it possible?"

"Yes." That one small word, spoken so matter-of-factly, makes my blood run cold.

"Can Torai hold them?"

"If he's there."

"But we don't know if he is."

"No."

Fuck. Again.

"Let's go."

"It's a day's ride from here to there."

"Don't care. We have to go now."

"It's not—"

"So help me, if you tell me it isn't safe, I'm going to throw you off this beast and go on my own."

"...fine."

And then we're moving, the beast picking up surprising speed as Ivan urges it into a full sprint. When I look back over my shoulder, I find Jerome keeping pace on his jubjub, but Percival is nowhere to be found.

"He's holding the city," Ivan says as if reading my mind. "That man is dangerous enough on his own to defend it, and he has several Oysters with him. They'll be fine."

He's actually *helping* us. It's strange. Welcome, but strange. I'm trying hard to trust him to stick to our alliance, but after everything I've been through recently, it's hard. The thin buzz of anxiety holds on long after I relax into Ivan's hold and let the scenery pass us by.

It's hours before we stop, and I am famished when we do. Ivan dismounts the big beast first then gently guides me to the ground. It's a good thing he has hold of me because my hips and legs are like rubber from so long in motion. The sun is at my back and nearing the horizon, and the air is much colder than I expect it to be. I shiver, and almost instantly I have Jerome's coat around my shoulders.

Ivan leaves me with him and guides the animals

to the river to drink. He comes back with a big leaf cupped in his hands. It's full of clear, cold water.

"Always water yourself when you water your animals," he says with a cheeky grin and holds the leaf up to me. It's a strange maneuver to drink from the leaf-bowl clutched in his hands, but I manage it okay. The water is crisp and sweet as it slides down my throat, and I can feel each individual cell in my body rehydrating. I didn't realize how thirsty I'd become.

I walk along the bank of the river for a bit to stretch out all the sore spots in my body, then take a seat beside a tree. The animals seem content to just stand there — a weird thing even from my world. Yeah, they're built differently, but the thought of spending my entire life on my feet is a scary one. That would hurt.

Jerome comes to sit beside me, his arms clutched around something that I can't see until he tips his treasure into my lap. The boyish grin on his face makes me smile. He's so proud of himself. My lap is now full of food: berries of varying shapes and colors, mushrooms, some greens, and a handful of tiny eggs. There's enough here for all of us to have at least two meals.

"Where did you find all of this?" I ask, looking at the bounty.

"The woods are full of lovely things to eat, if you know where to look." He winks at me when I look up at him, and my heart does a funny, little dance. It's really not fair that he's so beautiful and so stupidly charming. Ivan joins us under the tree, plucking a tiny, white mushroom out of my lap on the way down.

"Ooh, marshmorels!" He pops it into his mouth whole and crunches down on it.

"Marshmorels?" I lift one eyebrow at him and he grins.

"Try one."

I do. They pop like boba between my teeth and taste like marshmallow creme. The berries are exactly the opposite of what one would expect, too. Some taste vaguely like fruit jam while others taste like fried chicken and steak. The eggs, it turns out, are not eggs at all. At least, not any kind of eggs I've ever seen.

Soup eggs, Jerome calls them as he cracks one open and hands it to me. Inside is vegetable soup. It's even warm.

This little bit of whimsy does my heart good, but as always… it doesn't last.

I stand up from washing my hands in the river to find a blade at my throat.

"Move even a hair and I'll slice that pretty neck."

I freeze as requested. Stop breathing. Cut my eyes to one side, then the other, but I can't see who has me hostage. The bite of metal against my skin says he's fully prepared to kill me, too.

The buzz of fear hits me from both sides as my Rabbits also watch, frozen. Maybe it's for the best that I can't see my attacker. Then his laugh, deep and thick, raspy in the same way Edwin's was when he first started to heal, touches my ears and I shudder. That thought pings something deep in my brain and I freeze.

No. It can't be. Edwin said he'd be down for days. It shouldn't be possible, but...

"M-Morcar?"

"Very good, little Queen," he answers. "Perhaps you have more brains than I gave you credit for. Too bad they shall soon be smeared all over the ground."

"Let her go," Ivan snarls, hands opening and closing frantically, as if by doing so he might call his sword to his hand and end this new nightmare.

"Silence, traitor," Morcar hisses in his direction. He must turn his head because the blade moves, and a small line of fire erupts along my throat. Ivan's eyes flare wide, then turn hateful as he casts them over my shoulder. Warmth trickles down my skin and soaks into the collar of my shirt. "You no longer have a say in what happens here."

"The hell I don't. Remove your claws from her, you wretched beast, before I remove them from your body."

Claws?

Whatever it is, it doesn't push into my skin anymore, but it hovers close. I breathe shallowly, both to help dull the pain in my throat and reduce contact with the weapon. Another hand curls around my waist and tugs me back against a hard chest. His skin smells like blood and wind, and his entire body vibrates with unspent energy. He's like a coiled spring, ready to fly when released. *That* is scarier than anything else I've faced. Fear and anger make people unpredictable.

"You are more than welcome to fight me, Rabbit, but you will not make it in time to save your Queen's life. Surrender and I might *think* about letting you live."

"You're bleeding from both eyes, your nose, and that pretty hole in your throat, Morcar," Ivan prods. "I don't think you stand a chance without using a woman as a shield." He glances my way then locks his gaze on our opponent. "Not that she would have any trouble eviscerating you herself if you chose to play fair."

Morcar laughs. His grip around my waist loosens just a bit, knocking me off-balance. My left arm is free and pinwheels up to catch myself, but I don't go far before he tightens his hold. I keep my arm bent at the elbow.

He was in terrible condition last time we saw him. If he's still bleeding that bad…

He has to have a weak spot somewhere, I think. I just have to hope I find it before he tears my head off.

"What do—" I start but my voice comes out high and thin. I clear my throat and try again. "What do you intend to do with me?"

"You, little Alice, are a gift for the true Queen. I'd take your head and leave the rest of you for your Rabbits to fight over, but I wouldn't dare deprive my regent the satisfaction of ending your life herself." He chuckles, the sound as raspy as sandpaper on skin. "You've been quite the thorn in her side…though I suppose I should thank you. You *have* given me reason to do away with my idiot brother once and for all."

"If you want your brother dead so badly, why bother with me? Wouldn't it stand to reason that dispatching him first would make more sense? Leaving me unguarded?"

"You are unguarded now. Or are you too dim to understand that?"

He's not wrong about that, but I'm not going to validate the truth. I look over at my stunned Rabbits and try to affect boredom.

"I look pretty well defended from here."

He snorts, but I can feel the slight tensing of muscle as my jab lands. "And yet I was able to slip in and take hold of you?"

"You got lucky."

The snort turns to a snarl. *Bingo.*

His pride. That's the weak spot.

"If you were *actually* worth your salt, you wouldn't have to try and murder your brother. You'd already be in control of the Red Army." Every muscle in his body tenses, including the arm banded around me. His fingers curl into my side, and the sharp prick of claws digs into my skin just below my ribs. "You're just mad because Edwin is better than you."

Absolute panic filters down the Rabbit bond half a second before the world spins, and I'm jerked around to face Morcar. We're nearly nose to nose, his eyes black with rage. He's dirty and bloody. His breath smells like sulfur and death. And his fingers dig so hard into my arms that I'm certain he's about to crush the bones.

"You. Know. *Nothing*." His voice is low and deadly, more growl than language, and it carries that two-toned reverberation that comes with the shift.

"I know I can best you," I say calmly, then pull the magic close and swing my dangling fist into his side. The extra power isn't enough to do damage, but it is enough that I feel the crunch of already broken ribs as they shift under the skin. His hands tighten reflexively, then fly open as he stumbles backwards to clutch at his wounded side.

I run.

But I'm not fast enough. Ten paces away he's on me again, clawed fingers dragging me back against him, but the *swish* of a vorpal blade cuts the silence and the pressure releases from my arm. A soft *thump* echoes and when I look down, Morcar's left arm lies in the bloody grass at my feet. Ivan stands between us, armor fully formed around him and bloody blade glowing blue in the darkening dusk. The pain of amputation is delayed, because it's several beats before Morcar begins to scream.

"Run. *Now*."

I don't hesitate, turning and bolting toward… nothing. The animals are gone.

"Alice!"

I swivel my head toward the sound and find Jerome running my way at full speed. He doesn't hesitate when he nears, instead sweeping me up into a bridal carry and increasing speed when he hits the path.

The clash of metal-on-metal screeches through the air. I turn back just in time to see Ivan's knees buckle under the pressure of Morcar's advance. The air smells like blood and magic, and we're going the wrong way…

"We have to help him!" I shout over the wind rushing past my ears.

"You have to live!" Jerome shouts back, but his words sound distant. "This is our reason for living, Alice! To save you!"

"He is *not* going to die today!" I yell back. "Put me down!"

"No!"

"THAT IS AN ORDER! PUT ME DOWN NOW!"

He immediately halts, and I slide out of his arms onto my *very* unsteady legs.

"I won't let him die for me," I say more calmly than I feel. "Not today."

I turn, facing the fight that my Rabbit is clearly losing, and reach down into the earth for the magic which comes all too easily. It almost feels happy as it invades me, twines around my arms to gather between my palms. It shines bright, angry red as it coalesces into a hard knot, the raw power singeing my fingertips before I release the shot. It flies true, slamming with full force into Morcar's back where it explodes into a shower of magical fireworks so bright I have to shield my eyes. Ivan flies away, landing hard on his side and rolling until his back hits the tree we were recently under. When I look back toward the fading sparkle of magic, I expect to find scorched earth but... don't.

The man who held me hostage less than two minutes ago is now floating face-down in the river, his body being forced along by the current.

"Ivan!" He's holding his side and wheezing. At least he's awake.

"Ivan will live. He probably can't hear you because of the blast. Now can we go?" Jerome sounds impatient and his hands are already on my shoulders, trying to tow me backwards.

"He needs to come with us!"

"He needs to make sure Morcar doesn't swim to shore and come after you again. He'll be fine. *Now come on.*"

Jerome doesn't give me a choice as he lifts and tosses me over his shoulder. Again. I know I can be stubborn and contrary but damn it, this is *so* undignified! He gave me my shot, though. I took it and knocked the bad guy into the water. I guess I can't complain *too* much about being bodily hauled out of danger's way.

I'm thrown up onto the back of the bandersnatch and we're off immediately, the scenery whipping past us in a frantic blur that makes my head spin. We ride far and fast, Jerome not bothering to slow or look back as we leave Ivan behind to face Morcar alone. Maybe.

He *was* floating in the river, after all.

I close my eyes and reach out along our bond. The distance pulses like a toothache. I'm acutely aware of how far apart we are — farther than we've been since the bond snapped into place — but I don't find stress and frustration. The emotion behind the distance is one of relief. He's calm and in control. Just… distant. Distant enough that the corners of my eyes burn.

The important part is that he's okay, I tell myself and try to relax into the ride.

We go until the beast beneath us slows of its own accord. It pants like a dog as it all but stops in the middle of the woods—not the Tulgey Wood, thankfully—and collapses into an exhausted heap. Jerome and I dismount carefully and pick our way to the edge of the path to let the poor thing rest. My legs are shaky from the hard ride, and my head is wobbly, like we're still moving. I make it as far as the grass before my knees buckle, and I tumble to the ground.

"Where are we?" I ask, because nothing here looks familiar.

"Several hours north of the Rabbit Hole, and it appears we're going to be here for a while." He glances over his shoulder at the bandersnatch, which has fallen asleep right where it fell.

"Did we have to push it so hard?"

"We didn't. It sensed danger and ran on its own. They're much smarter than we give them credit for."

"But to run itself out like that?" I feel guilty now. It sacrificed its health to get me out of there. I appreciate the gesture, but... it's too much. I don't want to be the reason anyone or anything else gets hurt.

I lean back against the closest tree and curl in on myself, bringing my knees to my chest. It's not exactly an appropriate time to feel sorry for myself, but it also seems like we've got a couple of hours to kill while our critter naps. Just about the time my forehead hits my knees, Jerome settles in beside me and slides an arm around my body. He pulls me close so that instead of being a ball of skin, I'm draped across him.

"Stop that," he says gently, his lips brushing the shell of my ear with each word.

"Stop what?" I ask, playing dumb. He's going to tell me not to feel guilty.

"Stop courting misery." He kisses my temple. "It's quite unbecoming of a Queen."

I can't stop the sigh that falls out, and when I try to sit up, he holds me in place. It's mildly annoying.

"I don't want anyone or anything," I nod toward the sleeping bandersnatch, "hurt because of me. It defeats the purpose of being here to save them."

"Alice." The way he says my name… yeah, I'm in for a lecture. "Every ruler faces this dilemma. You cannot save everyone but mourning the losses of the dead and injured is an injustice to their legacy."

I lift my head and look up at him. "What?"

"If Ivan were to sacrifice himself to save you — which he has not, I'll have you know — your moping about would be an insult to that sacrifice. You must accept losses as part of war, but you must also *live* so that the lives lost aren't in vain." He pulls me up to look into my eyes. "Stop trying to sacrifice yourself for others. You're making our job so much harder than it needs to be." His words are stern, but the look on his face is gentle. I wrap my arms around his neck and hold onto him. He closes me inside the safety of his arms and the tears that have been threatening for the last several hours start to fall.

"I don't know what I'd do without you," I whisper into his neck.

"Probably spend most of your time in a ditch," he jokes back, which makes me laugh a little.

"You're not wrong."

"I love you, Alice." The confession is simple, but it lands on my heart like warm chocolate, melting and spreading through me with tingling satisfaction. "I never expected to find love like my parents had, but I cannot imagine life without you. Even at war, you are everything I never knew I wanted. So please… let us protect you the way we're supposed to."

Emotion chokes me, so I nod in response and burrow closer to him. We stay like that long enough that I doze off, and when he gently shakes me awake, the sun has set and the bandersnatch is sitting in the middle of the path, licking its paws like it has just had the best dinner ever.

We've got to get home soon, because I, too, am starving.

When I walk through the door to my room, *everyone* is staring at me. So many moderately alarmed gazes flare with surprise, then soften. Phineas is the first to cross the room and pull me into a bear hug despite the fact that I'm dirty, bloody, and partially singed from magical projectiles. He holds on tightly enough that I can't breathe for a minute, and when he settles me back on my feet, Edith latches on and squeezes tightly enough that I can't breathe again.

"You stink," she says against my shoulder, but hugs tighter.

"Casualty of war," I reply with a laugh and hug her back.

Ivan is next, and I nearly shriek when I see him before launching myself into his arms and letting him swing me around.

"How are you here already?"

"Found a door. I'll be back to the Rabbit Hole tomorrow, but for tonight, we're all safe."

I'm passed around the remainder of the circle like a party favor, Haigha and Percival being the only two holdouts on a full-house hug. Even Blade steps up and curls a gentle arm around my shoulders. Then they part and I realize that yes, *everyone* is in here.

That too-wide, too-sharp smile is the first thing I see, then the swirling, hypnotic eyes. My knees nearly buckle from the relief of seeing the Cheshire Cat awake again.

"Good evening, my Queen," he says, voice a low, rasping purr that does very naughty things to my insides. He rises to his feet, though not as fluidly as I'd expect, and favors his right side as he closes the space between us

"Koji…" His name is less than a whisper as one hand curls around my waist and the other around the back of my neck, and then his lips are on mine, gentle but insistent, and the rest of the world falls away. I forget absolutely everything, up to and including who I am, as he kisses me. I'm so lost in him that I forget to be gentle when I cling to him, fingers digging into his skin to keep him close.

A series of cheers, groans, and a high-pitched wolf-whistle finally break the spell, pulling me back down into reality while he slips back, kissing the tip of my nose and the space between my eyes before straightening.

"I owe you my life, my Alice." Honesty and devotion shine in his quicksilver eyes. "I was meant to die in that dungeon."

"As long as I live, I won't let them kill you." I wrap my arms around his middle and hug him again, then let him tow me over to the table where we all take our seats. This room is as full as my heart. It's good to see everyone all in one piece, even if Torai and Edwin look a little worse for wear.

"So…updates," I say once everyone is settled in their seats.

"Morcar is not dead," Ivan says from my left.

"The looking glass is secure," Jerome adds.

"Calloway is protected," Tag says.

"Securing the hostage has met…unforeseen struggles," Nacht admits from his brother's side.

"Struggles?" I ask.

"She is not held where one would expect her to be held."

"What does that mean, exactly?"

"King Humphrey has not imprisoned the small woman," Talon interjects, and every gaze in the room swings to him and his ethereal breeze that never seems to stop blowing. The mirage of wings flutters behind him, in and out of focus. "She has been offered a room in the Palace of Clubs, and his personal servants have been attending her. She is in no danger."

"He's squeezing her for information." The words leave my mouth in an angry rush and yet again, I see red. Of course, our former ally is using her. "I need to talk to Orvice about what she might know."

"Not much of worth," Talon responds. He's clearly still a dozen or more steps ahead of me. For that I'm both grateful and a little annoyed. *He's being helpful,* I tell myself. And he is.

"So, how do we get her back?"

"Let me handle that," Talon replies with a lazy smile and leans back in his chair, clearly done with the conversation.

"Fine, handle it. Next." I turn to Torai.

"The Oysters continue to defend Northumbria while also holding Coving. The Red Army has not attempted to advance beyond the gates of Callowary since they were overrun this morning."

That's good, at least.

"What about Coving? Was it a trap?"

"Yes," Percival says, "but not for the reason you might think."

"It was meant to separate me from the herd, right?" He blinks like I wasn't supposed to figure that out. "It worked. He ended up face-down in the river despite his best attempts to kill me."

That announcement stops everyone at the table mid-movement and they all look at me with a range of expressions from shock to approval.

"He wasn't as unconscious as we thought he was," I tell them. "We stopped on the road between Coving and Calloway to rest the animals and he attacked."

"Our Queen launched the meddling bastard into the river," Ivan announces proudly. "I dare say my Queen saved my life."

I toss a glare at Jerome, who stares back just as evenly as if I'd not said anything at all. I know deep down that he's right, but I'm still not ready to admit just how reckless I am.

"Well done, Majesty," Percival says with a sickly smile. He looks a little annoyed that I'm still alive. "Despite the odds, you've managed to survive again." Yep...definitely annoyed.

"Who's next?" I ask, moving away from that line of thinking because I'm really not in the mood for bloodshed in my bedroom.

Haigha and Aeromi say nothing, and Edwin has little to offer beyond Torai's report and a few mumbled words of appreciation for my help. Koji, on the other hand, rises from his seat and saunters over to where I'm sitting. With the smoothness of melted peanut butter, he slithers into my lap and wraps his arms around my neck. A scandalized gasp rises from the end of the table, followed by my sister's cheerful giggle.

"What are you doing?" I ask. My voice comes out raspier than I anticipate, and his smile spreads. The deviant knows full well what he's doing.

"Showing appreciation for my Queen," he says and bends to nuzzle along the side of my neck, purring.

"You already did that."

"It will never be enough."

"Can you please go back to your seat until we're done with actual business?" I ask as I manage to wedge my hands between our bodies and gently push against his shoulders. Koji doesn't resist, and surprisingly does what I ask.

"Fair warning, Majesty," he says as he sinks back into his seat, "I have a *lot* of appreciation to show you once this meeting adjourns."

The room fills with a combination of scandalized gasps and entertained whoops, all while I level Koji with my best *don't do that* stare. He just smiles back.

"Anyway..." I clear my throat and reach up to straighten the crown that hasn't moved at all, "Felina, any updates?"

"Lady Edith's training continues and I must say, she excels at everything she attempts." My sister beams back at me from the end of the table, a full, toothy grin turned toward me. "Tomorrow we begin fencing. She seems to be excited about it."

"I am!" Edith says. "It's going to be so much fun!"

She's adorable and idealistic and... entirely too naive for her own good. Battle isn't fun. I don't want her to see what it is really like, but the fact that Felina is training her to fight tells me I soon won't have much choice in the matter.

"Also, the Club Army appears to be preparing for an attack. We do not have much information on Humphrey's intended direction, but the White Army is also preparing."

"Indeed," the Unicorn adds from Felina's left. "The King of Clubs is quite aware of the struggle inside the Red Court and intends to use it as a distraction now that our forces are split."

"Might I also remind her Majesty that the White Court is currently without the majority of its most skilled fighters," Phineas says. It's just him and Felina, and my family is there. This is a problem.

"Blade?"

"Majesty?"

"How much longer will you be out gathering information?"

They look at Koji and then back to me. "If the Cheshire Cat is fit to return to duty, then I shall retire to the White Palace to wait at King Phineas's side."

Koji gives a lazy thumbs up. His face and body language betray absolutely nothing.

"I think that's our answer," I say, then turn my attention back to Blade. "Return to the White Palace as quickly as you are able in case it needs defending."

"Yes, Majesty," they say with a dip of their head. Their blue skin almost sparkles in the bright light.

"I, too, shall return to the White Palace upon completion of my duties," Nacht says. "Quite capable of defending the Queen, my brother is."

"Quite right," Tag agrees. "In the morning, I shall return to your side as well. Our beastly generals are more than capable of holding the front."

"That we are," Edwin says.

I nod in agreement, then cast my gaze around the table. Everyone is exhausted. Most of us are covered in some unholy mix of mud and blood. We've suffered setbacks and shared in victories, but this war is far from over. Emotion clogs my throat as I look at them. I know not everyone is likely to survive the coming fights… but I can't stand the thought of losing any of them. Through all of our trials, each and every one of them has become precious to me. Including the King of Diamonds.

"Haigha." His name comes out choked.

He turns to face me. "Yes, Mum?"

"Will you deliver a message to King Humphrey for me?"

"Certainly, Mum."

"Tell him that I'd like an audience with him away from the battlefield, and that I would like to negotiate for the return of the mouse woman."

"Your will be done, Mum."

CHAPTER TWENTY-ONE

Humphrey agreed to our terms all too easily. I know it's a trap. Phineas knows it's a trap. Hell, the cards probably even know it's a trap. But I'm one-hundred percent ready to walk right into it, head held high. I refuse to hide from anyone ever again.

Talon and I are in the throne room, dressed for travel and preparing our supplies, when the doors open and Haigha comes in. Percival rises from his place on the throne and crosses to stand beside me, his considerably taller shoulder positioned just behind mine and to the left. Ivan enters a moment later, arms loaded with a pair of saddle bags. He drapes them across the back of one of the pews and joins the circle. The messenger stops and drops to one knee, head bowed in supplication.

"Majesty," he says. The tone in his voice is different, and both Rabbits straighten.

This is not the March Hare.

"Yes?"

"A message for you."

"Proceed."

Haigha—Hatta—whoever he is—rises to his full height and looks down his long nose at me. The gaze feels condescending, but his heels snap together, and his hand flies into a formal salute.

"King Humphrey of the Court of Clubs extends his warmest greetings. He offers a kind invitation for The Alice's Court to attend a banquet at Castle Club this evening."

"This evening?"

"Yes, Majesty. This evening. I am afraid this offer is non-negotiable as the arrangements are already in progress."

I catch myself curling my lip in disgust and force my face back into a placid mask.

"Thank you for the message," I reply, nodding my head. The messenger snaps his heels together and offers a formal salute before his posture relaxes.

"Now, onto more important matters," he says, and the way his lips curl makes me take a step back—or rather, I would if it weren't for Percival at my back, keeping me in place. "What would her Majesty say is her greatest strength?"

I... I have no idea.

"I don't know. Why? Is this some kind of test?"

"Of course. Everything is a test."

I keep my gaze trained on him as I think through his question. My greatest strength? I don't have a single fucking clue what it might be. Any attempt at bullshit will be immediately called out. I might not know much about the madman before me, but I do know he's the only creature in this topsy-turvy world more perceptive than the Cheshire Cat.

"Resilience," I say after a long while. "And adaptability."

"Explain."

Hatta certainly takes no prisoners in his conversations.

"I've only been in Wonderland a short amount of time, but I've grown and changed, learned from my mistakes, and become more powerful than I ever expected. I know I have a long way to go to be worthy of the united crown, but I'm willing to put in the work, accept failure as the price of education, and pick myself up. And I'm willing to learn from my mistakes, no matter how painful they might be."

The former Rabbit stares down his long nose at me, gaze sharp and lips pressed into a solid line. I can almost see the cogs turning in his head as he mulls over my statement. Hatta watches like he's hunting me; his stare designed to make me nervous. To make me babble. To make me slip up and give away something.

I say nothing.

The hard line of his lips curves into a tiny smile, and he nods.

"A satisfactory answer," he says. "Congratulations, Majesty... I've no need to kill you where you stand."

"That's good to know, I suppose."

One sharp eyebrow lifts. "Are you saying you want to be killed?"

I school my features into an impassive mask. I don't need to let this nut know how annoyed I am.

"What I want is to not be challenged at every turn, but there's no hope of that happening. I gave you an honest answer. Do with it what you will."

His smile is no less dangerous for this new conversation, and when he turns to walk away without a response, the apprehensive shiver starts in my toes and works its way all the way up to the top of my head. I don't dare take my eyes off of him until he rounds the corner and disappears from sight.

"What are you thinking?" Ivan asks.

"I'm thinking I just walked into some kind of trap."

"I am inclined to agree," Percival says over my shoulder. "Rabbit or not, that creature is under no circumstances to be trusted."

"Wasn't he part of your court?"

"All the more reason to trust me when I tell you not to get too comfortable with him."

I stare after Hatta, the Carpenter's warning feeling a lot more prophetic than it has any right to be. I have to wonder, though... what would a betrayal by Hatta mean for Haigha as a messenger? As my friend?

"I'm glad he's on our side," I mutter.

"For now," Talon says like he knows something I don't.

"Are you saying he's going to betray me?"

"As King Percival said… I would be surprised if he doesn't."

We take the waystation to Goldrend and arrive at the gates of Castle Club on the back of four jubjubs, and the dark stone walls make me feel like we're ridding into the mouth of a monster that has every intention of devouring us whole. For all I know, this castle is alive. Nothing is outside the realm of possibility in Wonderland, and I'd be a fool to think otherwise.

Inside the gates we're met by humanoid guards in matte black armor. Some carry staves and pikes while others have swords strapped to their hips. None of them look happy to see us.

Talon is the first to dismount; I'm assuming because nobody in their right mind would attack a Caterpillar, and makes introductions. The guards eye me suspiciously, but they part at Talon's words. We dismount and follow him inside.

Where the White Palace is understated in its opulence, Castle Club is garish and ostentatious. Black and white marble surfaces are nearly indistinguishable beneath shining, gold accents.

Red drapes cover what I can only assume are walls and doors, blocking out who— or *what*— ever might try to peek in. Gold chandeliers dangle from the high ceilings, small orbs of magelight dancing at the tops of what appear to be daggers. What isn't gilded somehow manages to have Humphrey's face on it. Ceiling to floor tapestries hang along the walls of the main corridor, judgmental even for their lack of dimension. Ivan and Jerome both take a step closer as we're led past them and into the most hearts-awful space I've ever seen.

It's a ballroom with a black-and-white marble checkerboard for a floor and white marble walls. The space is easily ten times my height and so wide that the far wall won't even come into focus. And every single surface is covered in polished, shining gold. The lights themselves seem to be enchanted to make the decor sparkle. The whole space is a love letter to villainous excess.

"Ah, the little Queen has arrived!" Humphrey's voice isn't loud, but it echoes around the room, and I realize that the entire thing is designed for the complete overwhelm of his guests' senses. "Welcome to my home, Alice. I hope you find it to your liking."

I turn to face him. Talon places himself between us, continuing with his perfect performance. I suppose it's *not* a performance, though. This is his Caterpillar-face. Monsters like Humphrey don't get to see the softness under the facade like I do.

"Majesty," Talon says, bending at the waist. "May I present Queen Alice of the Court of Cards."

"The Court of Cards no longer exists," Humphrey replies. His face is a placid mask, smooth as porcelain and equally as unmoving, yet somehow that blankness exudes malice. "I do hate that it has taken so long for you to visit my humble home," he continues, focusing his dead-eyed, red stare on me over Talon's shoulder.

"My invitation to visit appears to have been lost in the mail," I reply curtly and move to Talon's side. "We both know you and I are no longer allies. Why don't we skip the pleasantries and get to business?"

"But a banquet is not a banquet without food and drink," Humphrey counters. He sounds more amused than angry.

"I'd rather not risk poisoning just to stroke your ego." I step around the Caterpillar so that I'm face to face with this horrible excuse for a King. Talon moves to the side, a silent referee for the brewing fight. "Tell me what you want in exchange for the woman."

A slow, vicious grin spreads across his face, and the rasp of porcelain follows it. I lock my jaw to keep from cringing at the sound.

"A no-nonsense Queen. Admirable."

"A Queen who doesn't trust her host not to poison her dinner," I reply, keeping my expression flat. Ivan coughs behind me, but I hear the snicker he's trying to hide.

"And surprisingly wise," Humphrey responds. What he doesn't know is that my heart is hammering hard enough to pound a hole through my sternum, and my lungs have chosen now to decide that breathing is no longer necessary. The smooth, emotionless planes of his porcelain face are terrifying in ways I didn't know existed. I liked it better when I couldn't see anything but his eyes through his helmet.

"Where's Estrella?" I ask. I'm stressed, lightheaded, and tired of tiptoeing around the point. I've been here five minutes, and I already want to go home.

"Who?"

"The woman you're holding captive. She's the wife of a stablekeeper."

He blinks at me like he's confused. The problem with porcelain skin is that it means he has a terrible poker face. No micro expressions mean no fooling me.

"Don't pretend like you don't know who I'm talking about. I want her back."

"Why would I hand anyone over to you?"

"Because despite the fact that I'm already your enemy, it would be a very bad idea to make me angry."

He chortles—actually fucking *chortles*—at me. My demand is funny to him. Not surprising, considering he's mad as a Hatter and as vicious as a Jabberwocky.

"Might I remind you that the last man who made me angry ended his reign of terror as battlefield confetti."

His laughter stops, but that sharp gaze lands square on me. He takes a step to the left and I answer, keeping my body even with his. "Is that a threat, little Queen?" When he stops, he has placed himself between us and the door.

Both Rabbits shift nervously behind me, and that's when I notice that Talon is gone. Jerome and Ivan are both armed to the teeth and preparing for bloodshed. I'm just not sure whose blood is going to spill yet. My money, honestly, is on mine. I swallow against the lump in my throat and square my shoulders.

"Returning Estrella is a request right now. It's only a threat if you make it one."

"A bold request."

"Have I mentioned that I'm getting bored yet?" I roll my eyes and punch my fist into the curve of my hip. "Because I'm bored." Because political posturing is not my favorite game. If our Caterpillar has done what I think he has done, I need to keep Humphrey talking for as long as possible.

"Are you always this impertinent?"

"Only when I'm faced with someone who doesn't deserve my time."

The smooth expanse of his face turns a blotchy red, the same color as his hair, even if his expression doesn't change. He's angry. *Good.* Ivan quietly steps closer to my side. He hasn't drawn his blade yet, but I feel the itch just as clearly as if it were my hand wanting for a weapon.

None of this was part of the plan... but we all know how easily plans change.

"What was your purpose in abducting that poor woman anyway?"

"Was she not the catalyst for your arrival?" he asks through gritted teeth.

"I was asked to come here and see about her, yes. But not because she's of any great, strategic value. Her husband came to me and asked for help. He's beside himself without her."

"You expect the plight of one of your allies to move my heart?"

"I expect nothing from a monster like you."

Smooth lips peel back from equally smooth teeth. I believe I've gone too far and I'm going to die a very slow, very painful death when I feel a spot of relief ping against my senses. Over Humphrey's left shoulder, I catch a flash of black fabric moving just beyond the open doors of the ballroom. I can't see who or what's moving there, but I'm not about to draw attention to it. As mad as this man is, it's likely he'll kill anyone or anything that gets within arms' reach and start by going out of his way to get his hands on me.

"If I had any intention of freeing that woman before, I certainly will *not* be doing so now," Humphrey says. His voice is low and venomous.

The King of Clubs is truly angry with me. I tense my shoulders and lock my hands into fists at my side to keep the adrenaline-fueled quivering of my limbs at bay and hold his gaze.

"If you refuse to release her, then this conversation is over. You leave me no choice but to take her by force."

Jerome releases a small, strangled sound, but Humphrey blinks in surprise.

"You would go to war over one pathetic woman?" He sounds truly baffled.

"If I'm unwilling to go to war over one woman, then I am not fit to lead anyone," I reply, crossing my arms over my chest. "No life is too small to protect because no life is worthless. I also object to your flippant dismissal of her as 'pathetic.'"

"Perhaps it is time to leave, Majesty," Talon says, having magically reappeared at my side. "Causing an incident on your first outing to Club Territory would be extraordinarily bad form, after all."

His expression betrays nothing, but the fact that the tension has bled out of my connections to both Rabbits seems important. I look over at him and he nods slightly.

"Perhaps you're right," I answer and take a step back. "After all, our host has been gracious enough *not* to slit my throat thus far." I smile up at Humphrey, who has returned to his anger. "I apologize for my abrupt departure. I'll need a raincheck on that poisoned banquet." I offer a delicate curtsy despite the fact that I'm in riding leathers and allow Talon to take my arm and escort me around the roadblock that is the King of Clubs.

I have a ton of questions, but I ask none of them. It's not until we're through the waystation and headed back toward Wonderland Castle that I'm brave enough to even look at the Caterpillar, much less think about having any kind of conversation. This topsy-turvy world is full of spies, after all. Fortunately, the biggest question I have is answered before I have to ask it. That answer also comes in the form of a bandersnatch carrying two people: Nacht and Estrella. The woman looks even smaller as he holds her in the saddle, and even from this distance there's no mistaking the nervous tremor rattling her hands and feet. Nacht offers a small nod and a half-smirk.

Mission Accomplished, that look says. Too bad it also means we've just instigated all-out war.

I arrive home to war.

No sooner did we leave Goldrend than the Club Army started its westward march, seemingly razing its own territory in the process. The messenger who met us at the waystation looked downright terrified to tell me.

I'm not particularly surprised at this turn of events. We just abducted a hostage from right under a mad King's nose. This scorched earth tactic of his also announces everything I didn't already know about our ally-turned-adversary: he's senselessly brutal and will stop at nothing to get what he wants.

At the very least, I'd hoped for a shower and a cup of tea before going to war, but alas…it is not to be. Wonderland Castle is a flurry of activity with Tag at the center, directing traffic like an old hand. Percival is nowhere to be found.

"Majesty." Tag pauses mid-flow to acknowledge me and offer a formal bow as we walk up. "Welcome home."

"Thanks, I think."

He offers a small smile before turning to a soldier who looks more like a bird than a person and issuing some sort of jargon-filled instruction that goes whizzing right over my head.

"I see you were successful in your endeavors."

"Thanks to your brother," I admit. "It's the first time I've been part of a reverse kidnapping."

"That you know of," Nacht offers, his voice close enough to my left ear to make me jump in surprise.

"Weirdo."

He chuckles at my weak insult and hands Estrella off to Talon, who offers to take her to visit her husband somewhere else in the castle. We've only been gone for a few hours, but it feels like weeks.

"What's going on?" I ask, falling into step between the twins as we move back toward the throne room.

"As the messenger explained, Humphrey has started his march and yes, he is destroying his own territory as he moves. The Club Army is stripping the land and the people bare, conscripting the able-bodied, and leaving the rest with nothing. King Percival has returned to Castle Diamond to prepare his people for the inevitability of Humphrey's assault."

"And to raise more undead soldiers, right?"

"A helpful ability in times of war," Tag says, and the epic side-eye he provides dares me to argue about the morality and ethicality of such behavior.

"The struggle to maintain control of Mercia and Northumbria continues to the North. Edwin and his army are skilled, but Morcar's control as sole General of the Red Army has presented… interesting… challenges."

"Such as?"

"The rules of war no longer apply," Tag says. "Morcar is a bloodthirsty beast, and the worst of the worst now revere him as a god."

That does not bode well for any of us.

"Can they hold him off?"

"For now."

One battle at a time, Alice. One battle at a time.

"I assume their holding of both lands will continue until we can do something about Humphrey?"

"No clue," Tag admits.

"Not likely," Nacht adds.

"What do we do?"

"Deal with the most pressing problem, of course," Tag replies. The brothers look at each other over my head. "Humpty Dumpty needs a great fall," they say in unison.

I bite the inside of my cheek to hold in a groan and turn for the barracks to armor up. I'd hoped to put a little bit more time between a couple of hours ago and now. "What time do we leave?"

"As soon as you are prepared, Majesty." Tag doesn't look at me as he says it. He's fully engrossed in his planning, and now that his brother is at his side, they have no further use for me. Except maybe to hold the standard as we ride off to war.

"Can someone get a message to Phineas about what's going on?" I ask as I leave the battle plans to the twins and head off to get ready. I don't wait for a response.

Of course I get no peace... Koji is in the garden, lounging in the sun along a low wall. He's half-dressed and fully shameless, partially shifted into cat form with ears and tail swishing in the breeze. From what I can see, his wounds have healed completely. Not even bruises peek between the lines of his swirling tattoos. His signature shit-eating smirk rests on his lips.

"I don't have time for whatever you're planning," I say in passing when he reaches a hand toward me in invitation.

"Meow," he drawls with a swipe of long claws

that scratch across the leather covering my hip. When I don't stop, he huffs a dramatic sigh and rolls off of the wall, landing on his feet to fall into step beside me. "The scurrying thither and yon is exhausting," he says, draping himself across my shoulders. "Seems a bit unnecessary."

"You do realize we're going to war, right?"

"My point stands," he says flatly. "War is boring. Too bloody for my taste."

"I imagine you've had enough bloodshed for a while, considering the last blood you saw was your own."

Koji says nothing, which tells me more than words ever could. Recent events have frightened him. There's something else, though. He's restless in a way that makes the magic tremble around him. It's not just his fear of bloodshed or the fact that he's not completely healed inside. He's planning something.

The armory is surprisingly empty when we enter, and when Koji pushes the door closed and slides the bolt into the latch to lock it, I know I'm in trouble. The light is dim and the air is thick with the scents of oil and leather. Footprints on the dusty floor tell me we've only recently missed the flurry of activity. I busy myself with riffling through the weapons racks, though I'm not really looking for anything in particular. My nerves are rising.

My whole body tenses when arms go around me and my back is pulled tightly against Koji's long, lean body. Lips drift lazily along the shell of my ear, and the rumble of his pull vibrates through me. He smells like magic and moonlight, a sharp contrast to the odors of battle surrounding us. I turn in his arms, stretching up to press my lips to his. His purr becomes a deep rumble, and next thing I know, my back hits the wall.

"Tempting little siren," he mutters against my mouth. "Dangerously addictive." Another kiss. "She who rules my heart."

I'm speechless, spinning out inside my head at the feel of his hold, his lips against my skin, and the sound of his voice rumbling through me. I could get so lost in this feeling, but his next words are as effective as ice down my spine.

"It has come time for the betrayal to start," he says softly. His voice is coated in sadness, but his lips don't lift from my skin... like by holding onto me, we can keep the truth from becoming true.

"Why now?" I force myself to ask. My voice is small and scared, and the heartbreak in my chest pours out with them.

"Her attention is focused on Edwin and the battle for the provinces," he says, and I realize as cold air drifts across my arms that he's moving away from me. "Queen Lucinda needs her informant at her side, spoiling the moves of the opposition. As long as I remain at your side — where I truly desire to be, my Queen — we all remain in danger." He lifts my hand in one of his and slides a bracer onto it.

"Feeding information to the Red Court is the easiest way to keep her from coming for you." Koji's touch is delicate as he turns my wrist over and tightens the straps against my inner arm. Each touch is so infused with love that it breaks my heart all over again. "A return to her good graces also means the ability to compromise Morcar's plans."

"Does this mean you'll help Edwin win?"

He nods while securing my other bracer, then picks up a pair of leg plates before kneeling at my feet. The reverence with which he touches me.

"As much as I would love to find a way to paint Morcar as the traitor, I fear that will not be possible. Lord Edwin has insinuated himself as your soldier a bit too well."

It's a fair assumption. After all, he betrayed his own kind to take me into Wonderland's most secure prison, then turned on them to allow Nacht to rescue me.

"But you will come back to me, right?" I can hear the desperation in my voice. It's...unbecoming. But Koji rises and smiles down at me.

"I will *always* return to you," he says, then clasps my face in his big, warm hands and kisses me tenderly. Despite his endless affection and pretty promises, I can't stop the tiny voice of doubt fluttering at the edge of my consciousness, trying to warn me that he really will betray me one day.

Neither of us says another word as he pulls back, then sets about coating me head to toe in shining, silver armor. There are no mirrors in this room, but that doesn't matter. I can see my own reflection in his wide, wet eyes. Between that reflection and the way he looks at me, like I'm the most wondrous creature in this twisted land, I finally feel like I belong.

Like I'm a true Queen.

Returning to the battlefield is not something I wanted to do on no rest after Koji tore my heart out and walked away, but here we are. Tag and I stand shoulder-to-shoulder at the top of one hill and stare across the valley at the Card Army. The situation is eerily similar to my last battle, where Humphrey fired on all of us, and I somehow managed to throw up a shield big enough to save the entire front line.

That feels like an eternity ago.

"Are you ready for this, Majesty?" Talon says from my left.

"Not even a little bit. Let's go."

The three of us swing up onto the backs of our jubjubs and start down the hill, both Rabbits following closely behind, at the same time Humphrey's negotiation party breaks from his front line. I measure my breathing to keep from hyperventilating and hold the reins tighter than I need to as we move closer and closer to what feels like inevitable doom.

We stop a respectable distance from one another while Humphrey, Talon, and I dismount. Talon moves at my side, back straight and that mystical aura encasing him again. He's back in Caterpillar mode... but the fact that he helped abduct an abductee from inside the castle of the man in front of us while I acted as a distraction... pretty sure that means he's complicit in my shenanigans and no longer entirely neutral in this war.

"King Humphrey," Talon says, his voice even and smooth, and bows.

"Quiet, traitor," he snarls. "Your words are worthless. Save them before I slit your throat."

"Leave him alone!" I snap, drawing the madman's attention back to me. "Your fight is with me, not him. Now quit with the theatrics and tell me why you've decided to destroy everyone and everything around you."

"It got your attention, did it not?" His voice is as raspy as I remember, and his expression just as flat, save for the burning hatred in his eyes.

"What do you want?"

"Want?" He scoffs and the sound is reminiscent of shattering ceramic. "What I want is you out of my way, little Queen. You are a pest."

"I'm not leaving Wonderland, so you may as well start wishing for something else. This fight is stupid and it needs to end."

"Then marry me."

"Excuse me?" I blink up at him, the words not

actually registering for what they are.

"You heard me."

"Yes, but I'm not certain what you mean."

"Exactly what I said, girl." The way he looks down his shiny nose at me is as infuriating as his patronizing tone. "Become my wife and unite the courts." Ceramic grinds against itself as his mouth turns up in a mockery of a smile. "And then offer your head to me in apology for your impudence."

I blink up at him, shock rippling through my system. Did he really just…

"No, I don't think I'll be doing either of those things."

Humphrey chuckles. It sounds like sandpaper. Then he draws his sword.

"Suits me fine. Either way, you're going to die."

Behind me the Rabbits' swords leave their sheathes, but I'm already annoyed with this whole scene. Before anyone can charge anyone else, I take a step back, plant my foot, and bring my hands together in a wide, sweeping motion. The gale that leaves my fingertips rushes outward and topples the entire Club army, their King included. He tumbles ass over teakettle backwards up the hill. When he comes to a stop, there's a long, jagged crack running down the side of his porcelain face. The rage burning in his eyes, even from across the field, is enough to make my blood run cold.

I thought we were at war before… now, I *know* we are.

CHAPTER TWENTY-TWO

Humphrey surprises me by following proper rules of engagement. He snarls at me across the field for a bit but doesn't advance again. His flunkies pull him up off the ground and lead him back to the bandersnatch he rode in on, and they recede beyond the hill.

Once he's no longer in my line of sight, both sides retreat a safe distance, and I discover that Tag has already directed the cards to set up camp. Rows upon rows of tents line what used to be an untouched swath of green land. The grass is gone, crushed under muddy boots and heavy equipment. Plumes of smoke rise from various fires. Messengers run to and fro, and this, I realize, is the part of war I've been sheltered from. The reality that the last home some of these soldiers may ever know is this muddy field. My heart aches at the sight.

"Come, Majesty," Tag orders, taking my elbow in his hand and guiding me through the labyrinth of white canvas toward a much larger tent. "There are no proper doors here. We must make do with messengers and scouts."

No doors. I'm cut off from my court. From my friends. From the false sense of security I've constructed over the last half a year. This little, ragtag bunch I've assembled is all alone unless we want to barge in on the next random house we find and commandeer their door. Even then, there's no telling what would await us when we exited.

The tent Tag leads me into is thrice the size of the others but equally as Spartan. A large table stands in the middle of the room. Neatly rolled maps march down its center in a perfect line. Chairs sit cattywampus, as if they were just thrown out and left for whoever might decide they want one. A small table with a pitcher of flower-topped water stands sweating on one side. A canvas flap toward the back is flipped up and secured with rope, and inside I see a row of cots.

"Welcome to the war room, Majesty," Talon says. When I turn to look at him, he nods, then offers a small bow. "I must take my leave. After all, a master of information is only such because he collects his quarry."

"Be safe," I tell him before he vanishes. My Rabbits wait patiently behind me while I find my bearings, but Tag steps toward the table and begins unrolling the maps and schematics, layering paper upon paper. I step up to the side of the table, and I'm immediately overwhelmed by the information. Tag, however, hasn't missed a beat. For all his insanity, he's perfectly on task and hyper-aware of everything happening all over the land.

While I'm mulling over the reality of our situation, the outer flap jumps back with a crinkle and a snap, and in strides Nacht. He moves like he owns the place — like he owns any place he enters, really — and steps up to the table opposite his brother. They speak in those weird, rhyming tones that make no sense before the darker twin turns his vicious gaze on me and grins like he's going to unhinge his jaw and swallow me whole. It takes everything in me and a little bit of magic not to take a step back.

Yeah, he saved my life. That doesn't mean he won't take it.

"Heard a nasty little rumor, Majesty," he says.

"Oh, yeah?" I try to feign nonchalance and fall very, very flat.

"The mome raths do *so* like to talk."

"What's the rumor?"

"That a certain precocious pussycat has made his way back to the lap of the bloody Red Queen."

Damn it all to Hell. I bite my cheek to hold in a grimace, but Nacht, of course, sees every minute change on my face.

"So it is true."

"Yes and… well, yes," I say. "But I can't talk about it here."

"Majesty," Nacht replies with a cluck of the tongue then turns to face me fully. "Every Tom, Dick, and Bill in Wonderland knows you've been betrayed by your favorite plaything. Anything you intend to say about him, you can say out loud before us and the mome raths."

But I don't want to. I know that, for Koji's sake, I have to keep his double-double agent status a secret. I just can't stand the thought of anyone thinking he's exactly the kind of character he portrays. He's too good for that image, carefully crafted or not.

"For all intents and purposes, we no longer have the Cheshire Cat as a messenger," I announce. Tag's eyebrows rise but he otherwise doesn't react. While we look back and forth between one another, a messenger scurries in, bows deeply, and hands a folded scrap of paper to Nacht. He reads the words and his eyebrows lift.

"It appears our allies are dropping like flies." When he turns the paper around, the writing looks like gibberish.

"I can't read that."

"Hatta has chosen his side, and it is not ours," Tag explains.

"What?"

Nacht's gaze sharpens as he looks down at me. "He's feeding Humphrey information." The paper crumples under his fingers and disappears from sight.

"The man most privy to White Court secrets has now turned Black. You should be very afraid, Majesty."

"Like I wasn't already…" I mutter as I fight the urge to curl in on myself.

"What was that?"

"Nothing." I glare at Nacht and his attempt to bait me before turning my attention to the maps. "We're two down and at war. Tell me, Master Strategist, what's our plan?"

Tag moves beside me, also looking down at the maps. "Our plan, Majesty, is to *not die*."

"Easier said than done, I assume."

"Correct."

Over the next hour, he explains the mechanics of war to me. Strategic positioning, asset placement, troop movement, supply lines, and information sharing. Most of it goes whizzing right over my head, but it doesn't stop me from at least listening and trying to make it make sense. As we move around the table, messengers come and go, passing notes to Nacht, who spends most of his time quietly conversing with the Caterpillar.

Once I sort of have a hold on how this will go, Tag turns to his brother.

"Report."

Nacht snaps to attention, back ramrod straight while his heels click together and one hand lifts to his forehead in a perfect salute.

"The Clubs have made camp and have no intention of moving on us for the time being. Word from the North is that Edwin continues to hold both Northumbria and Mercia. Approximately two-thirds of the Red Army has defected, favoring the beast over the brute. The Walrus and the Oysters have successfully quelled uprisings in the more rural areas. For all intents and purposes, Mercia and Northumbria are united and no longer under Heart control."

"That's good news, at least."

"There is more," Nacht says. "Reports from the Diamond Court confirm that the Carpenter is still in control of his lands as well. Lastly—"

"But not firstly," Tag cuts in.

"—but not firstly, Felina has requested The Alice's assistance at first convenience. There is... trouble."

"What kind of trouble?" I'm immediately on alert.

"It appears the Queen's sister is... a bit headstrong."

Fuck.

"Okay...how do I get there quickly? And is it safe to leave here?"

"To be fair," Ivan cuts in, startling me. He and Jerome have been so quiet that I'd forgotten they were here. "Nowhere in Wonderland is safe for you, Majesty. But the fastest path would be from Goldrend to Wabe."

"How far are we from Goldrend?"

"An hour, barring any *unforeseen circumstances*."

He means ambushes.

"Do I need to stay?" I ask, turning toward Tag.

"Only until the report concludes," he says, nodding back toward his brother. "Continue."

Nacht, at attention, accepts the note in Talon's hand, reads it, and announces, "The Cheshire Cat has arrived at Heart Palace and is at the side of the Duchess." He snaps his hand up in salute. "End report," he adds then clicks his heels together. My heart twists in my chest as he relaxes. Everything has gone so far off the rails. I'm standing here completely overwhelmed, butthe twins turn their attention back to the maps, and Talon steps up beside them, joining in the discussion.

Just another Tuesday in Wonderland, I realize.

"Ready, Majesty?" Ivan asks, offering a hand to me. I see the pity in his eyes and the unspoken *I told you so.* I want desperately to tell them of my last conversation with Koji, but even the magic is wary of my voicing that truth. The more people who think he's a true traitor, the safer he'll be.

"As ready as I'll ever be," I reply and take his hand.

I hate this. All of it.

The White Palace is a battleground all on its own.

It's late in the day when we arrive and I'm so exhausted I can barely hold my head up without assistance, but the dulcet tones of teenage hysteria snap me to attention before we ever make it inside. The sound of Felina's weary sigh leads us to the reception room where the tableau inside is almost enough to make me laugh.

My sister faces off against the Ace of Spades while the White King stands to one side, pinching the bridge of his nose and grimacing in frustration. A fop and two soldiers stand behind Felina, eyes wide and perfectly round as Edith screeches out her displeasure at whatever order she's just been given. Phineas catches my gaze when he opens his eyes and the way his widen act as a cry for help.

Please do something about this crazy child! that look says.

"Hey there, shrieking violet," I say, stepping up to her side, "what's got you in a tizzy?"

Edith immediately turns her blazing eyes toward me, her forehead creased in anger and her lip curled away from her teeth in what would be an intimidating snarl if she wasn't still a young teenager.

"It's *your* fault," she snaps, sucking in a breath with a hiss to really get started. I brace myself and wait. "All this work I've been doing, and I'm told I'm not allowed to fight? Why do you keep trying to baby me, Alice?"

"I'm not trying to baby you," I reply lamely because yeah... I sort of am. Even daring to say it out loud is patronizing enough that we both see right through it. "I need you safe until I know you're strong enough to protect yourself."

"How would you know?" Edith retorts, hurt pulsing in her voice. "You haven't given me a chance to show you." I cast a glance at Felina, who throws her hands up in exasperation, and drags a deep breath in.

In through the nose. Out through mouth. Woo-sah.

"Look," I say flatly because this argument is insane, "I haven't slept in two days. I've spent most of that time either facing off with psychopaths or in a saddle. I'm tired, hungry, and dirty. I haven't even been here for five minutes and I'm already being blamed for everything. Take. A step. Back." My expression must tell her everything my words can't. She steps back, but the fire doesn't leave her eyes. "We're at war, Edith. I've been in Wonderland for nearly a year and *I'm* not ready for it. You've been training a few weeks and while I have no doubt that you've excelled at everything you've done, I'm not sacrificing you for your own damned ego."

"You suck," she snarls. "You always look at me like I'm a baby!"

Fair. Because I do. "Maybe, but you're not going to the front and that's final."

"Who's ordering me? My bitchy sister or the bitchy Queen?"

"Both." She opens her mouth to argue again, but I keep talking. "You can be pissed all you want. Call me every name in the book and then make up a few if it makes you feel better. You'll just have to be mad at me and *stay alive*."

"Ugh." Edith stamps her foot like the child she is. "You're impossible. I never should have come here!" She turns on her heel and streaks away, long legs eating up the turf as I stand there and watch in shock.

"Should I go get her?" I ask, staring in the direction she ran. Felina steps up beside me and shakes her head, but before she can speak, my sister shrieks. We both break into a run, rounding the corner of the building in a panic.

Only to find Nacht standing at the gates, my flailing animal of a sister thrown over his shoulder and a shit-eating grin on his face.

"Lose something, Majesty?"

"Little rabbits run fast," I hear myself say.

Nacht's smile widens. "That they do."

"PUT ME DOWN!" Edith shrieks from over his shoulder. Her fists pound against his back and her legs kick wildly from the knees down. Only his arm slung across the backs of her thighs keeps her from tumbling ass over teakettle into the dirt.

"Quiet, little girl, or I'll strap you to a chair and gag you."

He'd do it, too. Edith seems to realize this, and all of the fight drains out of her.

"That's better." He strides past the two of us, as unbothered as a cat in the sun, but my sister glares at me as they pass. "What should we do with the little runaway?"

"My room," I say, and we follow along behind them in an increasingly ridiculous procession. Phineas falls into step at my right, a sigh of relief gusting out of him as we step through the gates. Behind us, Ivan snickers.

Somewhere along the way, we pick up both Blade and Aunt Margaret, but the most surprising part of this adventure is when we actually arrive in my room.

There's a new door inside. Off the sitting area, a sleek door of dark wood stands against the pale wall, marked with a tree whose branches arc up into a heart. Talon chuckles at the sight, then opens the door to reveal another hallway. At the end are two doors.

"Welcome to your new family suite, Majesty," he says. Even Edith has stopped fighting in favor of craning her head up over Nacht's shoulder to look. "Shall we investigate?"

"Sure…" I follow along behind him, and the others fall into step with us. One door is very clearly Edith's new bedroom while the other opens onto a room highly reminiscent of Aunt Margaret's whole house. It's a smaller sitting room, and her bedroom and bathroom are off to one side.

Aunt Margaret passes by us, looking around at the space. Edith pounds on Nacht's back, trying to get him to release her, but he looks over at me and grins. Apparently, he's enjoying his beating.

"Put her down," I tell him and the grin falls. He does as he's told, reluctantly, and while muttering something about ruining his fun.

"What is this?" my sister asks, stepping up beside me.

"Your new home."

"But what does it mean?"

I pull the chain containing my key from beneath my clothes and sure enough, two new keys dangle from it, tiny copies of mine.

"It means you're safe here and you can come and go as you please. Should something happen and someone gets inside, you two will have the same protection as me."

"But what if I want to be the one to protect you?" Edith asks, but her voice carries none of the fire from earlier.

"In time, you will." I curl my arm around her shoulders and pull her against my side. "But right now, you need to let us be the ones to do the protecting, okay?"

She huffs and blows her hair out of her face, but the fight has gone out of her. For Now.

"Fine."

By the time I make it to my bed, I'm so exhausted that I can barely function. Jerome all but carries me, my arm slung over his shoulders so he can support my weight. He does at least take my shoes off before tossing the blankets over me.

The problem with deep sleep in Wonderland is that it, like peace, never lasts.

"Alice, wake *up!* They're going to break down the door if you don't!"

My awakening is so violent that I'm disoriented and don't immediately recognize my sister's voice. I have no idea how long she's been standing over me, shouting in my face and shaking me like a ragdoll, but it doesn't feel like long enough. I have no idea how long I've been asleep. It feels like I just closed my eyes. But she's right; the pounding on the outer door is downright cacophonous.

"I'm coming…" I mumble. At least that's what I intend to say. What actually comes out of me is mostly unintelligible nonsense. I let Edith yank me out of the bed and stabilize me while I sway on my feet, then together we go pull the door open. Both Twins, both Rabbits, and a worried-looking King wait on the other side.

"What took so long?" Tag asks with arms crossed over his chest, his sharp gaze admonishing me.

"I was asleep."

He blows past me like I don't exist, and I take a stumbling step backwards to compensate. The rest follow him in, but nobody sits.

"I take it you have a report?" I ask as I push my knuckles against my lips to stifle a yawn.

Tag immediately goes into messenger mode,

snapping to attention and staring at a spot somewhere above my head.

"Report," I say, because I've learned that he'll just stand there until I do.

"The Club Army is fully mobilized and appears to be bound for Diamond territory. Reports say that Humphrey believes Castle Diamond to be unoccupied due to the Walrus's assistance with the northern rebellion. The Walrus and the Earl of Mercia continue to hold the liberated Red territory."

"Have we heard from Percival?"

"Only a messenger to report that the territory is well-defended."

"Arrogant as ever, I see." Tag nods but says nothing. "And Edwin is okay?"

"As far as we are aware."

He snaps his heels, signaling the end of the report. Tag's shoulders relax and he returns to himself.

"A request has come in from the North," Phineas says. "The Unicorn will lead a portion of the White Army to Mercia to assist Lord Edwin's defense so that the Walrus and the Oysters may rejoin the rest of the Club Army."

I nod along, trying to visualize the various armies as chess pieces… but I was never very good at chess. I'm thankful for Tag, who ingests this new development and files it away with the million other things he's remembering.

"Majesty, we need you back as quickly as you can get here," he says, and there's a distinct note of panic in his voice. "Our forces are strong, but we need our leader."

"As much as I love having you home," Phineas says, "he is correct. You are needed elsewhere."

I don't relish the thought of going all the way back to Wonderland Castle just to go to war again, but it appears that's what I'm doing. I bite my cheek to hold in a sigh and lean into Phineas' side when he wraps his arm around my shoulders.

"Give me half an hour," I say and head for the bathroom to shower off the first layer of filth.

We make it as far as Wabe before a messenger comes rushing up with a hurried bow and stutters a heart-rending message.

"The Oysters have been surrounded by the Red Queen's loyal forces," she says. The woman is unconventionally pretty, but she's also very, very tiny. She's perfectly proportioned but only comes to my waist. Tag has to bend to one knee to hear her and still looks down on her.

"Where is the ambush point?" he asks, perfectly calm and collected.

"On patrol near Coving," she says. "The Walrus is struggling to maintain his freedom, Sir."

"What do we do?" I ask.

"Proceed to the White Palace," Tag tells the messenger. "Inform King Phineas and have the

Unicorn move up the White Army's departure. We will send what reinforcements we can upon arrival."

She salutes him and runs along, weaving between us as deftly as a rogue. Moments later, we're passing through the waystation to Brillig and on the way back to Wonderland Castle.

We ride in silence for a long time, the events of the past three days tumbling over one another in my mind. The trek is weirdly peaceful, especially given the fact that war is all around us. It's almost like we're in a bubble, removed from reality. But even that bothers me.

"Hey, Tag?"

"Yes, Majesty?"

"If you had to guess, what are our odds of winning this war?"

He takes time to consider my question. A myriad of emotions pass across his face, but he doesn't speak until he's considered all angles. When he does, the answer surprises me.

"Roughly eighty-to-one."

My eyebrows rise. This is not a man who operates on emotion. He's really thought this through, and he still thinks it's a long shot. Truth be told, so do I. I've thought that from the beginning, but the idea of facing war on two fronts while sandwiched between only increases my fear that we're in an unwinnable situation.

Nacht scoffs from my other side. "This *divide-and-conquer* routine gets one nowhere at all. Majesty, you are too polite to engage with monsters."

"And what do you suggest I do?" I raise an eyebrow in challenge, but his smooth facade never cracks.

"Let me poison them all. If you have no enemies standing, you have no way to lose."

"Quite right," Tag agrees, though without much enthusiasm.

"Quite right, indeed," Nacht echoes and gives me one of those sadistic smiles that makes me want to run screaming into the night.

"There are two entire armies against me. Plus, Percival once the Red Queen is handled. There's no possible way."

"Do you doubt my abilities, Majesty?" He presses a hand to his chest and tips his bottom lip out in a perfectly manufactured pout. "You wound me."

"Oh, please… the only way to wound you is with a blade."

"Fair." His pout turns back into a grin.

"How exactly does one man poison thousands of people?"

"I have ways."

"He has ways."

They speak at the same time, and the stereo surround of their voices sends a chill of dread trickling down my spine.

I let the conversation drop. At this point, I have no idea how to respond. Nacht isn't joking and Tag seems to support him. They really are a terrifying pair.

We ride in silence all the way back to Wonderland Castle, where the army stands at the ready, divided into two factions. Before I can even get inside to wash off the road dust, Tag has me by the wrist, dragging me to one side of the courtyard where stands a locked door.

"If you would, Majesty," he says, nodding toward it. I do as instructed, and inside I find yet another deep, narrow closet stacked with card soldiers. Tag whistles and they snap to attention, eyes opening, and march out in narrow stacks. These cards' backs are a black-and-red chevron pattern, and their faces are bloodthirsty. I lose count of the decks somewhere around forty. "The reserves," he says of the more than ten thousand cards pouring into the open area.

"Where are we sending them?" I ask as he closes the door behind the last deck.

"You will ride North with Nacht and half of the army to assist in Northumbria. I shall take the other half east to assist King Percival with the defense of Brillig and Diamond Territory."

"When do we leave?"

"Now."

And we do. Within half an hour, we're through the looking glass and I'm astride a jubjub at Nacht's side, my Rabbits trailing behind on the angriest pair of these demon birds I've ever seen. That little shortcut is useful but disorienting as hell. We're halfway across the world in a blink. The instant travel is part of Wonderland I don't think I'll ever get used to.

Magic is fun.

I ride in silence at Nacht's side while he outlines our plan — arrive near Coving, drive back the Red Army, and bring Torai and the Oysters to safety. Leave the army with Edwin for defense. Run like hell before Morcar gets to me.

Simple, right?

I wish it was simple.

Because nothing in Wonderland is *ever* simple.

Nacht and I ride due north with stacked decks of cards in tow, faster than I've ever ridden before, but it's still the darker end of twilight when we cross the border into eerily familiar territory. Northumbria is anything but peaceful when we arrive. The sounds of battle greet us miles before we find the fray, but even that is not enough to prepare me for the absolute clusterfuck we find.

The battle is brutal, bloody, and not at all looking to be in our favor. The familiar image of battling beasts greet us, though this time Morcar appears to have the upper hand. Not because he's the better beast, but because Edwin is defending something.

No… *someone.*

Torai.

The Earl of Northumbria bears down on his older brother, teeth bared and wings flattened against his back as that long, serpentine neck coils to strike. Edwin shrieks, the sound loud enough to make my ears bleed even from this distance and raises a clawed foot in preparation to defend against the incoming attack.

"Cards, deploy!" Nacht calls and the decks of cards unfurl into perfect ranks. His voice is perfectly calm and collected, but it must carry across the battlefield, because Morcar's head whips toward us. We're far enough away that I can't see his features clearly, but the murderous blaze in those beady eyes is obvious enough "Attack!" Nacht shouts, and eight columns of perfectly ordered cards file down the hill with surprising speed. The ground beneath us rumbles enough to unsettle our mounts, and when I look around to find the source — because we did not bring enough soldiers with us to cause it — a larger contingent of card soldiers filters over the ridge to the west. In the midst of them, I catch sight of a familiar, horned helmet.

"It seems our Unicorn moves faster than expected," Nacht says and leads me down the path our soldiers have left for us. None of our noise, however, distracts the jabberwockies from their deadlock. "I suggest you draw a weapon, Majesty," he says. I take the sword from my back and allow Nacht to take the lead. Ivan and Jerome fall in beside me, armed and armored and looking delightfully deadly.

Morcar lets go an irritated screech that makes me want to turn tail and run. It hasn't been but a couple of days since he had me at his mercy, and

I'm not keen to return to that particular situation... but we really have no choice.

Our birds pick up speed and in moments we're cutting between Edwin and the Walrus, my vicious twin protector leaping from the back of his bird while producing a pair of deadly black blades. Our arrival gives Edwin the ability to take control of the fight, and the pair once again launch skyward, the buffeting air from their wings enough to knock me flat on my ass.

"Take care of him!" Nacht calls over his shoulder as the first Red soldiers break through the line of cards. I scramble back to my knees and crawl across the bloody ground to where Torai lies curled on his side.

"Let me see," I shout over the sound of clashing weapons. Jerome helps me drags Torai's arms away from his body revealing a nasty gash from mid-chest to just below his hip. His armor is flayed open.

Claw marks.

"This is going to be uncomfortable," I tell him. "Just hang on for me."

Jerome holds him steady while I dig my hands into the earth and drag power out of it. It let it fill me until I feel like I'll explode if I take on one more drop, then close my eyes and place my hands over the wound. Then, like Talon showed me, I push it into Torai's body.

The Walrus goes rigid under my hands. A scream tears from his throat. The sounds of battle grow louder, trying to draw my attention away from my task.

"We're losing it!" someone shouts. "Hurry up!"

I grit my teeth and continue to direct the magic where it's needed, finding the tattered threads of sinew and bone, politely-yet-forcefully asking for their assistance in repairing the damage. Were it not for Jerome wrapped around Torai, he would be thrashing. Shattered ribs pull back together; lacerated organs halt their bleeding. One by one, I rebuild capillaries and veins, then pull the muscles and skin back together. It's a rough job, rushed and messy, but the tension soon leaves his body.

I let the magic trickle away only to find Nacht standing over me, weapons poised to strike.

"Hate to interrupt, Majesty, but we have another problem. Big one."

I push myself to my feet and follow the line of his blade toward the middle of the field. Every faction has come to a halt. Red and White soldiers alike stare, weapons lax in their hands, as The Unicorn faces off against a soldier I've not seen before. Shining, golden armor reflects the fading sunlight, sending a kaleidescopic glare skidding across the ground. I raise my hand to shield my eyes from the worst of the blinding light.

"Who the hell is that?"

"The Lion," Ivan says from my left hand.

"One of the deadliest creatures in this world," Nacht adds.

"I thought you were the deadliest."

"I said *one of,* Majesty."

"What does this mean?"

Nacht turns his gaze on me. "It means our Unicorn is about to face the most difficult battle of their life." His sword falls to his side. "If you happen to be the praying type, now would be a good time to start begging whoever you worship for help."

Both warriors draw their weapons and take up battle stances. They are unhurried as they survey one another. Even from this distance, I can feel the confidence oozing off of both. When they finally start to fight, it's the most beautiful thing I've ever seen.

They move like dancers, parrying and thrusting, twisting and twining around one another. The Lion is significantly smaller than our Unicorn, but it makes no difference. They're equally matched and absolutely lethal with every single strike. The ring of metal-on-metal reaches our ears, and each new attack threatens to take my breath away.

Then a screech fills the air.

Oh, yeah... there are Jabberwocky fighting overhead.

We cast our gazes up as the aerial beasts lock claws and spin. Edwin manages the upper hand and sends Morcar flying away, only to have the smaller beast rocket back at full speed and slam head to chest.

I look back across the field to find the two warriors locked in battle.

But we also have a new problem. The armies have started to move again, and the Red Army is coming this way. We don't have enough soldiers in our contingent to hold them.

"What the fuck do we do?" I shout, taking a step back. Jerome and Ivan step in front of me, but Nacht stays at my side.

"You get rid of them," he says. "You've repelled larger forces than this."

I have, but not after healing a deadly wound. I'm tired, my limbs slightly jellied. I don't know how much I have left in me.

"Sooner rather than later, Majesty," Nacht suggests, his voice unaffected by his stance tense. "You are well aware that there are not enough of us to survive that many of them."

Fuck.

If it kills me, it kills me. But I've come too far. I am not going down without a goddamned fight.

I call the magic back up, focus it into a ball between my outstretched hands, and step forward. I spread my hands wide. The ball of energy hangs suspended in front of me, waiting for release. The sight of it doesn't deter the army. They keep marching, blades pointed in our direction.

I get one shot at this. And they're almost close enough.

"You guys probably want to duck," I say. All three men plus the cards around us flatten themselves against the ground and I bring my hands together against the magic. The ball explodes, and a wave of energy rockets outward, leveling everything on the field.

"Impressive," Nacht says. "Now… we must get you out of here."

Of course, his method of removing me from the field is to throw me over his shoulder. Only this time, I don't exactly mind. I'm depleted. I also notice that Ivan carries the Walrus in much the same manner. The cards close ranks behind us as we leave the field, and within two minutes, I'm on the back of Nacht's jubjub and he's wrapped around me, protecting me as we make a hasty retreat.

"What now?" I ask.

"Now, we regroup, decide a plan of action, and end this fucking battle.

CHAPTER TWENTY-THREE

A lone in my room with the four of the five most dangerous men in Wonderland…I never thought this would be a thing, but here we are. Percival, Phineas, Edwin and Tag sit at my table with me, cups of untouched tea in front of them while they glare daggers at one another.

"We need a plan," I say, which brings them all to attention. The four savage men look at me. "It must be flawless, and Humphrey can't know what we're doing until we're ready to strike. The four of you understand logistics much better than I do, so I need your advice on how we're going to surround him and take him down with minimal casualties."

"I am quite surprised you think you can surround the Mad King without his knowledge," Percival says. The derisive tone in his voice doesn't bother me anymore, though something tells me it should right now. Something about him has been off since this skirmish started, and the sense of wrongness has only grown since.

"We need to distract him," I say. "If he's distracted, he may not notice what we're doing until it's too late."

"Even distracted, King Humphrey will notice," Edwin says. "But I do believe there may be a way."

We look at each other across the table, and I get the feeling he's trying to tell me something without speaking. Whatever it is, I'm not getting it. Beside me, Percival huffs in annoyance.

"Can someone tell me what kind of fighter Humphrey is?" I ask. I know he's brutal given my experience with visions of Haigha's attack, but I don't really know much else.

"He's a madman," Phineas says. "He fights for the love of battle and nothing else. Once you get him started, it's nearly impossible to make him stop."

"Unless, of course, you sing him a lullaby," Tag says.

"You're serious?"

"As a vorpal blade to the heart."

I'm used to weird shit in Wonderland, but this might just be the weirdest shit I've heard so far. I'm supposed to stop a mad King by singing him a lullaby? How delightfully absurd.

"And how, exactly am I supposed to do that?"

"By distracting him, of course," Tag replies. That obnoxious smile appears on his lips again and it's my turn to huff. "Your other option is to kill him, and

I am not certain anyone at this table is skilled enough to do such a thing without *magical* distraction."

That sounds like a challenge, but I won't be the one stepping up to volunteer. I know I'm not skilled enough to take on a battle-hardened, mad monarch who has been in power three times as long as I've been alive.

"What sort of strategy can we use to distract him, then?"

"A modified clamshell."

The new, yet familiar voice causes all of us to turn. Koji materializes before us, leaning against the post of my bed and looking pretty rotten. His skin is pale and drawn and there's little color in his eyes. But he's upright and talking, and the sight of him makes my heart leap in my chest.

"What the hell are you doing here?" Edwin demands, eyes narrowing as every weapon in the room is drawn and pointed at Koji's throat. Bad kitties should be at the left hands of their monstrous Queens, giving her the wrong information."

"I grow tired of Lucinda's constant bawling over the loss of her favorite plaything." He hits Edwin with a pointed glare before turning to me and offering a waifish pout. "However, am I to regain my true Queen's favor if I stay away too long?"

"We can argue about your ability to regain favor later," I say. "Sit down and tell me your idea."

"You can't be serious." Jerome turns his angry gaze on me.

"As a fucking heart attack."

"You're going to let a traitor back in our midst?"

"There's more going on than you know," I say and make a point of turning to fully face Koji. "What's going on?"

"What our dear Carpenter has been quite remiss in telling you, Majesty, is that the Walrus' most successful attacks always begin with a clamshell formation." Koji slides from the bedpost to the edge of my bed. One hand clutches at his side in a way that most people probably wouldn't notice, but I do. Despite leaving to inform the Red Queen of our movements, he's in a great deal of pain. Jabberwocky scratches don't heal quickly for anyone, including magical creatures. "The Oysters split into three battalions, and while two close in on either side, the third waits for the target's loss of focus to attack."

"So, we surround him?"

"Yes. Even the Oysters are not formidable enough a force to take on the entire Club army, which is why I suggest a modified clamshell."

"You want to use several armies to box him in?" Edwin asks. Koji nods.

"There *is* a low place on the field," Percival says. "Perhaps using the clamshell formation to drive him into that valley would give us the advantage against him."

"That… could work," Tag agrees. "Provided we are able to position two armies in such a way that would put him at a disadvantage from the start."

"My darling brother believes me a traitor," Edwin says.

"Which you are," Phineas confirms.

"Semantics," Edwin replies, waving a hand dismissively toward him. "Which means my army will be fighting on two fronts. When the time comes, we will march from the north, bringing the full force of the Red Army with us. The clamshell must be placed to the east of the Club army. The only way this will work is if our forces are able to cut off any hope of retreat."

"Let the Oysters herd the Club cattle," Percival offers. "They are quite able to do such a thing and can operate with minimal instruction."

"Send a Rabbit with Torai," Tag suggests. "That will allow our Queen an awareness of their location and give the Walrus an extra commander."

Okay, I *really* don't like that idea. Not the *sending a Rabbit with the Walrus* part; the *being away from me* part. I don't like being separated from my Rabbits, particularly on a battlefield. But Tag does have a point, damn him. Even if plans change, they have a way to return to me. If only we had enough of those connections…

Well, I *am* supposed to take on four Rabbits as well as four Kings. I just don't have anyone else at the moment who fits the bill. And I honestly don't want to think about what it would take to get there. Two Rabbits and two Kings are enough for right now.

My people collection is getting seriously out of control these days.

I shake my head to clear those thoughts and focus back on my court. They stare back, waiting for an answer.

"So, the Oysters from the east, commanded by the Walrus and one of my Rabbits, the Red Army from the north, and...who from the south?"

"The White Army," Phineas says. "I shall bring our troops to the field."

"And your army shall complete the box," Tag says. "I will take command if my Queen wishes it."

This sounds like a great plan...except for one thing.

"Won't Humphrey see this coming?" I ask. "He's mad, but not stupid. Where will the distraction come from?"

"Leave that to me," Percival says, finally rejoining the conversation.

"How do you intend to distract him?"

The way he smiles makes my neck itch. "That is the question, is it not?"

"And what of me, Majesty?" Koji asks.

"You are to stick with your original plan," I tell him. "You're more useful controlling the Red Court's flow of information."

"But you will need a messenger, will you not?"

"We'll make do without you."

His expression falls. Understandably so, considering I've just told him he gets to sit out the battle while everyone else puts their lives on the line. I rise and move to stand in front of him, but he won't meet my gaze.

"Look at me, Koji." When he doesn't lift his head, I place my hands on his cheeks and lift his chin. "Do not ever doubt how precious you are to me. I'd rather have you safe in here than risking your life on the battlefield playing triple agent."

"Sentimental as her reasons may be," Edwin cuts in, "our Queen is correct. Your safety is more important than your ability to move unnoticed on a battlefield."

"You really should take better care of yourself," Tag adds. Each new statement causes tiny changes in the cat's expression. The troubled look leaves his eyes, and little by little, he looks more like himself.

"As much as I'd love to see you gone from my life," Phineas says, though grudgingly, "my wife adores you, which means I, too, must advise against your participation in this battle."

"I was not aware you cared so deeply for me," Koji responds, bringing a scowl to Phineas' face.

"I don't, you fool."

His surly retort causes everyone in the room to laugh. Koji relaxes, and a weight lifts from my shoulders. I run my fingers through his hair, pausing to scratch the small patches of skin just behind his ears while he purrs.

"So…do we have a plan?" I ask. The four men at the table nod. "Good. I guess that means it's time to head out."

I lean down to kiss Koji's cheek, then follow my Kings and generals out the door.

"This plan is completely mad," the King of Diamonds says.

"And that's different from everything else around here how?" Even this far above the battlefield, we still hear the screams of the dying. "There is no other way for this to end," I answer, as much to myself as to Percival. "It's my job to unite the lands, so that's what I plan to do."

He raises one eyebrow just a hair but otherwise does not respond. I let the silence hang until Nacht rides up on his heavily armored bandersnatch. He isn't bloody yet and all of his knives are around his neck, so that makes me feel a little better.

"A report, Majesty." He salutes, and the way he moves his foot in the stirrup suggests he would click his heels together if he could.

"Report."

"The vanguard has broken through the Club line." He hesitates, his expression telling me this victory has not come without a price. I wait, and after a too-long pause he begins again. "The Walrus is executing his shell formation as we speak, closing our opponents in quite well."

"But?"

What little color his face has drains.

"Nacht…what is it?"

"King Phineas," he replies. My heart drops. "He took an arrow to the knee on the first Club volley. Felina has removed him from battle and entrusted him to the Caterpillar for healing."

Injury I can handle. He's still alive, so I'm okay. I breathe out a stuttered breath and meet the twin's gaze. "We seem to be holding well."

"For now," he replies. "Once the White King returns to the battlefield —"

"Wait, *what? Returns?*"

"Of course, Majesty. He *is* the commander of the White Army."

Oh seven hells… this is not good.

"If he must." I sigh. "Continue your report, please."

Nacht looks worried, which unsettles me far more than an actual attack right this moment could. But then I remember who stands at my left hand and remind myself that an actual attack on my person is very, very possible.

"The Oysters are moving into formation. The Club army remains quite distracted."

"And how is everyone else?"

"Faring well."

"For now."

"Majesty, you should move into position and choose your lullaby."

I cringe. I'm not a singer, but if singing a lullaby to a mad king is what it takes to bring down the

Diamond Army, then so be it.

"I suppose you're right."

He nods. He's eager to return to the battlefield.

"Thank you for the update," I say. He bows as low as possible from the back of his bandersnatch and turns away.

And then there were three.

Ivan stands behind me and to the right, his mind a blurring tumble of emotions. He's ready to protect me from our "ally" beside me.

"It is time," Percival says. "Are you certain this is the path you choose?"

"Why? Is my darling husband so concerned for my safety?"

"Only that I may not be the one to take your head." He speaks with no inflection in his voice at all, a sound both chilling and reassuring. The smirk on his lips tells me his threat is still mostly harmless. Today is probably *not* the day I die.

"How sweet of you to say."

Percival lifts his helmet into one hand and turns toward his mount. Before he can move, I grab hold of his arm. The niggling voice of doubt echoes in my head.

"Remember that we're on the same side."

"As my lady commands," he replies and his sinister smile disappears behind his helmet.

I don't have a good feeling about letting that man loose unsupervised, but I don't really have a choice. This entire plan hinges on the distraction

Percival will provide in order to allow the armies unfettered movement. There is no other way to get close enough to that treasonous bastard Humphrey to end the fight otherwise. My hand-to-hand combat skills are not enough to take him on, and we both know it. But Humphrey, for all his physical might, cannot stand up to a simple lullaby as it precedes a magical coup de grace.

And we all know how good I am at exploding people.

Disgust ripples through me along with the memory of the Mock Turtle becoming meat sprinkles all over the battlefield, but I don't try to push it away. I killed a man that day. Even if he was an awful person and my actions were justified by the rules of war, the truth will forever be exactly as it sounds, and I have to own the fact that I'm a murderer.

I sit with that knowledge; let it ride on my shoulders where it belongs, while Percival prepares to leave. The black and blue jubjub makes no sound as he hoists himself gracefully into the saddle. And despite the fact that his stated mission is to kill me, Percival salutes me as his Queen before taking off.

Ivan takes Percival's place at my side, his eyes the only part of him visible under his armor.

"I will never understand how you've allowed yourself to trust that monster, Majesty."

"The only thing I trust is that he will try to kill me very soon," I answer, my gaze trained on the dust cloud in the distance that marks the first skirmish in this battle. The magic whispers on the breeze — begging, frantic. Desperate. Fear lingers in the air like the last drops of rain after a storm. It's infectious.

"I never in my life thought I'd say something quite so mad, but I agree with him," my Rabbit says.

I raise a questioning eyebrow at Ivan, but he doesn't make any move at all. "How so?"

"This plan is absolutely mad and destined for failure."

"Thanks for the vote of confidence."

"I never said it was impossible. Just mad."

"Either way, we're committed to it now."

"That we are." He lifts a hand to help me onto the back of my jubjub. "Shall we, then?"

No sooner do we start down the hill than a card messenger comes flying up, arms flying wildly over his head. I'm not sure how he manages to stay upright on his mount, but curiosity is quickly replaced by fear when I see the look on his face.

"Report," Ivan barks and the flailing soldier stops to execute a perfect salute and bow before returning to his previous action.

"The Unicorn, Sir," it says and the painted-on face flips and flops from happy to sad to scared to hysterical and back. "They're speaking nonsense…"

Ivan and I look at each other. Blade is a lot of things, but nonsensical is not one of them. He nods at me.

"Take me to him," he replies and wheels his mount in the direction of the card. "You're coming with me, Majesty."

"You're damn right I am!" I follow suit and together we race across the battlefield behind the messenger. I raise my magical defenses around the three of us to deflect stray arrows and burning balls of...I don't even know what...as we barrel straight through the middle of the fray. The air is thick with blood and smoke; small fires burn in patches of grass all around, intermingled with the lifeless bodies of card and humanoid soldiers alike. Black and red card backs fight both side-by-side and against one another in such a frantic mess that I can't tell who is an ally and who is an enemy.

"This part of the battle is not your concern," Ivan reminds me, obviously sensing my anxiety through our bond. I nod in response and find myself reaching out across that connection for Jerome. His presence pings in the distance, strong and steady, and I release a hard breath.

"You're right," I say aloud and force myself to focus on the task at hand: the Unicorn.

For a moment, it appears nothing is wrong with Blade. They fight with a cool and calculated composure that, quite honestly, frightens me. Each attack is as swift and precise as a snakebite, and three times as deadly. Soldiers—humanoid and card alike—fall like so many bits of scattered paper under their blade, and I am reminded again that I'm so glad they're on our side.

It takes no time at all for Blade to clear the field of enemies. When the last card falls, they flick the blade of their sword to clear it, sending droplets of blood scattering in a gory arc against the trampled grass. The ground is purple under their feet from so much carnage, and they see me, They stop and execute a formal bow. The gleaming horn atop their helmet is untouched and shines in the smoky light.

"Blade," I call out, "are you well?"

The response is exactly as the messenger said: nonsense. The words come out in a garbled mess that sounds more like radio static than words.

"I'm sorry... I don't understand," I say, hoping it's my ears and not something wrong with my White Knight.

They remove their helmet and speak again, but it's the same. The words don't make sense at all.

"Do you feel okay?" I ask. "Nod if you do."

They nod, and a look of concern crosses their features.

"Say your name," Ivan calls out.

The response sounds something like "dalb" and my Rabbit's eyes go wide before he curses. Quite creatively, I might add.

"Care to fill me in? I'm pretty sure our Unicorn would also like to know what's going on." I cast a glance toward them, and they nod.

"The Topsy-Turvy curse," Ivan says. Blade gasps, which surprises me because they rarely show any kind of emotion. Just that tiny flicker of awareness is enough to tell me exactly how serious this is. I look at Ivan, whose features have gone flat with frustration. "Do you remember the Crying Disease, Majesty?" he asks without taking his gaze from Blade.

"Yes."

"This is worse."

"Ssenyrw on htiw kaeps I. Ssenhgih, yrros ma I," Blade says, which makes no sense to me. I fight to keep my expression even and stop my nose from wrinkling in confusion.

"Do you feel okay?" Ivan asks my general and they nod. "No ill effects?"

Blade shakes their head. "Yad lla thgif dluoc I. Yako ma I."

Ivan pauses. "I... don't understand but you seem fine." Blade nods. "Can you maintain command?"

Blade shrugs.

Ivan turns to the messenger that brought us here. "Find Tweedledee," he says. "Bring him here and place him at the Unicorn's side." The messenger bows and disappears into the fray. "Hold strong, Unicorn," Ivan tells Blade, who nods in response. Our Queen is needed on the front lines."

And with that, we turn and head toward the main fray.

The King of Clubs isn't hard to find. All we need to do is follow the trail of playing card carnage. This particular trail chills me to the bone. It appears by the look of the cards on the ground that he's gone so mad that he's killing indiscriminately—his own soldiers as well as ours.

"Once again, this seems like a trap," Ivan says.

"I know it's a trap," I answer. "He's trying to bait me through fury."

"Do not fall for it."

"I don't plan to, Ivan." I did that once before and exploded a mindflayer. Granted, that solidified my position as Queen pretty easily and there are many who would tell me that particular mindflayer needed exploding… but I don't think I want a repeat performance.

We crest the hill, riding side by side, and a whirling dervish of carnage greets us below. Bodies of men and cards alike lay scattered all across the ground and the field is soggy with blue-black puddles and rust-colored mud. Oysters flank the valley on either side, holding their line while the White Court standard waves in the air from below. All that's missing is the Red Army to make a mess of the situation.

And then in the center, striking down anything in his path, is the demented King of Clubs.

"Bloody hell," Ivan mutters at the end of a gasp.

"Bloody Hell, indeed." I take a deep, iron-scented breath of my own. "It's so much worse than I thought."

"It usually is when full madness sets in."

This is a man who should never have attempted to use magic, much less use it in the way he has over the years. My first thought at the sight is one of panic, but then I remember I'm not only Queen, but of Paladian blood. According to every bit of my council, this won't happen to me. At least, they don't think it will.

The glint of shining silver to the south catches my attention. The Unicorn has arrived in position with Nacht at his side, the unified Wonderland standard flying proudly above the heads of their soldiers as it closes in beside one of the Oyster factions The north is also a mirror, Edwin's black-and-red armor shining in the bright sunlight, except he rides beneath the stolen Red Court standard.

We've closed the mad king in on three sides...

No, make that all four. Cresting the ridge behind Humphrey, due east of our position, is a second Wonderland flag. with two figures riding side-by-side. As soon as I put eyes on the Rabbit-eared figure, my anxiety settles. I hate being so far away from Jerome, but it's necessary.

He and the walrus complete the box, closing in the gap between the White Army and the Oysters. And a moment later, the sound of ten-thousand pairs of booted feet shakes the air around us.

"The last piece of the puzzle," Ivan says. When I look over my shoulder, Tag—Tweedledee himself—rides toward me with his head held high. The card army behind him is mine. And there is something breathtaking about the sight of the formerly savage assassin so cool and composed.

He really is a King, I think.

The bow he executes is similar to that of his brother. I nod back and return my attention to the carnage below. It's almost time.

The first rumble of thunder echoes across the land, and the electrical charge of unshed lightning makes the hair on my arms rise. It takes me a full thirty seconds to realize that this is Percival's diversion.

Fucking mindflayers...

All eyes rise to the sky above and the angry, swirling mass of clouds appearing out of nowhere. Lightning arcs away like grabbing fingers, reaching out and down to snatch up the unobservant.

The sudden storm is enough to give the King of Clubs pause. That ink-black helmet lifts toward the sky, and the carnage temporarily halts. Then just as he turns his attention back to the bloodbath, the storm turns into a vortex.

Roiling, angry cloud fingers reach toward him, twining in and out yet bound to one another by spindly bars of lightning. The sight is both beautiful and horrifying. A show of the Carpenter's true power.

Holy fuck am I glad his on my side.

...for now, anyway.

"Majesty?" Ivan asks, questioning why we haven't moved yet. I give a tiny shake of my head and close my eyes to listen to the currents.

Even without my vision, the scene before us is clear. The way the magic moves around me provides an accurate enough depiction. And yet, there's something else mingled in with it. Something old and dark and powerful.

Percival's face comes to mind, the roiling energy, a version of the darkness inside him. I listen to it, let it lead. Let it tell me when to move.

"What the hell?" Ivan mutters beside me. "Are we even necessary?"

"Yes."

It's time.

Percival's voice in my head is as clear as if he were standing beside me. The sound and sensation are so jarring that I jerk and nearly lose control of my mount. When I open my eyes, everyone is watching me. To battle it is.

"Cards, with me!" I shout. A battle cry tears from Tag's throat and, as if pulled along by strings, all four battalions move at once. Soldiers spill down the sides of the crater toward the swirling mass. Ivan and I take the lead, just as the other members of my court do, while the cards fan out to block any potential escape.

The storm tightens as we close in, and in the

very center we see flashes of silver—Humphreys' blades—cut through only to be lost once more. A loud, guttural roar shakes the air. My heart leaps into my throat, but I continue forward, halting twenty or so feet away from the eye of this murder storm.

I don't think I'll ever stop being afraid of battle. Jerome insists that it's healthy, but it feels... I don't know how it feels, honestly. Terror is so commonplace in Wonderland that this fear is almost a relief. At least I'm in control here.

I think.

"Humphrey!" I shout, drawing on my magic to increase the volume of my voice. The storm is so loud that my words would be lost otherwise.

My shout has no effect at all. The storm tightens, and my generals and I inch forward, careful to stay out of reach of the clouds.

"Humphrey Varai!" I shout again, my voice shaking the ground in its intensity, "lay down your weapons!"

Another strangled growl issues from the cloud, followed by a series of gasps from the soldiers.

"Sing the lullaby, Alice!" Ivan calls.

My mind goes blank.

I can't think.

I don't know the words.

Then the lazy whistle of the Cheshire Cat cuts through the noise. I pick up the thread and fill in the words to match his tune, projecting my voice across the battlefield.

"Twas brillig and the slithy toves did gyre and gimbel in the wabe... All mimsy were the borogoves... and the mome raths... outgrabe..."

Humphrey stops in his tracks and turns toward me. His armor protects every part of him, including his eyes, but I can tell I have his attention. I repeat the refrain, and his battle-poised arms lower.

"Majesty," Ivan says and points up at the figure descending from above the clouds. The song drops off my tongue as I follow his direction.

It's Percival.

Arms extended to either side, he sinks to the ground from the center of the vortex. His eyes are alight with the power of the lightning around him, gleaming like a pair of tiny suns. His feet touch down as gracefully as if he were dancing, and the storm parts around him. Humphrey's rampage halts. Fear flickers in his eyes. True, heart-rending fear. His features go slack, and the electric crackle of magic pulses around Percival.

"Remove your helmet, please," Percival asks Humphrey, but it is not a request. Humphrey can no more refuse than tell his heart to stop beating. So strong is the order that Ivan's helmet folds back, revealing the same glazed, vacant look in his eyes. All of my generals have done the same.

What. The. Hell?

I stand by dumbly and watch the scene unfold — The King of Clubs lifts his heavy, iron helmet from his head, revealing dirt-streaked, porcelain skin and a shock of sweat-soaked red hair topped by a club-studded crown. The helmet falls to the bloody ground with a dull thump and Humphrey's large frame follows half a breath later. Knees sink into the bloody mud, splashing up along the lines of his armor only to dribble back down. His head falls forward, a gesture of complete supplication. But the look in his eyes — that look is awful. He is no longer in control of himself and he's aware that he is taking one of his last breaths.

Keep your eyes open and watch, girl.

Even without Percival's voice injected into my brain, I know what's coming. Yet I'm helpless to watch as the Carpenter drops his sword with that same dancer's grace and, in one swing, shatters the neck of our rival. Shards of porcelain fly in all directions in a violent rain and Humphrey's head lands at Percival's feet. Cracks form along his chin and cheeks; one side of his jaw drooping as the fracture dislocates the joint.

The light in his eyes is the last part to fade; those angry orbs flickering toward me before growing dim. When he dies, he dies staring at me.

With one smooth flick of his wrist, Percival slings the blood from his blade, but I'm too stunned to register much. That is, until he lifts Humphrey's severed head and tears away the Club Court crown. He removes his Diamond crown and tosses it to the bloody dirt at my feet then replaces it with the new one before tossing the head away. It lands ten feet or so away and shatters.

I stare at Percival, mouth agape, and quite unable to move.

"So that's it..." Ivan says. His own incredulity is as obvious in his voice as it is in his thoughts. "We've acquired a third Kingdom."

"Not *we*," Percival says. His lip curls at the thought. "*I* have acquired a new court for myself."

"Your courts belong to your Queen."

"I invite her to try and take it." He hits me with a sharp glare, then bows reverently. When he stands, that deadly blade is pointed at my throat. "*En garde*, Majesty."

And now is when I die.

Drawing my own sword, I slide into a stance. The twins' lessons rise to the surface of my memory, and those memories are all that keep me from falling to the ground in a panic as I stare down my own death made flesh. I take a breath, release it, and prepare for the attack.

Percival is not fast to move. This long game is going to take us just a little bit longer. He watches me, no doubt using the anticipation to test my magical defenses. I can't feel him do it, but I certainly feel the magical wall around him when I try. The truly scary part is that I didn't feel it go up. Maybe it was up all along.

My mind is abuzz with my own anxiety and the combined anticipation and fear of my Rabbits, but they can do nothing. He called *me* out. These are the rules of engagement and they cannot interfere.

All the people I care about get to stand around and watch me die. Probably painfully.

Percival doesn't attack. He stands at the ready, unblinking, watching my eyes as if by doing so, he can see straight to my soul. Knowing him, he probably can. This man murders Kings and Queens and raises the dead for fun. I can't imagine he'd not take advantage of every tool in his arsenal right now. He and I both know I'm already outmatched. It's just a question of how long it takes him to take my head too. I was a damned fool to think he was ever anything except my enemy.

I'm way deep inside my own head when I realize what's happening. He's using everything I've told him—all of my insecurities and fears—against me. But as soon as I realize it, things change.

The fear ebbs and I remember just how far I've come. And because of that, the psychological warfare ends suddenly and brutally. There's barely a warning—only the slight narrowing of his eyes—before Percival strikes. His attack is as swift and precise as a snakebite, perfectly timed and absolutely deadly. I catch the swing with the back of my own blade at the very last second, but he doesn't bear down on me. Again, like a snake, he recoils and prepares for the next strike.

I keep up my defenses, parrying each attack but never finding an opening to launch my own. He's long-armed and light as a dancer on his feet.

As excellent a swordsman as a sorcerer. He moves around me as a petal in the wind, landing blow after brutal blow, wearing down my stamina. My breath soon comes in short gasps, and my racing heart begs to burst from my chest, but I don't drop my guard. I can't, or I'll die.

But I'm slowing down. My arms and legs burn from the exertion. My heart feels like its going to explode out of my chest. And Percival? He looks like he could do this all day. He probably can, because he's inhuman.

Even among the wondrous.

Three more murderous blows. Alarm bells ring in my head. Both Rabbits are screaming internally. The tension in the air is so thick it's nearly suffocating. Percival bears down on me and my left foot slips. My knee buckles and I go down.

He takes the shot.

The deadly, blood-stained blade comes careening toward my neck amidst a flurry of shouts. I throw up every magical defense I have and close my eyes as I throw myself to the dirt, certain I'm going to die.

A line of white-hot fire blooms along my side. Agony coated in numbness. But I live.

My eyes fly open and I see Percival's blade hangs just under my chin, my own blood dripping onto my armor. He's caught in the hold of my magic, struggling to break free. The sight re-strengthens my resolve as I continue to hold him. My side burns with a pain the likes of which I've never before experienced, and I know if I lower my arm, the shreds of my plate armor will bite into my skin. I struggle to catch my breath and stand, holding tightly to the magical leash binding the Carpenter. I've momentarily overpowered him. Right now, he can't move and is visibly angered by it. The way his hate-filled gaze follows me makes a shiver trip down my spine. Every bit of tenderness I saw out of him was a lie. I know that now.

End this now, I tell myself, and as I ready the killing blow, my resolve falters. I don't want more blood on my hands, no matter how necessary an evil it might be. With that one thought, the new King of Clubs breaks my hold. He regroups and smiles a sharp-edged smile.

"Quite impressive, My Queen. I expected you to die long before now."

"I'm tougher than you give me credit for," I reply and ready my blade. "I'm also tired of you."

"Then let us finish this."

Percival strikes. Our fight is fast and brutal. Blood seeps from the burning gash on my my side. My lungs and limbs scream, and despite both my will and my magical defenses, he overpowers me and drives me to my knees again.

"Raise the white flag, Alice." He leans harder into his sword.

"No."

"You cannot defeat me." Percival pushes against

our crossed blades, inching them closer to my throat. My side feels like it's going to tear in two.

"I would rather die than give in," I growl, straining to hold him off. He pushes harder.

"Fine by me."

Hot metal touches my neck, peeling back my skin. I can't hold on...

"No!" I screech through my teeth, a loud, desperate sound, and push as hard as I can, both with my body and with magic. A thunderous sound erupts all around me. Bloody dirt flies up. And Percival lands flat on his back near the decapitated body of the former King of Clubs. I waver on my knees, exhaustion replacing the magic as it rushes up and out of me. It pulses outward in white and blue waves, keeping him pinned to the ground and draining me over and over again. When I reach the point of incapacitation, I slam my mental shields in place and cut the magic off from the rest of me.

The flash of surprise across Percival's face when I glare at him says enough.

He rises to his feet, clapping.

"Impressive. I suppose taking your head will have to wait for another day. As much as you need killing, I simply cannot have all the fun at once. And I fear your zealots will end my life as soon as I end yours." I don't take my eyes from him as he takes a bow. "Farewell for now, Majesty..."

I move to take a step forward, but he throws his hands wide then brings them together with a sharp clap that echoes in the storm clouds overhead. With it comes a gale forceful enough to knock us all over like we're no more substantial than playing cards.

I tumble backwards, ass over teakettle as it were, and in my wild loop-de-loop, I see Percival and his new crown rise from the ground. By the time I stop rolling, he's gone.

The Diamond crown remains discarded in the mud, a layer of blood and grime dimming the sparkling silver surface.

As we all sit up and look around, we realize one thing at the same time — we own the battlefield. This fight is over. I'm bloody and bruised, bleeding and in pain, and more exhausted than I have ever been. But we're all alive.

And I am no closer to unifying Wonderland than I was half an hour ago.

We reconvene at the rear guard, bruised, bloody, and covered in mud. Ivan has peeled my ruined armor from my body. The discarded Diamond crown hangs loosely from my fingers. Despite the fact that I've taken full control of the Court of Diamonds, this doesn't feel like a victory.

Koji is still gone. Blade is cursed. Percival is on the loose. And Phineas...

The thought of my injured King sends my tired brain tumbling into a panic and I start to run. I vaguely register someone shouting at me, but I'll deal with whatever it is later.

Right about the time I reach the end of camp, large hands close around my waist and I'm lifted from my feet.

"Pardon me, Majesty, but stop thinking." Tag holds me tight against him until the fight drains out of me. "You haven't the foggiest where he even is."

And now I feel stupid.

"Please take me to him," I all but beg. Even though I'm exhausted, injured, and scared, Tag takes his time in calming me. He's heartbreakingly gentle as he places me back on my feet and brushes my matted hair out of my face.

"Soon," he responds. "King Phineas is no longer at camp. First, we must clean you up and treat your wounds."

"But Phineas—"

"—is perfectly okay," Tag confirms. "Wounded, but not mortally so." I sag in his arms, suddenly exhausted. "He will be more concerned to see his Queen fall to pieces at his bedside."

He has a point, damn him. So I allow Tag to lead me back to his bandersnatch and pull me into the saddle. I lean into his solid warmth and hold onto the arm around my waist as the adrenaline of battle fades. Now that I'm no longer staring my inevitable death in the face, I remember to actually be afraid. My whole body shakes from the jerking tremors.

"Report," he says loudly as someone rides up

beside us. He's still in General mode.

"The Red Army has retreated. Messengers have confirmed that Lord Edwin continues to hold both Northumbria and Mercia in the name of Wonderland. The Walrus and the Oyster Army are on the way back to the Rear Guard." It's Jerome's voice, which helps relax me a little. My Rabbit is safe.

"And the Unicorn?"

"No report. The Caterpillar is with them now."

Jerome falls in beside us, his jubjub looking as tired as I feel. It takes all my strength to meet his questioning gaze, but when our eyes lock, a flutter of relief touches the back of my brain. Tag maneuvers me toward the medical tent where a pair of dodo field nurses (no, really. They're a pair of dodo birds in candy striper uniforms) pulls me from his arms. One takes me behind a curtain while the other shoos the rest of them out.

The weird bird-ladies fawn over me like I'm a child, making such a fuss that I'm not even aware of the actual medical treatment until they're done. My hands are bandaged down to my fingertips and curiously, my side no longer hurts where I was nearly cut in half.

As soon as they give the all-clear, my entourage floods into the tent and I'm pulled outside.

"Now," Tag says with a dashing smile, "let us go see your King."

CHAPTER TWENTY-FOUR

"He's here?" I ask as we enter the inn.

"Yes and no," Jerome answers as he hands payment for the room to the innkeeper. "This is simply the fastest way to reunite the two of you."

We hike up the stairs and turn left. My brain is such a muddled mess that they have to remind me to open my suite where I go straight for Phineas' door, but Tag catches me by the shoulders and pushes me past it.

"Clean first, then King." Tag is gentle but firm as he maneuvers me into my room and begins the process of stripping the armor from my body. Blood, mud, and other detritus fall to the floor as he works. He's efficient, pulling each piece away and dropping it into a grimy puddle, all the while careful to keep his few actual touches in safe zones.

When I'm down to just my tunic and leggings,

however, I realize he's not going to stop there and cross my arms just as he reaches for the hem of my shirt.

"I've got this part," I say, stepping back. Tag smiles, humor dancing in his eyes. "You can go away now."

"Nonsense. I must not leave my Queen unguarded."

Unguarded from who, I wonder. Because the only predator here I see is him.

"I promise the shower monster won't eat me behind a closed bathroom door."

"But I might," he answers without missing a beat.

Oh. Well. Okay, then.

So much for platonic.

"All the more reason to close the door." I say, flustered, "and lock it."

Tag laughs, but the predatory gleam doesn't leave his sharp eyes. Now that he mostly makes sense, I'm no match for him. So I back away again, stepping over the threshold of the bathroom. He doesn't make a move as I push the door closed.

Once the door locks and the water is on, only then do I breathe a sigh of relief.

I am a jittery mess as Jerome leads me down the hall to Phineas' room. Both he and Tag have assured me that my King is okay, but the anxiety remains, growing heavier with each step. I don't know what I'm going to find, and I don't like not knowing.

Jerome knocks and a moment later the door swings inward, revealing our haggard-looking Spellbinder who seems just a little bit madder than she was yesterday.

To be fair, we're all just a little bit madder than we were yesterday.

"Majesty," Felina says. Her voice is as weak as her eyes, but she smiles at me. "Good to see you well."

"You too," I say. "Though you look like you could use a strong cup of tea and a nap."

Felina waves her hand dismissively. "A wink or two and I'll be right as rain. Tea would be lovely, though." She steps back from the door. "Do come in."

My anxiety spikes, but the sight of Phineas sitting up in the bed very nearly takes the wind from my lungs. He's handsome as ever and, aside from the dullness of exhaustion in the lines of his face, he appears otherwise unharmed. Pretty sure we have Felina to thank for that.

"My Queen," he says with a gentle smile. "What news of the battlefield?"

I stumble to the chair next to the bed but before I can sit, Phineas grabs my hand and guides me to sit beside him. Even after I land, I'm very aware of the fact that he doesn't let go.

"Humphrey is dead."

"The Club crown is ours?"

"Not exactly."

I give him the TL;DR summary of the battle and the events that followed. The lines in his face grow deeper the longer I talk. I intentionally don't tell him about the part where Percival almost succeeded in killing me, either. Even omitting that, his expression is unreadable when I finish speaking.

"That is... quite the tale," he says after a long silence. "I do not know of another King forfeiting his crown in such a manner."

"No other King has been rendered politically powerless by a Queen before either," Ivan says, surprising me. So focused was I on my King that I failed to notice the presence of my Rabbit.

"There is that." Phineas shifts position and winces. The flash of pain across his face reminds me that he was, in fact, gravely injured. I reach for him, but he waves me off and settles back against the pillows. "Do not trouble yourself, Majesty. I shall live."

"You haven't called me Majesty in months. Stop with the brave face and tell me what's wrong."

"Just a twinge. I promise I am fine," he assures me. "There are some things even magic cannot fix. The residual pain of being run through with a vorpal spear, for example."

"What?!" My mouth falls agape. "If that's the case then you should be dead!"

"Lucky for me, I have two highly talented Spellbinders at my disposal. "Phineas glances toward Felina, who smiles shyly and bows her head in acknowledgment.

"Lucky for all of us," I reply. "Though I've yet to see the other one. Any idea where our dear Caterpillar has gone?"

"Back to wherever it is Caterpillars go, I suppose."

"The Caterpillar remains at the side of the White Knight," Jerome announces. "Initial reports tell us it's quite the nasty curse our Unicorn has suffered."

"What curse might that be?" Phineas questions.

"The Topsy-Turvy curse, I'm afraid."

Who's-a-what?

Sensing my confusion, Jerome fixes his gaze on me and begins to explain. "Nasty as it may be, Topsy-Turvy is quite common. It's a curse most young mindflayers learn as practice. It's not lethal, but it is quite frustrating."

Not lethal is good. But I have more questions. Jerome doesn't make me wait to answer them, either.

"The most prominent side effect is that any conversation one attempts with our Unicorn will come out backwards. Depending on the ability of the mindflayer, they may also speak in perfect rhyme as well.

"Oh, great. We get two of them speaking the right way and the one with all the common sense goes wonky."

"It is the way of this world, I'm afraid."

Jerome nods and steps back against the wall. While I'm pondering this curse, Phineas lifts my hand from his lap and kisses my knuckles. Even injured, he's the sweetest. Just knowing these guys are nearby helps steady me.

"Now, my Queen, have you given any thought to your new King?"

"Tag," I say without hesitation.

I feel the amusement from the statue-like twin behind me. I hadn't told him this yet…but I also hadn't thought of it until just now, either.

Phineas blinks in surprise, then a small smile appears on his face.

"A wise choice indeed."

"How in Wonderland's name did you land on that decision?" Ivan asks. There's no malice in his voice. Only curiosity.

"He was a King before, was he not?" I ask and Ivan nods.

"Aye," Tag answers. "As it so happens, I was."

"There you have it."

"But… he's quite mad."

Tag takes no offense. In fact, the look on his face says he agrees.

"We're all mad, Ivan. This is Wonderland." He doesn't look convinced. "Besides, Tag has proven himself to be a competent — if not mildly ruthless — general."

"An iron fist with a soft touch," Phineas muses.

He lifts a hand to cradle my cheek. "A perfect complement for my lovely Queen."

I'm not one to blush easily, especially not lately, but this does it. Fighting the urge to be shy, I place my hand on top of his and smile at him.

"High praise indeed from the White King. Are you sure that hit was to your chest and not your head?"

Phineas laughs then groans. "I am quite sure, my lovely, little Royal Smartass."

Jerome clears his throat, reminding us that he, Tag, Felina, and Ivan are, in fact, in the room. It works to burst the bubble of flirtation and I straighten my back.

"Now that the battle is settled there is the matter of crowning a new King," he says. "I shall make the necessary preparations." Jerome executes a perfect bow and excuses himself, taking Tag with him.

After one final check, Felina also departs. Even Ivan steps out into the hallway, leaving me alone with Phineas for the first time in what feels like forever.

Phineas tugs the hand he's holding and pulls me against his chest. He holds me close, and I let him, listening to his strong and steady heartbeat—proof he's still alive. The stress of battle flows out of me and it becomes difficult to stay awake. The last conscious thought I have is that I am entirely too heavy for a recovering man as Phineas lifts me into the bed and tucks me in properly. Some tiny part of my brain thinks to argue, but he's too warm and I am entirely too comfortable.

It'll be okay. I can go get married again after a nap.

CHAPTER TWENTY-FIVE

For the second time in my life, I find myself dressed like a sparkly, poofy wedding cake and hauled down the center aisle of a throne room toward a new husband. Well, technically this is my third marriage... but we don't like that other guy.

Especially since he has a stated mission — as in he stated it again less than twenty-four hours ago — of killing me as soon as possible.

Jerome briefed me on how this would go while nearly strangling me with the corset and various other appliances under my dress, but every bit of it beyond the you'll be crowning a king this time part has vanished from my head like so many shards of a dream. I'm not going to lie... seeing Tag standing at the other end of the room, all clean and dressed up with that lopsided grin has me a little bit giddy.

I may or may not have a crush on my mad twin generals.

It's strange to be reversed here—I am the one standing at the dais, rising when the doors open, while my future King comes to me. Though I'm glad because we have a room full of witnesses (where did they all come from anyway?), the newly healed Orvice and his lovely wife in the front row, and there's a good chance I'd faceplant on the carpet-covered stone if I had to try and walk in this dress again.

Then, like magic, Tag is suddenly in front of me, kneeling with his head lowered just enough to show deference. His face is also turned just enough that I'm the only person in the room who can see the cheeky grin on his face.

"You are entirely too pleased with yourself, sir." My words are pitched low and meant only for his ears. The cheeky grin widens to show teeth.

"The Alice is soon to be mine," he says. I'm sure I should be annoyed by that statement, but I'm too amused by this turn of events to stay mad. "Speaking of, as much as I enjoy being your dedicated supplicant, do you have any intention of letting me off my knees anytime soon?"

"I don't know. I quite like the sight of you on your knees for me."

"Majesty, I shall bend to any position you please once you and I are wed, but our audience likely would not enjoy the show."

A loud throat clearing makes me turn. Talon stands beside me, looking as impassive as ever.

"If you are quite ready, might we begin this ceremony?"

I straighten my shoulders.

"Yes. Let's get this over with."

Tag snorts but remains kneeling. The Caterpillar produces a sword from somewhere—probably a pocket of holding in the nearby ether.

"We are gathered today to witness the union of Queen Alice and General Tag Tweed. Our Queen weds this man with the intention of crowning a new King. All those opposed to this union, speak now."

The room remains so silent that I can hear birds chirping outside. My court takes up the entire front row of this circus and every single one of them—except the missing Cheshire Cat, of course—grins so wide I fear their teeth might fall out.

"General Tweed," Talon says, turning toward Tag, who has yet to rise. "Do you pledge your unfailing loyalty to Queen Alice, to protect, to serve, and to provide partnership so long as Wonderland stands?"

"I do," Tag says with a wink directed at me. Like a damned schoolgirl, I blush.

"Queen Alice, do you accept the unfailing loyalty of General Tweed as his solemn vow?"

"I—" My voice comes out as a manic squeak, so I clear my throat and try again. "I do."

"Queen Alice, will you recognize and accept General Tweed as your lawful husband and partner, to share leadership duties, and to protect the sovereignty of Wonderland?"

I smile at Tag, who grins back. "I do."

"General Tweed, do you —"

"A thousand times, yes," he says and surges up from his knee to wrap me in his arms and spin me around. The throne room fills with laughter and cheers. I'm laughing too, and when he finally sets me back on my feet, tumbled and dizzy, Tag bends down and kisses my forehead.

"Can you go ahead and crown me King now?" he asks, grinning at me despite the impatience shining in his eyes. "I want to get to the good part."

"The good part?"

"Getting the Hell out of this party."

I laugh again. "You have to kneel for that part. You're taller than me."

"This is *not* how we do things," Talon interrupts, but a vicious glare from Tag makes him take a step back. "By all means…carry on." Sarcasm sounds strange on him, but I think I like it.

"Let's do this."

Tag kneels at my feet once more, reluctant to let me go even as Talon hands the newly polished Club crown over to me.

"General Tag Tweed, I hereby crown you King of the Court of Diamonds, ruler of the South, and Commander of the Oyster Army under General Torai DeWinter." I drop the crown onto his head, the soft waves of his hair brushing against my fingertips and will it to stay in place with a tiny touch of magic.

There. Complete.

"Rise Sir Tag, General of the White Army and King of the Court of Diamonds."

He rises to his full height, towering over me enough that he casts a shadow across my face. Tag bows and I curtsy. My sister sniffles. And then Tag totally breaks tradition by sweeping me up into the biggest bear hug, lifting me off my feet and forcing the ruffled layers of my dress to poof out in weird ways behind me.

The throne room devolves into pandemonium.

But I honestly don't care. I'm not interested in stuffy traditions. I'd much rather let life happen and allow joy to rule in the spaces where it can. So I hug him back and let the happiness linger.

The war will rage on with or without us. Right now, though, we need this moment of peace.

When we finally release one another, we share a smile. Then we turn to face the gathered crowd, hand in hand. Jerome steps forward and cups his hand around his mouth in preparation of an announcement.

"Introducing Tag Tweed, the King of Diamonds."

Tag clicks his heels together and leans forward at the waist, executing a perfect bow. He looks every bit the King I just made him. To be fair, though, he has done this before. I watch him, spellbound as the last vestiges of madness recede and a new strength of will takes its place.

"Many thanks, my lovely Queen," he says to me, then turns his attention back to the audience, a fist pressed to his chest above his heart. "I shall strive to serve this crown and our glorious Lady Wonderland fairly and faithfully." The knives at his neck clink together softly when he places his hand against his chest. "May the Queen of Cards reunite these broken lands. May peace rule forevermore!"

An inspired roar rises from the crowd. Even my eyes grow a little misty. Yes, I certainly made the right choice.

Tag turns back to me and takes both of my hands in his. He touches a reverent kiss to the back of each one, eyes twinkling with mischief."

"Now, my Queen... let us find and put an end to the Carpenter once and for all."

The battle continues in
Knight Club: Wonderland Wars Book 3

ACKNOWLEDGEMENTS

This book was truly a labor of love. I've lived in Wonderland for nearly a decade now, and the saying is true: We're all mad here.

Without my friends, I don't know where I'd be or if I'd have made it this far. Amy, Jen, Lexx, Misty, Nicole, Rey, and all the others... I love y'all so damn much. You just don't know.

And no Wonderland farewell would be complete without ackonwledging the morning crew of the Chester Waffle House. That place is my home away from home, and at this point, y'all are family.

To my family: thank you for putting up with me. My mom will probably never read this, but the fact that she's with me every step of the way means the world. My darling husband, Bill... he tolerates me. And my beautiful daughters keep the whimsy alive in my life, every single day.

Last but not least... you, dear reader. Thank you for taking a chance on me. Your support means more than words can express. Just promise me we'll meet again. Same Bat-time, same Bat-channel.

See you in Book 3.

ABOUT THE AUTHOR

SUSAN H. RODDEY writes dark speculative fiction and works as a book formatter, cover designer, and developmental editor. She is a voracious reader, wanna-be chef, and amateur gamer who lives in the Piedmont area of South Carolina with a house full of humans, cats, books, and yarn, and spends entirely too much time yelling at her sewing machine. She is also very food-motivated and can easily be bought with cookies.

Find her in all the places:
www.linktr.ee/SHRoddey

ALSO BY SUSAN H. RODDEY

Wonderland Wars
In Spades

The Shadow Council Archives
Gods & Monsters
Blood & Bone
Between the Dim & the Dark
The Broken Ones (Coming Spring 2026)

The Soul Collectors Series
Devil's Daughter
Armageddon Rising

Lingua Timore: 13 Terrifying Tales